BEYOND PULDITCH GATES

With best wishes + thanks —

[signature]

July 2007

HENRY HUDSON was born in Dublin's inner city in 1953 and began an apprenticeship in a power station in 1969. He worked in the power industry in various capacities before taking up a mature studentship in Trinity College, Dublin, in 1999.

IN MEMORY OF MY FATHER
HARRY HUDSON
A WORKER AND A TRUE DUB

Beyond
Pulditch Gates

Henry Hudson

WOLFHOUND PRESS

Published in 2001 by
Wolfhound Press Ltd
68 Mountjoy Square
Dublin 1, Ireland
Tel: (353-1) 874 0354
Fax: (353-1) 872 0207

© 2001 Henry Hudson

All rights reserved. No part of this book may be reproduced or utilised in any form or by any means digital, electronic or mechanical including photography, filming, video recording, photocopying, or by any information storage and retrieval system or shall not, by way of trade or otherwise, be lent, resold or otherwise circulated in any form of binding or cover other than that in which it is published without prior permission in writing from the publisher.

This book is fiction. All characters, incidents and names have no connection with any persons living or dead. Any apparent resemblance is purely coincidental.

 Wolfhound Press receives financial assistance from The Arts Council/ An Chomhairle Ealaíon, Dublin, Ireland.

British Library Cataloguing in Publication Data
A catalogue record for this book is available from the British Library.

ISBN 0-86327-888-4

5 4 3 2 1

Cover Design: Slick Fish Design, Dublin
Typesetting and book design: Wolfhound Press
Printed in Scotland by Omnia Books

prologue

PULDITCH ONE: FEBRUARY 1958

With the exception of the North and South Poles, there was no bleaker place than the construction site of Pulditch One. Sited at the mouth of the river and the navel of the bay, this miniature Siberia was lit by a myopic sun that peered through watery skies. April would bring showers, Easter and warmth. The upchurned ground was a glistening moonscape, dotted battleship-grey where puddles had frozen over. A vicious wind whipped through the raw concrete shells of the unfinished buildings. Its coldness shrank the balls and cracked the hands of the workers before it swept out towards the farthest corner of the site. From there, it steeplechased over a quartet of Nissen huts that grouped together like a school of hump-backed whales.

The biggest of the huts was Number One. It housed most of the labourers and a few of the tradesmen who worked on the site. Along both walls of the hut a line of lockers displayed yellowing newspaper cuttings on twisted arthritic doors. Amongst the displays was a youngish Queen of England with her teeth blackened, an Adolf Hitler moustache and two enormous cartoon tits. A potbellied stove stood centre-floor in the hut with its stack poking out through the roof. Apart from blistering pigeons that perched on its stack, the stove kept the hut warm while its hotplate razzled the bottoms of two big cast-iron kettles. It was coming up to lunch-time and the age-blackened vessels waited for the gritty tea that would turn their clear dancing water into a reeking stewy brew.

Bernard 'Barney' Coogan, mess-hand (or Senior Janitor as he preferred) mopped between the rows of tables and long wooden benches in Number One hut. He was just forty-one years of age but looked older. He was broad and barrel-chested with a shock of hair the texture and colour of wire wool. His face was weathered and lined with thin purple veins that betrayed twenty-five years spent on building sites from Dundee to Dover and everywhere in between. He'd had a hand in building many power stations for the Brits, but Pulditch One was his first on home soil. Barney's legs were stiff and moved slowly, a souvenir of a fall from a scaffold a few years before. His hands were shovels made flesh and their thick stubby fingers were browned by nicotine. Light tan at the knuckles they darkened all the way down to the oily crud that was permanently embedded under his fingernails. He owned no suit and only one tie, a black one in case somebody died. He wore overalls to, in and from work but always put on a fresh pair whenever he took the missus out for a drink. Once a month he washed his hair in Sunlight carbolic soap. He used the same stuff to slop out the floors in the mess huts so he never had any bother with grease or lice.

It was just five to one when Barney finished mopping out the floor. He put his mop and bucket away and fished in his overalls for his watch. He moved the minute-hand forward five ticks and went outside to crank the lunch-time siren. He knew Gussie Gallagher, the site foreman, would be listening. Gussie had put Barney 'on report' because he had accidentally cracked a cistern as he mopped out the site office toilets. Barney owed Gussie a big one and he was determined to repay him. He decided he'd teach the bow-legged little bollix to stuff his cistern where the monkey stuffed his nuts.

part 1

chapter 1

PATSY

Home to Patsy and Timmy Talbot was the garret room of number fifteen Larnham Street. Measuring sixteen by twenty feet, the room was the third home they had rented since their marriage twelve months earlier. A collapsing roof and a lunatic landlord took care of the first two, they only had this one on a nod and a wink and there was no hope of a rent book. The house was built nearly two-hundred years before to keep one family in luxury, but by 1958 it was a four-storied, crumbling tenement, one of thousands scattered all over the north side of Dublin City. When she moved in, Patsy was befriended by Mrs Coffey, a small, rotund, silver-haired widow who lived most of her sixty-five years in a big front room on the first floor of the house. Across the hallway, in the room opposite Mrs Coffey's, lived a thin, severe-looking spinster called Lily Caffrey. She worked in an office somewhere in town. Patsy reckoned she was in her fifties. The other tenants called her Miss Caffrey to her face but Sourarse behind her back because she never smiled or talked to anyone except Patsy and Mrs Coffey. Even then her conversation was brief and to the point. Religion seemed to be her only interest and she spent a lot of time in Dominick Street Church.

Although it was midday, Patsy had the curtains closed because she was about to have a bath in a basin. At forty weeks pregnant, her huge bump was totally out of proportion to her slim willowy frame. She stood at five-foot-five in her bare feet and a halo of honey-blonde hair framed her impish, high cheekbones. She had a soft generous mouth and small white teeth. When she smiled, her pale blue eyes could light up a room. That said, the same eyes could ice-blast an offender through a block wall. She was feisty and somewhat headstrong, more attractive than beautiful. Many men lost their hearts to her but none ever won hers in return. Then one night she spotted Timmy Talbot at a dance and decided there and then that she would marry him. She arranged an introduction and let him pursue her for two years before she finally 'agreed' to become his wife.

Patsy opened the sweaty brass tap that hung over the trough where she had set a white enamel basin. The tap spat a harmless belch of water that splattered into the basin. It began to gurgle and gag and she thumped it in exasperation. Somebody further down the house had their tap open so the water couldn't make it to the top of the house. Rapping the tap sometimes gave them the hint, but if that didn't work she would have to do without or get dressed and go all the way down to the tap in the yard. As her swollen stomach brushed the cold, glazed skin of the trough she thought of a kitchen she had seen in an American magazine. Everything matched and it had a shiny metal sink with hot and cold taps looping over it like the necks of silver swans. Drifting for a moment, she saw herself in such a kitchen before a sudden gush from the tap snapped her back to Larnham Street.

Beyond Pulditch Gates

Taking the half-filled basin from the trough, she laid it on a towel to stop it slipping on the linoleum floor. Then she topped it up with a kettle of water she had heated earlier. She had the mirror on the sideboard draped with a sheet because she knew that seeing your naked body was a sin. As she crumbled a square of bath salts into the basin she thought of Monica Dillon. They were the best of mates when they worked together in Graves' paint factory. Monica gave Patsy the bath cubes as part of her wedding present and they laughed because Patsy had no bath in which to use them. That was the day the foreman told Patsy she would have to pack it in when she got married. Patsy knew who made that decision, and more importantly, she knew why.

Richard Graves was her boss's son and the manager of the section where Patsy and Monica worked. He had asked her out several times but Patsy always refused. One night she was working alone in a storeroom when he crept up behind her and shot his hand up inside her overall. He tried to clamp his mouth over hers, but in rage and fright she raked his face with her nails and slammed her work-boot into his ankle. He roared in agony and let her go. As she ran away he yelled that he'd make her the sorriest bitch in creation. After that night Patsy kept well clear of Richard Graves. She never told anyone what had happened. She was terrified Timmy would go after him with a hatchet. Worse again, he might think she had encouraged the creep.

Patsy never returned to the factory after her wedding. Some time later she heard Monica Dillon had packed in too. Ever since, the very thought of Richard Graves made her blood boil, so to soothe herself she stepped into the basin and used a flannel to dribble the warm scented water down her body. Had she known the word 'sensual', that is how she might have described the feeling. It was like the tingling that sometimes came on her when she lay at night beside Timmy. She would become hot and moist and a strange, empty feeling would gnaw at her. Then she would ache to reach out and touch him and sometimes, as if by telepathy, he would sense her need and turn to her. Sometimes he would ask if he could take off her nightie and sometimes, provided the light was out, she'd let him.

She bent over to wet the flannel and it was as if a cork popped high up inside her. She squatted and steadied herself by gripping the thin navy rim of the basin. As warm sticky fluid trickled down the inside of her thighs she felt both fear and elation.

TIMMY

Timmy Talbot shielded his eyes against the sun that sat low for one o'clock in the day. Standing six-feet tall, he weighed in at twelve-and-a-half stone. He had a sallow complexion that tanned at the first hint of sunshine. His hair was ebony and swept back off his forehead in a shiny Brylcreemed wave. A silk of fine dark hair covered his chest then narrowed down to his navel and beyond. Many took him to be Italian or Greek until they heard his accent. Physical labour kept his body trim and made his shoulders broad while his face was chiselled and rugged from working outdoors. It was a face that suggested strength and toughness but it slipped easily into one of his warm and friendly grins. Then his black, deep-set eyes would sparkle, and it was these dark, dangerous diamonds that won Patsy's love before she even knew his name.

He was thinking about her when the lunchtime siren wailed its way across Pulditch.

'Nosebag!' he called to the gang working on the platform above him.

Beyond Pulditch Gates

A plasterer and his mate immediately heaved themselves over the side and aped down the bare bones of the scaffold. Saint Joseph tidied away his carpentry tools and descended in the recommended fashion via the ladder. From all corners of the site, a ragged trickle of men appeared and headed for the huts. Catcalls and insults were exchanged without malice. The Child O' Prague chased Mackerel and swore to break his face for slipping a lump of ice down the back of his neck. Timmy couldn't resist joining in. The three of them crashed through the door of Number One hut and ended up in a heap on the floor.

'The door!' Barney yelled. 'Close the blee...'

His warning came too late. The pot-bellied stove sucked in the icy blast, paused, then belched back a gas that ponged like rotten eggs. Barney lost the head.

'Youse three are a right pair of wankers if ever I saw one! The place'll be smellin' like Sing bleedin' Sing!'

'Prison?' Mackerel grinned.

'No! Fuckin' gas chamber! Now gerrup offa that floor, I'm only after washin' it!'

Apologies were offered but kiss-me-arsed by Barney. Jackets and hats were hung on nails driven into the timber beams of the hut. Lockers were prised open with screwdrivers. No one, except Saint Joseph, had a key. Lunches, mugs or jam-jars, decks of cards and the previous night's newspapers tumbled into the arms of the diners. Saint Joseph entered a moment later carrying his biscuit-tin lunch box. He unlocked his locker and carefully lifted out a china cup. It had a gold-painted rim. Barney reckoned if Joseph had a saucer to match he could have said Mass.

Alfred John Jameson was called Saint Joseph for two reasons. One, he worked on the site as a first-fix carpenter and two, he was very religious. He was frail and whey-faced. Unlike others of his profession, he had no shoulders so it seemed that his arms came straight out of his neck. Although he was thirty-seven years old, he looked more like a schoolboy. He had used the same barber since he was six and the barber still gave him a six-year-old's haircut with a dopey fringe that just invited mickey-taking. Saint Joseph didn't drink, smoke, swear, back horses, chase women or even choke the chicken when the pressure built up. He still dressed like his mother used to dress him. Charcoal suit, black shoes, white shirt, blue tie and gobshite jumpers, the type kids give their uncles for Christmas. Apart from work and being lead trumpeter with the City and District Brass and Reed Band, his only other interest was Mass every morning, sodality every month and evening devotions in between. He served his apprenticeship with his uncle and worked with him until he died. The business folded and he found himself in a Labour Exchange. In his innocence, he said he didn't mind where they sent him to work.

When he arrived on the Pulditch site, he thought he'd landed on Mars and that was before he met the Martians in Number One hut. He owned the only decent locker in the whole caboose. It stood alone in a corner away from the lower orders and their crude exhibits. A picture of Jesus with his chest torn open and his heart on fire hung on its door. To balance things up, Barney had his legless locker propped on a beer crate, and from its well-battered door Lenin stuck out his jaw urging the masses to kick up quick and inherit the earth. Mackerel McKenna's locker was adorned with faded photographs of footballers and racehorses and below these was daubed in big red letters, 'KNIPEMKCUF'. It took Saint Joseph a full lunch hour to work it out and then he wouldn't talk to Mackerel for a week.

Beyond Pulditch Gates

As usual the occupants of the hut slid themselves and their lunches in parallel along the benches and tables until each sat at his allotted spot. Then the spouts of the kettles moved along the tables, bowing into each receptacle a steaming browngold liquid. Milk-bottles and sugar bags moved in a square dance to the ragged music of a communal teaspoon stroked from the Gresham Hotel. The shiny side of baker's paper squeaked as lunches were unwrapped. A voice sighed wearily.

'Shite! Jam again!'

'Yer lucky,' another retorted, 'I got a bleedin' prairie!'

Saint Joseph whispered to Barney.

'What type of sandwich is that?'

Barney thought for a moment before answering.

'It's when there's fuck all between the cuts of bread only air and space!'

Twenty minutes later the sandwiches were eaten and scum formed on the dregs of cold tea. The men of Number One hut relaxed. Some slept. Some talked. Some read. Others played poker using sets of ragged-edged cards. One set proclaimed Guinness was good for you. Another had the same donkey carrying the same load of turf fifty-two times up the same boreen. Mackerel said the poor thing must have had a pain in its bollix carrying the stuff. There was consternation when Saint Joseph explained to Mackerel that there was no need to worry about the donkey. He'd only carried it once and the rest of the cards were copies. Then Mackerel produced a deck smuggled in from England. When Saint Joseph saw what was on them he said that he'd never have a minute's luck. Not that it worried Mackerel.

Mackerel had been christened Michael, but when he was twelve his father skipped off to England and never came back. Michael

15

had to leave school and lie about his age to get a job in a fish factory. His mates immediately christened him Mackerel and it stuck. He was a long, skinny kid and he stayed that way. He had wide honest eyes, a funny face, a loping walk and limbs that turned to rubber whenever he did his Norman Wisdom routine. Leaving school was no hardship because it never did him any good in the first place. Instead Mackerel studied on the streets and learned to survive where others would starve. If it took ten, twelve or twenty hours a day to get what he wanted, then his thin wiry body worked them.

There was a girl in his life once. He was besotted and for months he spent every penny he had on her. It never dawned on him to ask why she never introduced him to her friends or family. They went out shopping and she put her eye on an expensive gold watch. When Mackerel said he couldn't afford it she went into a sulk. A few days later she asked him to read her an article in a magazine. It wasn't a request, it was a challenge and he failed. She called him a thick and walked out. He never bothered much with women after that.

Mackerel was waiting for his turn to deal when Horizontal Harvey lifted his head from the bench where he was resting.

'Hey, Timmy, did the mot fall asunder?'

'Not yet,' Timmy mumbled.

'It must be a bicycle pump yew have. It's a ball o' wind under 'er shift!'

'Leave that talk where it belongs,' Mackerel snapped, 'in the gutter!'

Horizontal turned with a laugh and a riddle of farts to snooze again. Mackerel nodded over to Barney and then over to Timmy, who was staring at the orange glow behind the slatted door of the

Beyond Pulditch Gates

stove. Barney took the hint, eased over to Timmy and offered him a Woodbine.

'Never mind that gobshite Harvey. He'll never die of a brain haemorrhage!'

Timmy smiled. They lit up and let two fireflies dance in the air.

'Ye had a decent brood yerself, Barney?'

'I had, Timmy. Eleven all told. Eight still alive, thank God!'

'Ye lost three kids?'

'It happens! But don't yew worry, the first is the slowest. After that, it's a doddle!'

Barney stood up and stretched. He sighed, and shuffled off down the hut.

Timmy watched him weave his way through the tables. Hairy Mary, Man-in-the-Mirror, Fixit 'n' Fukkit, Clean and Oily Paddy were all playing cards. The Child O' Prague lived up to his name by staring out the window. Saint Joseph was reading *A Pilgrim's Guide to Lourdes*. The Pox was tying fishing flies onto vicious-looking hooks. His name was Jimmy James, but with The Pox everything was poxy this and poxy that so he more or less named himself. Horizontal Harvey snored and then broke loud and riddling wind. Timmy reckoned the shagger was a razorbill in another life because he could shit while asleep on a nine-inch ledge. Further down the hut Willie Kearns was expounding socialist theory to a group of new recruits. They looked like they didn't give a rollicking rex how unfairly the world was divided. Kearns was known as 'Red' Kearns because he was always on about burning down the banks and building a workers' paradise. Yet for all his bluster, Kearns was never caught dopey by Gussie. Some said he was just a jam-pot, but others quietly questioned his endless good luck. Kearns was the sort that if his right hand ever

17

met the left one they'd have to be introduced because Kearns would never let one know the other existed.

Ruuppturruppptuppp. Barney ran the handle of his brush along the corrugated roof. 'Gerrout yiz hoors, yiz are way over the time!'

A torrent of abuse washed back, especially when he hoisted one end of Horizontal's bench and dropped it with a bone-jarring thump. The cards were dealt for one last hand while Saint Joseph performed his daily lunchtime ritual. First he swept his crumbs off the table and tidied away his cup. Then he took his lunch-box back out to the carrier bag of his bike. Kearns finished his diatribe with a triumphant thump on the table. The Pox tied off the last of his flies while whistling an aria from *The Pirates of Penzance*. Man-in-the-Mirror gazed into a small shard of mirror glued inside the door of his locker. Hairy, so called because he was as bald as a billiard ball, went outside to flick out the dregs of his tea. Seconds later he dived back in again.

'On the ball! It's Gallagher!'

The scatter was straight from the Keystone Cops. A four-handed lift flung Mackerel out a side window to run and warn the lads in the other huts. Cards, cups and fishing flies disappeared. Hats and jackets were whipped off nails as their owners made for the door. Barney watched Gussie's bandy legs waddle furiously towards the huts.

'Gotcha,' he whispered. 'Gotcha!'

Gussie Gallagher trembled as he neared the huts. He'd heard there was nothing as exciting as sex. He'd never had it or even come close but it would have to give some whack to beat the thrill of hunting lazy whores out of their huts. Scatter, that's what they were to do whenever he appeared. They were to scatter like rats just as the occupants of Number One hut were doing. He scanned

Beyond Pulditch Gates

huts Two, Three and Four. There was no sign of movement so he veered off to hit Number Four for a start.

As a five-foot-eight, fourteen-stone bully, Gussie never went around anything if he could go straight through it. With his hooped legs, hanging belly and flushed face he looked like a load of giant beef tomatoes lumbering along in a gaffer's brown coat. Despite the cold, fuss sweated his brow and armpits. His flat cap was too small for his head, his neck stretched the grimy collars of his shirts and as for his tie it was hard to say where pattern began and food stains ended. Gussie didn't wash too often or put creases in his clothes. He was a rough-and-tumble gaffer who got things done by putting the fear of God into everyone else. He was also a grade A, Class One gobshite who really believed he'd finally made it as a manager.

Number Four hut, usually occupied by the scaffolders, was empty so Gussie waddled around to hit Number Three where the steel-erectors were always slow about showing their faces. It too was deserted. When he found Number Two devoid of plumbers and painters, his excitement switched to intense vexation. When he finally crashed through the door of Number One it too was empty except for Barney who was tiddling the floor with a sweeping brush. Gussie decided to take at least one scalp from the hunt.

'The siren!' he bellowed.

'Out the front!'

'I know where the hell it is! Why it was five minutes early for the break?'

'Sure that couldn't be! I sets me watch be the BBC World Service!'

'Never mind the bloody BBC! From now on the siren will be up at the site offices where I can keep me eye on it!'

19

'But I'd have to hoof all the way over every time there's a break. Me ould legs'd be murdered!'

'Well now, Mister Coogan, if you're not capable o' doing yer work there's plenty o' men who would be! Understood?'

'Understood,' Barney mumbled, but as Gussie buffaloed away he swore that somehow he'd nail the short-arsed, snot-gobbling, bow-legged little bastard. Just then Saint Joseph appeared in the doorway. Barney went for him.

'An' where the fuck were yew?'

'Out at my bike. Why? Did I miss something?'

LIFE

The plasterers worked on under floodlights until seven o'clock that night. Gussie detailed Timmy to stay back to clean up after them. When he had finished, the night-watchmen fixed him a mug of tea before he headed off towards Ringsend to catch a bus. His boots crunched along the sparkling ribbon of road that the moon and frost laid out before him. Ever since Patsy told him she was pregnant, he watched in amazement as she swelled and filled with life. The idea fascinated and frightened him. He often wanted to take her in his arms and share it all with her, but he never could. The rules had been there for generations. Women's work was women's work.

As he walked on, a voice deep inside echoed his dead father's wish that Timmy's first son would bear the name of Timothy. The tribe touched the nerve it wanted. Timmy felt himself go chin up, chest out and shoulders back. Men were about to fly in space but the grip of the cave was as strong as ever. Past, present and future generations of Talbots marched with him as he strode on towards the winking lights of Ringsend. Then a thin flash of yellow streaked across the night and disappeared. A soul on its way to Heaven. Suddenly Barney's remark about his three dead children spiked Timmy's heart like a shard of ice. It left him cold, alone and listening to the wind banshee through the leafless skeletons of the trees. He ran the rest of the way to the bus stop.

Ten minutes later the number three bus crunched up a gear to tackle the rise at Wallace's coal-yard. A blazing coal fire painted on the wall praised the quality of Wallace's English Mossbank Nuts.

'On late?' Timmy asked the conductor.

'Last car! I do dread when it's as cold as this. It's like drivin' on glass when ye hit them cobblestones. Doin' blue yerself?'

'Below on that Pulditch job. Casual for now but I'm keepin' me fingers crossed.'

The conductor leaned back remembering.

'We used ta spend every summer down at Pulditch when we was kids. Swimmin', fishin' an' lookin' for birds' eggs. Wan desolate kip in the winter. Still, I suppose it's an ideal place for a power station!'

He picked up his ticket machine, rattled the coins in his pouch, and went to collect fares. Timmy wiped the fogged-up window. A succession of shop names rolled by. Stanley Woods and Burney for cars. Murphy's for a pint before the boat train from Westland Row. Hatchell's for pork, Hopkins' for overalls and Flitterman's for tweeds and hobnailed boots.

The Liffey looked black and forbidding as the bus crossed the bridge into O'Connell Street. The Lemon's Lady in her bonnet and hooped skirt glittered demurely above a sign that claimed her sweets, like her, were pure. There was no such coyness about the flashing red Caltex sign on the corner a few yards further up. On the opposite corner the grimy windows of De Valera's *Presse*s

(*Irish* and *Evening*), glared down Middle Abbey Street at their blueshirt competition. The bus stayed neutral and passed on. It dropped Timmy at the top of Parnell Square, and minutes later, he turned the corner into Larnham Street.

When he got to the hall-door of the house, he noticed another pane of glass was missing from the ribs of the fanlight above it. The door groaned as he pushed it open then kerplummed shut, trapping him in the dank, gloomy hall. A radio was playing céilí music somewhere above. Out to the rear, the Hafferty's were winding up to their nightly row. Mrs Coffey called down from the top of the stairs.

'Is that yerself, Timmy?'

'It is, Mrs Coffey. Is everything all right?'

'I don't think Patsy's too hot!'

Timmy took the stairs in fours. Mrs Coffey nodded him into their room where Patsy was lying on the bed. Her face was waxy and her eyes were closed.

'It started at dinner-time,' Mrs Coffey whispered. 'I said she'd be safer below in the Roxy but she wouldn't budge till yew got here.'

Timmy moved to the bed and touched Patsy's hand. She opened her eyes. They were two terrified pleas for help.

'Timmy! I was waitin' for ye!'

'Sorry, I had to work on!'

'Ye poor thing. Ye must be famished.'

While Mrs Coffey helped Patsy to dress, Timmy ran up to Smokey Joe's (alias Maguire's Select Lounge and Bar) to phone for a taxi. Patsy swore she'd never be carted off in an ambulance with the whole street watching the spectacle. Unfortunately the option of a taxi or an even an ambulance was stymied by a battered penny

Beyond Pulditch Gates

jammed in the slot of the payphone. Timmy was frantic. He was about to run all the way down to the taxi rank at O'Connell Street when the gods sent in the cavalry. A BSA with sidecar attached came sputtering round the corner. Astride it was one of the regulars from Smokey's. Timmy waved him down and told him how he was fixed. Bikers love nothing more than an emergency. He revved his machine to a roar.

'Bring 'er down, ould son! We'll be there before ye can say Jack Johnson!'

That was how Patsy and Timmy Talbot travelled to the ancient halls of the Rotunda Women's Lying-in Hospital (alias The Roxy) for the birth of their first born. Patsy, jammed into the sidecar, puffed more in fury than in labour, while Timmy had the balls blown off him as he clung to Patsy's bag and the biker's belt. The biker seldom got a chance to show just what a BSA with sidecar attached could do. He leaned very far forward when bombing down streets and very far over when slewing around corners. It was all very dramatic, inelegant and utterly unromantic. On the other hand it was memorable, effective and quick because seven minutes after they left Larnham Street they were standing at the hospital porter's desk. He made them sit down on a long bench then he rang upstairs to send down a nurse.

A few moments passed in silence, then the footfalls of an approaching nurse handcuffed their hands together. A porter steered a wheelchair behind the nurse who was a big red-faced woman. Timmy noticed she wasn't wearing a wedding ring. It struck him that a woman like that couldn't have the faintest notion of what it was to have a baby.

'Mrs Talbot?' the nurse flicked a clipboard into the crook of her arm.

Patsy's eyes glazed like a snared rabbit. Timmy answered for her.

'It is! I mean, she is!'

'Our first, yes?'

'Well, we're only married a year!'

The porter smiled as the nurse extended her ringless hand.

'Now, Mrs Talbot, if you'd like to sit in the chair, we'll bring you upstairs.'

Timmy felt Patsy's nails dig deep into his flesh. Was she in pain again? Was she saying, 'Don't leave me'? Or was she saying, 'You bastard, it's your fault I'm left like this'? Patsy eased herself into the wheelchair.

'Right!' Timmy picked up her bag. 'Where to?'

The nurse put up her hand.

'Oh, no, Mister Talbot, this is where we ladies do our bit!'

She took the bag from his hand.

'Call back in the morning and the porter will tell you if there's news.'

It was time to kiss and encourage but Timmy did neither.

'I'll see ye then, Patsy,' he mumbled.

'See ye, Timmy. Let me Ma know I'm in.'

Then the porter wheeled her down the long corridor towards the lifts. As they turned the corner Patsy looked back, and for an instant their eyes met. It was a look that Timmy could never describe, nor did he ever try to. It was one of the few moments in a man's life that he holds silently in his mind and carries with him into eternity.

When Timmy got back to Larnham Street he eased the hall-door closed behind him but there was no escaping the kindness of Mrs Coffey. Her door was ajar and the light of her room spilled out

Beyond Pulditch Gates

into the darkened hallway. As soon as she heard him she was out to insist he come in for something to eat. Timmy felt both guilty and grateful. Being a widow, Mrs Coffey had little enough for herself, but she was, like so many of her generation, willing to share what little she had. Timmy looked around the plain but tidy room. Above the mantelpiece were two black-and-white photographs. One was of Mrs Coffey's dead husband, Padso. The other was of a young tousle-haired man in a pinstriped suit with wide trousers and lapels. He was arm in arm with a pretty young woman who held a small bouquet of flowers. It was the wedding photograph of Mrs Coffey's only child Billy and his wife Marie. In the first year of their marriage Billy was laid-off three times, so they had packed up and headed for Australia.

Timmy sat at the table while Mrs Coffey clattered a black iron pan onto the gas stove, flattening its yellow-blue flame. A daub of lard went skating across it and rashers and sausages quickly followed. As the grease heated a sausage burst and the rashers wriggled in protest. An egg was cracked on the rim of the pan and plocked on beside them. It turned white with the fright. Minutes later a mammoth fry clattered down in front of Timmy along with cuts of turnover bread and a cube of slushy butter. Beside the overflowing plate, Mrs Coffey plonked a mug filled with hot, strong tea. It was only then that Timmy realised how hungry he was. As he ate, Mrs Coffey buttered a crust of bread and sprinkled it with sugar. She poured herself a mug of tea and began to talk of babies, of who was born when and where. Then she told Timmy about a woman who had just had her ninth son.

'When the Sister asked her what was she gonna call the baby yer woman says, Enda. Enda, says the Sister, that's a good Irish name. Irish me eye, says yer woman, that youngfella's the enda' me and shaggin' labour wards! Yer man at home can tie a knot in it from now on!'

Their laughter caused the teapot to shake.

It was one o'clock before Timmy got to bed. Sliding between the cold, clinging sheets he missed Patsy more than ever. He missed her warmth and the gentle scent that surrounded her. He missed her fury when he'd slip his cold hands down the back of her nightie. It wasn't true fury, but the kind of fury that usually ended with them warming each other. His eyes begged for sleep but the alarm clock was determined he'd hear every second of what promised to be the longest of nights. He wondered if she was in pain? Was she frightened? Did she hate him for making her pregnant? Maybe it was happening right there and then. While he lay alone in the dark was she struggling among strangers under the blazing lights of a delivery room?

The luminous hands of the clock were glued at a quarter past one. He was exhausted, but the best he could do was to close his eyes. An instant later, the clock was clattering like a demented hornet around the saucer on which it stood. Timmy groped in the dark and stubbed it silent. He cursed himself for setting the alarm arseways. Then his eyes focused and he realised the big hand was at twelve and the little one at seven. The number one bus left Parnell Square at twenty-five to eight and would take him to the gates of the site. If he missed it he'd have to take a number three and walk from Ringsend. If so, he'd be late and Gussie Gallagher would put him on report. Within minutes he was skittering quietly down the stairs, unwashed, unshaven and lunchless.

Outside the night was struggling to keep dawn from seeping under its navy skirts. The cold was bone-snapping and the

Beyond Pulditch Gates

glistening paths had laid booby traps wherever they'd snared a pool of water. It was twenty past seven when he pushed open the hospital door. The porter's desk was empty. Timmy paced up and down the waiting area. Time changed its mind from the night before and the second hand raced around the face of the clock above the porter's desk. He considered barging on into the hospital but he was afraid he'd get Patsy into trouble. Twenty-five past came and went. His litany of prayers rapidly changed to a string of profanities. What he wouldn't say to that porter when he finally showed up.

At twenty-eight minutes past he did and Timmy almost cried with relief.

'Me wife! I left her in last night!'

'Surgical or maternity?'

'She's having a baby but I'm in a terrible rush for me bus!'

He knew by the porter's face that he didn't quite make the connection. Nonetheless, the porter lifted the heavy black phone on his desk.

'Name?'

'Talbot, Patsy Talbot!'

The porter's finger spun the dial once, twice, three times. There was a pause that the clock chose to ignore.

'Hello, it's the front desk. Have yiz a Patsy Talbot up there? Yiz have! She is? How soon? I see. Right oh, thanks a lot!'

He clattered the phone back together.

'She's in the labour ward. They said she's fine.'

'Did they say when there might be some word?'

'That's all ye ever get outa them. Sometimes things goes fast, sometimes they take forever. If yer handy to a phone ye could givvus a ring later on.'

Timmy felt his stomach drop. The only phones on the site were in the offices and he'd have to ask Gussie Gallagher if he could use them.

'I'll do what I can!' Timmy blurted then he turned and ran like hell for the bus.

A Very, Very Good Girl

Patsy's labour stopped and started throughout the night but now was at its height. In an adjoining cubicle, a woman screamed as though being ripped apart with a tin-opener. Patsy refused to cry aloud. Sweat blinded her. Pain washed over her in ever closer waves, but still she gritted her teeth and pushed or panted as instructed. Two young nurses were at either side of the delivery table, while a midwife worked between her legs that were splayed and held aloft in stirrups. A doctor stood in the corner well back from the messy spectacle he was supervising. The instant he breezed into the cubicle, the hair on Patsy's neck rose in revulsion. He was the spitting image of Richard Graves. Sometimes he stepped in to check progress. When he did, he spoke to the midwife like a vet speaks to a farmer who is helping a heifer to calve.

The woman in the adjoining cubicle screamed to Jesus, her mother and the world for help but Patsy was too preoccupied to hear. She gulped for air, gulped again, then bore downwards. The midwife's face turned white.

'You're too soon, Mrs Talbot! Too soon!'

Patsy was no longer on the couch. She was floating high above it watching her baby poke its glistening crown into a treacherous floodlit world. A voice that sounded like hers bellowed a long unconquerable roar. Even the adjoining cubicle fell silent. She gulped, pushed and roared. Then gulped, pushed and roared again.

Beyond Pulditch Gates

It was left to her son to answer. He bawled back his outrage at being hoisted aloft like a plucked and buttered chicken. It was twenty-five minutes to eight.

Patsy wanted to hold and hug her son into existence but in seconds their last physical link was tied-off and severed. Then he was whipped away to be washed, weighed and made presentable. Kissing the birth-goo off your own child was considered bad medicine. The doctor appeared at the foot of the table.

'Now, Mrs Talbot. I'll take the afterbirth and then you'll need some stitches. I've some student chaps outside. I wonder if they might pop in and watch?'

The request was killed by Patsy's icy glare. The doctor stitched in silence.

Despite her discomfort, Patsy never flinched, and bravely fought the blackness of exhaustion that crept in all around her. She was thinking only of Timmy. He'd be frantic for news and now he had a son but didn't know about it. She wanted to be the first to tell him and the first to hand him their baby. Then the doctor stood back and patted her on the buttock.

'Four of the best!'

He peeled off his gloves like a magician wrapping up a rather clever trick.

'All things considered, you've been a very, very good girl!'

Patsy was too tired and sore to retort to the smarmy little shite. Instead she just closed her eyes and within seconds she was asleep.

OPERATION ROXY: PHASE ONE

Timmy just made the bus. Clean and Oily Paddy were already aboard and Horizontal Harvey was sprawled over one of the long back seats. Clean Paddy was just that. He was small and dapper with shiny shoes and permanent creases in his trousers. Though he helped the plasterers, dust or dirt never stuck to his overalls and he always finished the day looking like he was on his way to a dress dance. Oily Paddy was small like Clean Paddy but that's where any similarity ended. Dirt came to Oily like iron to a magnet. He called himself Site Lubrication Officer, but everyone called him the greaser. He was tough and blocky and his clothes and cap were so greasy they shined. The Child reckoned Oily could stand out in a monsoon and never get wet.

In Townsend Street, the bus picked up the other great double act that worked in Pulditch. They were known as Fixit and Fukkit. Although they were the best of mates, they were like the North and South Poles – they cancelled each other out. Fixit was a tall, thin, nervy man whereas Fukkit was small, fat and cocky. Fixit never cursed whereas Fukkit never did anything else. Fixit drank his tea black while Fukkit took it with three sugars and a good sup of milk. Fixit followed Everton while Fukkit followed Liverpool. The only thing they had in common was that they both helped the electricians. Whenever Gussie barked that he wanted something done, Fixit would say;

'Yes sir! I'll fix it straight away, sir!'

Fukkit would let Gussie waddle away then he'd sigh:

'Ah, fuckit! We'll do it in the morning!'

At six minutes to eight, the number one deposited the boys outside the Pulditch gate. They saluted Dockets Hannigan in the watchman's hut. He was known as Dockets because a duck couldn't carry its feathers in or out of Pulditch without showing Dockets a docket to cover them. They were almost at the huts when Barney came out. The boys knew Gussie made him move the siren over near the site offices the day before. Clean Paddy led with the chin.

Beyond Pulditch Gates

'Gonna blow the siren, Barney?'

'No, me bleedin' nose!'

He humped off towards the offices.

'Ouuchh!' squawked Oily. 'I can't see that arrangement lastin'!'

'Neither can Yiiiiii,' Horizontal yawned.

Fixit stopped and thought for a moment.

'They should fix the siren somewhere agreeable to everyone!'

Fukkit shook his head.

'Naw! We should fuckit inta the Liffey with Gussie Gallagher tied t' the handle!'

They were pulling on their overalls and sneaking a quick mug of tea when they heard the siren. It was short and flat like a top-table fart. Mackerel shook his head sadly.

'Is Barney afraid o' the bleedin' thing? Gussie's put the fear o' jayziz inta him!'

The Child wagged an admonishing finger.

'Yew of little faith! Know you not there is more nor one way to shag a cat!'

Saint Joseph jumped immediately.

'No! No! You don't shag cats ... you skin them!'

The place erupted and when Barney came back into the hut he was smiling too, but no one had the courage to ask him why.

A few minutes later The Pox screeched his bike to a halt outside.

'Mornin', Poxes!' he bellowed into the hut.

A torrent of abuse washed back out at him that was fielded and returned with interest. As the verbal battle continued, Barney noticed Timmy staring into his locker. A carpet of bristles covered his chin and his clothes were crumpled. He eased over to him.

'Well, Timmy? What's the read?'

31

'She went in last night but when I called down this mornin' they said she's in the labour ward. I've ta ring back every hour but how the hell do I get near a phone down here? Ye heard Gussie. Nine, nine, nine only!'

Barney thought for a moment.

'Well, if Mohammed can't ring the mountain!'

He winked to Hairy who drifted over beside them. Barney whispered in his ear.

'Let the air outa the front tyre on the dumper!'

Hairy disappeared unnoticed amid the turmoil of The Pox saying good morning to the tin-roofed asylum.

Ten minutes later Gussie was shown the flat-bottomed tyre.

'Ah, damn it in an' outa hell that's the second one in a week! Are they made o' bloody liquorice or what!'

Barney tut-tutted and said it was probably a nail. Gussie was almost crying. He kicked the tyre and then turned on Hairy.

'Did ye try blowin' it up?'

'No joy! Besides, it might blow out with a load up. If that happened someone's balls could be rightly in a sling!'

'Especially if someone got hurted!' Barney rubbed it in gently.

Gussie hopped from foot to foot. It was his decision not to buy a spare tyre to replace one that had been ripped the week before. Then Hairy lit up like an apostle at Whit.

'I've a mate up town who'd do it straight off! I'd be up and back be the tea break!'

'That's the shot!' Barney cried. 'Least said, soonest mended!'

Gussie wavered for a minute wondering what, if anything, was behind this sudden bout of co-operation. At the same time his arse, while not exactly out the window, was definitely parked on the ledge.

Beyond Pulditch Gates

'Well, get the bloody thing off! There's a meetin' here for the top knobs at twelve o' clock so I want every man and machine at full belt when they get here!'

Hairy began to struggle with the wheel-nuts. That was the signal for Timmy to make his entrance from where he was hiding at the back of the huts.

'I'll need a hand,' Hairy grunted. 'These bloody tyres weigh a ton!'

Timmy was the bait and Gussie took it like a barracuda.

'Hey, you, Talbot! Give this man a hand!'

Timmy dutifully trotted over to pull on the wheel-brace.

'Not too fast!' Hairy whispered. 'Not too fast!'

A few minutes later a van that contained Hairy, Timmy and the tyre trundled out the gates and headed for the city. Satisfied it was safely away, Gussie turned on Barney.

'I see ye moved the siren!'

'As instructed, Mister Gallagher! Today's timin' will be perfect!'

OPERATION ROXY: PHASE TWO

Timmy was sure they'd both be sacked.

'Gussie will go mad when he finds out we went all the way up to the LSE! There's a hundred garages between Pulditch and North Frederick Street!'

Hairy pulled out a yellow and black Gold Flake packet.

'I told him I was goin' where me mate works. That just happens to be the LSE!'

Timmy obliged with a match as Hairy went into his Bogart routine.

'So ye see, blue-eyes, we's gotta pass the Roxy while we's goin'!'

The cigarette dipped on his lower lip and the rising smoke made him squint.

'Of all the gin-joints in all the woild she's gotta have a babee in the Roxy!'

They had just murdered 'The Marseillaise' when Hairy dropped Timmy at the hospital with a shout that he'd be back in ten minutes.

When Timmy pushed open the door the porter was perusing the runners and riders for Kempton. He looked up, recognised Timmy and grinned.

'Howye Da! Ye made it back after all!'

Timmy opened his mouth but nothing came. The porter asked and answered for him. 'A boy! They rang down just after ye went! Mother an' child is well and restin'!' Timmy wanted to whoop and shake his hand but instead he blushed and looked down at his feet.

'Any chance they'd let me in to see her?'

'No way! Visitin' is two ta three in the afternoons, seven ta eight at night!'

As Timmy waited outside for Hairy his eyes scanned the windows of the hospital. A nurse came and went like a white ghost. A woman in a dressing gown peered out at the brightening city. Somewhere behind the rows of glinting glass, the two most important people in his life were resting, unaware that he was only yards away from them. The van backfired as Hairy pulled up beside him. Timmy wanted to get word to Patsy's mother so a few minutes later the van sat in the lane behind her house while the boys sat inside milling rasher sandwiches and mugs of tea.

OPERATION ROXY: PHASE THREE

The hut was quiet after the early-morning riot with The Pox. The ten o'clock tea break was strangely muted. Clean Paddy read from his newspaper that the nuclear arsenals of Russia and America

Beyond Pulditch Gates

were doubling every year. Oily Paddy carefully considered this along with what he'd just picked from his left nostril. Then he looped his thumbs into the pockets of his overalls à la Perry Mason.

'That may as well be, but can the bastards pull a pint without poisoning someone?' Heads nodded because everyone knew that, while plutonium might be dangerous, a bad pint was absolutely deadly. Barney thumped his mug down on the table.

'D'ye know lads, dem Russians wouldn't know a good pint from a nip of gnat's piss!'

Red Kearns was incensed.

'If ye said that in Moscow you'd be dumped in the Liffey!'

Then Oily unlooped his thumbs and leaned forward like a judge giving a verdict.

'Whatever about the Russians, them Yanks is ten times worse. I sailed in an' outa New York when I was with Irish Shippin' and I wouldn't wash me feet in the ditchwater they put up as beer!'

Knowing Oily, the boys reckoned America had reason to be grateful. The Pox decided to keep the pot simmering.

'Ah, now, Paddy, fair's fair! The yanks give the Irish a great look in.'

'Well said,' Saint Joseph piped up, 'some of their most famous people are Irish! They're politicians and priests, not to mention actors!'

'Like who?' Oily insisted.

'Barry Fitzgerald!' Saint Joseph flashed back triumphantly.

'And where d'ya leave his sister?' Mackerel demanded.

The hut went silent then Barney asked him what sister he was on about.

'Ella!' Mackerel grinned.

A sluice of tea-leaves took off in his direction.

35

'Ellohhbee!' a voice yodelled from the door. 'The van's back!'

The boys were waiting when the van pulled up and Timmy stepped out.

'Well?' The Child demanded, 'A boy or a child?'

'A boy!' Timmy roared.

Men instantly shook his hand, slapped his back, said fair play or I'd never doubt ye. Everyone pulled out fags and lit up to celebrate, but the celebrations were short-lived. A lookout whistled a warning. Gussie was on the move. In a flash, the tyre was bounced from the van and rolled to the waiting axle. The rest of the boys disappeared, leaving Barney to supervise Timmy and Hairy, who were pulling on the wheel-brace when Gussie came stomping around the corner. He went straight for the jugular.

'Well, bejaysus it's the prodigal sons! Did yiz have a nice time in New York?'

Hairy stopped pulling.

'Couldn't help it, Mister Gallagher. The damage was worse nor we thought. I was yapsed me mate done a nixer on it! Only charged me two quid!'

'Two quid!' Gussie choked. 'Did ye get a receipt?'

'For a nixer?'

Gussie started his hopping routine again. Then Barney put in the sucker punch.

'What time is these big wigs havin' their powwow?'

This seemingly innocent enquiry stopped Gussie in mid-hop.

'They'll be here any minute!'

He eyed Hairy suspiciously but knew he was shanghaied.

'All right! All right! I'll get the money outa petty cash but ye'll see none of it unless that bloody dumper's moving in five minutes flat!'

Beyond Pulditch Gates

As he stormed off, Timmy wiped sweat from his brow.

'Two quid! For a blast o' free air! We'll be sacked!'

Hairy shrugged his shoulders.

'That's inflation for ye!'

It was the oldest joke in the book, but Hairy and Barney had to hold each other up they were laughing so much. Timmy leaned against the dumper because his knees were shaking and he thought he was going to be sick.

PERFECT TIMING

At ten minutes to noon George Keyes, the Chairman of the Board arrived in Pulditch. He had a retinue of head-office acolytes trailing behind him. True to his word, Gussie had the whole site going full tilt. The dumper criss-crossed in front of the cranes and cement-mixers while the men were stuck in, flat out and giving it whiskey. Keyes was very impressed when he viewed the scene from the window of the second-floor site office. Over coffee and biscuits, he was introduced to the site engineering team. The grovelling gaffer was left until last and Gussie blushed like a teased bride when described as a foreman of reputation with experience on both sides of the Irish Sea. That meant he was one almighty bollix, which suited management down to the ground. Then they all gathered round a table to hear a presentation from Keyes. Gussie was allowed to stay, not at the table, but on a wooden stool tucked away in a corner.

Though he was a middle-aged widower, Keyes was dressed in one of the latest mohair suits. He wore a brilliant white shirt, silk tie and chunky gold cufflinks. Keyes wasn't tall but he had a commanding Napoleonic presence. A full chin, decent paunch and silver hair oiled back off a red, polished face told of his fondness for good food and wine. Keyes was the patron of an art gallery, an orchestra and some high-profile charities. He used these activities to keep tabs on the rapidly changing business and political scene. A new breed of 'business' people was emerging. Their talk was of nods and winks, strokes, what politician was in whose pocket and the astonishing power of the plain brown envelope. Keyes wanted people on his team who understood this new game and how to play it. It was his beloved daughter, Catherine, who found him the ideal man to slot into Pulditch.

At one minute to one, Barney Coogan sauntered to the siren that was directly below the window where Keyes was speaking. At exactly one o'clock according to the BBC World Service he wound it up and let it rip. The blitz had come to Pulditch. Keyes stopped speaking and glowered at the site engineers who in turn glowered at Gussie who felt his anal sphincter loosen. He leapt up, cracked his head on a shelf, and brought down an avalanche of site maps, drawing pins and paper clips. He waded through them on his way to the window where he waved furiously at Barney who smiled, waved back and cranked even harder. Gussie drew a finger across his throat but Barney just shrugged as if to say he was going as hard as he could. An instant later the site accountant was snarling into Gussie's ear.

'Never mind the semaphore! Get out there before that lunatic gets us all sacked!'

Gussie clattered down the steps to where Barney was cranking.

'No! No! No!' he screamed.

'Whaddya mean go, go, go!' Barney bawled, 'I'm fuckin' goin' as hard as I can!'

Gussie nearly beheaded himself as he dived to halt the spinning arm.

'Whaaaaat! Whaaaaat in Gaaaawds name do you think you're dooooing?'

Beyond Pulditch Gates

'Blowin' the siren! An' bang on time too!'

'But the Chairman...!'

'Whaddabout 'im?'

'He's ... He's halfway through his speech!'

'So?'

'So he can't finish it with a fuckin' air raid on outside the window!'

'Oh! So ye don't want me to blow it then?'

'No, I don't! I mean I do! But not here!'

The accountant appeared at the top of the steps.

'Gallagher! Mister Keyes is waiting to finish!'

Gussie glared at Barney but Barney had switched to imbecile mode.

'Where will I put the siren this time, Mister Gallagher?'

Gussie wanted to roar up his drainpipe sideways, but to the impatient tapping of the accountant's foot, he said he'd leave that to Barney to decide.

Gussie grinned sheepishly as he slithered back into the room. It was hard to grin with a drawing pin stuck in his foot.

The head-office gang around the table were outwardly grim but inwardly delighted. The Marx Brothers routine with the siren made the site gang look incompetent and the word was out that the position of station manager was about to be filled. It was a plum position so they were like hounds in traps when Keyes said he wished to finish his remarks with a special announcement.

'Now that construction is under way, it is time to appoint a station manager to Pulditch One. The manager's responsibility will be to ensure that the Pulditch One project finishes on time and within budget, and thereafter to run it in a safe and efficient manner!'

39

Eyes flashed all round the table wondering which of them would work the oracle. They were all stuck to their chairs when Keyes told them the appointment was already made.

'The appointee will be from outside the company. He's the son of Theo Graves, one of the most enterprising businessmen in the city and his name is Richard Graves!'

FIRST IMPRESSIONS

Hairy got the two quid out of Gussie and slipped one of them to Timmy as they headed for the bus that evening. Timmy rushed home and soon stood stripped to the waist at the trough. He wetted his shaving brush in the marmalade jar that served as a shaving mug then daubed its scalding bristles across a lopsided stick of shaving soap. He whitened two days of stubble, then slowly dragged his razor through it. Northlite De Luxe it said on the blade, but its effect was far from luxurious. Timmy felt layers of skin lift off his face. When globules of blood appeared, he used the waxed blade wrapper to seal the cuts. He washed his hair, which was something he usually did at weekends. Kettles and pots of water were heated, cooled, emptied into other vessels and finally poured over his head. This tricky procedure is known only to those who have studied the art of washing their hair at a kitchen sink.

When his hair was washed he stood naked in a basin of warm water and used a cube of carbolic soap and a timber-backed nailbrush to scrub himself down. The alarm clock ticked quietly as though exhausted by the ordeal of childbirth. Timmy pictured the scene in the hospital. Patsy would be in a quiet room with the baby in a crib beside her. She'd smile, put her finger to her lips and then gently lift the baby into his arms. He went over it again as he began de-soaping himself. As with hair washing, this complicated

Beyond Pulditch Gates

procedure is known only to those who have mastered the even more refined art of having a bath in a basin.

He dressed in his wedding suit and Brylcreemed his hair into straight shiny lines. His grey crombie overcoat was belted closed with a leather-covered buckle, while its collar stood up to spits of sleet that harried him all the way to Kirwan's sweet-shop. His weekly treat for Patsy was a quarter of powdery bonbons that she waited for with the eager expectancy of a child. That night things were on a different plane. Hairy's generosity gave him room to be choosy. He settled for large box of chocolates. On its lid, two small kittens played in a basket of wool and around one corner it was sashed by a flash of blue shiny ribbon. He asked the assistant to wrap it in brown paper.

When he got to her ward, Patsy was sitting up in bed chatting to her mother. In that second he was proud of her, loving her yet peeved that she wasn't alone. Sitting with their backs to him were two of her mother's neighbours, Mrs Sammon and Mrs Kyle. Better known as Laurel and Hardy, one was short and fat and the other tall and skinny. Timmy reckoned their mouths were for foggy nights at sea. As he moved towards the bed Patsy looked up, their eyes locked and loved.

The foghorns swivelled together and Mrs Kyle held out a green-wrapped bundle.

'There ye are, Timmy! Yer son an' heir!'

The whole ward turned to look. Timmy turned Charlie Chaplin. He forgot the chocolates were under his arm and they thudded onto the floor. He knocked over a chair as he retrieved them from under the bed.

'A few sweets,' he mumbled as he slid them onto the hillock of Patsy's knees.

'Ah, Timmy! Ye shouldn't have!'

It was smiles all round as he gingerly lifted the baby into his arms.

His son was small and pink. A light silk of hair covered his head and, though his eyes were clamped shut, his hands were open like a goalkeeper about to parry a shot. His fingers were translucent with tiny orbs of pink at the tips. Timmy went to tickle them but was suddenly aware that despite soap and scrubbing, his fingers were still ingrained with dirt. His nails too were gapped and broken like the teeth of an abused saw. Instead he touched the light soft skin of the baby's face with the back of his finger.

'He's grand! A real Talbot!'

Then he handed him back to his mother-in-law's neighbour.

Sweat poured down his back. Maternity hospitals were strictly for women. Doctors apart, men had no business there. Their involvement finished with spurts of semen approximately forty weeks before. When a child was born men were to stand back and later stand at a bar and buy drink for their mates. They in turn would congratulate him on doing the business and advise knocking a few more out of her while she was young. This last piece of logic presupposed the older children would rear the younger ones of the brood. It was something akin to Bedouins giving advice on the most effective way to build an igloo.

The final half-hour of visiting was for fathers only but Patsy's mother and her sidekicks were in for the long haul. It was only when a nurse glared 'Get out' that they stood up to go. However, Mrs Sammon wasn't surrendering without a fight and began to call down a litany of saints and martyrs to protect both mother and child. This was a master-stroke on which the nurse didn't dare impose. After what seemed like an age, she left with the dreaded

Beyond Pulditch Gates

promise that they'd be up to visit again. Mrs Kyle made one final sortie when she returned to remind Patsy that she needed to be churched. The nurse took the baby to the nursery and at last they were alone.

Patsy fiddled with the bedclothes.

'They mean the best.'

Timmy nodded. Silence fell. To break the ice he handed her the chocolates a second time and watched her prise open the wrapping.

'They were the best in the shop!'

Patsy knew they were. The assistant forgot to tear off the pricetag.

'They must have cost a fortune!'

Timmy squeezed her hand.

'Thanks Patsy. He's lovely!'

She smiled back but Timmy saw trouble in her eyes.

'What's up?'

'Me Ma wants us to call the baby Jack, after me Da!'

The tribe slapped Timmy on the back of the neck. Was he a man or a mouse? Would he be the one to break the line of Timothy Talbots? Then he remembered a thin streak of light flashing across the sky. He squeezed her hand even tighter.

'Whatever you want, just as long as he's healthy!'

THE AMMO BOX

That evening Gussie Gallagher sat in his room and read that morning's *Irish Independent*. It was a good Fine Gael paper that gave no quarter to lefties or republicans, though they had begun to carry more and more ads for drink, smokes and other kinds of debauchery. At nine o'clock his landlady, Mrs Gorman, would bring him up a supper of cocoa and two slices of toast. They would

Henry Hudson

exchange pleasantries then she would go downstairs again. As he ate he'd turn on his radio for the news, and if Irish music followed, he'd listen while preparing for bed. Thick hardback manuals describing the plant being installed in Pulditch were stacked by the head of his bed. He knew the boiler-house manuals inside out and next he'd tackle the cooling water intakes from the river. That evening he'd been unable to concentrate on either his paper or the manuals.

The incident with the siren haunted him. He couldn't understand why Barney Coogan shafted him over the siren, having saved his neck over the dumper tyre. There was no logic to people like that and to Gussie everything depended on logic. Discipline, rank and order, that was the only way things could work. There had to be superiors and inferiors, with nature demanding you crawled to the first and crucified the latter, which reminded him that he'd have to get on the right side of that new Graves shagger whenever he turned up.

He picked up the *Indo* again. In the deaths column he saw a name he recognised. Fanning. It said the deceased was late of Ballyjamesduff and that he died after a long and painful illness.

'Good!' Gussie hissed. 'May they all die roarin'!'

Then he read that the man died fortified by the rites of the Holy Catholic Church.

'The rites of the Holy Catholic Church! Christ, some people have neck. Wasn't it one of the Fannings brought shame to our doorstep. Well, Dixie Fanning didn't best Gussie Gallagher! No, by Jesus, I made damned sure o' that!'

He flicked the page over and found himself looking at a quarter-page ad for Clery's sale. A pen-sketch of woman accompanied a list of bargains available in the women's department. She was wearing

Beyond Pulditch Gates

a corset stretching from her breasts down past her hips. A tab hung from either side of the corset holding up her stockings. For the fuller figure it said. His eyes lingered so he could be disgusted some more. Her legs were crossed and he began to wonder.

'No! No! No!'

He flicked over page after page until rescued by a headline that read, Pontiff says large families are not a social evil. Gussie grunted approval. That was the kind of thing the *Indo* ought to be printing.

When Mrs Gorman delivered his supper she remarked on the bravery of the men who were crossing the South Pole. Gussie declared it madness and a criminal waste of money. She didn't stay long. When his supper was eaten Gussie eased over to the door and locked it. Then he went to the fireplace where a small turf fire battled gamely against the freezing draughts that attacked down the chimney and through the warped window frames. He eased two loose bricks from the far side of the fire-place then reached in and pulled out a metal ammunition box. When he opened it, a wad of notes sprung open like a jack-in-the-box. He counted his money every night, and on Fridays, when he added to it, he counted it twice. It stood at one thousand, nine-hundred and eighty-five pounds. Satisfied that all was in order, he put his money away, got into his pyjamas and climbed into bed. He looked around the room with its one anaemic light bulb poking from a lampshade that looked like a coolie hat. The wallpaper was well in place before Hitler startled the world. It was a kip. Yet it was nothing to the privations he'd known. Real hardship was to be riven by rickets so that your legs bent outwards like the prongs of a hay-fork. Hardship was to survive on a few lousy acres of bog a mile off the road between Cavan and Ballyjamesduff. Hardship was to struggle on with just him, his mother and Josie, his brainless slut of a sister who had dragged them all to the edge of disaster.

Gussie had nursed his mother through five years of illness before she finally died. Despite his best efforts, he had fallen inexorably into debt, so when the doctor and the undertaker sent final demands for payment, he had no choice but to sell the place and head for England. From then on he thought of nothing but making enough money to return and buy a parcel of land as near as possible to the old homestead. He planned to put a marble headstone on his mother's grave with Jesus pointing her way to Heaven. On Sundays he'd sit in the front of the church and let the locals begrudge behind his back. That would make it all worthwhile and obliterate the memory of Josie, Dixie Fanning and all the godforsaken sites he'd worked from Greenwich to Glasgow. Never again would he take the gaffer's job and all the shite that went with it. Gussie Gallagher would be a landowner just as he was always meant to be.

When sleep closed his eyes the woman in the ad was waiting. She had her back to him but he could see her corset strain against the ample flesh of her body. Her legs were crossed and her suspenders bit into her stockings, holding them captive. This was no pen-and-ink drawing but a Black Widow spider whose hands slowly teased the web of her body.

'Will I, Gussie? Would you like to see more?'

His mind screamed she was a Jezebel, but his body begged her to continue. Her thighs eased apart a fraction.

'Enough, Gussie? Is this enough?'

'No! No! Show me everything!'

'Everything? You want to see ... everything?'

She whipped around and she was hideous. She fell on him with a spine-chilling cackle. No longer full and sensual, she was a bony,

Beyond Pulditch Gates

rancid cadaver straight from the bowels of Hell. He screamed. There was a clap of thunder and he was awake. The light was on and he was alone. The works manual was on the floor. He was wet all over but especially so below.

'Sweat,' he reasoned, 'it has to be sweat!'

He was still willing himself to look when there was an urgent rap on the door.

'Are you all right, Mister Gallagher?'

'A manual, Mrs Gorman! I was reading some stuff. Let it fall. Sorry!'

'Did you hear someone scream?'

'Scream? Me? No!'

'It's ten past two! The rest of the house is trying to sleep!'

'Eff you and ten past two!' he hissed.

When Mrs Gorman went, he eased down the bedclothes. A spreading disc of piss was gluing his pyjamas to his lap.

chapter **2**

LETTING GO

Ten past two and the sobs of Monica Dillon had every other girl in the dormitory awake. Most cried with her, but none dared go to her for fear of being caught by a raiding nun. Besides, they knew that like them she would have to confront her pain until it numbed her body and then went on to numb her soul. She would have to learn that her crime was worse than murder. It had to be because killers sentenced to life imprisonment eventually got out, whereas she might never be free again. She would scrub clothes, polish floors and iron vestments until she grew old and toothless. Her only glimpse of the outside world would be during an occasional Sunday afternoon stroll. Then, under the watchful eye of a nun, she would walk two-abreast in a line of other sinners with her head bowed in a suitably contrite fashion.

Before daybreak, she and the other girls would be hauled from their beds to kneel in the cold oratory. There they would hear from a flop-jowled priest that, in spite of all, the Man from Nazareth loved the whorish Magdalene and so there was hope for

Beyond Pulditch Gates

them. Breakfast would launch them into yet another gruelling battle with the steam and heat of the laundry and the redeeming righteous-ness of the nuns. Fallen women had to receive the wages of their sin. Their cracked hands and blistered fingers reminded them that as they were scrubbing dirt from clothes they were scrubbing sin from their souls.

Monica was twenty-three. She was small with short black hair that bobbed around a flat and badly proportioned face. She had thin, weak lips under a button nose that was pushed up close to big, blue eyes that cried easily. Nature gave her a full figure and heavy legs that refused to reduce despite numerous diets and exercise. In school she took a lot of teasing, so she became the class joker. Her humour and ever-present smile disguised her lack of confidence and a desperate need to be told she was beautiful. From the day she started work, Monica spent every spare penny she had on clothes, make-up and high-heeled shoes to give her the height, shape and look she wanted. As usual, her father cut the ground from under her. He said she looked like a slut and that she'd come to grief in the end. He was right in the second part. Monica was no match for a suave sophisticated lover who wined and dined her while insisting she was the most beautiful woman alive. His insistence on keeping their 'love' a secret only added to her enchantment. Within weeks she was in his bed. Within months she was pregnant but her lover didn't want to know. Within days of telling her parents she was with the nuns.

Her baby kicked and Monica pleaded with it to stop growing so she could protect it forever in the shelter of her womb. Some girls never got to hold their babies, as the nuns took them the moment they were born. Others got to keep them for weeks or even months until they got the dreaded call to bring their baby to the Superior's office. Then Monica thought of Lanky Sarah and her tears rolled freer than ever.

Sarah Kelliher was a tall beautiful girl who came from the west of Ireland. The girls christened her Lanky. She used to sleep in the bed opposite Monica's and croon the dormitory to sleep with haunting Gaelic lullabies. Sarah was the first to befriend Monica when she arrived in the convent and they became inseparable. In quiet moments, they told each other their most intimate and painful secrets. In the final weeks of her pregnancy, Sarah wrote three times begging her family to take her home. To get the letters posted she had to bribe a young trainee gardener with cakes snared from the convent bakery. No reply ever came or if one did, it never reached Sarah. Her son was two days old when a posse of nuns came to the dormitory where she was nursing him at her breast. It took three of them to subdue her while a fourth prised the baby from her arms.

Sarah loved too much and could not live the nightmare. She finished it the following day. As a suicide, she could not be buried in the convent grounds, so she was interred in an unmarked Health Board grave in Glasnevin. Apart from a clerk who recorded the number of the grave, the only others present were the undertakers, the gravediggers and a priest who prayed that God the Father would forgive her two great sins. He didn't mention her earthly father who insisted that Sarah be sent to the nuns and that her name never be mentioned again. Neither did he refer to the man who lied his way between her thighs. He reckoned she'd probably led him on and sure everyone knew that boys would be boys.

BROTHERS

Dublin Corporation binmen were on strike and no refuse had been collected for several days. As usual, the newspapers were down on

Beyond Pulditch Gates

the striker's house. With the Russians launching yet another sputnik, the whisper was that they were not alone under the bed, but watching from outer space as their Irish agents masqueraded as binmen. The fact that ninety-nine per cent of the strikers were card-carrying Catholics seemed to bypass the editor's desk. It was lunch-time and Number One hut was crowded with most of the workers on the site. They were discussing the strike and how they might help the strikers. Smoking and crudity annoyed Saint Joseph but the whiff of Moscow sent him into a pure blue funk.

'This strike is communism!' he cried. 'Pure communism!'

Barney Coogan looked to Heaven.

'What has communism got to do with binmen gettin' an increase!'

'It's part of their plan! They won't stop until we have Bulganin for Taoiseach!'

'I though he already was!' chirruped a voice from the back.

Mackerel shook his head in despair.

'Just imagine, the hammer and chisel flyin' over the Mansion House!'

Saint Joseph bit and corrected Mackerel regarding his choice of tools. A typhoon of tea-leaves, cheers and foot-hammering followed in an eye-blink. Barney rapped the shaft of his brush on the floor until order was restored.

'Who gives a rat's what's over the Mansion House. It could be Santy Clause for all we care! This meetin' is to see how we can back up the Corpo lads!'

Red Kearns jumped to his feet.

'Brothers, we should all walk out in sympathy!'

Saint Joseph turned white but everyone else knew Kearns was only flying a kite. On a show of hands it was decided they'd all chip in a dollar a week to help the binmen's strike fund. Saint Joseph refused to give in case he helped the Russians. Instead he promised to send his sub to the nuns who ran the Penny Dinners in Henrietta Street.

Timmy sat in the middle of the crowd and his heart soared. This at last was more like it. If they all stuck together they could end the nightmare that had haunted so many workers for years. As long as he could remember, workers had to take the boat to England and even further afield rather than stay and face the icebergs of poor pay and unemployment. All his uncles were away and Timmy remembered how hard his father worked just to hold onto his job. He was a helper on a lorry for a furniture removal firm. He'd leave the house before daybreak, and from then until darkness, he would travel the length and breath of the country. Most of the time he was tasked to load antiques and furniture from the country houses of doddering gentry. One by one they were returning to Blighty to die with old decency and tiffin on the lawn. Despite their wealth, few offered the lorry-men as much as a cup of tea, so they survived on flasks, jam sandwiches and the back-hand generosity of native housekeepers.

Timmy remembered, as a small child, lying awake behind the curtain that divided the single room his family called home. He'd struggle against sleep until he heard the squeal of brakes as the lorry pulled up in the street outside. His mother would have a stew or a coddle ready. He would hear the scrape of the pot and the flick, flick, flick of the flint lighter as she lit the gas beneath it. She would then ease open the door to the landing so that his father could see his way up the darkened stairwell. When he stepped inside he'd say quietly:

'How's tricks?'

Beyond Pulditch Gates

'Not a bother.'

She'd put the food on the table and as he ate she'd sit with him sipping a cup of tea.

'How did the kids do at school?'

'Not a bother. Where were yiz today?'

'Cashel first then over to Limerick. Sligo tomorrow. Bastard 'iv a road too!'

Sure that his father was safely home Timmy would close his eyes. When his mother shook him and his brothers awake the following morning, his father would be gone on his travels again. When he died suddenly at fifty years of age the doctors said they weren't really sure what killed him. Ever after, Timmy would never leave unchallenged the ancient and idiotic adage that hard work never harmed anyone.

TEMPERANCE

The following Saturday, an ad hoc meeting was called for lunchtime in Number One hut. The subject was whether they should enrol en masse in the newly formed National Pint Drinkers' Association. This body aimed to fight the penny increase that had just been levied on the pint. The Child opened proceedings by calling down a blessing on the Minister for Finance.

'May he be lowered balls first into a bath of boilin' acid!'

Oily Paddy jumped to his feet.

'Too good for the fucker! Men, the two-bob pint is starin' us in the face!'

Missiles over Lambay Island wouldn't have evoked such deathly silence.

'There'd be a revolution!' Hairy cried. 'Jaysus, there'd have ta be!'

53

The Pox tied more flies and whistled 'The Drunken Sailor' just to get up Hairy's nose.

Then Saint Joseph stood up.

'For problems regarding drink the only association worth joining is the Pioneers!'

Despite the cheers he kept at it.

'Remember Dublin's most famous apostle of temperance!'

'Leave my ma-in-law outa this!' Fukkit demanded.

'It wasn't talking about her! I was referring to that saintly man, Matt Talbot!'

Fukkit nearly swallowed his smoke.

'Is it that scabby short-arsed lunatic yer on about? I remember him all right! Ye couldn't go for a piss in any pub in Dorset Street unless ye took yer pint out with ye. Drink it offa sore leg 'e would!'

'But he used to wrap himself in chains!' Joseph pleaded.

'Yea! Most o' them round his wallet!'

'That was before he saw the light and went back to Jesus!'

'Well, it's a pity the light didn't shine 'is way to the bar while it was at it! That hoor never wore a track in lino from goin' up to buy drink!'

The debate got rowdier and more manic by the minute. When The Child volunteered to be the Pulditch delegate to the inaugural meeting of the NPDA he was cheered to the rafters. When he looked for a collection to defray his 'expenses' he was covered in tea-leaves. The Pox stopped the meeting dead when he stood up and solemnly announced that he had a murmur on his heart.

'So fuckin' what?' sang a hutful of voices.

'I just want yiz to know that I don't give a rattlin' bollix how much the poxy pint goes up as long as they leave the brandy alone!'

Beyond Pulditch Gates

In reply a smelly sock, later claimed by Oily Paddy, took flight from the crowd. It glued itself like a limpet to the door of a locker just above the Pox's head. Everyone waited for it to fall on him but it didn't. It just hung there.

'It's a golfer's sock,' Hairy whispered.

'How do you know?' Saint Joseph whispered back.

'Because it has nine holes and it smells like it's wiped a few as well!'

Gussie was due to go on the move so Barney suggested the meeting be reconvened on the following Monday. The Child winked to Fukkit who sidled outside. The men were pulling on their jackets and hats when The Child grabbed the sock and slapped it on the hotplate of the stove. It smouldered for an instant, then a blue-green flame shot upwards releasing fumes straight from the trenches of the First World War. It was all great craic until someone shouted, 'Gas!'

The plumber's mate panicked.

'I don't wanna die! I'm too young!'

This set everybody thinking and resulted in a blind charge to fresh air.

Fukkit was outside with a screwdriver wedged into the bottom of the door. He heard an ominous rumble inside then a massive thump struck the other side of the wall. The door, safely wedged into its frame, stayed put but the wall just shuddered for a second, then with an almighty crash, fell out onto the rock-hard mud. A decent whack of the Pulditch construction crew fell out with it. There was a moment of silence, then Fukkit heard the stamping hoof and grinding teeth of an infuriated bull. There was no need to look around.

'Yer sacked!' Gussie bellowed. 'An' the rest o' ye is sacked along with 'im!'

55

Henry Hudson

At last his prayers had been answered. He'd caught a nest of commies destroying company property and holding a meeting during overtime hours. Sending them up the road with their cards in their hands and his boot up their backsides would square the balls-up with the siren and show the pinstripes that Gussie Gallagher wasn't a man to be messed with. With a dismissive about-turn, he hopped back to his office giving the lads no chance to plead for clemency. He had his report on the sacking half-finished when there was a gentle rap on the door. Gussie knew it was the commies and that they'd be begging to have their jobs back. Pleasure piled on pleasure when he pulled open the door and saw Barney Coogan standing, cap in hand, with a contrite look on his face.

'Mister Gallagher,' Barney began, 'the lads assed me ta come over an' ask ye....'

'The answer is no!' Gussie snarled. 'No! No! No!'

'But d'ye not wanna hear the question?' Barney asked innocently.

'I know the question! An' the answer is no!'

'So yer back'll be all right for Monday mornin' then?'

'Me back?' Gussie snapped. 'What has me back t' do with it!'

'It's just that the brickies was wonderin' if yer back'll be up ta unloadin' the cement an' breeze blocks what's gettin' delivered here a' Monday!'

Gussie remembered and turned white. One of the civil engineers had ordered thirty tons of cement and ten-thousand breeze blocks to be delivered on site first thing on the Monday morning and he had just sacked the crew who'd have to unload the bloody stuff. Being a blockhead he decided he'd tough it out.

'Sure I'll get some o' the others t' do it!'

Beyond Pulditch Gates

'What others?' Barney smiled. 'Sure ye know us, wan sacked, all sacked!'

Gussie knew he was snookered or more to the point, he'd snookered himself.

'Gimme a minute!' he croaked, and slammed the door in Barney's face.

He stormed over to his filing cabinet and kicked it, nearly breaking his big toe. When he finished cursing and swearing at his toe, God, the world and the filing cabinet, he had no choice but to hoof back across to Number One Hut and ask the huffing occupants to come back to work. He thought they'd all be delighted but they said they'd have to have a meeting to consider the position. Otherwise, they'd wait and have a face-to-face with their union official on Monday morning. Gussie had bent himself over a barrel and invited the bastards to shove a bargepole up his arse. It was four o'clock before they emerged from the hut to say they were back on side, but by then it was time to start packing up for their one-day weekend. Worse again, the carpenters had to be paid overtime to put the end wall back up in the hut. The Lemon's Lady always said Saturday was the best day of the week, but all she had to do was eat sweets. She never had to deal with a nest of hut-wrecking commies.

Nightwords

Patsy and Timmy were lying in bed. Patsy whispered so as not to waken Jack.

'If kids did that I'd tan their behinds! Imagine grown men demolishing a hut!'

Timmy started to giggle and within seconds she was biting the corner of the sheet to stop herself from screeching aloud. He was grateful to hear her laughing. Since Jack's birth, she'd been like a panther on the prowl. All offers of help were gently but firmly rebuffed. She was so protective towards the baby that Timmy felt he had to ask permission to pick him up. This laughing woman beside him was more like the Patsy he married. He ran his hand down onto her hip.

'We can't, Timmy. Not till I go back to the hospital.'

'I know! I just wanted to ... to....'

Patsy gently eased his head down onto her breast. He could hear the beat of her heart as she undid the top of her night-gown. Then she found his mouth with her nipple and fed him her warm sweet milk. It happened in silence. They never referred to it again.

The bell of St George's Church tolled three and Timmy felt her roll over again.

'Patsy?'

'Sorry, can't settle.'

'What's up?'

'Nothin'.'

Timmy's hands rested on her shoulders and began a gentle massage.

'Come on, out with it!'

'Remember Monica Dillon? Worked with me in the factory?'

'Gave ye bath salts for a wedding present? How could I forget!'

Patsy turned to him. Her voice was low and troubled.

'She promised she'd keep in touch but she never did, not even when I had Jack.'

'Maybe she didn't hear.'

'If anyone would hear it'd be Monica! Anyway, yesterday I decided I'd take Jack up to her house to let her see him. She lives up near Mountjoy.'

Beyond Pulditch Gates

'You carried him all the way up there! We'll have the pram next week!'

'I know! I just got this urge to see her!'

'I thought women only got longings before a baby came! So, what happened?'

'They live over a shop so when anyone knocks on the hall door they pull back the curtains to see who it is.'

'And?'

'I knocked and her Ma pulled back the curtains. Then a hand pulled 'er away from the window. I tried knocking again but they just didn't want to know!'

'After you walking all the way up there!'

His anger woke Jack who screamed hunger through the sleeping house.

'Oh, for Christ's sake, Timmy! I don't know why I bother tellin' ye anything!'

A guillotine of hurt sliced their bed, leaving Timmy to fume at the ceiling while Jack sucked at the nipple he'd tasted just a few hours before.

DAYBREAK ONE

Despite Monica's pleading, her daughter came into the world ahead of schedule. Her labour was slow and tremendously painful. At its height she begged the midwife for something to ease her agony. The midwife's eyes flashed at the nun who was at the foot of the bed but she said suffering was an ideal way to atone for sin. Monica snapped two of her teeth as she bit on a stick and grunted her baby into the world on that cold February Sunday. They had just five minutes together. Monica kissed her and named her Patsy in the hope that she'd inherit the strength and compassion of her friend, Patsy Talbot.

The pain of giving Patsy life was nothing to the agony of giving her up. As a nun carried the infant away, Monica finally understood why Lanky Sarah just couldn't go on and why she'd chosen the oratory to finish her pain. Only the red glimmer of light above the tabernacle could understand what it was to feel so rejected and alone. Only that glimmer would know what it was to be cut down in shame and buried in secret in a stranger's grave. One of the nuns, a pinch-faced pixie called Sister Hilda (the girls called her Batface) insisted that at best Sarah was in Purgatory and even then she'd be there for a very long time. Killing herself in the oratory was the gravest offence Sarah could have given to God. Monica was often tempted to tear the malignant bitch asunder but she held her tongue. She would polish and scrub, iron and sew and when the time was right, she'd escape. She would find her daughter, or like the pitiful Lanky, she would die in the effort.

MUNICH

Dawn was needling Thursday awake as the freewheel of Barney's bike clicked to a halt outside the gateman's hut. One of the night watchmen stepped out wringing his hands as if to strangle the cold.

'Jayz Barney, that's brass monkeys for ridin' a bike! Any word on the binmen?'

'Never mind the binmen! Did yiz hear about United?'

'Naw, the radio's bollixed! Did they win?'

'Their plane crashed! Taking off from Munich yesterday evenin'!'

'My Jaysus! Anyone hurted?'

'There's nearly twenty killed! A lot o' them was players!'

The watchman called for his mate to come out, and by the starting siren, the whole site was talking about the terrible news.

Beyond Pulditch Gates

The only exception was Gussie Gallagher who ignored everybody, went straight to his office and slammed the door behind him.

He spread the *Indo* across his desk then read and re-read the advert for Shanahan's Stamp Auctions. To be sure he had it right he read the text of the ad aloud.

'Profit from stamps without risk with a full safeguard for your capital and the probability of an outstandingly large profit within four months!'

If he invested the two thousand in his ammo box and if it paid back thirty per cent he'd have a profit of six hundred pounds after only four months. If he invested the same two thousand twice more then by the end of the year he'd have near enough four thousand quid. A wad like that would go a fair way to buying a nice little place back in Cavan. Then the local smart-arses could never laugh behind his back again. He knew them and their vicious, back-stabbing ways. They'd have had great fun sniggering about his sister Josie being shafted by Dixie Fanning, the greatest whore-master in the county. Well, Gussie took care of her and her whoremaster and the same smart-arses were still wondering what became of them.

Whoever rapped on the door didn't wait to be invited in. Thinking it was one of the men, Gussie turned to attack but just in time he saw the shirt and tie. The man was mid-twenties, about six feet in height, trim and broad-shouldered. His teeth were white and even, while his nut-brown hair was a perfect compliment to his almond-coloured eyes. Gussie was no judge of fashion but his suit and shoes looked expensive. He looked like he'd stepped from the Craven A ad in the *Indo* – the one where a well-groomed and attractive man offers a cigarette to an equally well-groomed and attractive woman.

61

'Mister Gallagher?' the man asked.

'In the flesh!' Gussie snapped to grovelling peasant and whipped off his cap.

'I'm Richard Graves!'

'The new manager is it! Oh, awful pleased to meet ye, Sir! Awful pleased entirely!'

Gussie fumbled his cap from hand to hand. It was only by letting it drop that he managed to shake hands. He noticed that Graves had soft, work-shy fingers and pink, manicured nails. He held the handshake to give him more time to weigh up the new arrival. Though Graves had a Kirk Douglas chin, a straight, strong nose and blemish-free skin, he had a hard, sly mouth. Gussie's mother always said a hard, sly mouth meant a hard, sly heart. Gussie's animal instincts concurred. Richard Graves was not a man to be trusted but on the other hand Gussie's mother was dead and Graves was his new boss. If he played ball, then Graves would see him right. Gussie tightened his grip.

Graves had to pull his hand away from Gussie's sweaty paw.

'I thought I'd drop down and introduce myself. I hope you don't mind?'

Gussie snapped into his bedad and bejaysus mode.

'Mind? Mind is it? Sure yer as welcome here as the flowers o' May!'

'I'd like to meet some of the men, if that's okay?'

Gussie turned to the window intending to invite his new boss to take his pick. It was only then that he realised the site was deserted.

Richard Graves grinned as he watched the idiot foreman tear off towards the site huts. What a capture. The whole bloody outfit asleep way after start-time. An impulsive man might make tracks

Beyond Pulditch Gates

to George Keyes and hang the lot, but that would give him only one bite at the cherry. His first day on site, and already he had the drop on Gussie Gallagher, and crawlers like that were most useful when they felt vulnerable or threatened. Like a trained dog, all they craved was an occasional pat on the head and one more biscuit than the rest of the pack. He adjusted his position so he could see out without being seen himself.

SACRILEGE

When Timmy heard the news about United, it was as if someone had thrown a bucket of icy water over him. He could recite the seed, breed and generation of the entire Manchester United squad. Charlton, Edwards, Taylor and Blanchflower. All the boys were in the hut speaking in shocked whispers. Clean Paddy said he once shook hands with Matt Busby. Oily Paddy shook his head sadly.

'Liam Whelan's brother, Christy, works for the Corpo. He's probably out on strike!'

'That's the last thing on his mind right now,' Timmy sighed.

Someone asked how many caps Liam Whelan won for Ireland. The Child said four.

'One against Holland in '56, one against Denmark, and two against England!'

'Sounds right,' Barney agreed.

'I dunno,' Hairy mused, 'I think it was only three.'

Fixit said Scanlan was United's best player but Fukkit wouldn't have it.

'Scanlan couldn't lace up Denis Viollet's boots.'

Then The Pox, who knew as much about football as a bat's arse knows about snipe-shooting began a yarn about bunking into Old

Trafford when he worked in Manchester during the war. He was mid-story when the door crashed open and Gussie came in with his safety valve about to lift.

'Where the shaggin' hell d' yews think yews are? Billy bleedin' Butlins?'

Every eye in the hut glared back, but Gussie ploughed on in.

'Not two minutes ago I looks out the window an' what do I see? Men at their work? No, be Jaysus! They're all in here warmin' their arses be the fire!'

Timmy was about to dive at him but Barney trapped his arm and his anger.

'Sorry, Mister Gallagher! We were just talkin' about United.'

'United? United who?'

'Manchester United! They were in an air crash last night. A lot o' them was killed!'

'I don't give a shite if half o' Manchester went with them! There's a brand new manager above in that office and all he can see out there is fuckin' seagulls! Now the next man I catch offa the job is sacked! Sacked! D'ye hear me!'

Gussie could see no shape in the window as he ploughed back towards his office. At least Graves wouldn't see the embarrassing exodus from the huts. Maybe the hoor wasn't as cute or as cool as he looked. Meanwhile, back in Number One hut, Timmy Talbot was spitting fire.

'Ye shoulda let me burst 'im! That's a robot that is! Has he no shaggin' feelin's?'

'No,' Barney replied, 'and he'd still have none when he hands ye yer cards! Never let that bollix sting ye inta deckin' him. He'd cream himself at the thought of sackin' one of us!'

Timmy shook Barney's grip loose.

Beyond Pulditch Gates

'So we just stand here and take that shite? Is that what yer tellin' me?'

The Child put a calming hand on Timmy's shoulder.

'What we're sayin' is there's more than one way to shag a cat!'

'Skin!' Saint Joseph dived in. 'How many times have I to tell you, cats aren't for shagging! They're for skinning!'

There was silence for a moment then a volcano of laughter, whistling and locker-hammering erupted. It drowned out the carpenter's frantic attempts to correct what history would record as one of his best ever spokes. Then another mini-riot erupted when Mackerel asked The Child how he held the cats while he shagged them. This in turn gave Hairy the chance to tell yet again the one about the man who tried to make love to a tigress. Oily cut him short.

'We know! We know! Claude Balls!'

Hairy was miffed and threatened to tell no more jokes. Oily raised his eyes to Heaven. 'Thanks be t' Jaysus!'

As the men scattered to the four corners of the site, Barney, who had nodded to Timmy to hold back, closed the door behind them.

'Siddown!'

Timmy sat like a chastened schoolboy. Barney produced two Woodbines and shared them. He sat opposite Timmy and blew a long streamer of blue-grey smoke that snaked upwards to caress the bare bulb hanging above their heads.

'If I never teaches yew wan thing, I'm gonna teach ye this. When yer up against a bull-necked bollix like Gallagher ye use brains, not brawn!'

'But Barney...!'

65

'No buts! That bastard is itchin' to sack someone to put the fear o' Jaysus into the rest. When yer casual like us ye only shoot if the duck is sittin'. Otherwise....'

'Otherwise what?'

'Lunacy! Act the sack, play the dumdum and the dumber the better! Understood?'

Timmy nodded. Barney examined the glowing beacon on the tip of his cigarette.

'My nephew done a week's trial with United wanst. He didn't make it but if 'e had then it might have been him on that aeroplane. So, when it comes to Gussie Gallagher, yer not the only one wants ta shove a banger up 'is bum!'

Sunday

On the following Saturday night, Timmy went down to Smokey's for a pint. He rolled home long after closing time, fell over a pram in the hallway then stumbled up the darkened stairs. Patsy was furious because she knew everyone in the house would hear him. He was only inside their room when he began to feel sick. Patsy held his head while he vomited noisily into the trough. The rancid smell and the yellow-brown spew splattering against the walls of the trough was bad enough, but his whining about United and Munich was unbearable. For the first time ever she felt cold towards Timmy. Not angry, not murderous, just cold that a sad but distant tragedy could reduce a grown man to a blubbering slob.

'Typical bloody Irishman!' she hissed. 'Never miss a chance to wallow in it!'

When he finally finished retching she dumped him onto the bed to sleep.

Beyond Pulditch Gates

She boiled kettles of water and scoured out the sink. Then she poured full-strength Jeyes Fluid down the drain to kill the smell. She had just climbed into bed when Jack woke up. He wanted food and a fresh nappy. Patsy lifted him out of his crib and untied the back of his gown. Scuttery mustard-coloured shit had escaped his nappy and was halfway up his back. He'd have to be changed from head to toe. She went to the tallboy and pulled out a fresh nappy and gown. The gown was embroidered on the front with the word, 'Baby'. It was a present from Miss Caffrey who had quietly left it up a few days after Patsy took Jack home from hospital. Mrs Coffey said Jack would win a million some day because Sourarse Caffrey had never done anything like that for any other baby before. Patsy held the gown to her cheek. It was scented by the bath cubes she kept in the drawers. The bath cubes made her think of Monica Dillon. The next time they met she'd warn her to have nothing to do with men. They just weren't worth the effort.

When Jack was changed she fed him and he howled whenever her nipple slipped from between his milk-greased gums. As he fed, Patsy let her eyes roam around the room that was papered in a faded twists of red and yellow roses. The ceiling fell in a sharp taper from inner to outer wall following the slope of the roof above. There was only one door in the room. Half a dozen coats clung to it on a large brass hook either by a loop in their necks or else crucified on wooden hangars. Next to the door was a double-sided dressing table topped by a mirror, and beside this a four-high chest-of-drawers. On top of the chest was a glass dome that held a collection of stuffed birds. Mrs Coffey gave it to them after they moved in so Patsy felt obliged to keep it on display. Beside the dome was a heavy walnut-framed radio with a large dial and four gold-topped knobs.

Their bed and Jack's crib accounted for the second wall. Along the third was a dresser that held their food, delft and cutlery. Beside this was a small foldaway table with two matching chairs. Like the radio, they were bought on the never-never from Cavendish's in Mary Street. In a corner wedge sat a small fireplace with a black enamel surround, cracked red tiles and a sagging ribcage of metal bars on which to build a fire. A brass log-box depicting an unfortunate fox being chasing by a pack of hounds stood beside it. Above the fireplace was a timber mantelpiece on which stood a carriage clock that hid letters, bills and notices awaiting attention or disposal. Timmy called it their filing cabinet.

A sash window that fell open in summer and jammed shut in winter had punched a square hole in the fourth wall, the one that looked out over the backyard. Below the window, the temperamental brass tap snorted down into the yellow stone trough that was spider-webbed with a million hairline cracks. Under the trough, a curtain disguised a rough two-tiered timber frame on which basins, pots and pans vied for space. It also masked a lidded enamel slop-bucket, the necessity for which can only be attested to by those who've lived four floors up in a tenement house. To the left of the trough was a gas stove that was on the drip from the Gas Company in D'Olier Street. To the right, nearest the door, was a French-polished tallboy. This held their underwear and bed linen. That was it, apart from the well-worn lino on the floor and a cracked light shade on the ceiling. Their world. Four walls, a door and a window.

NIGHTWALK

Man-in-the-Mirror decided that he would walk all night if he had to. Though it was bitingly cold he reasoned that once he was out and moving, death couldn't sneak up on him. The news from Munich

Beyond Pulditch Gates

terrified him. Twice they had tried to take off. Twice. Snow and ice and God knows what, but still they tried. Not for all the tea in China would he go up in one of those aeroplane things. He was thirty-seven years of age and everyone said he was the spitting image of Danny Kaye. They were right. He had a thin, pointed face that usually had a harassed or quizzical look. His eyes danced around his head as if afraid to stay still for a moment. He kept his hair long in winter so he wouldn't catch cold and shorn in summer so he wouldn't get lice. He kept his weight strictly at ten-stone-ten because he had read that this was the healthiest weight for someone his height and age.

He was at the bottom of Grafton Street so he made his usual stop at Switzer's window. With the aid of a street light, he examined his reflection in the plate glass. He didn't think he'd aged at all that day. Nonetheless he searched for any new wrinkles. Pulling his comb from his pocket he fixed his already perfectly groomed hair. Then two coppers turned the corner from Dawson Street so he dropped to one knee and fumbled with his shoelace. The shiny peaks of their flat-top caps tilted towards him masking four barn-owl eyes that drank him in from head to toe. Rednecks. Acting the gobshite but missing fuckall. When they passed he pushed on up towards St Stephen's Green.

His father died in 1928. He was eating his tea when he suddenly turned purple and smashed face-first onto the table. The doctor said it was a massive aneurysm. It must have been a powerful thing because they said he never knew what hit him. Man-in-the-Mirror turned seven the day his father was buried. His mother cried a lot after that. She refused to eat, got very skinny and spent all day talking to his father. When he finally picked up the courage to tell her she couldn't talk to dead people she screamed and slapped his face. Not long after, another doctor came.

His aunt came too and packed two suitcases. He thought they were going on a holiday like the time they went to the seaside when he was five. Then the doctor took his mother and her suitcase away and he never saw either again. He went to live with his aunt in her house in Scarfe Terrace. Thirty years later, he was still there. His aunt, as with everyone else who touched his life, had been claimed by the unerring hand of death. It was only a matter of time before it came looking for him. His only chance was to stay awake.

At daybreak he returned to Scarfe Terrace where he had a hot but hurried breakfast. Then he dressed in his heavy jacket and trousers, pulled on his working boots and got his rake and hoe from the outhouse in the tiny backyard. His only social outlet was keeping a rented allotment near the railway line out in Cabra. February was the time to weed it out and plant the first of the lettuce and leek seeds he'd bought in Rowan's seed shop earlier in the week. He would spend his morning quietly working out in God's good air and listening to other allotment owners exchanging tips and bemoaning the obstinacy of the rock-hard ground.

SUNDAY

Jack slept late and Patsy was glad to lie in. They usually visited her mother after Mass on Sundays, but by the cut of Timmy he was unlikely to pass muster. Beside the bed lay a sheet of newspaper that had escaped his slobberings of the night before. A headline read, 'O'Casey Play Withdrawn'. Patsy picked up the page. Sean O'Casey had withdrawn a play from a theatre festival in Dublin because the organisers wanted to interfere with the script. She sighed, remembering the first O'Casey play she'd seen. The programme for *The Plough and the Stars* described Rosie Redmond as 'a daughter of the digs'. Though she knew it was an actress playing a part, Patsy watched transfixed as for the first time in her life a prostitute became flesh before her. She'd heard about such women. How they'd do business in lanes or dingy hotels only to have men throw them their money and slink away like a dog having serviced a bitch. Anger flashed through her as once again she remembered that awful day of the dogs.

The Graves had a mongrel bitch named Molly who roamed the yard of their factory. She was a gentle mutt and Patsy always had a word and a rub for her whenever they crossed paths. It was afternoon and Patsy was working alone in a storeroom. She heard cheering and whistling in the yard below and went to the window to investigate. The lorry-drivers were watching a large German Shepherd dog circling Molly. The dog circled and sniffed. Checking. Patsy wanted to cry out a warning but instead she stayed quiet. The dog clambered up on Molly's back. The men guffawed as his hind paws scrambled for a grip on the polished cobbles. When he finally penetrated, Molly yelped in fright and the men guffawed even more.

Patsy's eyes stung with tears as she watched the dog pummel himself against Molly's hindquarters. She turned her head away only to see Richard Graves standing in the shadows at the back of a truck. He was watching and wiping his mouth with the back of his hand. Another cheer caused Patsy to look back again. The dog was trotting triumphantly out the gate. That night she worked on late. She was just about to pack in when she heard a sound behind her.

Lying in the semi-dark she shivered as she remembered the cloying hand of Richard Graves groping inside her clothes. She could smell the cheesy fug of his breath as he panted in her ear like a dog. The fury she felt then flashed once more. All she was to

Richard Graves was a witless bitch, a handy mark to be mounted then left alone to face the consequences. She closed her eyes and damned him to the hottest part of Hell. Then a distant church bell reminded her it was Sunday. It was a sin to wish anyone to Hell but especially on the Sabbath Day. Patsy thought about that rule for a moment then wished him to Hell anyway.

MONDAY

Lunch had just finished in Number One hut when Clean Paddy popped his head out of the vee of his paper.

'Some crowd o' lunatics is walkin' across the South Pole. On foot!'

Saint Joseph was in like a light.

'An expedition! Led by a German named Fuchs!'

'Yeshowerah,' Mackerel said to no one in particular.

'Beg pardon,' Saint Joseph rose for it beautifully.

'That's 'is first name! Ye ... sho ... wer ... ah!'

Saint Joseph was very impressed. The name rolled round his tongue.

'Yeshowerah Fuchs!'

The tea-leaves and bread crusts were airborne before he realised what he'd said. For this major offence, Saint Joseph sent Mackerel to Coventry by way of Gdansk.

To restore harmony, Clean Paddy changed column and subject.

'Says here the Corpo lads had a meetin' in Matt Talbot Hall yesterday. Called a minute's silence for Liam Whelan.'

'Fair play!' Hairy acknowledged the tribute.

Clean Paddy read on.

'Fair play t' them again! They're gettin' ten bob a week of an increase.'

Beyond Pulditch Gates

An uneasy murmur rippled along the benches, sloshed off the walls and receded into silence. Everyone was tuned to the same station. If they can, then why can't we? Pay and conditions at Pulditch were barewire and management was determined to keep them that way. The Pox's pipe changed sides in his mouth.

'Well, if we want the same, we'll haveta start poxin'.'

There was a long pause because knowing The Pox that meant anything from a go-slow to blowing up bridges.

'The man's right,' Red Kearns declared. 'Are we men or mice?'

Barney rapped his heel on the floor.

'Put a bit o' cheese down there and we'll soon find out!'

Hairy squeaked and tiddled Man-in-the-Mirror's ankle. He shot clean over the table with fright then, to the cheers of the others, he went after Hairy with a tin-opener.

'Settle! Settle! For fuck's sake settle!' Barney roared.

When peace reigned again Fixit stood up.

'I'd say a work to rule would fix it!'

'Fuckit!' says Fukkit. 'Let's hit the tar and have done with it!'

Oily Paddy squidged snot between finger and thumb.

'Fair do's, if yer gonna do it, do it right!'

Clean Paddy shivered.

'It's very cold to go on strike. We could all catch pneumonia!'

He was lucky all the tea-leaves had been used on Saint Joseph. The only thing they all agreed was to call in their unions. The plumbers, the mates, the fitters, electricians and painters all agreed to contact their delegates. The plasterers said they'd love to contact theirs because the bollix had just done a danny with their subs and his secretary. Then Saint Joseph piped up.

'Before I could picket I'd have to get guidance from a priest.'

The Pox shot a hook up a mayfly's hole.

'Great idea! We'll put the poxy placards up in Latin!'

Barney placed three words on the air with his fingers.

'Strikus onus hereus!'

'Whaddafuckseesayin'?' Mackerel asked Oily.

'Latin,' Oily sniffed like an Oxford professor.

Mackerel eased himself onto the bench beside Horizontal's head.

'Big deal! Sure I can speak that meself!'

'You can?' Saint Joseph was astounded. 'Say something then.'

Mackerel paused, squared his jaw and raised his hand like Charlton Heston.

'Hail Caesar!' he cried and farted full bore into Horizontal's ear.

There was murder. Instantly.

DOLOROSA

Queen of Heaven. Star of the Sea. Refuge of Sinners. The nun droned the nightly litany and the women answered, Pray for us. Mother most pure. Mother most chaste. Mother Undefiled. The mothers who weren't echoed back another 'Pray for us'. For Monica Dillon, the nightly rosary was a time to fantasise about her daughter. She dreamed little Patsy was with a kind, caring couple who lived in a house by the sea. They were wealthy and would take her on foreign holidays. She would have a pony and learn to speak French. Monica lost track of which of the Mysteries they were chanting. Was it The Joyful, The Glorious or the Sorrowful, or was it the one where flesh was scarified until screams of agony transformed into cries of everlasting joy. The nun kissed the crucifix on the end of her Rosary beads.

'Hail, Holy Queen, Mother of Mercy. Hail our life, our sweetness and our hope!' Monica wrung her hands together. Hope? What hope? The nun droned on.

Beyond Pulditch Gates

'To thee do we cry poor banished children of Eve!'

All the woman's fault. Adam as usual had nothing to do with it.

Supper consisted of silence, Marietta biscuits and milk. Nothing would cross their lips until after communion the following morning. When supper was finished, Monica was sent to the chapel with vestments for the priest. She cut across the convent yard and in through the sacristy door. She was laying out the vestments when she heard noises in the chapel so she eased open the door that led out onto the altar. In the pallid light of a candle she saw a nun prostrated at a life-sized statue of The Crucifixion. Her hands caressed the bloodied feet that were riveted together by a square-topped nail.

'I'm here,' she wailed softly. 'Take me! Use me!'

Monica froze. Richard Graves used to make her beg at his feet. Plead for his love. Life raft on his promises of marriage. Then he would impale her on his red-tipped spear until he drew blood. The nun's cries grew more intense. Monica couldn't decide if they were cries of pain or pleasure. Then the idea hit her. She hadn't time to think about the consequences. Taking a deep breath she whispered her feet across the herringbone parquet. Just outside the wavering circumference of candlelight, she halted.

'Good evening, Sister!'

The body in the habit stiffened then slowly turned and looked at her. The face was pinched and red-eyed. It was Batface, the one who swore Lanky Sarah into Purgatory. Wetness glistened on the hairs that barbed her upper lip. Monica spoke very softly.

'The vestments are in the sacristy, Sister. Now I'll report to Mother Superior.'

'No! Please don't tell her! Please, Monica! I'll pray for you!'

'You'll do a damned sight more than pray for me. I want to know about my daughter. How she is, where she is and who she's with.'

'I'll find out anything I can.'

'Look in your files and you'll find out everything.'

'It's not that easy.'

Monica turned away.

'Have it your way.'

The bluff worked.

'All right,' Batface croaked, 'I'll just need a little time.'

A few days later, Monica was polishing candlesticks in the chapel when Batface appeared beside her. She picked up one of the sticks as though inspecting her work.

'Your daughter is with a family in Dublin called Sheridan. The father's a carpenter. They have two older children, a boy and a girl.'

'And Patsy?'

'Settling in well, according to reports.'

Another nun came into the chapel. Batface handed the candlestick back to Monica.

'Polish that again! It's filthy!'

Batface swept into the sacristy taking the other nun with her and Monica dashed to the toilets and retched until she could retch no more.

The Grim Reaper 1

Gussie didn't show by tea break so Barney suggested ringing around the undertakers.

'Why so?' Clean Paddy asked.

'Because the fucker must be dead!'

Saint Joseph blessed himself to deny such profanity.

The Pox pulled hard on his pipe.

'Speakin' o' death, it's Belfast an' the oven for me when I kick the bucket.'

Beyond Pulditch Gates

'I'll go up with ye,' Hairy volunteered.

'To accompany the remains?' Clean Paddy enquired.

'Naw! T' light the bleedin' gas!'

Saint Joseph blessed himself again. Hairy kept it going.

'I heard bodies bein' cremated sits up in the oven.'

'You'd sit up too,' Oily retorted, 'if a thousand degrees was fryin' yer arse!'

Timmy hopped it for Saint Joseph.

'Does the church still bar cremation?'

Joseph drew himself up stiffly.

'Indeed it does! And to that end I'll defy the godless British and be interred!'

Mackerel was gobsmacked.

'Jaysus, Joseph, I never knew yew were in the IRA!'

The difference between interned and interred was being explained to Mackerel when Man-in-the-Mirror walked out leaving his lunch orphaned on the table behind him.

With Gussie missing, the boys extended the break to watch the steel-erectors lifting girders for the boiler-house roof into place. Steel-erectors were mad bastards. They had to be because they skipped across girders with only a hundred and fifty feet of pure air between them and the deck. The girders were being hoisted aloft on the hooks of long-armed cranes. Each end of the girders was drilled with rows of holes and these had to align with those drilled in the ones already erected. The erectors achieved this by using hand signals to talk to the crane driver below. Single finger. Vertical. Spinning rapidly. The hook rose quickly. Spinning slowly the hook moved likewise. To lower the hook the finger inverted. Single finger. Horizontal. Spinning. The hook moved in the direction of the finger at the spinning speed of the finger. A finger to the nose then flicked in a particular direction moved the hook a pick that way and no more. As one of the main girders was being slid into place the erector whistled down to the crane driver, rubbed his crotch then pointed towards the river. Saint Joseph was fascinated.

'What on earth does he mean by that?'

Fukkit put him wide.

'He wants it moved a pussy-hair left!'

'Well I'll be!' Joseph gasped. 'Imagine moving something as big as that the thickness of a cat's whisker!'

The lads had to look away so he wouldn't see the tears rolling down their cheeks.

On the next lift things turned treacherous. Restraining ropes attached to the each end of the girder were paid out from the ground as it ascended. Suddenly the girder lurched and trapped one of the ropes against an upright. Sliced through, the severed rope snaked crazily downwards. The rope-man at the opposite end pulled but couldn't stop the girder from hammering into an upright. It struck only inches above an erector's snow-white face. It rebounded, swung away, but then came back for a second bite. The erector was slithering down the upright when it struck. He held on though his feet pedalled air like a landing swan. The girder swung away again only to return with the menace of a blooded shark. Blinded by its own rage it missed the upright and went dancing off into space allowing the erector scramble to the safety of a lower beam. From high above them the boys could hear his gasping prayer.

'Fucccck meee! Oh, fuccck meee pinkkkk!'

'Well, well, an' what have we here?'

Gussie had come to work after all.

'Enjoyin' the excitement are we?'

Beyond Pulditch Gates

The boys about-faced to the one-man firing squad. They'd left the parlour open and the spider was about to eat them all without salt. Instead Gussie just smiled.

'Let ye get back to yer work an' don't be distractin' them erectors!'

No one moved. It had to be a booby trap.

'Today, gentlemen! If ye please!'

They backed off like gunfighters waiting for Gussie to draw, but he just waved them away like a master sending labourers to the harvest. Safely back on the scaffold they were like men who'd just crossed a minefield and come out without a scratch.

'I'm tellin' yiz men,' Hairy insisted, 'we'll have to build a grotto!'

Saint Joseph was delighted.

'I know! We'll build one to Matt Talbot inside the main gate!'

'Me bollix! We'll build one to Gussie right under them girders!'

Meanwhile, back in his office Gussie Gallagher was strutting up and down and swinging an umbrella like a real toff. He was one cute hoor. A lad. More than that, he was an investor. Two thousand pounds. On the nail. Invested. To double within the year. The thought made him benign. He could have screwed the shaggers for being off their jobs, but they were working class and irresponsible. They'd never be investors. That afternoon he smiled at Barney as he mopped out his office. Barney went to the window to see if the sun was spinning.

It was the same story later that night when Mrs Gorman brought up his supper. She wondered what transformed her normally po-faced lodger into a second Prince Charming. With the receipt for his investment locked safely in his ammo box, Gussie slept like a baby. He dreamt he was looking out on fields of wheat and fat, milk-filled cattle. Voices whispered behind his back.

'That's Gussie Gallagher, he owns the place!'

'Not *the* Gussie Gallagher?'

'The same! Ireland's biggest investor!'

No book fell and woke the house. The landlady didn't hammer on the door. His pyjamas remained dry. Only for the alarm clock, he might never have woken at all.

BROTHERS

Early morning and the boys and the cement-mixers were side by side and going full tilt.

As usual, Red Kearns was breastfeeding his shovel.

'I'm tellin' yiz, lads! We should go into that shaggin' office and lay it on the line. Ten bob on the rate or we bring the place to a standstill!'

Clean Paddy was unimpressed.

'Let the unions handle it. We claim, they refuse to pay, we serve strike notice.'

'Bollix! We'll be at it till Christmas!'

'Maybe,' Oily mused, 'but there's no point sticking yer dick in a meat-slicer! If we go unofficial, the union won't touch us. We could be left outside for weeks.'

'Or for good!' Oily Paddy wagged a warning finger.

Kearns shook his head in disgust.

'Youse should be up in Clery's gettin' measured for bras. I never met such a crowd o' bleedin' ouldwans in all me life!'

He stormed off and was still missing at tea break. Hairy asked Barney where he was.

'Probably behind the brick-stack prayin' to Karl Marx!'

'Blasphemy!' Saint Joseph cried. 'And God punishes blasphemy with blindness!'

'Yer dead right!' Mackerel said solemnly. 'That's why I always sleep with me hands outside the blankets. Better get frostbite nor end up like Ray Charles!'

Beyond Pulditch Gates

Saint Joseph threw up his hands in exasperation.

'One cannot go blind from playing one's piano!'

In seconds, a hutful of blind piano-players were tinkling the tables. Saint Joseph didn't get the joke, nor did he get the follow-up Hairy told about the Chinaman.

'There was a Ming from Peking who robbed a bank in Nanking, got fifteen years in Sing Sing and spent all his time there wa ... wa ... waving out the window!'

Red Kearns heard the cheers and laughter coming from Number One hut. The boys were busy so he was in the clear. Bending low he dodged between hillocks of sand and mortar before slipping under the wire fence that encircled the storage compound. He sensed his way through the labyrinth of stacked crates and when he reached the appointed spot he crouched on his hunkers and waited. Minutes later Gussie let himself through the gates of the compound. He carried a clipboard and moved along the crates until he came to a particular one where he stopped and pretended to jot down its markings.

'Kearns?' he growled. 'Ye there Kearns?'

'I'm here, Mister Gallagher.'

'What's the word?'

'They're going on strike! They want ten bob a week. They're callin' in the unions to make it official. I'm playin' along, Mister Gallagher. So if ye hear I said somethin' ye'll know I was only putting up smoke.'

'Communists! The bastards are everywhere. They'll even have a shaggin' sputnik flying over us next week! Right, gimme names.'

'How d'ya mean?'

'The ringleaders!'

Kearns felt his blood run cold. Individual hangings were never his style. Mass executions were much more comfortable.

81

'Come on, Kearns, I haven't got all bloody day!'

Kearns gave Gussie the ones he thought he'd like to hear.

'Well, there's Barney, Oily Paddy, The Pox and that gobshite Mackerel.'

Gussie wasn't impressed.

'Ah, I cudda told ye them meself!'

'But there's Clean Paddy, Saint Joseph an' young Talbot. They're in on it too!'

Gussie whistled genuine surprise.

'Ye won't forget this t' me, sure ye won't, Mister Gallagher?'

There was no reply. When Kearns peeked out from behind the crates Gussie was gone.

Lifeline

Nuns from the convent regularly went into the city and sometimes took one of the girls in with them. Monica made sure she was with Batface on her next trip. They sat beside each other on a bus as it slowly took the hump of Binn's Bridge at Drumcondra. From the upper saloon Monica looked down into a deep grey-walled ravine where train tracks waited innocently to take lanky Sarah home again to Mayo. The bus stopped directly over the canal that sided the railway. A sheet of water skimmed over a set of lock-gates and rainbowed into the darkness under the bridge. A snatch of a song glittered across her mind. Somewhere over the rainbow.

'One call,' Batface said sullenly. 'We agreed only one!'

'One call,' Monica whispered. 'I promise.'

To her left, Croke Park stadium was grey, open and empty. To her right, Mountjoy Prison was grey, closed and full. Her parents' house was only streets away. Given any hope that their door would open to her, she'd have run for it there and then.

Beyond Pulditch Gates

She thought of how many times she had asked Richard Graves if she could tell people they were an item, but he had always insisted they kept their relationship secret. It was only when she became pregnant that she realised why he had wanted it that way. For the thousandth time, tears of pain and anger trembled behind her eyes, though she managed to keep them in check until the bus screeched to a halt outside the Savoy Cinema in O'Connell Street. Next door was the Gay Child shop. Its window was filled with dresses, ribbons and things to make little girls beautiful. Monica sobbed, but Batface knuckled her ribs and led her quickly across the road to Gill's, a shop of polished brass and darkened wood that sold religious books and furnishings. There was a phone-booth outside and Batface left Monica there while she went on into the shop.

The booth tanged of damp and stale piss. Monica zinged coins down into the black enamelled box. She dialled, there was a click then a distant voice reminded her to press button A. She did and the voice cooed loud and clear.

'Graves and Company. How may I help you?'

Lousy Lotty was still on the switch. An eternal spinster with dandruff like hailstones on her well-padded shoulders. Monica tried to disguise her voice.

'Hello, I'm trying to trace a girl who used to work with you. She was Patsy Burke before she married but now her name is Talbot.'

'May I ask who's enquiring?'

'An old school friend. I'm home on holidays from England and I'd love to see her if I could.'

'Well, we normally don't give out such information....'

'Please!' Monica begged, 'I only have a very short time!'

'Just a moment!'

There was short muffled conversation then Lotty was back on again.

'One of our office staff says she lives near her cousin in Larnham Street. She thinks it's number fifteen.'

'Thank you.' Monica whispered and hung up.

She lowered her head against the cool metal dial and sobbed. Then, as she turned to leave the booth she saw them coming towards her. The woman was pushing a pram. A boy and a girl were either side of her. It was exactly as Batface said. Monica tumbled from the booth and ran in front of them. The woman pushed the children behind her.

'Go away! Get outa me way or I'll call the guards!'

'But that's my baby! That's my Patsy!'

The woman whipped back the hood of the pram.

'That is me dirty washin! Now get outa me way before I run ye out of it!'

Suddenly Batface was pulling Monica away. The woman called after them.

'Ye shouldn't let that sort out near people. There's places for the likes o' her!'

Redemption

Gussie played it cute like a good investor should. He waited until he got Graves on his own before announcing what he'd discovered about the strike. He thought Graves would be delighted with his detective work but instead his new boss just buried his head in his hands.

'As if we aren't far enough behind. If they go out we'll be rightly in the stew!'

Gussie shadow-boxed a quick right jab.

Beyond Pulditch Gates

'I say we hit them! Hit the bastards before they hit us!'

'But how?' Graves sighed.

'Leave that ta me, Mister Graves, Gussie Gallagher knows how ta handle reds!'

'And how *do* you handle them, Gussie?'

'Ye puts yer arm around their shoulders then slip yer knife inta their ribs!'

Graves looked at Gussie. The man was a grade A gorilla but he knew how the gang in overalls ticked. Graves picked his words carefully.

'I wouldn't want to be ... embarrassed. D'you follow me, Gussie?'

'Then stay in yer office an' leave it all t' me! Ah, Mister Graves, if'n I had the time I could tell ye a thousand an' wan ways ta shaft them godless commies but first things first. I'll be back in ten minutes!'

Graves gave two vicious fingers to Gussie's retreating back. There was nothing about treachery that bandy blockheaded bastard could teach him. He'd grown up with it. When he was small his mother promised that she'd never leave him. When he was ten, she did. Though his father often beat her senseless he never forgave her for leaving him behind. Theo Graves took up where his wife left off. He promised Richard they'd stay together but within months he packed him off to boarding school. His banishment had nothing to do with his education. With him around, his father couldn't squire his 'lady' friends in comfort.

Richard arrived at the school determined to grow up fast and unforgiving. He spurned the suspect bonhomie of the brothers and priests. He did likewise with the comic-book company of boys his own age. Instead he sought and won the friendship of a prefect five years his senior. This friend helped him with studies and picked

85

him on his side for football. He also got to hang around with the other seniors. They had endless jokes about pussies and pricks and rhymes with words Richard neither knew nor understood. One such chant would be started by one and taken up by the others.

'Gimme five F's for doin' it with wimmin!'

'Find them, fool them, feel them, fuck them aaannndddd forget them!'

Then they would all convulse in laughter but Richard never knew what they found so funny. He thought they'd know that love was all about being fooled and forgotten. Love was a lie followed by treachery and escape.

Five minutes later, Gussie paused outside Number One hut and heard laughter boom inside. It was safe to proceed. He slunk around the back to where a posse of bikes were tangled together like saddled drunks. Sleeving sweat from his brow he approached Saint Joseph's bike. It was propped against the wall, away from the roughnecks. A feather of snow tickled his ear as he unfastened the buckles on the carrier bag and pulled out the biscuit tin that Joseph used for a lunch-box. It was empty except for a few rubber bands, so Gussie slipped a brand new theodolite from his pocket into the box. He snapped the lid closed and buckled it back into the bag. Then he slithered back to the offices. It was a quarter to five. Within the hour he would have sweet and total revenge on the gang in Number One hut.

chapter **3**

ANOTHER WAY

It was called a post-natal clinic but it was more like a production line. A fussing nurse swept a doctor in and out of a line of curtained cubicles. They didn't bother to pull the curtains fully behind them, so privacy went out the window. Patsy was sitting directly opposite one of the cubicles so she couldn't help witnessing what transpired between the doctor and a woman he was examining. Probing her midriff and between her upraised knees, his questions about her most intimate bodily functions were clipped and clinical. Then he picked up her chart and began to scribble.

'Still taking the invalid stout?'

'Yes, doctor.'

'Anything on your mind?'

'No, doctor.'

'Right so, take it easy for a few weeks and maybe we'll see you again next year.'

'Thank you, doctor.'

Within seconds he was in an adjoining cubicle doling out more of the same.

When her turn came, Patsy lay on the couch and prayed that she'd soon enjoy the relative privacy of the street. She was there a while when the nurse stuck her head through the curtains.

'Sorry, doctor's called away. We're trying to get a stand-in.'

Patsy cursed quietly at the ceiling. The men were busy so the women could wait. Naked from the waist down with only a blanket to preserve her dignity she began to think of how it was the woman who always had things done to her. It was the woman who was pumped with seed, who spewed up morning after morning, then swelled out like a flesh-coloured balloon. It was the woman who struggled and screamed new life into the world. She had to feed it, wash it and wipe away its tears and shit. Then after six exhausting weeks, a prig in a white coat would tell her she could start all over again.

A few minutes later the cubicle curtain opened. Ensuring they were closed behind him, a doctor shyly approached the couch. He had spiky red hair, freckles and wore wire-rimmed glasses. He looked like an overgrown schoolboy, his voice a soft lilt from somewhere in Scotland.

'Sorry aboot the delay, it's my first day here and I couldnae find the bloody place.'

Laughter broke the ice and Patsy found she could answer his straight, quiet questions with an honesty that at first frightened but then exhilarated her. This man was different. She felt no embarrassment as he examined her, having first explained how and why he would do it. When he finished he pulled up a chair and sat down.

'How are you coping?'

'Okay, I suppose.'

'Ever feel you can't?'

'Sometimes.'

'Do you cry?'

'Yea. I dunno why but when I start, I can't stop.'

'Good! A good bawl is better than a thousand tablets.'

'Speaking from experience?'

'Aye! Every Saturday, regular as clockwork.'

'You serious?'

'Aye! I support Dundee United!'

They laughed again and he began to write up her chart.

'You can resume sexual relations if you're up tae it. Use a lubricant, take it easy and you'll be fine.'

The point of his pen stabbed a full stop.

'Now, your turn tae ask the questions.'

She hesitated, afraid that he might be appalled by what she had to say.

'I wouldn't like to get pregnant again. I mean, not straight away.'

'I dinnae blame ye! But they tell me we're no allowed t' prescribe condoms an' such. Dinnae ask me why but we're no. However, there is somethin' ye could try. It's no foolproof but it's the best I can offer.'

On a sheet of paper he drew what looked like an inverted pear with two thin arms either side of it.

'What is it?' Patsy asked

She saw disbelief flash across his face.

'That, allowing for my bloody awful drawing, is a sketch of a womb!'

THE STING

At finishing time the hut-dwellers began walking or cycling towards the gate. The snow that was forecast began to scatter a fine silvery covering on the ground. Dockets stood well in out of it.

'It'll never stick.' he mused to Gussie.

'What won't?'

'The snow.'

Gussie gulped relief. For an instant he thought the idiot had tumbled to the set-up. Dockets scooped a snowflake and watched it melt into his palm.

'What am I supposed ta be lookin' for?'

'Contraband. Company property bein' misappropriated.'

'Misafuckin' wha'?'

'Robbed! Now get out there and do yer job!'

Man-in-the-Mirror, Hairy and The Pox were the yellow jerseys. They were heads down and pushing when Dockets flagged them down.

'Sorry, lads, security check.'

The Pox wasn't impressed.

'Fuck's sake, Dockets! This is no time for the Lone Ranger act. There's a poxy blizzard headin' in from Howth!'

Dockets flicked his eyes over his shoulder at Gussie.

'Tell that t' Bollix-the-bore!'

One by one he did his duty on the boys. Cyclist. Walker. Cyclist. Walker. Gussie grinned up at the office window where Graves watched the shakedown. Then God touched Gussie because the last two cycling towards the gate were Barney and Saint Joseph. One would be guilty of theft and the other of aiding and abetting. This was one crucifixion where neither thief would be saved.

When Barney and his bike were cleared, Dockets turned to Saint Joseph. He undid the straps of the back-carrier on his bike, stuck in a perfunctory nose then began to do them up again.

Beyond Pulditch Gates

'There's a box in there!' Gussie blurted.

'Oh, for Jaysus sake!' Dockets griped as the snow turned shitty and blinded him.

He reopened the straps, pulled out the box and popped it open. Despite the slicing cold Gussie felt warm all over.

Dockets tipped the lunch-box upside down.

'Like our front room, fuckinwell empty!'

Gussie's bowels exploded and he felt himself touch cloth. He turned sheepishly to the window where Graves looked on like Quasimodo, except his hump looked an awful lot bigger. Barney looked to the darkening sky.

'Ye know Mister Gallagher, ye should wear yer wet gear stannin' out here!'

'Exactly,' Saint Joseph agreed, 'and not only that but I keep rubber bands in my lunch-box. I snap them around my wrists and ankles. I find them excellent for keeping out the breeze.'

The boys pedalled off with snow scattering snowflakes of purity under their wheels. Dockets turned back to Gussie.

'Fair play t' Saint Joseph. Dem rubber bands is a great idea. Ye could have somethin' shoved up yer sleeve and it'd never fall out!'

Night Moves: One

Patsy's face glowed red. Periods were something you never discussed, not even with your husband. Timmy picked his words carefully.

'So, this doctor reckons if we only do it when ... when you're ... eh ... ye know ... there's a good chance ye won't get pregnant?'

'He drew a sketch for me. It has to do with the linin' in me womb.'

Celibacy for three weeks out of four wasn't appealing, but they both knew too many families where a birth in January was followed by another in December.

'Okay,' Timmy nodded, 'we'll give it a try!'

Patsy always put herself off-limits whenever she bled, but now she'd have to do the opposite. Yet if that was the price of avoiding an annual trip to the Roxy, she was willing to pay it. She had plans. Plans for Jack. Plans for herself and Timmy, and thanks to a breath-of-air Scotsman, they didn't include a clatter of kids before she was thirty. That night she slept with her back to Timmy. She was aware of a thousand ideas nuzzling her brain and a lone undisciplined penis nuzzling against the cotton of her night-dress.

Like his erection, Timmy's mind just wouldn't lie down. Something was adrift but he was damned if he could put his finger on it. The woman lying beside him wasn't the same one he'd married. It was as if Patsy was striking out on a road of her own and it worried him.

'Bloody sure it should worry you,' the tribe hissed in his ear. 'Is that a prick or a posy between your legs? Bad enough giving away your name but now you'll be left with a bloody pigeon's family!'

Timmy turned into his pillow but the tribe kept it up.

'No way will your brothers settle for a one-off job! And where do you leave your father? Seven sons. Seven, by Jaysus! Stallions! That's what the Talbots are. There was never a gelding in our stable!'

When the clock veed its arms to ten-to-two he was still awake. Though the tribe was silent he knew it was there, watching him huffily from the darkness.

Night Moves Two

Ten-to-two and Gussie Gallagher couldn't curse enough. He was afraid to walk the floor for fear of waking Mrs Gorman. He lay in bed fuming over the cruel joke God played on him at the gate. He'd

Beyond Pulditch Gates

sent a snowstorm so Saint Joseph would discover the theodolite and ruin his hour of glory. Odds-on that black-enamel bastard Barney Coogan had it and would exact some price to hand it back. Gussie clenched his hands in despair.

'God, God! Why did ye do it? After all I've done for ye! Amn't I fightin' commies day in day out below there in Pulditch? Didn't I pack me own slut of a sister off t' England?'

He paused for a moment so God would feel guilty.

'An' didn't I do for the bastard that put 'er up the spike?'

God didn't answer so Gussie answered for him.

'Fanning was no fuckin' hero when I jumped out from behind that hedge. There was only one thing bulgin' in his trousers that night ... and that was shite!'

Gussie had used a slash-hook to impale Dixie Fanning just as Fanning used his prick to impale his sister. He had squealed like a pig and clawed at the metal crescent buried into his chest but to no avail. He died as Gussie dragged him across an abandoned bog to a deep, water-filled hole. There Gussie weighted him down with a sandbag and rolled him in. Fanning was known for flitting between different beds so almost a week passed before he was missed. A search was raised but no trace of him was found. Some said he'd skipped to England to escape yet another irate father. Others said the fairies took him because Fanning's uncles had dug up a fairy fort. The local publican said he was in great form the night he was last seen. Gussie said nothing and left them all guessing.

Night Moves Three

Theo Graves had bullied and cheated his way to owning his own paint factory. Slack-bellied, slack-arsed and heavy-jowled, he permanently tanged of sweat. He had a big, raw, red face, fat lips and a mouthful of crooked brown teeth. To compliment his constant scratching and belching, Theo had the table manners of a warthog. Although he had managed to buy his way into a decent golf club, he couldn't understand why, unlike other businessmen, he was never asked to the stand at race meetings or invited to dinner before a recital or a show. That was why Theo couldn't believe his luck when his son Richard started dating Catherine Keyes. Her father was George Keyes and Theo was convinced that a marriage between Richard and Catherine would finally lift him over the plate-glass barriers of Irish society.

It was two a.m. and Theo and Richard were in Theo's study. They had been arguing for hours and the row was still going on. When Richard said he didn't love Catherine, his father almost came over the desk at him.

'Love my arse, Richard! You've spent years pumping anything in knickers and love never once came into it! Remember Mona whatsername!'

Richard threw his eyes to the ceiling.

'Her name was Monica, Monica Dillon.'

'I don't give a shite if she was Mona Lisa! Only a gobshite stuffs one of his own staff!'

'Look Dad, I'll talk to Catherine and explain to George.'

'You'll explain fuckall to George Keyes except when and where you'll marry Catherine! Dump her and we'll both be in the shite! You'll be out of Pulditch so fast it'll make your head swim and I'll never sell another tin o' paint in this city!'

He turned to the drinks cabinet and rattled his way through a phalanx of bottles in search of the brandy.

While his father cursed his way through the drinks cabinet Richard moved to the window. His breath fogged the chilly glass

Beyond Pulditch Gates

and his fists drummed on the frame until it shuddered. It would be bloody awful being married to Catherine. She was all right to ride but that was it. He was about to dump her when her father offered him the job in Pulditch. He had leaped without looking. It was only when George Keyes shook his hand and welcomed him into the family that he realised just how deep he was in. Catherine began to talk as if they were engaged, and if both fathers had their way, they very soon would be. The idea terrified him.

His finger penned 'PB' on the misted pane. Patsy Burke, the woman who still fuelled his wildest fantasies. Seven times he had asked her out and every time she had said no. He had tried everything to break her down, but the more she refused the more it tortured him. Then one day in the factory yard, he watched a big male dog roughly service a cowed and compliant bitch. The incident haunted him until later that night he crept up behind Patsy as she worked alone in a storeroom. She was neither cowed nor compliant. Instead she screamed, raked his face with her nails, and smashed her workboot into his ankle. She was a wild, fiery bitch. She was trouble, but no matter how many women he had had she was always there, teasing and taunting his manhood. Patsy was the irresistible challenge, the Everest to an addicted climber.

His father broke his reverie by handing him a fat round glass midriffed with brandy.

'Look, Richard, you were bloody lucky that Monica's father didn't come after you with a shotgun. I'd have made you marry the big-arsed lump myself, but shopkeepers are shagall use as in-laws. Now nothing on paper, but the day you marry Catherine your name's on twenty per cent of the business. Whaddya say?'

Richard let the brandy and the offer soak in.

Henry Hudson

'Thirty! The Keyes wouldn't want their daughter marrying a pauper!'

Theo spat on the palm of his hand and held it out.

'Twenty-five!'

Richard looked at the callused paw with its grubby nails and nicotined fingers. He wondered how his beautiful, elegant mother could ever have loved such an almighty Philistine. Nonetheless, he slapped down hard on the opened palm.

'Twenty-five it is!'

'Ah, ha! You're a chip off the old bollix and no mistake!'

Richard wanted to vomit, but he mirrored his father's beaming smile. A quarter of the pot wasn't bad for a start.

THE COWBOY

The following morning the snow and the story were all over Pulditch. The bastards had tried to set up Saint Joseph. The man himself was staring at the picture of the Sacred Heart that hung on his locker door. Barney was thumping a table.

'It had to be Gallagher! Dockets was noddin' us through but he insisted on openin' the lunch-box! Lucky we found it when Joseph was puttin' on his wet gear!'

Mackerel spotted Saint Joseph moving his lips.

'Askin' where 'e was last night?'

'Actually,' Joseph smiled, 'I was thanking him for the blizzard.'

Mackerel screwed a finger into his temple.

'Thick as treacle. Imagine sayin' thanks for a snowstorm!'

Barney fired the end of a Woodbine.

'Well, I'm not much on religion meself, but it meant we needed our raingear. Otherwise we'd have never twigged that spyglass thing!'

'So what's our move?' Timmy pushed.

96

Beyond Pulditch Gates

'Already made. The Pox'll be back fairly soon.'

'Where's he gone?'

'Up to our union hall, for The Cowboy.'

'Cowboy Flanagan?' Hairy gulped. 'He'll have us on the tar before ye can blink!'

Barney pulled hard and long on his smoke.

'If they wanna play Wyatt fuckin' Earp then we'll give them the OK Corral!'

'What about the other unions?' Timmy asked. 'They should all be in on this!'

Barney shook his head.

'There's times for talk and times for action. Now, the way I see it is this. The Corpo and the busmen already landed half-a-note a week. Then yesterday the Labour Court nodded eight bob a week for a deal between the buildin' unions and Fibsee.'

'Fibsee?' Hairy asked. 'Whodefuck is Fibsee?'

'F.I.B.C.A.E.I.,' Saint Joseph explained, 'Federation of Irish Builders, Contractors and Allied Employers of Ireland.'

Oily was amazed.

'Jaysus, ye'd need some envelope t' write to them!'

Barney began to think aloud.

'If there's eight in the net then ten is only a matter of squeezin' a little bit tighter. All the better if ye have something to squeeze with!'

Mackerel tuned in straight away.

'An' we have that teedoddelite!'

'He means theodolite,' Saint Joseph explained to the rest of the hut.

Hands reached for cups as though choreographed, but he was saved by the sound of two bikes squishing to a halt in the slush outside.

97

'Ahoy, all indoor poxes!'

The Pox dismounted. Beside him, his face reddened by the breeze and the effort of cycling from the city, was The Cowboy Flanagan.

He was a small elfin man who had pushed a lot of living into his fifty-five years. He had a crumbly, weather-beaten face. He wore a flat cap, a crombie overcoat and bicycle clips that double-wrapped his trousers around his short skinny legs. His eyes were a soft mischievous blue. His false teeth clicked whenever he was thinking and his gnarled hands had been no strangers to the pick or shovel. With The Cowboy what you saw was what you got. He was an old-style, dyed-in-the-wool trade unionist bred in the cockpit of the 1913 lockout. During one of Jim Larkin's protest meetings, a policeman's baton opened both his father's head and his ten-year-old face. His father and The Cowboy wore those scars with pride. As he creaked his leg slowly over his bike it was hard to credit that this thin frail man could strike fear into the hearts of the biggest employers in Dublin. Once dismounted, The Cowboy took a relieving stretch.

'Taaaay onnn?' he croaked into the hut.

'Two minutes,' Mackerel called back.

'Good! We'll have a cuppa rosy while yiz are gettin' the boys together.'

In the opposite corner of the site, the door of Richard Graves' office was shut but his shouting could still be heard.

'God almighty, what a bloody mess! They have our brand new theodolite, they know we know they have it and that we can't say anything without hanging ourselves from the yardarm! Now that headcase Flanagan is in on the act. Christ, he's the bane of my father's life. He still thinks he's back with Larkin in the lockout.'

Beyond Pulditch Gates

Gussie was shell-shocked. He was devoid of God, hope or a brand new theodolite.

'Mister Graves,' he raised his hand like a schoolboy.

'Gussie, if this is another of your bright ideas I don't want to hear it.'

'But I know Flanagan of an old day. He's a horse-trader. We could do a deal.'

'What kind of a deal?'

'Let them meet and blow off steam. When it's over we lost the theodolite but if we found it we could work extra overtime next week. We was gonna work it anyhow!'

'You think they'll buy it?'

'With that gang a principle's a principle, except on double time!'

Outside, lines of telltale footprints led across the snow to Number One hut and puffs of black smoke belched from its stovepipe. A conclave in overalls had gone into session.

Ten minutes later the walkout began. Led by a slow-pedalling Cowboy, the entire crew abandoned ship and headed for the gate. Saint Joseph dithered, but having said a good Act of Contrition, he grabbed his bike and joined the exodus. Dockets saw the tribe approaching and stood-to at the gate.

'Boom's lowered.'

'Well, unlower it!' a voice bounced back at him.

Dockets decided he'd do an Alamo.

'Gimme wan good reason,' he drawled like John Wayne without the height.

Twenty excellent reasons whizzed towards him in the shape of big mushy snowballs. He was like Nanook of the North as he lifted the boom, and to make things worse, a chorus of Bing Crosbys started singing 'White Christmas' as they passed.

'Where yiz goin'?' he called, shaking off snow like a dog shakes off water.

'Grealish's!' a dozen voices answered together.

They were just gone when Gussie came ploughing across the snow at him.

'Why didn't ye stop them!'

'Me tommy gun jammed an' I'm fucked if I could find me bazooka!'

'Where are they goin'?'

'Grealish's pub and they wouldn't let me check their bags neither.'

'Run after them. Tell them to come back!'

'Do I look like a bleedin' husky?'

'They can't go to a pub on company time! There's work to be done!'

'Listen, the only things that work on a day like this is polar bears an' penguins. Now if ye'll excuse me, I have a site to lock up!'

'Lock up? Ye can't!'

'Well, it's that or leave the place swingin' wide open. So make up yer mind, 'cos I'm bolloxed if I'm stayin' down here on me tod.'

CONTACT

The mantle in Mrs Coffey's paraffin stove was broken and the nearest place to buy a replacement was The Central Hardware in Parnell Street. Patsy wouldn't hear of her wandering around in the snow, so she went while Mrs Coffey sat in with Jack. Mrs Coffey was dozing by the fire when she heard a gentle rap on the door. When she opened it, she was startled to see a nun standing on the landing. She had a black cloak wrapped around her and the hood of the cloak pulled forward, almost hiding her thin pinched face. The skirts of her habit were wet from the slush and she looked chilled to the bone.

'God save ye, Sister!' Mrs Coffey whispered.

'And you. I'm looking for Mrs Burke. I ... I ... I mean Talbot.'

'Oh, ye mean Patsy. She just slipped downtown for a message but she'll not be long. Come in an' heat yerself be the fire. Ye can have a cuppa tea while yer waitin'.'

The nun hesitated, her little sparrow head twittering indecision.

'I'm not sure I should. I really can't delay.'

Mrs Coffey saw an envelope in her hand. She was just about to ask if it was for Patsy when the nosy ouldwan who lived on the floor below called up the stairs.

'Is everythin' all right up there? Is somebody sick?'

Panic seized the nun's face and she flashed the envelope into Mrs Coffey's hand.

'I have to go!'

'But, what'll I tell Patsy, Sister?'

'Tell her ... Tell her I'll be in touch.'

'When?'

'Soon.'

With that, the little nun skittered back down the stairs with her head lowered to avoid the neighbour's toothless gawp. Mrs Coffey prided herself on being a Christian, but this time she made an exception. Leaning over the banisters she glared down at the offending nosy parker.

'Are yew related ta Charles Dee Gawl be any chance?'

'I am not indeed!'

'Well, ye certainly look like 'im, especially round the nose!'

She swept back inside and slammed the door, giving the nosy parker no time to retort.

GREALISH'S

The Cowboy Flanagan had a genius for organising sit-ins, walkouts, strikes and sing-songs. It gave Timmy a brilliant feeling

Henry Hudson

to march behind him with the rest of the lads as they headed towards Grealish's. As they passed through Ringsend, they were cheered from footpaths by people who seldom had anything to cheer about. Along the quays, their ranks were swelled by dockers who were into a third month of the stevedore's dispute. At City Quay Church, mourners waited po-faced until a departing cortège was out of sight, then they quickstepped in behind them. The parade took a final recruit as it crossed the Liffey at Butt Bridge. A certified lunatic, he wore farthings in his ear to stop aliens filling his head with subsonic propaganda. They were almost at Grealish's when Hairy warned Saint Joseph that the decor inside was unique.

'They call it Little Dresden.'

'After a porcelain?' Saint Joseph lit up.

'Naw! After an air raid!'

Saint Joseph thought he was joking until they got inside.

Mouldy flock wallpaper sagged from the walls like an old man's belly, while vicious de-balling springs poked up through the seats. Beer crates propped up Formica-topped tables that were pock-marked from the carpet-bombing of careless cigarettes. The floor was a haphazard chessboard of red and black where tiles had lifted but were never replaced. The drinkers' side of the bar was worn smooth by a million leaning elbows and the timber seats by half as many sliding backsides. On the barman's side brass-handled beer-pulls stood erect like unpolished soldiers waiting to fill tumblers on the double. A cash register with its tray lolling open showed '9d.' on a white flag in its window. That was the price of a pint the day it jammed, and it never registered another sale. Nailed to the inside of the front door was a battered sign. Under layers of fossilised flyblows, a grinning seal balanced a pint on the tip of its nose. He

Beyond Pulditch Gates

was watched by a ruddy-faced keeper. Their names were written under them. One was called My Goodness and the other My Guinness.

Grealish's opened at seven a.m. to facilitate night workers. At least that's what they told the judge who signed the license. Among its regulars were dockers, drovers and ghost-shift bakers along with police and firemen from nearby stations. It also provided asylum to escapees from newspaper offices, ships that docked in the night and cures for those who'd been on the batter the night before. Along with its two-footed flotsam Grealish's was home to five dogs (all named, none licensed) and a clowder of cats. These felines incessantly pissed, purred and poled each other but wouldn't mouse to save their lives. Its only bow to exotica was a scrawny parrot. This unfortunate creature spent its days gazing from a cage at the reeky boredom of the Liffey. He was traded to the publican by a sailor with solemn assurance that once settled in it would recite all of 'The Ancient Mariner' and the occasional gem from Dylan Thomas. The regulars prodded and poked it for weeks trying to make it talk. Asked for the thousandth time to say Pretty Polly it finally snapped.

'Ah, Polly me bollix!' it screeched.

It never spoke after that because it was missing Hawaii and dying of lung cancer from the smoke.

The Cowboy stood centre-floor of the pub like a wagon-master, letting the boys circle him whatever way they could. As pints were pulled by the tray-load, he complained that he'd struggle to sing with the phlegm on his chest. His dilemma was cured by Red Kearns who produced a Jemmy and pep. The Cowboy clapped Red on the back.

'Daycent man, Red! Yer Da'll never be dead when yewr alive!'

Henry Hudson

He dropped the mixture at a shot.

'Ahjaysthatsgreat! Right lads! Yiz know the read. We stay put till the gaffers make a move.'

As he had the floor he had call on the first man to sing. He called on Hairy who blushed and played shy.

'I only know wan song!'

A cacophony of voices encouraged him to sing it.

'But I only know wan song.'

'We're not fussy.'

'But I only know wan song.' He did a Saint Peter and dropped the ball a third time. The Pox's short-string patience snapped.

'Yew shudda been a poxy Chinaman! Ye know more fuckin' wan songs nor a Chinese laundry!'

The place erupted but gargle (unlike tea) was too precious to throw.

Hairy held the head and murdered 'Moonlight Becomes Yeeww'. When he hit the final squalling notes tomcats came from everywhere to see which of their brothers had hit the jackpot. Having obliged the company, Hairy had the shout and called on one of the painters. The call was answered with a heartfelt version of 'The Dying Rebel'. This quivering dirge prompted Oily to whisper that the Brits shudda shot the shagger who wrote it as well. Clean Paddy followed with 'The Old Bog Road'. It was about a dead mother, springtime and her flower-covered coffin. On the third chorus Mackerel moaned that if they got any more bodies they could open a bleedin' undertakers. He was stunned when (so as not to hog things to themselves) Clean Paddy called on one of the mourners to step forward. One did, and honouring the funereal mood, gave a hands-apart version of 'When I Leave This World Behind'. The lunatic uncoined his ears so he could hear, while Mackerel clamped his hands over his so he couldn't.

104

Beyond Pulditch Gates

An hour later they were backing Barney through the dah-dee-dah-dah-dah-dah-dee-dah-dee-dah dah bit of 'New York, New York' when a young boy eased his way inside.

'Where's Mister Flanagan?'

Hairy had himself parked on a sack folded onto a beerkeg just inside the door.

'Who's askin'?'

'Two fellas outside in a car. They gimme a wing to ass 'im to come out.'

Hairy waited for the last Nehuuuuuu Yorrrrkkk and through the explosion of applause and cries of 'Inchicore!' that followed. Then he signed to The Cowboy that they had company and inched open the door to have a look.

'Graves an' Fucky-the-ninth, outside in Graves's car. Must want a powwow!'

The Cowboy hitched up his trousers.

'Okay men. Sing like fuck so they'll think yiz don't give a bollix what they do! Barney, yew come out to ride shotgun for me!'

As the two men squared up to the doors, Oily whispered,

'Jaysus, it's like watchin' High Noon!'

It was an inspired spoke because The Child (who was standing near the window) took it up immediately. He began in a low worried voice:

'Do not forsake me oh my dahlin'...'

A hundred hands drummed thighs for the rum-diddly-dum bit, giving The Child a chance to get his wind.

'...On this our weddin' dayhay, Do not forsake me ohhh my dahlin', Wade! Wade along!'

Barney and The Cowboy stepped out into the street. All they were short of was Gary Cooper, a grandfather clock and a train.

105

Henry Hudson

The two in the car heard the singing as the doors swung open.

'I thought you said they'd be shitting themselves,' Graves snapped.

Gussie wrung his cap in his hands.

'They will be if we stick it out. Singin' never put bread on a table.'

'And it never roofed a boiler-house either!'

Graves wound down the window as The Cowboy and Barney approached.

'Nice car' The Cowboy nodded. 'What is she?'

'Standard Ten.'

'Musta cost a quare penny.'

Barney drove the nail in deeper.

'De Luxe model too. Five and a half? Am I right?'

Barney knew the cost of a Standard Ten Deluxe was exactly five hundred and forty nine pounds because he genie-wished for one every time he read the ad in the paper. Graves ignored their baiting.

'You're unofficial. A lightning stoppage isn't playing the game.'

The Cowboy leaned down to him.

'Neither is tryin' to do people! Anyone with a theodolite to their eye can see that. Anyway, we was gonna hit yiz for more shekels wan o' these days so now that we're out....'

Graves gripped the wheel as if trying to choke it.

'I'll need time. I'll have to consult.'

'Consult who ye like but remember, I'm after pushin' me bike up here from Pulditch and I was up t' me bollix in snow while I done it. So don't come back here with some Mickey Mouse offer!'

As if to back him up 'Oooohhhklahoma' soared from inside where a mourner was conducting a run-through of all-time greats. The Cowboy slapped the roof of the car.

Beyond Pulditch Gates

'Well, fuckitinanyway! I'm after missin' me turn to sing!'

He turned and stormed back into the pub.

'...an' the wavin' wheat, it sure smells sweet.' slipped out as the doors flapped wildly in his wake.

Barney shook his head at the men in the car.

'That's him up ta high doh! He gets like a bear with a briar up its arse if 'e misses his twist! Yiz better come back carryin' like the Aggy Cann!'

He turned away leaving Graves hammering the steering wheel in frustration.

'The whole bloody site locked up and all they care about is whose turn it is to sing!'

Gussie was almost hysterical.

'They can't sing forever! Play hardball and they'll crack! They're communists! The Archbishop 'imself said they've no moral fibre! No backbone!'

'But what they have got is our brand new theodolite and us by the mebs. We'll have to find a phone and ring George Keyes.'

'Yea! He'll know what t' do.'

'And what am I, a house-painter?'

'Oh, no, Mister Graves! I didn't mean yew couldn't make a decision. I meant....'

Graves cut the grovel dead by firing the engine and driving off at speed.

107

chapter 4

The Visitor

When Patsy returned from her errand, Mrs Coffey was waiting with the letter and a pot of hot, strong tea. Patsy opened the envelope and read the letter. Mrs Coffey saw the colour drain from her face.

'Ye okay, Patsy? Ye look like ye seen a ghost.'

Patsy handed her the letter.

'What do you make o' that?'

Mrs Coffey put on her glasses and read aloud.

'"To Mrs Patsy Talbot, Please arrange with the bearer to contact Miss Monica Dillon on an urgent personal matter." Who's Monica Dillon, if'n ye don't mind me askin'?'

'A girl I used to work with in the paint factory. I haven't seen her in years.'

'So why would she send a message like that?'

'That's what I'd like to know. And that nun didn't say when she'd be back?'

Mrs Coffey raised her eyes to heaven.

Beyond Pulditch Gates

'She never got the chance. That nosy cow below started bawlin' up the stairs like a Mullingar heifer an' put the kibosh on it. Gawd forgimme but I'll swing for that gummy rip wan o' these days.'

'An urgent personal matter,' Patsy mused. 'Any ideas?'

'I'd write ye a list if I had a month t' spare. Best wait till that nun shows up again.'

'If she shows up again.'

Mrs Coffey creaked up out of her chair.

'True, but first things first, any joy on me mantle?'

Patsy pulled it from her bag like a magician.

'Wallah! An' I got us fresh turnovers in Johnston Mooney's on me way back up.'

'Fresh bread! Patsy, ye should run for President!'

When Mrs Coffey left, Patsy poured herself more tea and thought about the nun's strange visit. She tapped her spoon on the side of her mug.

'Why would Monica send me a letter instead o' comin' t' see me herself? And how come a nun arrives to deliver it?'

The clock on the mantelpiece dinged noon. Jack woke and smiled at her through the bars of his cot. Patsy wedged the letter behind the clock, intending to show it to Timmy when he got home. Then she moved over to the cot and caressed Jack's hand. His tiny fingers immediately closed around her reassuring finger.

REVELATIONS

Graves and Gussie had just driven back through the unmanned gate when George Keyes drove in behind them. A war council started in Graves's office. Graves laid out The Cowboy's demands but he decided to play tough in front of Keyes.

'We know exactly what they want thanks to Mister Gallagher.'

Gussie glowed like a Halloween pumpkin.

'But,' Graves spat dismissively, 'they won't get two shagging shillings, so they can whistle up their kilts for ten! Amn't I right, George?'

There was silence, then Keyes whipped the floor from under him.

'I dunno, Richard. After all, we did hand them a theodolite to beat us with.'

Keyes rapped a thinking four-finger jig on the desk.

'Flanagan will be onto the Fibsee deal and that's an up-front eight shillings on the rate. Maybe we can do a body-swerve. We'll offer five up-front and five for conditions money to be stitched in later on!'

'What?' Graves and Gussie gagged together.

Keyes just sighed wearily.

'Look, I wouldn't give Flanagan the steam off my piss, but the last thing we want is to be hauled to the Labour Court. The buggers up there think there's a sleigh and reindeers on the roof. Every day is Christmas according to them! Paying five and five means we get back to work and still look three points under the Fibsee rate. Jig things whatever way you like as long as the five up-front holds firm!'

Keyes stood up to go.

'And it'd be nice if we could get our theodolite back while you're at it!'

A short time later Graves and Gussie pulled up outside Grealish's for the second time.

Graves leaned back wearily in his seat.

'Go in and ask Roy Rogers to come out.'

Gussie nearly choked.

110

Beyond Pulditch Gates

'Ye want me ta go in there? Among that gang?'

Graves gave him a long hard look. As Gussie heaved himself wearily out of the car, a voice which he thought he recognised warbled:

'Oh, what a beautiful morning, Oh, what a beautiful day. I've got a beautiful feeeellling, everything's going our wayyyhay!'

A fulsome choir backed the voice to the hilt.

'Everything's goin' our waaayyy!'

It was true, and it made Gussie as sick as the bird who was inside on the bottom of his cage praying in parrot for the Birdgod to take him.

The singing nose-dived when Gussie came through the doors. The barman's right hand froze in mid-pull and the tumbler in his left tilted in mid-air. Even the parrot struggled upright for one last look. Gussie felt like a Jew in Mecca.

'Mister Graves wants ta see ye again. Seems there's a bit of a misunderstandin'.'

The Cowboy did a Jimmy Stewart:

'Waaal, gimme a minute an' I'll mosey on out.'

Gussie had to smile and nod gratefully, but beneath the smile he was vowing to scarify every shagger there. On his way out he locked eyes with Red Kearns but his stool pigeon never blinked.

The Cowboy rubbed his hands together.

'Right, we're in business! I wants a real good song! Somethin' with a bit of umpfh. Wan they'll hear out in Howth!'

Brains were racked but they'd already sung the decent ones.

'Come on,' Barney urged, 'givvus a real ball-tingler!'

Mackerel couldn't resist.

'We'll give them a blast o' the natural Antrim!'

He formed a bugle with his hands and blew the first few bars of 'Amhrán na bhFiann'.

'Dah, dah dee dah, dah dee dah, dah, dahhhh!'

'I'll dah dah dee dah yew,' The Pox snapped. 'We're not layin' wreaths at the GPO! Dem pair o' poxes has t' think we don't give a rat's arse how long we've ta stay out!'

The Cowboy looked around him.

'Sing Three Blind Bleedin' Mice if yiz haveta but for fuck's sake, sing somethin'!'

'Last night as I lay sleeping there came a dream so fair...'

Heads turned to the corner of the bar. Jaws dropped in disbelief. Saint Joseph had his eyes closed and his hands twined in front of him. His voice was crisp, clear and rising. '...I stood in old Jerusalem beside the temple there. The light of God was on it. The gates were opened wide...'

The Cowboy could have kissed him.

'Someone give that beaut a medal!'

Line by line Saint Joseph drew the room like a magnet.

'...It was the new Jerusalem that would not pass away. It was the new Jerusalem that would not pass away!'

The boys were a dam waiting to burst and they did in a torrent of song.

'Jerrewsallemm! Jerrew...sallem! Lift up your gates and sinnnggg!'

The Cowboy nudged Barney towards the door and they stepped outside backed by every man in the bar.

'Hosanna in the hi ... eye ... est, Hosanna to youuurrrr kkkinnng!'

Graves and Gussie were ashen-faced as The Cowboy leaned into the car again.

'This better be good. That song's one o' me favourites.'

'Five shillings up-front on the rate,' Graves choked, 'and five condition money.'

Beyond Pulditch Gates

Barney pursed his lips and The Cowboy was clearly less than impressed.

'Condition money is like a mooch off Marilyn Munroe. Ye might get it all the first week, but after that?'

A reprise of the chorus soared inside.

'Okay, Okay!' Graves snapped. 'If something we misplaced was to turn up, the condition money would be stitched into the rate later on!'

'How much later on?'

'Half in June and the rest at Christmas.'

The Cowboy checked with Barney who wrinkled up his nose to say they were almost there.

'Easter an' August,' Barney growled, 'an' we'll shake on it!'

Graves chose his words like a Pope arguing with a Protestant.

'On the clear understanding that all that's on paper is five per cent and the theodolite shows up by lunchtime tomorrow!'

The Cowboy eye-checked with Barney who nodded okay.

'Fair enough! We'll see yiz startin' time tomorrow!'

'Tomorrow!' Gussie spluttered. 'Why not today?'

'Because I still didn't get me turn to sing!'

The Cowboy about-turned and marched back inside. Barney shrugged his shoulders and followed him. Gussie was livid.

'Sniggerin' bastards! We'll see who's laughin' if they come lookin' for a job when that site's finished.'

Graves fired the engine into life.

'We'll have to build the bloody place first. Meanwhile, if they're not coming back, you'll have to man the gate!'

Inside the pub, the parrot was up and at it. He hadn't seen such action since the shipwreck off Tahiti. He watched open-beaked as the men who had been outside were carried around the bar, followed by

113

cheers, applause and a lusty rendition of 'Happy Days Are Here Again'. His lap of honour finished and The Cowboy moved centre-floor, where he accepted another Jemmy and pep, this time from a beaming Timmy Talbot. He sipped then began to tap his foot in time.

'An old-cowpoke came a' ridin' out one dark an' windy day! An' upon a ridge 'e rested as 'e went along his way!'

Someone howled like a coyote as The Cowboy let rip with the song that gave him his nickname.

'When all at once a mydee herd o' red-eyed cows 'e saw, comin' at 'im up the hill and down a flashing draw!'

The human herd were in and riding hard behind him.

'Yippiee eye ayh! Yipp eye oohhh! Ghost riders in the skyeye!'

The parrot decided to postpone his demise. Below him Timmy Talbot stamped and sang, his eyes flashing with pride and happiness. He was singing for himself, his Da and thousands of others who had never won a round against life.

'Ghhoossttt riiiddderrrs innn the skyeyeeyeeye!'

The song finished to wild cheers and clapping. The mourners were up on the tables. The lunatic threw his farthing earplugs into the air and the parrot lost it completely. Fluttering up onto his perch he squawked at the top of his squawk.

'Polly me bollix! Polly me bollix!'

There was silence and then the pub exploded with the biggest cheer of the day.

OLD GHOSTS

Timmy came home like a conquering hero. He was hours late, well shot and singing.

Burnt dinners usually earned him a night in the doghouse but instead Patsy found herself laughing, as one minute he was

Beyond Pulditch Gates

Dockets plastered with snowballs, then the lunatic with farthings in his ears. She cuffed him playfully for aping the unfortunate man. Timmy grabbed her and swept her up in his arms.

'Oh, what a beautiful morning! Oh, what a beautiful day!'

'Timmy! That ould witch underneath'll have a kitten!'

'Ah, we'll buy 'er a broomstick outa the back-money!'

He let her slide slowly down his body. The room was silent but for their ragged breathing. Patsy gasped as Timmy nuzzled the nape of her neck.

'Haven't you had enough excitement for one day?'

'Nope!'

'Oh, Jesus, Timmy. It isn't the time yet!'

He nuzzled her again and her need overcame her fear.

'Come on then,' she whispered.

While she slipped off her knickers Timmy unbuttoned his trousers and released a massive pulsing erection. She eased herself down on the bed.

'Be very gentle and please, pull out! Promise ye will!'

Timmy eased himself down beside her.

'Don't worry, I'll save the rough stuff for Gobshite Gallagher and that new clothes horse of a manager!'

'Clothes horse?' Patsy tittered as he fluttered his hand between her knees.

'Ye'll never believe it! His Da owns the factory where ye used to work!'

Patsy felt her stomach heave and her thighs clamp shut.

'No! ... I mean ... it's not ... Ri ... Richard Graves?'

'The very lad! ... Now, where were we?'

He ran his hand up inside her legs but Patsy pulled away.

'No! Please, Timmy, I can't!'

115

Timmy looked stunned then he jumped off the bed turning his back to her.

'I'm sorry, Patsy. I thought ... I thought ye wanted to.'

'I do! Honestly! But I'm ... I'm just too nervous!'

Timmy quickly buttoned up his trousers.

'Maybe it's as well. The Roxy got enough business out of us this year!'

There was silence for a few seconds then Patsy's sobs racked his back with guilt.

'Jesus, Patsy, I wasn't forcin' ye.'

'It hasn't anything to do with you, love.'

'O' course it has to do with me. Jesus, it'd be easier to get inta Fort Knox!'

Jack woke in fright and began to bawl. Almost on cue, the complaining thump of a brush-handle began to tom-tom on the ceiling below them. Timmy stamped down furiously with his boot.

'Ah, fuck off, ye gummy ould shite!'

He stormed to the door, tore his coat down off the hanger and slammed the door behind him as he went. The letter wedged behind the clock on the mantelpiece watched Patsy and Jack cry each other to sleep.

NIGHTMARE ONE

Monica heard a bell ringing and voices calling somewhere in her sleep. She turned and pleaded into her pillow.

'Oh, please, it can't be morning already!'

A hand shook her and a voice panicked into her ear.

'Monica! Monica! Get up! The place is on fire!'

As she struggled upright Monica saw that smoke was already seeping up through the cracks in the floorboards and an orange

Beyond Pulditch Gates

glow was dancing menacingly outside the windows. A nun was standing centre-floor.

'Everybody! Take a blanket and get out! Go down the back stairs and hurry!' Monica saw Annie Murray, one of the girls who was heavily pregnant trying to struggle out of bed. She went to help her and had just wrapped her in a blanket when a massive thud hit the wall of the dormitory. The windows shattered and the lights went out, causing pandemonium amongst the girls. Annie leaped backwards, fell over and smashed her head off the iron bedstead. She slid unconscious to the floor.

A whorl of smoke caught Monica by the throat as she tried to pull her upright again. Goaded by a malicious breeze, tongues of flame lapped their way onto the window ledge. They teased the curtains for a moment, then leaped into the room. Monica pleaded with Annie to wake up, but the figure in her arms would not budge. Smoke was now billowing all around them, so Monica stumbled to the Sacred Heart altar that was fixed to the dormitory wall. Flinging the flowers away she soaked the altar-cloth in the water from the vase and tied it round her mouth and nose. Two seconds of yellow flame seared across the ceiling singeing her hair and lighting the sad-faced statue. She cried defiantly at its flickering heart.

'Once! Just for once, will ye help me!'

Monica dragged Annie out onto the landing where a stumbling body collided with them then lurched onwards into the choking stew. Another crawled past on all fours gagging in wordless terror.

'Help me!' Monica pleaded. 'Please, help me!'

But nobody did and precious minutes passed as she hauled Annie along the wall of the corridor until she touched the railings of the banisters at the top of the stairs. Her eyes streamed water and her lungs sucked for precious air. She felt her knees begin to buckle, but just then a grandfather clock that stood in the hallway below struck midnight. Like a ship lost in fog, Monica began to pull Annie slowly down the stairs towards its pompous chimes. It seemed to take forever and Monica's brain started to give up the fight. Instead of making her struggle for air it began to invite her to sleep.

'No!' she told her self over and over. 'Awake! Y've gotta stay awake!'

The face came out of the swirling blackness. It was a baby's face, a pale button-nosed disc of innocence.

'Patsy?' Monica gagged.

The baby screwed up its face as if frightened. At the same time Monica felt her arms pull on something. She was desperately tired yet she pulled and pulled. She had no idea what she was pulling or why she was pulling it. It didn't matter as every pull brought her closer to the baby she once held in her arms. They were lying at the bottom of the stairs when a huge whorl of flame claimed everything above head-height. Monica used the last of her strength to drag Annie into the space under the stairwell. If they were going to die, then they'd die there, together. Monica had long since given up on God, religion or eternity. Instead she comforted herself by remembering the few precious moments she had with her daughter. They would be the last thoughts she'd ever have.

She had no idea how long they lay there but as another huge flash of flame lit the hallway Monica opened her eyes a fraction and saw a blurred black shape moving towards her. A narrow beam of light blazed from an eye in the front of its head.

'So,' she thought to herself, 'this is what death looks like!'

She felt no fear, closed her eyes, hugged Annie and waited for their final darkness to descend. Instead huge gloved hands grabbed

Beyond Pulditch Gates

her around the shoulders and hauled her out of the hideaway. Then other hands grabbed her legs and she was carried along through a tunnel of fire and black choking fumes. She felt as she was being carried forever but then suddenly she was out of the searing heat and into cold, clean air. Many more hands reached out and hurried her clear of the building. Moments later, Annie Murray was carried out behind her. Monica was laid on a stretcher and lifted into a waiting ambulance. Inside the ambulance an oxygen mask was placed over her face. She gulped in the life-giving gas.

Nightmare Two

The night-time city was sinking under inches of greying slush. Man-in-the-Mirror had been walking for hours when he spotted Timmy Talbot staggering out of a pub. It was well past closing time and he was in a bad way, so Man-in-the-Mirror offered to see him home. As he linked Timmy towards his house all he got out of him was a rambling babble about tribes and stallions. When Timmy was safely delivered, Man-in-the-Mirror walked back to Dorset Street and turned for Drumcondra. Near Binn's Bridge he checked his reflection in the window of a chemist shop. As he did so, an urgent ringing came chasing behind him. A fire brigade thundered past. Another followed, tailed in turn by the clanging of an ambulance. He couldn't stop himself from hurrying after them. As he neared the Tolka Bridge, he could see an orange-red glow in the distance.

By the time he got to the fire, one entire wing of the convent was ablaze. Begrimed and sweating firemen snapped more and more hoses into dribbling standpipes. Fire tenders revved their engines to power pumps and arc lamps that deluged the building with water and light. A flop-jowled priest with a pyjama leg poking

119

out below his cassock was flicking holy water at the already saturated walls. Flames licked high into the sky, then lay down only to flash again a moment later. A fireman perched like a black shiny beetle on the tip of an extension ladder. He powered a scuttering lance of water through a top-floor window, sending billows of steam tumbling out into the darkness.

A few feet from where Man-in-the-Mirror stood, a group of people was surrounding a newspaper reporter. They all wanted to add their bit to the grisly story.

'I seen a woman fallin' from a winda! Her clothes was afire!'

'They got some o' them out but a whole load o' them had to jump!'

'The place went up in minutes!'

Man-in-the-Mirror knew he'd been brought to the gates of Hell. He began a silent prayer as a cremated roof-truss collapsed into the conflagration below. He couldn't finish the prayer, so he turned and trudged away. Minutes. That's all it took for death to turn three solid stories into a crematorium. He was heading back towards Tolka Bridge when two ambulances powered past him. He stopped, said a prayer from start to finish then followed them into the city.

NIGHTMARE THREE

Dixie Fanning's eyes stared blankly as Gussie tied a sandbag around his hips.

'Now, me bucko! Let's see ye charm yer way outa that!'

Bubbles of blood soughed from Dixie's lips in a long slow curse.

'Ggguussiiee!'

Gussie cried and leaped away.

'Noooo! Yewr dead! Yew haveta be dead!'

Beyond Pulditch Gates

The moon confirmed that the slash-hook was still rooted in Dixie's chest. Gussie chided himself for being so jumpy. Nonetheless, he moved gingerly towards the body and prodded it with the toe of his boot. Then he grabbed it by the shoulders and dragged it to the edge of the hole. For an instant, their faces were only inches apart and the body sighed his name again. Gussie heaved it out into the bogslop.

'Fuugghhh yeewww!'

It lolled for a moment on the surface.

'Sink! Sink ye bastard's animal! Siiinnnkkkk!'

A debaucher to the end, Dixie Fanning slowly rolled over and for the last time eased himself into a dark engulfing wetness. To keep him that way, Gussie pitched turf into the hole for a solid hour, yet his sweat was cold as ice. Moonlight danced a ragged jig on the surface of the water as the ribs of peat plopped into the dark-brown void. Then suddenly the moon slipped behind an inky cloud. Plunged into darkness Gussie yelled and clamped his eyes closed in terror.

When he opened them again he found himself lying on the cold linoleum floor of the watchman's hut. He lay still for a moment then dragged himself up to kneel against a chair. Sweat coursed down his face.

'Dear Jesus! How many times have I to tell ye! I did it for yew! I ran that slut Josie away and then I done the whoremaster that put her in shame! Now I'm doin' night-watchman because of that crowd o' bloody commies! What more do ye want? What more do ye waanntt!'

When he finally dragged himself to the window he saw a red glow somewhere on the north side of the city. It sat on the earth like a miniature sunset. Gussie reckoned it was a fire and a big one at that.

chapter 5

PULDITCH

A few weeks after Easter, Fixit and Fukkit were putting lights along the roof of the riverside pumphouse. They sat down together for a few minutes so Fukkit could have a smoke. Suddenly Fixit was on his feet and pointing towards the Kish Bank lightship.

'There they are!' he cried. 'There they are at last!'

'There what are?' Fukkit demanded.

'Swallows! Swallows! The end o' winter!'

Fukkit stood and looked seawards. In the distance he could see a black arrowhead of birds weaving their way towards land.

Fixit pulled himself up proudly.

'My grandfather used to fish out of Ringsend. He always said that year after year the first place swallows landed in Dublin was here!'

As if to confirm his words the leader of the flight dipped the birds downwards until they were almost skimming the water. A landing was only minutes away. The two-man welcoming

Beyond Pulditch Gates

committee stood-to to greet the returning migrants, but at the last second the flight leader took the flock upwards in an almost vertical climb. The black whirring mass just cleared the heads of the two startled men. Banking sharp to the left, they headed out towards Sandymount Strand, then banked again to make a second pass over the Pulditch site. Panic seemed to thunder through their wings as their leader searched for a safe landing spot in the concrete nightmare below.

Twice more the swallows swept low over the site, but then they headed back out over the bay towards the rough but unspoilt safety of Lambay Island. In the weeks that followed willow warblers, chiffchaffs and a dozen other species would follow suit. Apart from gulls and cormorants, Pulditch had few feathered visitors that summer. The only song to be heard during that long hot season was the raucous bawl of Gussie Gallagher being answered by the quickening tinny ring of brickies' trowels. Behind them came squads of plasterers, floor layers, pipe fitters, electricians and carpenters. For a long time it looked as if the various parts of the building would never come together, but then corridors and stairs began to open. High above the ground, catwalks were connected, and by late summer, a man could walk from one end of the building to the other and always have a roof over his head.

The place was really taking shape when Autumn finally slipped into the frame. It was a gentle season, though its copper-coloured reign was short. Winter gripped early, but by then the bulk of the construction work was finished. Inside the building, erectors were assembling the turbines and the boilers to run them. Outside, a crew of roadmakers was laying tarmacadam through the site. The station chimney was almost complete, as was the pump house down at the riverfront. During all this frantic activity, the roof of

Number One hut continued to leak and the stove continued to belch amidst the daily rows and riots, but all were patched up somehow or other. Christmas brought a splash of warmth and colour before another hard, cold January weaned 1959.

Timmy Talbot had never worked so hard or so long in his life. No hour was sacred, no day or night spared in the frantic push to ensure that by mid-year Pulditch One would be up and running. He often felt guilty being away from Patsy and Jack so much but the need to keep his job and the prospect that maybe, just maybe, he might land a full-time job in the new station, kept his nose firmly to the grindstone. He was so preoccupied, that he never noticed January slipping into February and Patsy had to remind him that Jack was a full year old. In March, a carpet of buttercups and daisies spread themselves across a stretch of ground just behind the station. Timmy often took a moment to admire their brave and bright display. A week into April, diggers ploughed the lot as they began to lay foundations for the station oil tanks.

It was evening on Friday the first of May, feast of St Joseph the Worker, and a well-oiled Oily Paddy was holding the floor in Grealish's.

'Whoo... Whoo tipped Mister What for last year's National at eighteen-ta-wan?'

Hairy acted the dum-dum.

'What kind of a half-arsed question is that? What who tipped What?'

'No! No! I'm sayin' I'm the who who tipped What!'

Timmy took over from Hairy.

'Lemme get this straight. You're sayin' you were the who who tipped What when he won at eighteen-to-one!'

Beyond Pulditch Gates

'Essactly!'

'And why should we give a fish's tit what horse ye tipped?' Barney snapped.

'Because, I'm tryin' ta show yiz me credentials!'

'Do an' ye'll get six months!' Mackerel warned. 'Flashin' Fagin's out around here!'

'Not dem credentials! The wans that's gonna make us million-bleedinaires!'

The Pox incensed the barflies with pipe-smoke.

'What are we gonna do? Jesse James a bookie's?'

Oily drew himself up into his barrister pose.

'We, are gonna buy ourselves a racehorse.'

'We're gonna buy a wha'?'

'Youse heard me! One head, one tail, four hooves and a prick if it's a stallion! I'm a personal friend of a trainer in the Curragh and what's more, 'e knows me name!'

Pissed as he was they all stopped to listen. Even the parrot was squawkless.

Oily took a gulp of beer, burped and continued.

'Issimple! We all puts up a ten spot t' start and a wanser a week after that.'

'For how long?' Hairy demanded.

'Until we have enuffa readies to buy the bleedin' thing!'

'Say we did buy it,' Barney spat a pick of tobacco, 'what'll it live on?'

'The Curragh! The shaggin' place is covered in grass!'

Hairy stopped in mid-sip.

'A racehorse is like a bally-dancer. It has to be washed down, brushed up and have it's arse wiped when it's finished! And another thing, hay doesn't grow on trees!'

125

'Too right!' Mackerel slapped his knee. 'It grows in bales and bales costs money!'

Even the parrot was breaking its bollix when the door suddenly flew open. Saint Joseph filled the saloon door like a sheriff in a cowboy picture. Then the boys remembered why they were there in the first place. He'd organised them to go to City Quay Church for a feastday devotion to his namesake. He should have known better than to allow a rendezvous in Grealish's because the place was a notorious glue-pot.

'Well, well, well! So this is how Irish workers honour their patron saint.'

Though the parrot's mother always told him to be proud of being a bird he decided to act sheepish like everyone else. Mackerel's mother never told him he was a fish, but she did leave him a watch. He plucked its strapless body from his pocket.

'Is that the time! Youse are some shower for keepin' me talkin'!'

It could have gone either way, but Saint Joseph wasn't all sour-apple.

'I said a prayer for you all. God knows you need it!'

The place erupted and the parrot wished they'd make up their minds.

When Saint Joseph got himself into a seat and a shandy into his hand, Oily restated his equine proposal. Joseph agreed to bunce in provided it didn't come under the ambit of gambling. Then The Pox threw a spanner in the works.

'Hang on a minute. As soon as that site's finished we'll be history.'

'So?' Oily rejoined.

'So what happens the poxy horse?'

It was a good question and one the whole place had to ponder. The parrot got pissed off and went to peck at himself in his mirror. It was Saint Joseph who broke the duck.

Beyond Pulditch Gates

'Who says we'll be history?'

'Well, ye know yerself,' Hairy replied. 'Pulditch is the same as any other site. As soon as it's up, we're out!'

'Most of us maybe but not all. I was fixing a shelf in the offices today and I overheard Graves on the phone. He was saying they'd soon be advertising for bodies to run the place.'

Timmy jumped in immediately.

'Ye mean, permanent staff?'

Saint Joseph swizzed his shandy back to life.

'I'm only telling you what I heard!'

Waiting

Patsy Talbot waited patiently to hear from the little pinch-faced nun, but she never came back. One day she was passing a local convent and called in on spec to see if they might be able to help. She was met with a polite but impenetrable wall of silence. When she mentioned her predicament to a priest in confession he told her to go home and mind her own business. Stung by his rebuke Patsy took the bull by the horns and called on Monica's parents again. It was a wasted effort. When she got to their house, she discovered they had sold it and moved. The woman who bought it said they left no forwarding address. Patsy knew by her face she was lying. As she walked away she decided she'd have to confront an old ghost and ring the paint factory to see if anyone there might be able to help.

Lousy Lotty was delighted to hear from her. They chatted for a moment about old times, then Lotty asked if her friend had been in touch.

'What friend is that?' Patsy asked.

'Your old school pal,' Lotty chirruped. 'She rang here a few months ago and asked for your address! One of the girls here

127

knew where you lived so I gave it out to her. I hope you don't mind?'

Patsy felt her knees weaken but she steadied herself and played along.

'Oh, no. Not at all!'

'She was just so anxious to contact you.'

'Was she? I mean, o' course she was.'

Patsy remembered little of the conversation that followed. When she got home she called into Mrs Coffey and told her what happened.

'An' ye reckon it was this Monica who rang the factory?'

'I'd put me life on it!' Patsy insisted. 'So, what am I gonna do now?'

Mrs Coffey thought aloud.

'That nun who called was wrapped up like a hock-shop parcel but if we could figure out which order she belongs to we might be able t' find 'er.'

'But who'd tell us that?'

'Our friend, across the landin'.'

'Ye mean....'

'Sure she's religion mad! If anybody can clue us in, she can.'

'I dunno. She's a bit ... ye know ... private.'

'Ah, she's all right under that ould puss o' hers. I'll have a word with 'er.'

A few minutes later Mrs Coffey was back. She had a thick paperback booklet in her hand.

'Told ye she wouldn't let us down. This is the Parish Guide to the Archdiocese of Dublin an' every convent an' chapel in Dublin's in it.'

Patsy studied the booklet.

'Well, there's me, a Catholic all me life an' I never knew such a thing existed.'

Beyond Pulditch Gates

'Nor did I! Sourarse she may be, but the woman knows 'er religion!'

'We really shouldn't call 'er that.'

'What?'

'Sourarse. I mean, she's not that bad!'

'True, but a smile, ever now an' again wouldn't kill 'er.'

'I wonder why she's like that?' Patsy mused.

Mrs Coffey toyed with the pages of the booklet.

'I do see terrible sorra in 'er eyes betimes. She never says nothin' but....'

'But what?'

'But nothin'! Me addin' two an' two and getting ten. Lessee what we're up against.'

They sat at the table and read though pages and pages of entries. When they were finished Patsy sighed wearily.

'There's so many places that nun could be! It's lookin' for a needle in a haystack!'

'Well,' Mrs Coffey rolled up her sleeves, 'no better women t' find it!'

Monday, 1 June 1959

Saint Joseph had heard right. Permanent positions were being created in Pulditch and applications closed on the last Friday in May. Graves and Gussie ripped gleefully through the pile of applications. They did the ripping in Gussie's office where Gussie picked up one that looked liked it was written in Greek.

'Mackerel! Mackerel McKenna lookin' for a job! Lord Jaysus, I wouldn't let that gobshite run sheep never mind a shaggin' turbine!'

Graves held another one aloft.

Henry Hudson

'"Dear Sir" Spelt d-e-r-e, "I would" w-o-u-d, "like to apply for a job", full fucking stop!'

They had every reason to scoff. They had old scores to settle and the day of reckoning had finally arrived. They had made two stacks for the applications. Stack One was for the home-and-drieds. Stack Two was for those who, as long as their dicks dangled downwards, would never get a job in Pulditch. Man-in-the-Mirror, Hairy, Clean and Oily Paddy were already in Stack Two along with The Pox and The Child O' Prague. Gussie lifted the next sheet.

'Here's one I'll enjoy burnin'! It's from that ould creepin' jeeziz of a carpenter! A great man ta sing Jerusalem. He'll go down a bomb on the dole queue!'

Saint Joseph joined Stack Two as Graves considered another neatly written page.

'How about young Talbot?'

'A Communist!' Gussie snapped.

Timmy's application instantly joined Saint Joseph's. Gussie had Red Kearns's application in his pocket. While Graves was distracted Gussie, slipped it into Stack One. Then Graves smiled and held out the letter he'd been reading. It was written in an open, childlike scrawl and signed 'Bernard B. Coogan'. Gussie grabbed it and shook with excitement.

'Gotchya! At long last ye hoor's bastard, I fuckinwell have ye!'

He approached his first ever orgasm as he dropped Barney's paper on top of Stack Two.

When they were all finished, Graves stood and stretched like a cat in sunshine.

'I'll have a word with the typist about the letters I want sent out. If I move sharpish she could have them in the post this evening.'

Beyond Pulditch Gates

Gussie began to gather up Stack One.

'In that case, Mister Graves I'll bring these down to 'er now.'

'No! No! Gus! You're management. Let her come up and collect them. See you tomorrow!'

Graves had been sniffing around the typist for weeks. Having her type up a letter gave him an ideal excuse to get close to her. They exchanged smiles and small talk as she typed a stencil of the letter he wanted sent out. He stood beside her as she ran off a sheaf of copies, then sat with his knee touching hers as he signed them using a flashy gold-nibbed pen. He could see she was impressed, yet experience told him she was the sort of filly who couldn't be rushed. It'd take time but if she shagged as well as she took shorthand she'd be worth the wait. He smiled as he stood up to go.

'Mister Gallagher has the names upstairs. Perhaps you'll have a word with him?'

Distaste clouded her face and he wondered if anyone liked the smelly, sappy-headed moron.

Upstairs, Gussie pulled the morning's *Indo* out of his drawer. He'd been too busy to read it earlier, but he knew what it would say before he even unfolded it. There'd be trouble in Cyprus, riots in Alabama and warnings of the red menace on every second page. Right there and then, he didn't give a shite. He scratched himself and sat well back into his seat.

'As the man said, I'm management!'

He put the paper face down on the desk. That way he could read it from the back page towards the front ones where the *Indo* usually carried their pen and ink ads. Every day he did a mental heads or tails as to whether it would be plumpish Miss Twilfit in a full length girdle or the skinny strip of a wan in Kayser baby doll pyjamas. He was disappointed on both counts because the *Indo*

131

couldn't have half-naked women anywhere near a piece concerning Cardinal D'Alton.

Gussie read the headline aloud.

"'CARDINAL D'ALTON SAYS GOODWILL COULD BRING A SOLUTION TO PARTITION'"

He flicked the page over narkily.

'As if we haven't enough shaggin' leeches 'iv our own.'

He flicked over another page and the headline hit him like a hammer. 'STAMP COMPANY COLLAPSES'. Gussie choked out the lines that followed.

"'Four directors of a Dublin Stamp Auction firm will appear in Dublin District Court today charged with conspiracy to defraud.'"

He was charging down the stairs when the typist stepped from her office.

'Oh, Mister Gallagher! About the names of....'

'On me desk!' he snapped and barged out past her.

'Pig,' she muttered, then went on up to his office where she found the papers on the corner of his desk. She'd have tidied away the scattered newspaper if its owner wasn't such an ignorant shit. Minutes later she was typing names and addresses onto the letters Richard Graves signed before he left.

Passing Ships

Gussie knew there was a solicitor's near the Regnum Christi Place in O'Connell Street, so he headed there. Arriving without an appointment he browbeat the secretary into letting him see one of the partners. Gussie told his story but the solicitor couldn't help.

'I'll be honest, Mister Gallagher. This stamps business is on the tom-toms and if they're correct, which they usually are, then the whole lot's down the Swanee!'

Beyond Pulditch Gates

'But I put in two thousand pounds. I got a got a cast-iron promise! Outstandin' profit within four months.'

'What you got was the 'probability' of an outstanding profit. You can drive a double-decker bus between promise and probability.'

'I saved that money week be week! Years 'n' years it took me! Kept it in a box!'

'What about a bank?'

'Didn't trust them.'

'A pity you didn't.'

'I'll sue! I'll sue their arses off!'

'You'd be wasting my time and your money.'

'Then I'll go to the papers! Get it on the radio! Can't ye advise me t' do that?'

'Provided your tax affairs are in order.'

'This has shag all t' do with the taxman!'

'Go public on this and it very soon could be!'

Minutes later Gussie was back out in the street. He decided to make an anonymous call to the papers demanding action. What that action was and who would take it he didn't know, but nonetheless he hobbled blindly across the street towards the phones in the GPO. He never saw the car that was approaching at speed.

The car jammed on. Monica Dillon and a nun who was sitting beside her on the back seat were pitched forwards.

'Bloody lunatic!' the driver called after Gussie's retreating back.

'Dear, oh, dear!' the nun cried. 'Are you all right, Monica?'

'I'm fine, Sister.'

'That madman nearly got us all killed!'

Monica was beyond caring. Since the fire she had been moved from convent to convent in Dublin, but now she was being moved almost thirty miles away, to a place in Wicklow called St Jude's. The irony wasn't lost on Monica. St Jude was the patron saint of hopeless cases. It seemed the fates were determined she would never contact Patsy Talbot. Without Patsy Talbot she would never find her daughter. More and more, Monica wondered why the same fates hadn't done the decent thing and let her and Annie die together under that stairwell.

The car began to move again. They had just passed the Gay Child shop, and on the opposite side of the street, the phone box that stood outside Gill's shop. Now they were opposite the round grey pillars of the GPO. Monica caught a fleeting glimpse of an elderly woman standing outside it rocking a baby's pram. She shivered remembering the terrible time she got off Batface over the scene she caused when she confronted a woman with a pram. Batface had allowed her make one call, just one lousy phone call. Then she promised for months to go back to Larnham Street, but she never did and now she never would.

Her charred remains were found in the chapel where the fire started. Beside her lay the twisted ribs of a metal candle-holder. Painters who were working in the chapel had left drums of paint and white spirits near one of the statues. The firemen reckoned that somehow the candle had ignited these and caused the inferno. There was talk that they had to smash their way into the place because all the doors were locked from inside. There was no talk of what the nun was doing alone in a chapel in the middle of the night. Instead the subject was buried quietly and quickly, just like the girls who died in the fire.

Monica closed her eyes and felt weary to the bottom of her soul.

'Oh, look, Monica!' the nun cried. 'Clery's! Have you ever been in?'

Beyond Pulditch Gates

The nun didn't take the hint of Monica's silence. She blundered on.

'Now I know you're a city girl, but you'll just love this new place. It's at the foot of the mountains. It has the most beautiful chapel and, oh, the gardens! St Jude's is a home from home.'

Monica's eyes stung with tears. She hadn't seen home since she told her father she was pregnant.

'Patsy, Oh, my poor, poor Patsy,' she sighed quietly.

The nun frowned.

'Patsy? Patsy who?'

'Nobody, Sister! Just someone I used to know!'

Mrs Coffey rocked Jack's pram to send him back to sleep. The screech of brakes as a hoop-legged lunatic stepped out in front of a car had woken him and he began to whimper. Mrs Coffey watched the lunatic barge his way across to where she stood. On the opposite side of the street the car began to move on down towards O'Connell Street Bridge. The lunatic had just plunged through one door of the post office when Patsy stepped out of the other.

'Right,' she declared, 'that's another six letters gone!'

'How many's that now?'

'Eighteen. Though be the looks of it I could send eighty an' still get nowhere.'

Mrs Coffey set the pram in motion.

'Some convent somewhere has ta have somethin' on Monica Dillon so it's only a matter o' time before that somethin' shows up.'

'But it's been over a year as it is.'

'All things come t' them that waits, Patsy. All things come t' them that waits.'

The two women walked slowly up the street towards Parnell Square.

Outsiders

Early the following morning, Barney was sitting with Saint Joseph in Number One hut arguing over the introduction of PAYE. Saint Joseph was all for it.

'It'll be the best thing ever happened! Paying your tax every week instead of having to pay it all together at the end of the year.'

'I dunno about that. The farmers and the pinstripes is stayin' out on the prairie. No way they'll run into a corral like sheep t' be shaved.'

Saint Joseph never understood Barney's suspicion of governments, farmers and pin-stripes. Just then The Pox pedalled to a halt outside. He leaped off his bike and barged into the hut pulling a flash of white paper from his pocket.

'Morninnnn' poxes! Run yer poxy mince pies over that!'

He slapped the letter on the table. He'd been offered a job in Pulditch.

By the starting siren Mackerel, Oily Paddy and The Child did likewise. Dockets was in deep shit. He'd opened a book on who'd get jobs, and the first four home were rank outsiders. Timmy hoped against hope there'd be a letter waiting for him at home that evening, even though the boys who got them took some slagging. Cries of 'Crawler!' and 'Lick-lick!' pinballed up and down the hut. Hairy pushed between Mackerel and Oily.

'It's like bein' in Willwood's factory! I'm surrounded be bleedin' jam-pots!'

'I don't see any jam-pots!' Saint Joseph complained.

'Not real jam-pots. A jam-pot is a fella who falls inta a sewer and comes up with a cheese sandwich!'

'Oh, dear,' Saint Joseph turned green. 'Wouldn't that make him sick?'

Beyond Pulditch Gates

The place went bananas. It went bananas squared when Oily admitted that he had brought in cheese sandwiches for his lunch.

Manpower

Gussie came in late. He'd put in a fearful night in the company of old and insistent ghosts. Bankrupt and weary, he climbed the stairs to his office where Red Kearns jumped out at him from the corner. Gussie nearly shit himself.

'Bloody hell, man! Are ye tryin' ta gimme a heart attack?'

'Are you tryin' ta give me the elbow?'

'Elbow? What elbow?'

Kearns was purple with temper.

'Don't act the fuckin' eejit with me! Where's me letter?'

'What letter?'

'One like a lot o' fuckers got this mornin'! Dear Sirs sayin' they have a job in Pulditch! I swear, if you've jibbed on me I'll hang your arsehole higher nor heaven!'

'No! No!' Gussie blubbered, 'I put ye in the pile meself, personal.'

'Under or over Mackerel?'

'What are ye on about? There's no letter gone out to him.'

'So what The Pox and Oily Paddy got this mornin' was early Christmas cards?'

'They got no letters! Lookit!'

Gussie snatched the scattered pages of the *Indo* up off his desk. When he saw the single stack of letters he knew immediately there'd been a monumental balls-up.

The typist gave him a withering look as he barged in on top of her.

'Listen here, Missy! What letters did ye send out yesterday?'

She handed him the applications she had taken off his desk.

137

'I sent appointment letters to all these people as per Mister Graves's instructions.'

'Who in Christ's name told yew these were the ones to go out?'

'You did! Remember you almost knocked me down on the stairs? I asked you where they were and you said on your desk.'

Gussie said nothing. He just turned and walked out. Kearns dived on him the minute he came back into his office.

'Well? What's the read?'

Gussie let Stack Two fall around his feet like confetti.

'If in all this world I could pick fuckers I'd most like ta shoot, I'd pick these!'

He looked down at the papers scattered on the floor.

'But I didn't have them shot!'

'Then what did ye do?' Kearns demanded.

'I've just offered every one of the bastards a job here in Pulditch!'

SALVATION

Patsy heard Timmy thunder up the stairs. He almost took the door off its hinges as he burst into the room.

'Patsy! Patsy! Did I get a letter?'

She pointed to an envelope wedged behind the clock on the mantelpiece. It had the company crest in one corner. Timmy was all thumbs as he tried to rip it open.

'It's about the jobs! Some of the boys got word this mornin'.'

Patsy calmly took it off him, sliced it open with her nail and pulled out the letter.

'"Dear Mister Talbot, I am pleased to inform you that your application for a position as a general worker in Pulditch One has been successful."'

Beyond Pulditch Gates

'Yeessss!' Timmy punched the air.

'Hold it! This offer is subject to a satisfactory twelve-month probationary period.'

'Ah, I'll do that on me head!'

Patsy was so excited she never noticed who signed the letter. Timmy plucked the letter from her hands and kissed it. Then he began to kiss her full and open on the lips.

Minutes later her nails were raking his back as he drove himself high up inside her. The tribe, The Roxy, mysterious nuns, even the spectre of Richard Graves stayed away as they rowed together. Timmy called her name as his body stiffened then relaxed with a shuddering sigh. They lay unmoving for a long time. Patsy knew there was a risk she might become pregnant, but right there and then she didn't care. Jack snoozed in his cot and the brush in the room below stayed mute. A daddy-long-legs danced across the ceiling and she wondered what the leggy insect might make of the sight on the bed below. Timmy's trousers accordioned around his ankles while her stockinged legs clamped his bare white buttocks. The insect was as worn out as the lovers. He settled on the lightshade and within minutes all three were asleep.

Letting Go

It was late on a hot June night when Pulditch One finally saw action. A burner ignited with a yellow-red roar in the combustion chamber of one of the boilers and within hours the boiler was making steam. A week later, the first of the turbines was run-up to speed. It was tripped and tested, tested and tripped, until finally it was ready to be synchronised onto the national grid. That test took place between midnight and dawn and for six heart-stopping hours, it exported five megawatts before it was taken off again.

During July and most of August, boilers and turbines were run-up, shut down, adjusted then run-up to be tested all over again. Staff too were being trained and tested as rigorously as the machines for which they would soon be responsible.

As the construction work tapered off, those who were hitting the road began to drift in ever increasing numbers. Not a Friday night went by that Grealish's didn't ring to songs and speeches of farewell. When Number One hut was finally abandoned, Clean Paddy went all sentimental.

'We should burn it! The apaches always burn their huts when the tribe moves on.'

Mackerel wouldn't have it.

'Well, I seen all the John Wayne pictures an' I never seen a Nissen hut in any o' them!'

In the end, Number One hut was left standing to serve as a stores, and the boys transferred to new locker rooms inside the station. They had tiled floors and lines of pristine lockers clamped against newly emulsioned walls. They had washrooms and showers. They even had hot water.

September 1959

Pulditch officially opened on Sunday 10 September, and staff were allowed bring a guest for the day. Patsy shivered when Timmy first asked her to go. Richard Graves was in Pulditch. Nonetheless, as they approached the gates she returned Timmy's proud grin. He felt her grip on his arm tighten, but he put it down to excitement. A huge crowd turned up, including the five P's as the Pox called them: Priests, politicians, press, poseurs and the proletariat poxes who built the place. Pulditch was a riot of flags and bunting and a brass band played on a podium just inside the gate. Its array of

Beyond Pulditch Gates

brightly coloured balloons were under close guard by Dockets who had landed the gateman's job. The Lord Mayor was chatting to some people on the podium and Patsy admired the magnificent gold chain that hung around his neck. Timmy nudged her with his elbow.

'See that fella standin' beside the Lord Mayor? The one in the flashy suit? That's George Keyes. He's the Chairman o' the Board!'

'A big wig?' Patsy grinned.

'The biggest!' Timmy laughed as he led her on into the station.

He brought her through the turbine hall and she could feel their powerful pulse as they toured around them. She didn't fancy the boiler-house. It was hot and noisy and the narrow open-grate catwalks seemed to go up and up forever. She had great fun trying to guess who was who among Timmy's workmates because he used their proper names to introduce them. She never thought the legendary Pox would wear a dicky bow, whereas she picked out Oily Paddy from fifty yards away. Timmy led her around as though he'd built the place on his own. He was proud of Pulditch, he was proud of her but most of all he was proud of the faintest swelling around her waist. Patsy was three months pregnant.

They were walking outside when they bumped into Barney who insisted they head for the refreshment tent. There bottles of ale were decapped for the men while Patsy had a bottle of orange. Timmy and Barney were like magnets. Within minutes a crowd gathered round them and a noisy debate began as to how many IRA internees were still in Belfast Jail. Patsy left them to it and strolled out into the sunshine. She'd been fascinated by the height of the chimney and wandered over to stand at its base. When she looked up she felt as if it was falling away from the white scudding clouds at its tip.

141

'Two-hundred-and-seventy-six feet, base to top!'

The voice sent a shiver up her spine. Taking a deep breath she turned to face Richard Graves.

'Hello, Patsy. Long time, no see. How come you're gracing us with your presence?'

'My husband works here! Timmy Talbot?'

Graves felt like kicking himself. He knew Patsy had been dating a bloke when she worked in the factory but he had never made the connection between her and Timmy. He was furious that a mere labourer had succeeded where he had failed.

'So, you're not Patsy Burke any more?'

'No. I'm Patsy Talbot and bloody proud of it!'

'Hey! Hey! Relax! I just want us to be friends!'

'I was never your friend! I was your employee, worse luck!'

'Careful, Patsy! Timmy's on probation and I might have to assess him!'

'And I might have to go the police about what happened in that storeroom!'

Before another threat could fly, a woman's shrill voice called from behind them.

'Richard! Richard!'

'Oh, shit,' Graves mumbled

A tall flame-haired woman hurried towards them. Patsy took her in an eyeblink. She was wearing a beautiful silk suit with a matching handbag and shoes. Her face was fine and well-featured, and as she got closer Patsy saw her make-up was perfect. Money, thought Patsy and lots of it. The woman didn't wait for introductions.

'Richard! Where have you been? Daddy wants you on the podium. The Lord Mayor is about to cut the ribbon!'

Graves turned white.

Beyond Pulditch Gates

'Eh, Patsy, I mean Mrs Talbot, this is my fiancée, Catherine Keyes! Catherine, this is Mrs Talbot. Her husband is on the staff.'

Patsy decided to make the shitbag squirm. She shot out a hand in hello.

'The name's Patsy. I worked under Richard before I was married. Strange how our paths keep crossing.'

'Do they?' Catherine said icily. She barely touched Patsy's fingers then pulled her hand away.

'Oh, I could tell you stories,' Patsy giggled.

'I'm sure you could but you'll have to excuse us.'

Graves winced as Catherine linked herself to his arm and frog-marched him away. Patsy watched them go.

'Keyes?' she asked herself. 'Now why is that name so familiar?'

She was almost back at the refreshment tent before the penny dropped. She stopped dead as the old familiar rage trembled through her. Trust a bastard like Graves to snare the head man's daughter.

BALLOONS ONE

Night-time, and Gussie Gallagher sat on his bed beside his ammo box. It was empty but for moonspill. Building Pulditch should have been the making of him, but instead he was virtually starting from scratch. Having straightened the notes and faced them right way round he counted ten fivers twice. On the floor beside him a column of the *Indo* was defaced leaving only the hands and feet of a brazen black-clad whore. Served her right, her and her Little X corselet at only 69/11d. He sighed as he took a fiver from the wad. He'd have to buy a new 'going-out' cap because he'd lost the one he had earlier in the day. That was yet another trial from God. A trial like the bastards in overalls, his slut of a sister and the man he shredded just like he shredded the crumpled ad at his feet.

BALLOONS TWO

The moon looked like a big off-white disc of cheese as Man-in-the-Mirror strode out along the seafront at Clontarf. Across the bay he could see the lights of Pulditch and the tall dark hulk of its smokestack. He laughed remembering the consternation there'd been down there earlier in the day. The Lord Mayor had just cut the ribbon to declare the place open. Then a raft of balloons was released by George Keyes, the Chairman of the Board. They were fifteen feet in the air when it was discovered some smart shite had tied Gussie Gallagher's good 'going-out' cap to the end of them. The boys held an immediate steward's enquiry and the nod went to either Mackerel or Barney. Man-in-the-Mirror walked on chuckling quietly and wondering if Gussie's cap was still aloft.

BALLOONS THREE

Patsy was out of bed and looking at the moon that sat above the crooked chimneys of Larnham Street. Timmy and Jack were asleep. Mrs Coffey baby-sat for Jack while they were in Pulditch earlier in the day. When they got home, she showed Patsy a photo she had found in an old religious magazine. It was a photo of a group of nuns on retreat in a country house. Though the black-and-white image was smudged and grainy, Mrs Coffey was certain that the nun on the left of the picture was the one who called on the day of the snow, the one the nosy neighbour had frightened away. The caption under the photograph named her as Sister Hilda. Patsy scrutinised the nun's thin, pinched face. The black piercing eyes peering out from under her veil made her look hawk-like. There was something about her that frightened Patsy back into bed beside Timmy. She wrapped herself tightly around him until sleep came and took her.

Beyond Pulditch Gates

BALLOONS FOUR

The moon was a balloon above Saint Jude's. Monica Dillon sat in the window of her room and looked out over the high dark walls of the convent grounds towards the distant twinkling tiara of Dublin Bay. She had just finished writing another page of her secret diary. The keeping of diaries was strictly forbidden, but Monica clung to the hope that someday her daughter might get to read her words and understand all that happened and why they were parted. Along with words to young Patsy, she recorded events that happened in Saint Jude's and the stories of some of the other girls who were in situations like her own. Monica kept the pages hidden in a box at the back of her wardrobe and she planned that someday she would stitch them all together in the form of a book. She took one last look at the moon, pulled the curtains and got into bed. High above, an unseen clutch of gaily coloured balloons floated over the navy outline of the Wicklow Mountains. Though weighted by a dark, flat disc they rose quietly and effortlessly, like a child's prayer.

chapter 6

Changing Times

In the months that followed, Timmy settled into Pulditch and Jack grew taller by the day. Patsy tried in vain to track down the mysterious Sister Hilda. She even wrote to the mother house of the order to which she belonged but, as with so many of her other letters, no reply ever came. Patsy meant to follow it up but then she suddenly developed problems with her pregnancy. She woke one night in severe pain and began to haemorrhage. She was rushed to the Roxy where they performed an emergency operation that saved Patsy but not her baby. When she came out of the anaesthetic a nurse said she'd had a little girl. Neither she nor Timmy were allowed to see the baby nor did they get a birth or death certificate to say that she'd ever existed. The hospital arranged her burial, and again neither she nor Timmy were present. The doctors said it was better if things were finished and forgotten as soon as possible. Patsy tried to forget but she couldn't. Every time they talked about it she cried and Timmy went silent.

Beyond Pulditch Gates

So they talked about it less and less, but the pain waited like a readied snare for an unguarded word or the sight of a new-born baby being pushed in a pram.

A year later, two rooms became available on the first floor of the house, so they moved down and took them over. The front room was the bigger of the two. During the day they cooked and lived in it. At night a bed settee folded out and it became a bedroom for Jack. Patsy and Timmy used the small back room for themselves. There they continued to walk the tightrope of the safe period or 'jumping off at the lights' as Timmy called *coitus interruptus*. In 1963, Patsy became pregnant, but she lost the baby just as she had before. In 1966, the same thing happened and Patsy had had enough. She sought out her 'breath-of-air' Scottish doctor and discovered he was practising in a private hospital on the south side of the city. Though it cost a lot of money to see him, Patsy gladly paid it.

He listened to her story then wrote her a prescription for cycle regulating medication otherwise known as 'the pill'. He told her that if anyone asked she was to say she was having trouble with her periods and not just trying to avoid being pregnant. She tried several chemists before she got the prescription filled and even then the chemist eyed her suspiciously. Patsy decided that Ireland's symbol should change from the harp and shamrock to the wig and gavel. Every fucker was a one-man judge and jury. Two years later, Patsy would have her suspicions confirmed. She would learn first-hand that when it came to the proletariat, Ireland had no shortage of judges, wigs or gavels.

part **2**

chapter 7

PULTDICH: FRIDAY, 22 MARCH 1968

The semi-skilled lads were in the big locker room for a dinner-hour meeting. They were also divided for and against going on strike. Timmy Talbot had been elected deputy shop steward to Barney Coogan and they sat together at a table at the top of the room. Barney was on for hitting the gate. The boys trusted Barney and had followed him over the top many times since Pulditch opened, but the rules of battle were changing. A new breed of union official stalked the world. Red Kearns was one of them. Five years earlier, he had left Pulditch for a job as a full-time delegate in the union. The Child said the fucker must have won it in a luckybag, but within six months Kearns was The Cowboy's assistant. Within twelve he was his boss, and The Cowboy was effectively sidelined. Kearns wouldn't hear of a stoppage and sent down word that if they went out they'd be out on their own.

Barney called the boys to order.

'The semi-skilled above in the railway works is out already. Their tradesmen got the same increase ours did. So just like us, they got left behind. They got a pain in their arse waitin' for the unions to do somethin' so they grabbed the bull be the bollix an' did it themselves! Now, we've been warnin' and warnin' we was gonna do somethin' but we've done fuckall! So I say come next Tuesday we do the same as the lads in the railway. We hit the tar an' be done with it!'

Clean Paddy was dubious.

'I dunno, Barney. Ye heard what Kearns said about unofficial action! It's not like the old days, one out, all out.'

'Ah, eff Kearns!'

Mackerel jumped to his feet.

'Eff 'im again, Barney! But if the trades givvus the fingers an' the shift goes in we'll be out till the fat lady farts!'

Timmy chalked '80' on a makeshift blackboard.

'Look at it this way: Up to '66 we were on eighty per cent of the tradesman's rate. They went out and got twenty-one pound a week leavin' us on thirteen. Now Kearns says the best we'll do is one lousy pound of an increase!'

He chalked a large '67' and circled it.

'Accept that and we'll be on sixty-seven per cent of the trades-man's rate. Thirteen per cent worse off nor we were two year ago!'

Barney eye-challenged the room.

'We've had a six-week overtime ban an' got nowhere. So it's piss or get offa the pot!'

On a show of hands they decided for strike and the meeting broke up.

As the room cleared, Barney slid a newspaper over to Timmy.

'Top o' the page.'

Timmy read a warning that some sort of unofficial action was imminent.

'That bastard Kearns is singin' to the papers. He'll hang us all yet.'

Beyond Pulditch Gates

'He'll have plenty of help to work the trapdoor. Read the end bit.'

'"The Minister for Labour may invoke the Electricity Special Provisions Act should the threatened industrial action take place. The Act allows for fines and or imprisonment where action interferes with the production or supply of electricity."'

Barney pulled two Woodbines free of their packet.

'This is it, Timmy ould son. They've a pain in their tits with strikes. CIE, Unidare, Potez, the dockers, and now us. They're gonna nail someone's arse to warn the rest!'

'Well, if we do get banged up we won't be short of company. Says here EI just got a restrainin' order stoppin' the picket outside their place in Shannon. They'll have to send the gangsters home to make room for us all!'

'Wouldn't be the first time, Timmy. They'll always find a cell for workers.'

They smoked in silence, like soldiers waiting for the order to fix bayonets.

GUSSIE: FRIDAY, 22 MARCH

The *Indo* carried a full report on the opening of a murder trial. Gussie locked himself in his office and read it dot to dot. The prosecution said the murdered woman met the accused man at a party and agreed to sex if he'd pay her three pounds. They went up a lane but then she upped her price. The man was enraged, strangled the woman and dumped her body. Even before he finished reading, Gussie reached his verdict. 'Provocation, pure an' simple. Another good man driven to the edge be a slut!'

His hands trembled, but Gussie shook more in fear than outrage. The body of Dixie Fanning had just been discovered. Workmen found it when they drained the bog where Gussie dumped him. The

153

papers said the remains were well preserved and Fanning was quickly identified. The police promised a thorough investigation. The press milked the body-in-the-bog routine and then lost interest. Gussie prayed the coppers would do likewise. He spent many sleepless nights worrying if they'd connect Fanning and his sister, Josie. Some local busybody was sure to repeat the gossip.

He closed his eyes remembering many years before on Dún Laoghaire pier when he marched Josie onto a mail-boat bound for Holyhead. She was three months pregnant. Given a choice between the boat or the nuns she opted for England. He remembered tears coursing down her face as he shoved an envelope into her hand.

'There! That's the last shaggin' penny ye'll ever get from us, Josie Gallagher! Now yew never darken our doorstep again! As far as me an' Ma is concerned, yewr dead!'

His last sight of her was as she hauled her cardboard suitcase up the gangplank. Gussie didn't trust her and waited until the ship was well off the quay before he walked away.

PATSY: FRIDAY, 22 MARCH

Patsy was reading the *Indo* when she came on a report of a murder trial where a man was accused of strangling a woman and dumping her body. The prosecution said the murdered woman agreed to sex for a price but then looked for more. This infuriated the man and that was why he killed her. The defence presented the accused as a decent and upright man more sinned against than sinning. Patsy imagined the toffee-edged voice of his barrister as he described the dead woman as a tart and a tease who had asked for everything she got. The courtroom would be full of men: On the bench, in the jury, prosecuting, defending, taking the coats. Though

Beyond Pulditch Gates

they were going through the motions of a trial, deep down Patsy already knew what their final verdict would be.

A few minutes later she heard the hall-door groan open and then boom shut. The sound of footfalls tattooed on the stairs then Jack and one of his friends tumbled into the room. Jack was carrying a brown paper bag.

'We got the candles, Ma. They were a tanner each but six for half a dollar.'

Patsy had given him three shillings and he handed her a six-pence in change. His honesty suddenly overwhelmed her. Could a man who'd murder a woman ever have been as innocent? Tears threatened so she flicked the sixpence back to him.

'Share that an' take a candle each down t' Missus Coffey and Miss Caffrey.'

Jack took a pair of candles from the bag.

'Why is everyone buyin' candles, Ma?'

'It's in case yer Da an' his mates leaves us all in the dark like Protestant Bishops!'

Patsy hugged herself as the boys and their laughter galloped back down the stairs. She still had her plans for Jack, one of them being to move him to a house where he would have his own room and where he wouldn't have to wash in a metal bath or share a toilet with thirty others. All the Corpo had offered them was a house or a flat somewhere, sometime. That was unless Larnham Street fell or she had three more kids and claimed for overcrowding.

The other thing that made her determined to own her own hall-door had happened three years earlier. From the day he was born, Patsy had encouraged Jack to love books and reading. On his seventh birthday she took him down to join the Capel Street Public Lending Library. She proudly led him up its wide linoed stairs to where the

155

children's department squatted under a low attic ceiling. Her pride quickly turned to humiliation when she was told she couldn't sign his application form herself. Not being a property owner she'd have to get a guarantor in case the Luddites in Larnham Street used the books to light the fire. Patsy swore she'd never be humiliated like that again. Every week she headed for Blessington Street to add a few pounds to her book in the Stephen's Green Loan Fund. It was a hard, relentless struggle made no easier by knockers who jibed that a labourer's wife saving for a house was either a gobshite or a snob. Mrs Coffey told her to tell them all to mind their own effin' business.

PULDITCH: TUESDAY, 26 MARCH

Despite the sharp, cold morning, all the lads were outside the gates before eight o'clock. They smoked, stamped their feet and spat. Man-in-the-Mirror stood alone as if glued to the wall for support. A few yards away a police car was parked. The cops usually dawdled down the road twice a day, saluted Dockets in the gate-hut, then pushed on down to the lighthouse wall. They'd wait for a while to put a skin on things, then dawdle back up the road again. Now they were stuck at the gates and looked like they intended to stay there. Hairy ran his eyes over the car.

'I never understand why they patrol down here. All they'll catch is pneumonia.'

Oily Paddy lowered his voice.

'I hear they pike inta cars where fellas is dippin' their wicks with youngwans.'

'Nonsense,' snapped Saint Joseph, 'A car is no place to make candles!'

Fixit and Fukkit gave out placards. One man complained the handle on his was loose.

Beyond Pulditch Gates

'I'll fix it,' said Fixit.

'Ah, fukkit,' said Fukkit, 'just carry it be the edges!'

Barney split the lads into teams of four; the first team lifted their placards and began to walk up and down outside the gates. A sergeant hauled himself out of the squad car. As if on cue the eight o' clock shift cycled down the road. They stopped at the picket line.

'Coppers down already?,' the shift leader called to Barney.

'Yep. Looks like they're waitin' for someone to try goin' in.'

'I wonder what's the game-plan?'

Barney gave him a sly wink.

'There's only wan way yiz'll find out.'

In reply, the shift leader moved his bike within a foot of the picket line. The picket kept moving, neither blocking nor leaving his way clear. The sergeant looked to the sky but the gods left him on the hook. He walked slowly over to the pickets.

'Now then, lads. Under the Electricity Industry Act what ye're doin' is illegal and if ye persist I'll have to charge ye with a breach of the said Act.'

For a moment the only sound was the flittering of the wind then he sighed and pulled a notebook from inside his coat.

'Name?'

'Talbot. Timothy Talbot.'

Hairy, Oily Paddy and the plumber's helper followed him. Four more were lifting placards onto their shoulders when the shift leader suddenly led the rest of the shift through the gate. Mackerel kicked the ground in disgust.

'Bastards! That was the last thing we needed!'

'Patience,' Barney whispered. 'Now givvus a Woodbine, I'm gummin'!'

The Child produced the cigarette.

Henry Hudson

'Jaysus, Barney, I don't know how ye can be so shaggin' cocky.'

'It's like the man said, there's more nor wan way to shag a cat.'

GUSSIE AND GRAVES: TUESDAY, 26 MARCH

Gussie tumbled into Graves' office, doffing his cap as he came.

'Misser Graves! Misser Graves! They're bet! Bet clean t' be Jaysus!'

'Who is?' Graves slithered his copy of *Playboy* behind his desk.

'The gang at the gate! There's a copper bangin' their names in a book. The eight o'clock shift's gone in and the trades'll do likewise. O' course they think they're gonna sit on their arses without their mates, but I'll soon have them hoppin'.'

'I wouldn't count on it.' Graves snapped.

The phone rang. He snatched it up.

'Graves here. I see. I'll be right over.'

He let the receiver clatter down into its cradle.

'That was the shift engineer. The eight o'clock shift are in to shut down the plant. They're leaving one unit on for essentials but otherwise, we are out of business!'

'Co ... Co ... Communism!' Gussie choked.

'No, fucking eejitism! The surest way to glue Irishmen together is to rattle the keys of a cell. Go see what's happening at the gate!'

Gussie lumbered off and Graves retrieved his magazine. The woman draped across its centre pages reminded him of Patsy Talbot. The day he discovered she was married to Timmy Talbot he pulled his file to find out where they lived. For months afterwards he had cruised around Larnham Street hoping to catch a glimpse of her. On the rare occasions they met at staff functions, her cold politeness made her even more maddeningly attractive.

He often fantasised about waking up beside her instead of Catherine. Their marriage was a sham from the start and rapidly

158

Beyond Pulditch Gates

descended to a shambles. Weeks after their wedding he was on the hunt for fresh meat. If Catherine knew, she said nothing. All she wanted was to be pregnant. When it didn't happen she went for tests that showed it never would. Everyone, even her father, blamed that news for launching her into drink and despair. Graves signed her in for one useless treatment after another. While she was away he always made hay but no matter how many scalps he took Patsy Talbot stood like a far-off range of mountains, inaccessible, challenging. The phone rang again. He flung the magazine into a drawer, clicked into his management strut and headed for the shift engineer's office.

BROTHERS TWO: TUESDAY, 26 MARCH

The tradesmen arrived at half-past eight, heard the boys were booked and refused to go in. Word spread that there was trouble, and within the hour the press showed up. Though they never gave strikers houseroom, the prospect of workers in cells made irresistible headlines. When the sergeant saw the reporters and cameramen he radioed for reinforcements. They duly arrived in the shape of two wobbling bicycles, pedalled by a pair of red-raw bogtrotters who were even greener than his rookie driver. No sooner had they arrived than a squad of shiftmen marched out of the boiler-house and headed for the gate. A rousing cheer greeted their approach and Barney stuck out a hand to greet their leader.

'Fair play! Never let it be said yer mother reared a jibber!'

The shiftman crushed a butt under his foot and swung a right hook.

'Well Barney, we don't mind this...'

He swung a left hook.

'...an' we don't mind that! But when it comes to this....'

159

He nodded over at the police car.

'Fuck that!'

The cheer that greeted such a profound spoke was taken by the two young coppers as the start of a riot. They went scurrying behind the car while the sergeant went for the radio. There was a brief exchange with headquarters then he turned purple.

'Whaddya mean, summons them all? I'd need the shagging Book o' Kells!'

The radio cackled an unsatisfactory reply.

'Bloody easy for you to say! It's like the Patrick's Day Pafuckinrade down here!'

The radio cackled again then went dead.

'Shaggin' penpusher!'

He flung the handset back into the car, nearly decapitating the ashen-faced figure in the driver's seat. He snapped his fingers at his reinforcements.

'Take over. I'm goin' up to Irishtown to find out who's runnin' this circus!'

'But what'll we do, Sergeant?'

'If it's carrying a placard and it's moving then book it!'

Which is exactly what they did, although the boys neglected to tell them they'd been booked earlier on. Mackerel went one better. He got the poor hoors so confused that they both took his name. There and then he entered legal history as the first man to be done three times for the same thing in the same place in the same morning. Man-in-the-Mirror had his name taken only once, but once was enough. He hoped they'd only get a fine because he'd never handle being locked up. Unable to walk, to escape and worst of all, hearing a metal door bang shut behind him. Off Tuscar Rock a plane had slammed down into the sea just as his father slammed down onto

Beyond Pulditch Gates

their table. No warning. No mayday. The *St Phelim*. Gone. Those last few seconds knowing there was no escape. Falling. Knowing. Munich far away. Wexford only down the coast. Death drawing nearer. Coming for him. Jesus. He leaned back against the wall.

St Jude's: midnight, Tuesday, 26 March

Sister Frances Dunne was just twenty-six years of age. She had a slight frame and wore her auburn hair cropped close around her neat, well-featured face. She had deep green eyes, gentle hands and a voice that seldom rose above a whisper. People sometimes took her for a softie, but they soon learned she had steel in her spine. If she thought something was wrong she would do her damnedest to put it right. She was professed in 1966 just after the Second Vatican Council ended in Rome. She saw it as an omen for her to bring the 'new' church to the abandoned, to prisoners, and to those without hope. Two years later, she was posted to St Jude's where she thought she'd find all three together as the place was described as a home for 'wayward' women. When she got there she found that the women were not wayward, crude or immoral but unusually gentle and subdued. What they all had in common was that when they were young they had been used and abused by lovers, by families and sometimes just by life itself. One of them tended the gardens. Her name was Monica Dillon. The rest spent their time embroidering vestments and altar-cloths or baking communion wafers for churches. Otherwise they sat in their rooms or walked the grounds like trusties in an open prison. They showed little interest in events outside St Jude's. The world had abandoned them long before, and in the lonely years that followed, they had learned to return the compliment.

It was nearing midnight and Sister Frances was at the kneeler in her room trying to complete her night office but her mind just

161

wouldn't focus. Her thoughts were haunted by the story of the women. She asked herself over and over how it happened, why it happened and most of all, who let it happen? Then the lights flickered and went out. Warned of possible power cuts she had a candle and matches at hand. She lit the candle and went to check that everyone was all right.

MONICA: ST JUDE'S: TUESDAY, 26 MARCH

Monica Dillon had just got into bed when the lights failed. She froze and the only sound she could hear was the Lambeg-thumping of her heart. Then other sounds filtered along the corridor. She gasped as an orange flicker tinged the fanlight over her door. Fire had returned to finish the job it botched ten years before. Monica screamed and scrambled into the corner of her room her hands covering her head against the terror of the approaching flames.

It took Sister Frances some time to calm her down. In the glow of the candle she cradled her like a baby in her arms. As her terror receded, Monica realised that for the first time in over a decade, she was being held by another human being. She tried to pull away but the arms held firm so she allowed herself be rocked and comforted.

'Talk to me,' the nun whispered. 'This place is so full of pain. Let me share it.'

Monica learned bitter lessons about trusting nuns but there was something different about the new arrival. Besides, if all went to plan Monica would soon be beyond worrying about nuns or anyone else. She eased away from the nun, and reaching in under her wardrobe, she pulled out a wad of papers that were crudely sewn together.

'We're not allowed keep proper diaries so I had to make do with these. Ye can read them on one condition.'

'Which is?'

Beyond Pulditch Gates

'Nobody, and I mean nobody else ever sees them. Agreed?'

'Agreed,' the nun whispered. 'Agreed!'

When the nun left, Monica reached into her hiding place once more and pulled out a wrapper filled with white round pills. She had more than enough for what she wanted to do – all she had to do was to decide when she would do it.

Larnham Street: midnight, Tuesday, 26 March

The lights had gone out just after teatime and Jack and his mates had great fun running up and down the stairs with flashlights they had bought from Hector Grey's novelty shop. A button moved a coloured disc in front of the bulb, changing the light from red to blue or vice-versa. The batteries had collapsed about the same time as the boys.

Timmy was lying in their candlelit room when Patsy eased in from where Jack was sleeping.

'He's flat out,' she whispered. 'He hopes the bloody strike never ends!'

Timmy watched as she undressed. At every move the soft gold light touched her skin like an artist's brush. She had her back to him and was just about to pull on her nightdress when he reached out and touched her shoulder. She stiffened then turned and faced him. Her proud brown nipples were already erect. She went to blow out the candle but he stopped her.

'No! I want to look at you.'

Patsy didn't object. They'd never made love by candlelight before. Timmy's body looked different too. His eyes flashed like black diamonds and his skin was honey-coloured. She eased onto the bed beside him.

They had just begun to move together when a tattoo of blows thundered on the front room door. Timmy cursed as he scrambled

163

off the bed and into his trousers. Grabbing the candle he stumbled through the front room and pulled the door open. Two policemen stood on the landing. One had an envelope in his hand.

'Timothy Talbot?'

'Yea, what's up? Is someone hurted?'

'A summons. Dublin District Court, eleven a.m. tomorrow morning. The charge is illegal picketing contrary to the Electricity Special Provisions Act.'

'Yiz'll have half o' Larnham Street out o' their beds.'

'Just doing as we're told. G'night, sir.'

They were gone as quickly as they had arrived. Jack sat up sleepily in his bed.

'Da? Is everythin' all right, Da?'

'Everything's fine, son. Go back asleep!'

When Timmy got back inside, Patsy was sitting with the bedclothes up to her neck. He handed her the summons.

'I'll say one thing for them, they don't waste time.'

'D'ye think they really will lock yiz up?'

'Who knows?'

He reached out to touch her.

'Sorry, Timmy but I just couldn't relax.'

She swung herself out of the bed and he saw just a flash of the dark soft thatch between her thighs before her nightdress plunged down to her ankles. Apart from very little sleep, the only thing they shared that night was tea and toast.

Law and Order: The Four Courts, Wednesday, 27 March

The chaos at the gates of Pulditch moved on twenty odd hours and three miles upriver to the rotunda of the Four Courts. The boys

Beyond Pulditch Gates

were gathered in a huddle when Mackerel sauntered in. He was time-warped into his best Teddy boy outfit with his quiff dripping Brylcreem and his crêpe-soled shoes squeaking across the tiles. He was dressed more for a gig in the Carlton than a trip to the 'Joy.

'Well, be the lord Jaysus,' Hairy chirruped. 'Look what the cat dragged in!'

'Lay it on me, baby,' Mackerel drooled.

'There's a pox of a judge inside that'll lay it on ye,' The Pox snapped. 'Ye can bee-bop yer bollix when yer up in the 'Joy wavin' out the window of A wing!'

A few minutes later Oily Paddy lumbered in.

'The time o' night them coppers picks ta turn up. Imagine bein' in the asses' gallop when some big redneck bangs down the door to hand ye a summons!'

Everyone laughed at the chances of Oily being in that position. Timmy hoped no one noticed how he reddened.

Suddenly the doors boomed open and The Cowboy Flanagan thundered in.

'I'm only after hearin'! They're lookin' for blood and no mistake. It's Foreskin Childers they should call that shaggin' minister! Where's Kearns?'

The lads shrugged. Man-in-the-Mirror jumped forward.

'He should be here! It's his job to get us off!'

A few awkward moments passed before Kearns appeared with an enormous black-gowned man who sported a fluffy white beard and armful of papers.

'Look out for reindeers, lads,' Timmy quipped. 'It's Santy in a wig!'

Kearns and the barrister stopped in the middle of the rotunda, then Kearns came over to the boys alone. He ignored The Cowboy and talked to Barney.

165

'That man over there is Jay Jay Sedgebrook, barrister-at-law. Although yiz are out unofficial, the union has just retained him to represent yiz!'

Barney curled his lip.

'Big fuckin' deal, Kearnsie! I've paid subs to the union for yonks an' all I ever got was a badge for me coat an' a calendar at Christmas. So excuse me if'n I don't bend down an' kiss yer arse!'

'That attitude won't help. They can do yiz for breakin' the Electricity Act so listen to Jay Jay's advice an' folly it.'

Kearns wheeled round and walked back over to his wigged companion. The Cowboy gave his back the fingers.

'He's come a long way since the cement-mixer. That little bollix used to eat his sambos offa shovel!'

Minutes later they were all gathered round the rotund barrister. He told them he would seek a deferral to give him time to prepare a defence.

Monica: St Jude's, Wednesday, 27 March

Monica was pruning roses when Sister Frances came up and stood beside her.

'I read your diary.'

'And?'

'Have you any idea where your daughter is?'

Monica shook her head.

'I stopped looking a long time ago, Sister.'

'And her father?'

Monica shook her head again.

'None of it matters now but I'll show you what does matter.'

She beckoned the nun to follow her. The only sound was the crunch of their feet on the pebbled pathway. They turned a corner

Beyond Pulditch Gates

and passed a row of whitewashed crosses. The grass around them was neatly trimmed and each one was chiselled with INRI and the name of the nun interred beneath it. Monica led on towards the furthest corner of the grounds where a rough, high wall surrounded an area on four sides. They walked around it until they came to a narrow opening cut into one of the walls. It had a wrought-iron gate that was padlocked. It barred the way into a rectangular patch where weeds and rough knee-high grass rustled in the cold March wind. Monica touched the padlock with her fingers.

'You know what they call this place, Sister?'

'We call it the Dolour Plot.'

'And we call it Hell's Acre! Unconsecrated ground with a padlock and a big high wall to keep us fallen women in our place!'

Monica gripped the bars of the gate.

'The Pope called a meeting when all the bishops went to Rome, right?'

'Vatican Two,' Sister Frances replied.

'Everything was supposed to change: Mass, altars, everything!'

'Everything will change, Monica. I promise you!'

'Not according to your man, McQuaid. I read it in one of those religious papers. He came down off the plane and said it's stay as yiz are boys, nothing will disturb yer 'Christian' lives. That'll be great comfort to the poor bitches in there!'

'Monica, please!'

'When I go I'm goin' in there and the sooner the better.'

'You mustn't say things like that.'

'Why not? They're the only family I have now and I'd rather be in there with them than out here with so-called fuckin' Christians who won't even cut the grass over their graves.'

A silence fell between the two women and then Monica raised her hands in apology.

'I'm sorry, Sister, I'd no right t' swear in yer presence but if ye really do wanna do somethin' useful then make sure I'm the last wan ever goes into a place like this.'

Monica turned and walked away leaving the young nun to gaze into the godforsaken plot. She was trying to imagine the depth of its sorrow and betrayal when the black fluttering shape of a crow dropped from the trees above her.

'Gaw! Gaw!'

The cold wet touch of death slithered across her soul.

'Gaw! Gaw! Gaw! Gaw!'

The hellish cries chased her all the way back to the house.

JUSTICE: THE FOUR COURTS, WEDNESDAY, 27 MARCH

Judges are not allowed to have a pain in their bollix, but they can have discomfiture in their testicles. This judge was hit by instant discomfort when the Clerk of the Court did the 'all-rise' routine as he entered. There before him was a courtroom tribalised with barristers, strikers, the press, and to top it all his piles and his wig were itchy. He was depressed even further by the sight of Jay Jay Sedgebrook lurking behind a wall of legal volumes on the defence counsel's table. He envied the judge in the next courtroom. He was handling a murder trial and murder trials were straightforward. All you needed was a defendant and you either gave him life or let him go, whereas anything to do with strikes or strikers was always a dog's dinner stewed in a kettle of week-old fish. The sticky bit of the Electricity Act had to be implemented and he was the one they had picked to implement it. To cheer himself up, he thought of fishing for salmon in a quiet mountain stream. That failed, so he

Beyond Pulditch Gates

switched to sinking cool gin-and-tonics in the bar of the Ormond Hotel. That too died a death when the Clerk stood and called the case. To get things going, the judge invited a barrister who was representing the Department of Labour to address the court.

The barrister stood and intoned a weary why-me mantra demanding that the Act be implemented and that picketing should cease forthwith. As he droned on the judge fought hard to stay awake, but when the barrister finally finished, the judge nodded in his direction;

'A very reasoned and well-presented argument, if I may say so!'

That meant the little twit was as boring as watching paint dry on a damp Sunday afternoon.

Having paid his respects to the government, the judge peered down his nose at Jay Jay.

'Mister Sedgebrook? You represent the defendants?'

The barrel-shaped barrister barrelled to his feet.

'I do, m'lud. However, unlike my learned friend I have not had sufficient time to consult my clients and prepare a case. The court should be aware that most of these summonses were served less than twelve hours ago.'

'Urgency, Mister Sedgebrook. The same urgency that allowed this court to issue an order late yesterday restraining thirty-five named persons from picketing. The dogs in the street know that.'

'With respect, m'lud, are those same dogs aware that these men were picketing before that order was made?'

'Well, it's made now, and as its existence and the legislation under which it was made is common knowledge, further picketing will be regarded as contempt of my court!'

Jay Jay was out of rope.

'A moment, m'lud.'

He sat down.

'Well?' Kearns whispered.

'Well, if they go back on picket today, they bring their pyjamas in here tomorrow.'

'Pyjamas? What for?'

'Prison,' The Cowboy snapped. 'It's a place with bars that don't serve drink.'

'Shite,' Kearns whimpered.

'Volumes of it,' Jay Jay sighed. 'Otherwise known as the law!'

As the court rose, the judge and Jay Jay exchanged one-up and I-owe-you-one nods.

An hour later, the boys were back on the picket line, but by then the law had pulled its act together. The police were waiting, and aided by Gussie Gallagher, they began to identify and book each man in turn. Barney nodded Gussie aside.

'Listen,' he whispered, 'Man-in-the-Mirror's ould pots is not the best. He'd never be able for the slammer if it came to the push.'

'So?'

'So the lads'd really appreciate it if he was off the list o' runners, understand?'

'Do I look like Vincent Dee Paul?' Gussie sneered and stamped away.

To add injury to insult he grabbed the nearest policeman and took him straight over to Man-in-the-Mirror. The boys were incensed and The Child swore to even the account and to add a decent bit of interest to boot. Meanwhile, the cops kept taking names. By late afternoon, the boys were all served with fresh summonses to appear in court again the following morning.

chapter 8

PULDITCH: THURSDAY, 28 MARCH

The Pox slipped quietly into Pulditch before daybreak. They were all due in court later, and Barney had asked him to suss how things were on the deck. He scouted the turbine floor first. Only one turbine was running. Normally all the machines would be at three-thousand revs-a-minute and roaring defiance as they faced into the breakfast peak. Instead they were like grumpy geriatrics tumbling thirty times a minute. This technique was known as barring. It prevented their shafts from sagging, which would happen if they were suddenly stopped and left to cool. In the boiler-house, only one boiler was in action and this was feeding the running turbine with steam. In the control room, the emergency cover crew was doing their damnedest to keep the show on the road. The boilers that were shut down creaked and groaned as they shrank due to loss of heat. If the dispute lasted more than a few days, they would have to be pumped with chemicals to stop their innards from rusting.

From the boiler-house, the Pox slipped over to the riverfront. In the pump-house, three of the four cooling water pumps were switched off and left to freewheel at the whim of the tides. Rolling slowly on their bearings, they issued faint pitiful cries like a trio of orphaned dolphins. From the pump-house, he walked to the oil farm where extra steam was being fed to heating coils in the bottom of the storage tanks. This ensured that the black smelly goo they contained stayed fluid enough to pump. His recce finished, The Pox headed back towards his bike. It was only then that he noticed the singing. He stopped to listen. The birds were back in Pulditch. They strutted across roofs, roosted along handrails, or rocked one-footed atop the flagpoles that stood inside the gates. The Pox drew comfort from the ragged chorus of shags, gulls and plovers. It even crossed his mind that, if the strike dragged on, the swallows might make a comeback for the first time in years. He quietly whistled the first few bars of his favourite aria. Then he remembered the appointment in court later in the morning. The notes died on his lips as he mounted his bike and pushed off towards the city.

LARNHAM STREET: MORNING: THURSDAY, 28 MARCH

Mrs Coffey sent Jack up to Patsy to ask her to come down to her room. There she introduced her to a tall, thin woman whose hair was pinned up on her head in a bun.

'Patsy, this is Annie Leahy, my Billy's mother-in-law. She's sellin' her house in Rose Street. I thought yiz might like to chat.'

Patsy felt her heart jump.

'I know those houses. Up be the playground. They're lovely!'

'It's no Buckin'ham Palace,' Mrs Leahy conceded. 'But it's dry an' solid.'

As Mrs Coffey poured them tea, Patsy steeled herself to ask the vital question.

'Don't mind me askin', Mrs Leahy, but how much are ye lookin' for it?'

Beyond Pulditch Gates

'Two an' a half on a twenty per cent deposit.'

Patsy did a quick sum. Twenty per cent was five hundred. She was in with a chance.

'How soon would ye have to know?'

'Fairly sharpish. Me solicitor wants it all tied up before I go.'

'Go where?'

'Australia.'

'Australia!' Patsy cried. 'God, I wish I had yer bottle!'

'Billy has 'is own firm now and Marie runs the office. Has 'er own car an' all.'

'But I thought they have a couple o' kids?' Patsy whispered.

'Three! They have a nanny but she's leaving, so Marie wants me to take over.'

'Imagine!' Mrs Coffey declared. 'Gettin' paid to mind yer own granchilder!'

Mrs Leahy winked at Patsy.

'O' course, I wasn't the only one asked out.'

'Oh, Mrs Coffey!' Patsy cried. 'That'd be brilliant!'

Mrs Coffey shook her head.

'There's room for wan more in the grave beside Padso. That's far enough for me.'

Mrs Leahy shrugged her shoulders.

'Each to their own but the ould shite I married left me six kids in ten year then snuffed it. I had enough o' him to last me two eternities. Y'know, whenever Marie writes she says Irish wimmen is right eejits. Tribes o' kids and not a bob in our pockets. Out there if a woman has a brain in her head and no lead in her arse, the sky's the limit!'

Then her voice fell as though she was passing on a state secret.

'There's even places ye can go if'n ye don't want any more kids. Ye can walk in offa the street all legal and above board. If there was a place like that here thirty year ago I wouldn't have ended up like Ould Mother Hubbard!'

Patsy was astonished at Mrs Coffey's reply.

'Neither would thousands of others! Anyways, it's all history now. Ye'll soon have sunshine an' more money than the shower here ever gave ye for yer pension!'

The three women drank their tea in silence. Mrs Leahy was thinking about Australia. Mrs Coffey was thinking about her beloved Padso. Patsy was thinking of how great it would be to own a dry, solid house in Rose Street.

JUSTICE: THE FOUR COURTS, THURSDAY, 28 MARCH

The judge sat sphinx-faced as Barney took his place in the dock. The Clerk of the Court asked him his name.

'Coogan,' Barney barked. 'Bernard Coogan.'

'Thank you,' said the Clerk.

Then he began to read out the charges against one Bernard Coogan, that on Tuesday, the twenty-sixth day of March 1968, and again on Wednesday, the twenty-seventh day of March 1968, he did place and maintain a picket on the Pulditch Power Station in contravention of the Electricity (Special Provisions) Act of 1966. The judge gave silent thanks when the windbag finally sat down. He rapped his gavel and invited Counsel for the Minister for Labour to take up the baton. He repeated the same dirge before calling a police sergeant to the witness box. The sergeant confirmed that the man in the dock was indeed the Bernard Coogan he had booked at the gates of Pulditch on the dates in question. Counsel for the Minister thanked the sergeant who nodded towards the judge and then went back to his seat.

Though the judge wanted to get straight to the hangings, he had to give Jay Jay a chance to say something in the men's defence, so

Beyond Pulditch Gates

he invited him to address the court. Everyone knew it was a waste of time. Heads were wanted and heads would roll, but nonetheless Jay Jay gave it his best shot.

'M'lud, working men have few enough weapons with which to pursue their legitimate rights. Now, the most effective of these is the right to withdraw their labour which, in the economic marketplace, is the most valuable thing they have to barter.'

The press, who had been using their pens to pick their noses suddenly leaned forward.

The judge knew Jay Jay was a master at the speech-from-the-gallows act and how, given an audience and time, he could make Attilla the Hun look as harmless as Heidi.

'Mister Sedgebrook,' he snapped. 'We all know men are entitled to strike. What they are not entitled to do is to hold the country up to ransom.'

The Pox shot to his feet.

'If anyone's holdin' this country up t' ransom it's the poxes in the pinstriped suits!'

The court erupted and it took several furious raps of his gavel before the judge restored order. It took every ounce of Jay Jay's grovelling skills to save The Pox from being done for contempt. Placating the judge was all he could do. Their position was shaky enough, but The Pox had not alone ripped the knickers off it, but left the wig in tatters as well.

When things settled, Barney was asked by the quivering judge if he would refrain from picketing again. Barney said no. To gasps of astonishment, he was fined fifteen pounds for contempt of court. Jay Jay rose to protest, but the judge waved him back into his seat. When Barney refused to pay, he got three months in default. The circus was up, the lions were loose and the ringmaster had lost it. Pressmen scrambled over each other in a rush to the door. The Clerk, Counsel for the Minister and the sergeant played chances in the witness box to repeat the exercise on each of the boys. They were making great progress, but then one Michael McKenna was called to the dock.

The Clerk and the Counsel for the Minister did their bit. The sergeant was leaving the witness box when Mackerel piped up.

'What about the other two?'

'What other two?' the Sergeant scratched his head.

Mackerel nodded to the two rookie guards mousing at the back of the court.

'Noddy and Big-Ears! Do they not have their spoke? After all, they booked me too!'

The judge glared at the two reddening policemen. One really had ears like a cauliflower and the other nodded like a cuckoo shot out the door of a wind-up clock. He had a chilling vision of '*The State versus McKenna*' being quoted in every courtroom in the civilised world. He appealed to Jay Jay to help him out.

'Mister Sedgebrook?'

Jay Jay knew his honour was in a sling and as he owed him one for the day before, he just shrugged and left him twanging.

'Baawstid,' the judge swore quietly then he turned menacingly towards the Sergeant.

'Sergeant?'

'Men?' the Sergeant turned in turn on the rookies.

They gulped, that's all they said.

Oily Paddy rose to fulfil a lifelong fantasy of doing a real live Perry Mason.

'If I might be permitted.'

'What the fu...!' everyone said, but quietly so as not to offend his lordship. As for his lordship, he was too stunned to say anything.

176

Beyond Pulditch Gates

Meanwhile Oily looped his thumbs behind his lapels and nodded all legal-like at Mackerel.

'It is true that yesterday, being Wednesday, my colleague did indeed have his name taken by the police for picketing.'

He let his words sink in before delivering the punchline.

'However, on Tuesday, he had it taken not once, not twice, but three times!'

He shot three fingers into the air.

'An' remember, that before the cock crew three times the Jews done Jesus 'cos 'e jumped ship and started the Jesuits!'

There was an instant riot that would have matched Number One hut in its heyday.

'Recess!' the judge nearly put the gavel through the bench. 'Recess!'

Then he stormed off towards his chambers where he planned to tear someone's testicles out through their teeth.

Minutes later, he was circling his chambers like a lion with a thorn in its tit.

'Let me get this straight. On Tuesday morning this McKenna fellow was booked three times for the same thing in the same place by three different policemen?'

'So it would appear,' Counsel for the Minister snivelled under his wig.

'And what about yesterday?'

'Oh, yesterday he was booked only once.'

'He'd win the Olympics for being booked! Jesse Owens has nothing on him!'

Jay Jay rubbed the blister raw.

'May I ask which of the four summonses is he facing? And if he does three months for the first summons, what about the other three?'

177

The judge eyeballed the Counsel for the Minister.

'Well, you heard the man! What now?'

'We proceed! Picketing's a national bloody pastime. It has to stop!'

'Says who?' Jay Jay quipped.

'The government!'

'Is this the same government whose fathers fought with Connolly in the GPO?'

The judge hammered his fists down on his desk.

'For God's sake Jay Jay don't start, I'm flustered enough as it is! Now, no matter what happened at that gate, I will not allow those people make an ass of the law! Have they no sense of morality, no shame, no self-respect?'

'But your honour....,' Jay Jay pleaded.

'I don't want to hear it, Jay Jay! You tell them that either they back off or they take a long drop on a short rope and that's final!'

From deep within his robes he produced a fob watch and flicked it open. Time-checked, he used its fine silver chain to arc it back inside his robes again.

'We go again in five minutes!'

JUSTICE: THE DEAL, THURSDAY, 28 MARCH

They were in a quiet corridor at the back of the Four Courts. Graves smoked. Kearns paced up and down.

'You said a fine! A fine and a fixy-up! You said that if the boys lifted the pickets, we'd square things up between us!'

Graves shrugged his shoulders.

'That was the signal we were getting but someone obviously changed their mind.'

Kearns had been shafted with a splintery pole and he knew it.

'No one shites on Red Kearns! No one!'

Beyond Pulditch Gates

'So you've said,' Graves sighed wearily.

Kearns went face to face with him.

'Youse are bloody lucky it's me an' not The Cowboy youse are dealin' with.'

'And why's that?'

'If youse fucked around like this with him he'd have yer dicks for doorknobs!'

'Look, you want to play in the boardroom so you'll just have to learn the rules.'

'Rules?' Kearns fumed. 'What fuckin' rules?'

'Exactly,' Graves sneered. 'Now, I hope that judge gets the finger out, I haven't had a crumb since breakfast.'

JUSTICE: PATSY, THURSDAY, 28 MARCH

Mrs Coffey offered to keep an eye on Jack, leaving Patsy free to head for the Four Courts. As she hurried on, she tried to marshal her thoughts. Borrow what they were short for the deposit. Get a mortgage. Buy Rose Street. Convince Timmy. No. Wrong order. Convince Timmy. Get the money and then buy Rose Street. She had four hundred saved. Borrow one more and they'd have the deposit. She'd get a job if that's what it took. Timmy would have a fit. So what? Oh, god, what if he really did go to prison? She was hurrying along Bachelor's Walk when a delivery van flashed past her. Dillon's Wine Merchants. Patsy immediately thought of Monica Dillon. Her search for the nun and for Monica had drawn a blank on all sides, and as time passed, Patsy just stopped asking. Instead she resigned herself to the hope that one day either of them might make contact with her. She was still thinking about them as she approached the high green dome of the Four Courts.

179

Henry Hudson

A few minutes later, she eased inside the packed courtroom. The only free seat was next to a sweaty, bull-necked man who glanced at her as she sat in beside him. The smell of body odour hit her at once. Her eyes searched for Timmy among the group of men huddled at the front of the courtroom. She picked out the wild Brillo-pad hair of Barney Coogan. Beside him was the one who wore a bow tie and sang opera, but never wore socks, the one they called The Pox. She hoped Timmy would see she was there. Then she saw him and willed him to look around. His head flicked round towards her. She was sure he saw her but just as quickly he looked away. Maybe he couldn't pick her out in the crowd. When he looked around again she'd wave.

JUSTICE: GUSSIE, THURSDAY, 28 MARCH

Gussie sat at the back of the court bewildered by the pantomime that was unfolding before him. The judge who was hearing the case was supposed to be as tough as nails, but instead he was acting like a brainless baboon. The gang in the dock were communists who deserved nothing less than a short shrift up to the slammer. He felt uneasy being in the same building as a man on trial for murder, even if it was only a tart he'd throttled. Sweat slimed his bri-nylon shirt and he felt that every policeman in the place was looking at him. At the same time, he was annoyed that he hadn't been called as the star witness having fingered the reds so the coppers could book them. The judge was still cooling off in his chambers when a woman slipped in and sat beside him. Gussie decided she had a whorish look. That was it, a mate of the murdered slut who just got her courtrooms confused.

JUSTICE: TIMMY, THURSDAY 28 MARCH

They were waiting for the judge when Horizontal Harvey poked Timmy in the ribs.

180

Beyond Pulditch Gates

'Oi, lover-boy! Yer mot's here t' hold yer hand.'

Timmy froze hoping that it was only a wind-up. He eased his head around and glimpsed Patsy's face. He immediately looked away pretending not to see her. Was she trying to make a complete fool of him? None of the other wives were there fussing like a mother hen. Why couldn't she accept that some things were strictly men only? God knows he took enough flak from his brothers over one kid in ten years, and even more over Patsy's outspoken ideas. He dreaded to think what they'd say if they discovered she was on the pill. At least when he was jumping off at the lights there was some chance he might ring her bell. Even doing it when she bled, there was some hope, though the tribe fumed in disgust to see her lying with her back to him on an old sheet with her protection lowered just enough to let it happen. Watching her squat over a basin to sluice away his pointless and bloodied semen, it would sneer that only he had to piss he wouldn't need his prick at all.

Barney elbowed him back to the courtroom.

'Timmy! Wakey, wakey!'

'Sorry, Barney. I was miles away!'

He sat upright and squared his shoulders. He was a man among men and this was man's work. Women had no place here. He wouldn't turn around. He couldn't. If the boys noticed, they'd make him knickers of the week. Yet he loved her. He wanted to turn and see her concern and to let her see his in return. Barney was saying that the fuck-up with Mackerel was their last hope, otherwise they were all models for the slammer. Timmy squared his shoulders again to let them see he wasn't worried. He was a man and men didn't get frightened. He was one of the boys. He loved her. Patsy.

181

Justice: Patsy, Thursday, 28 March

As the court waited for the judge to return, Patsy thought about the power he had. He could order people to be quiet, to speak or even to go to jail. Education, that was what gave people like him their power. Just like priests and politicians could rule people's lives, not because they were decent or honest, but because they knew how to set the rules to suit themselves. No way would a judge's wife and kid be turned away from a library, so Patsy was determined that Jack would never experience such humiliation. She'd raise him never to bow the knee to anyone. Come hell or high water, she'd see to it that he got a bloody good education along with a home of which he could be proud. Sometimes Timmy threw cold water on her plans and the huffy silence that followed could only be broken by a row. It was usually caused by an unwashed cup or a shirt left lying on the floor, but the real thorns were kept well-buried.

She could only guess at Timmy's frustration at her being on the pill. She knew his brothers gave him a hard time because he wasn't producing the yearly Talbot, but there was no way she would be bullied by the same caveman attitudes that killed her mother. Despite living in one room and being permanently on the bread-line, the woman had dropped babies like a brood mare drops foals. Thirteen deliveries and four miscarriages had left the neck of her womb poking out of her body before she was sixty. She died after an operation to put it back in place. That was why Patsy counted to ten whenever the family got together and began the good ould days routine. We were poor but we were happy. Mammy loved babies and that's why she had so many. It was all bullshite. Patsy lost count of the nights they sat out on the cold dark landing after the midwife arrived from the Roxy. What she would never forget was her mother's strangled screams as she shunted yet another sibling

Beyond Pulditch Gates

into the world. A whole generation later, the dog collars were still waving the stick. Contraception was out, but men had to have their rights and women had to have their kids. That way God could look down from Heaven and see that all was right with the world.

A voice snapped her out of her reverie.

'All rise.'

Everyone stood up. The judge bundled into his seat. Then the same voice called again.

'Be seated.'

Patsy sighed. In church. In court. In the bedroom. Control. Everywhere. Control.

JUSTICE: THE VERDICT, THURSDAY, 28 MARCH

Justice, if justice it was, was swift and merciless. Mackerel was called back to the dock and the judge glowered down at him.

'Now, Mister McKenna, do you wish me to have you incarcerated?'

'Oh no, yer honour, if I ever gets married I wanta have kids!'

'I'm talking about the slamming of a cell door.'

'Jaysus, yer honour, that'd be agony. I was only picketin' the place not blowin' it up.'

'Mister McKenna! Will you desist in this picketing?'

'Resist? The McKennas is famous for resistin'! Me Uncle Paddy was in Boland's Mills an' still shootin' long after Dev shit 'imself an' waved the white flag at the Brits.'

'Mister McKenna, for the last time, will you stop picketing?'

'No can do, yer Honour.'

'Fifteen pounds fine. Will you pay it?'

'No can do again, no offence.'

'Oh, it is an offence and I'm giving you three months for it.'

Seconds later, Mackerel was leading the boys towards the cells.

As they went, the judge leaned back and let a fart in slippers. He was more than capable of a decent howitzer, but this was more of a soft gentle blip to salute the unshakeable fairness of the Irish courts and all who sailed therein. He checked his watch again. He'd have time to get home and have tea with his wife. Then she'd go out to choir practice, leaving him free to go scouting for the girls. A session with those two would put a perfect end to a great day's work. The black-haired one could get a snowman to stand and the red-haired one could get him to squirt. A shiver of anticipation ran through him as he stacked his papers and books on the bench before him. All done, he nodded to the Clerk of the Court.

'All rise,' the Clerk demanded.

All rose and then judge rose and left in a fussy rustle of black, leaving the Clerk to wonder what smelly shagger had egg sandwiches for lunch.

Justice: Patsy, Thursday, 28 March

As he was being led from the dock down to the cells, Timmy turned and caught Patsy's eye. A faint, almost embarrassed smile flickered across his face, then he was gone. Minutes later, she was out in the rotunda of the courts being jostled by a milling crowd. She had to see Timmy before they took him away. She needed someone to help her. A barrister was weaving his way past and she caught hold of his sleeve.

'Excuse me, Sir. Can I ask you about a case that was on today?'

'Innocent. They've just announced it.'

'Innocent?'

'You were referring to the murder trial, m'dear?'

'No. I was wonderin' where they'll take the men who were out on strike?'

'Siberia, I hope! And the sooner the better!'

Beyond Pulditch Gates

He moved away, leaving Pasty like a lost child. The man who sat beside her in the court bundled past in a waft of stale armpit. He was grinning like all his birthdays had come together.

'Patsy?'

The voice spidered up her spine and she turned to face Richard Graves. He held his hands up in apology.

'Patsy, I'm sorry Timmy went to prison. Really I am!'

'It's a bit late bein' sorry now!'

'I did everything I could for them but this is coming from the very top.'

She was sinking in a bog of desperation and Graves of all people was her only lifeline.

'I have to talk to Timmy, I just have to!'

'How come?'

Desperation made her reckless.

'We have a chance to buy a house and I just need a hundred pounds to make up the deposit. I can get it off the loan company but I have to okay it with Timmy first.'

'I'll see what I can do. Are you on the phone?'

'No.'

'Your address then?'

'Larnham Street, number fifteen, first landin' on the right.'

Graves went through the motions of writing it in his diary even though he knew where she lived, the colour of the hall-door, her son's name, her husband's earnings. He could have filled the diary with what he knew about her. All except the final, fascinating page.

'Right! Number fifteen, Larnham Street. Later on. Say about ten o'clock?'

He said it very loudly and the people around them turned to look. Patsy reddened.

185

'Okay, ten o'clock.'

She turned and almost ran out of the court. Graves strolled after her. A dozen witnesses just heard her invite him up to her house. He knew she had a kid, but with Timmy being minded up in Mountjoy, it was too good a chance to miss. The first thing he needed was someone to help him slip the noose with Catherine. He hadn't far to look. A bulky bow-legged shape was waddling towards Queen's Street Bridge.

JUSTICE: GUSSIE: THURSDAY, 28 MARCH

Gussie Gallagher was like a dog with two mickies. The reds were on their way to the clink and the man who was up for strangling the slut got off. There was a god up there after all. He had spotted Richard Graves as they were leaving the court and was about to go over when he saw him move in on the whorish-looking one. Flog it to the world she would, he knew by the cut of her. Gussie was cute enough to know that if Graves had pulled a piece of skirt he wouldn't want company, so he decided to hold his own private celebration. He'd have a bottle of ale on the way home, and to hell with the expense. He was crossing Queen's Street Bridge when his day was crowned by the sound of Richard Graves calling him from behind.

'Gussie! Gussie! Hang on there, old son!'

He waited for Graves to catch up. He was smiling and he punched Gussie lightly on the shoulder.

'Right, Gus! The reds are dead! Let's celebrate! The drinks are on me!'

PRISONERS: THURSDAY, 28 MARCH

They were in a big room at the back of the courts waiting to be loaded into Black Marias to take them to Mountjoy prison when the Pox made a proposal.

Beyond Pulditch Gates

'That for the duration of our stay at the state's expense we will, to a man, adopt an official policy of poxin'!'

A show of hands was called for. Mackerel was appointed teller.

'Carried synonimously!' he said and sat down.

Oily got things off to a flying start by producing a ham sambo out of his pocket.

'In case I got hungry,' he explained.

Opening his shirt, he produced a dog-whistle clipped to a chain around his neck.

'Givvus a bunt up t' the top o' that winda.'

Hands whooshed him up to the open fly-window above the main window in the room. Oily blew a long silent whistle and within minutes a flurry of dogs came reefing into the Bridewell yard. He blew once more, and when a decent pack had assembled, he dropped the ham sambo down between them, the wall and the Black Marias. Two warders and three policemen were trying to separate the reefing mutts when Oily cupped his hands to make a megaphone.

'Meeeaowww!' he wailed softly, 'Meeeeaowww!'

A soggy ham sandwich lobbed among a dozen dogs is trouble. Adding a hint of pussycat is a sure-fire recipe for a canine riot. The dogs went bananas. The coppers ran and a warder had his ankles ripped. It took ten minutes to clear the yard of dogs so they could get the warder into an ambulance and another forty-five to get a replacement warder down from the 'Joy.

Up at the prison, the Governor wasn't impressed. It was bad enough having to lock up strikers, but his ear and his arsehole were twitching since he got up that morning and twitches meant trouble. True to form, he was already down a warder, and an hour after they were due in their cells, the strikers were still firmly anchored down at the Four Courts. Things got no better when,

187

almost two hours late, the boys were herded into the reception area of the prison. As soon as they'd been signed in, they were ordered to strip. Timmy nearly hit the roof.

'Strip? We will in our brown bollix strip!'

'But ye have to be deloused,' a warder wheedled.

The boys knew he was a culchie. His accent had its head in Kerry and its feet in Cork.

'Deloused?' Barney fumed.

'Dassright.'

'Yew! Yew with pigshit still glued behind yer ears! Yew wanta delouse us!'

The Pox jammed his pipe under the culchie warder's nose.

'The only Sunlight yew ever saw was up in the sky 'cos ye never saw none in a poxy fuckin' soap dish!'

Another warder stepped forward. He was a Dub and Dubs are born with an innate sense of knowing that when there's a major bout of poxing in progress it's best to go with the flow.

'Now, now, lads there's no joy in us cuttin' the balls o' one another, after all we're workers just like youse are. So, how about a shower? Just get yer toes wet so's we can cross it offa the list then we can all get inside an' get a bite to eat.'

'What's on?' Clean Paddy demanded.

'Dublin weddin' cake!' the redneck warder decided to be witty. 'Bread an' jam!'

'Bread an' bleedin' jam!' the boys moaned together.

'Is there butter on the bread?' Hairy demanded.

'No, 'tis dry,' the redneck blundered in up to his armpits.

The Dub warder shook his head. Talk about sticking an awl in an alligator's arse.

Oily Paddy snapped into his Perry Mason stance.

Beyond Pulditch Gates

'Dry bread is for feedin' the seagulls! I want Johnston Mooney's fresh turnover buttered both sides an' brang on a plate or else!'

'Or else wha'?' the witty warder suddenly realised he'd never worry Oscar Wilde.

'Or else ye can stick yer shower where the sultana shoved 'is raisins, up the smelly end of 'is camel's hump!'

The Dub warder flicked his cap back on his head. At the rate they were going there'd be no getting the head down later in the shift.

After a long row they finally agreed on a shower, but the boys were in and out in a flash. The culchie warder was hopping but it was that or another university debate about the temperature of the water or the angle of the spray. As regards delousing powder, he was asked if he'd like the can pushed up his jacksie *à la* battering ram or side-on, because the boys weren't fussy where it went as long as it wasn't over them. To make things worse every few minutes a normally solid Alsatian guard-dog would smash its head against the shower-room door as if trying to get in. Meantime, in every other section of the wing, other dogs were at the same act trying to get out. The Governor suspected it had to do with the mob who'd just arrived. Locking up strikers was a latter-day Pandora's Box. Trouble with a capital T.

He was sent for when the boys refused to eat their meal. As he pushed open the door of the dining hall, he intended to show he meant business.

'Good evening, gentlemen. I'm the prison governor.'

'An' I'm Bugs poxy Bunny,' the Pox snapped. 'Only a rabbit can live on a leaf o' lettuce and a marble some gobshite bought as a tomato.'

'The bread's hard,' a voice chirruped from behind.

189

'An' stale,' another moaned.

'I'll keep the slice o' corned beef,' yet another rejoined, 'me pigeon loft's leakin'!'

The Governor adopted his best prison-governor stance.

'That food is standard prison fare.'

Hairy adopted his best James Cagney stance.

'Maybe for bank-robbers an' burglars but not for card-carryin', tax-paying, god-fearin' members of a trade union. Now, that is shite and we are not eatin' shite!'

'Fine,' The Governor bluffed. 'Then don't eat at all.'

'Okay, lads, yiz heard the man. He wants us to go on hunger strike.'

The Governor's face lit like a distress flare then he turned on his heel and stormed out. The Dub warder shook his head again. It had all the makings of a very long night.

A little while later, the boys were being led towards the cells when Man-in-the-Mirror grabbed the Dub warder by the sleeve.

'I'm innocent!' he pleaded.

'O' course ye are,' the warder nodded. 'Just take yer time an' ye'll be okay.'

The warders had a list and filled the cells accordingly. Man-in-the-Mirror heard his name being called. He froze. Then the warder called another name. Man-in-the-Mirror felt a hand take his arm. Timmy Talbot eased him towards the cell door.

'C'mon, that's us.'

His feet felt like lead weights as he allowed himself be led inside.

'Jesus,' he prayed, 'Jesus, please don't let them put me in here.'

The door banged shut behind them and the awful sound echoed down a thousand nightmares. In the dark. Hammering. Screaming. Please. Please. Let me out.

GUSSIE: THURSDAY, 28 MARCH

Dead on nine o'clock, Gussie rang Graves at home as they'd arranged. He could have used the call-box in the digs, but he decided to use the public phones up at Ballsbridge. Besides privacy, he needed to clear his head, having sunk several bottles of ale with Graves after leaving the court. Graves answered the phone, hummed and hawed, then said he'd be over straight away. Then the line went dead. Gussie reckoned Graves was either pissed or up to something. Knowing Graves it was the latter. Either way he'd done his bit and that was him in the clear.

Power wasn't due off in the area until midnight so he took the long way back to the digs. That way he could scout past the whores who traded along the canal. They'd have heard the result of the murder trial so they'd have to think twice about upping the ante when they took on a customer. He allowed himself to be disgusted by what they got up to in the warren of alleys around the Pepper Canister Church. How did they manage it? Did they lie down or did they do it standing up? Suppose it was raining? He crossed the bridge at Percy Place and turned right towards Grand Canal Street. He spotted two of them under a streetlamp on the opposite side of the road. A redhead and a blackhead. He flicked his eyes towards them again. Leopard-skin jackets. Imitation. Cheap plastic boots. The third time he looked they were waiting. The red-haired one hauled up the front of her skirt.

'Ah, here, have a good fuckin' gawk while yer at it!'

Gussie felt like he'd walked into a lamp-post because he had walked into a lamp-post. He was sure he'd shattered his dentures as he stumbled away chased by the laughter of the girls.

He was only inside the door of the digs when Mrs Gorman came out to say a man was waiting in her parlour to see him. She knew better than to ask what happened to his blackening eye and made herself scarce. Gussie went into the parlour and the man stood up.

'Mister Gallagher?'

Gussie spotted his notebook and snapped into his say fuck-all mode.

'An' who might yew be?'

The man flashed a silver badge.

'Detective Sergeant McBride. I'm with the murder squad. We're investigating the discovery of a body in a bog close to the place where you used to live.'

Gussie felt his stomach drop but he kept calm and put up the antennae up for any trick questions. They both sat down and McBride took a photograph from the notebook.

'That's Dixie Fanning, the man found in the bog. Did you know him?'

Gussie acted the gobshite.

'Well now, it's a long time since I stood in that neck o' the woods.'

'But did you know him?' McBride insisted.

'Us Gallaghers is private people. We didn't mix much.'

'Maybe so but I believe your sister, Josephine was 'friendly' with him?'

'Ye better ask her about that.'

'I would ... if I could find her.'

'Ye found me,' Gussie snapped.

'Only by chance,' McBride retorted. 'So your co-operation would be appreciated!'

Gussie realised he'd made a blunder. He moved immediately to mend fences.

'Lookit, our Josie went foreign years ago and not a word from 'er since. She could be in Timbuktu for all I know.'

Beyond Pulditch Gates

'How come she went?'

'Ah, she never saw eye t' eye with the mother.'

McBride pursed his lips.

'Strange. The locals say she and your mother were like sisters they got on so well.'

'What would they know? Two women in a kitchen never works out.'

'Don't mind me asking ... but was she 'okay' when she left?'

'Okay?'

'I mean, years ago, if a young woman left home suddenly....'

Gussie saw his chance to wrong-foot the copper.

'My sister was as pure as the driven snow! An' any Gallagher ever got was got between the sheets of a marriage bed! Ye can tell that to the locals too!'

The bluff worked. McBride backed off.

'No offence, Mister Gallagher. Anyway, I've taken up enough of your time.'

'Is that it?'

'For now. If you should remember anything about Dixie Fanning or if you should hear from your sister, I'd appreciate a call.'

He gave Gussie a card with his name and phone number on it, said goodnight and left.

MONICA: NIGHT-TIME, THURSDAY, 28 MARCH

Monica once heard one of the groundsmen describe what happens to migrating birds who are blown off course and never make it to their destination. He said that no matter how well bird-fanciers care for such creatures, most crouch in a corner, cover their heads with their wings and die. Monica empathised with the unfortunate birds. She too had been blown off course a decade before, and found

193

herself stranded in a strange and distant place. Deprived of her daughter and her family, she sought solace in her gardens and the friendship of the other women, but the pain of her loss and despair worsened as the years went on. Like those lost birds, she too had decided her journey was pointless and so it had to end. For once Monica played it cute. She started to complain that she was having nightmares about a ghostly nun who followed her carrying a lighted candle. She asked for sleeping pills to help her sleep. Usually such a request would be turned down flat but Monica knew that the last thing the nuns wanted was to revisit anything about that dreadful night. She got her pills and saved them up until the chosen day arrived.

From early morning Monica busied herself seeing that all the plants were watered and that seedling trays were set on the green-house shelves. Late in the afternoon, she hung her gloves and hand-fork on a hook behind the green-house door and walked away beneath grey cotton wool clouds that were already losing raindrops. Back in her room, she washed and changed, then she slowly swallowed all the pills she had saved. She took her time washing each one down with a sip of cold water. When all the pills were gone she lay down on her bed. She closed her eyes and imagined herself holding her infant daughter in her arms. They rocked together and gradually slipped into a deep and peaceful sleep.

There was silence for a long time then she heard distant voices chanting a prayer she had heard so many times before. Poor banished children of Eve, mourning and weeping in this valley of tears. Monica knew all about mourning and weeping. Hers began the day Richard Graves turned away when she told him she was pregnant. When she opened her eyes she found herself looking down on her own lifeless body. It was neatly laid out on her bed.

Beyond Pulditch Gates

Candles burned either side of the headboard and a brass crucifix and bowl of holy water were on a table beside the bed. A crisp linen sheet was pulled up to where her hands were twined across her chest. The nuns and the other girls knelt around her bed in a horseshoe of rattling rosaries. Sister Frances knelt behind them. Monica could see that she was crying.

Closing her eyes again, Monica found herself on a road that cut through a bleak treeless valley. In the distance some people stood by the side of the road. As she drew near them she recognised her father. He was dressed in his Sunday suit and hat, the ones he wore to church. Her mother as usual stood half-a-step behind him. Beside them were Batface and the flop-jowled priest from the convent laundry. The faces of all four were grey lifeless masks. She thought her mother was about to speak but instead she looked bitterly at her father's back then dropped her gaze to the ground. Monica passed on, leaving them in that dank and dismal limbo. Soon the road began to rise and she felt the sun on her face. She crested the brow of a hill and came face to face with a beautiful young girl mounted on a magnificent white horse. Monica knew immediately who she was.

'Patsy,' she whispered. 'Oh, Patsy!'

The girl offered Monica her hand. She felt light as a feather as the girl pulled her up behind her. Unbidden, the horse began to walk, then trot, then gallop, until it left the ground and they began to rise. Up, up they went until Monica could see the valleys with rivers of tears and mountains like gnashing teeth fall away below them. Together, triumphant, they raced out into the navy vastness.

At that moment in a small tidy bedroom of a small tidy house somewhere in Dublin, a woman called Mrs Sheridan is tucking her daughter into bed. The power is off, so the room is lit by a single candle. She checks to see that the candle is safely wedged into its holder.

'Now, Patsy, be careful of that candle like a good girl.'

'I will, Mammy.'

The girl snuggles down and cuddles her teddy.

'Mammy, how far away is Austrahalia?'

'It's Australia and it's about twelve thousand miles.'

'Is that far?'

'Far enough.'

'Why are we going there?'

'I've told you already. Because there's lots of work for Daddies, lots of sunshine for Mammies and lots of friends for kids.'

'And we'll be safe there, won't we, Mammy?'

Her Mammy kisses her forehead.

'Of course we will, love. Now, sleep tight and don't let the bugs bite.'

'G'night, Mammy.'

The curtains are drawn against the night and the cold so neither see the bright streak of light that flashes across the sky above the house.

Mountjoy: Night-time, Thursday, 28 March

Timmy lay on his bunk watching Man-in-the-Mirror. He was standing on a stool with his face jammed into the tiny opening of the cell window.

'Air! More Air!' he cried over and over.

Timmy felt sorry for the poor bastard. At the same time, a window opened in March was fine if you were an Eskimo, otherwise it was sit there and shiver. With that a chorus of dog-howls filled the air. Timmy clapped his hands together.

'Me life on ye, Oily! Me fuckin' life on ye!'

He stood up behind Man-in-the-Mirror so he could hear better. He was just in time to see a star shoot across the sky. A soul on its way to Heaven? An omen of ill luck? Someone you love in trouble? Bah, an old wives' tale. He climbed back onto his bunk, huddled into his blanket and thought of Patsy. He was sorry he hadn't waved to her in court.

PATSY: NIGHT-TIME, THURSDAY, 28 MARCH

She put Jack to bed in the back room and he was asleep long before Graves was due. The power was off and she had two candles lighting. Their soft warm glow mellowed her. Maybe time had changed Richard Graves. Maybe he regretted the day of the dogs and that was why he offered to help her. She wanted the house in Rose Street more than ever because Larnham Street was a lost cause. Mould rose a foot above the skirting board that bellied to follow the outward bulge of the walls. It was time to get out and now that she had the chance she wasn't going to lose it. Timmy would be furious, but she'd explain Graves only offered to help for old time's sake. She heard a soft knock on the door and when she opened it Graves was standing on the landing.

'Hello, Patsy,' he said softly.

'Well?' she demanded.

'I'm sorry. I'm pulling every string I know but so far, no joy.'

He rubbed his hands together.

'Bloody icebergs out there.'

Guilt made her ask him in and offer him tea. He pulled off his coat and watched the candlelight tease her silhouette around the walls as she moved back and forth across the room. An image of a black panther flashed into his mind. The woman he was watching could cuddle a cub or tear a man's heart out but right then she was vulnerable. There was no sign of her kid, her mate was away and she was desperate for money. He had her where and how he wanted her. Over tea and small talk she seemed to relax so he made his move.

He pulled an envelope from his pocket and put it down on the table.

'There you go, Patsy.'

'What's this?'

'That's a hundred cash and I can fix up a mortgage whenever you need it.'

'I can't! I couldn't take that!'

'Why not?'

'It'd take me forever t' pay ye back.'

'Oh, it needn't take that long.'

He reached out a put his hand on her knee. She jumped to her feet.

'Out! Get out, ye little creep, an' take yer fuckin' envelope with ye!'

'There's a hundred pounds in there!'

'I wouldn't let you near me for a million!'

He stood up and towered over her. Fear shot through her.

'Get out! Get out or I'll scream my bloody head off!'

'You uppity little bitch. I have a hatful of witnesses that you asked me up here!'

'Please! Me son's asleep inside!'

'Then we'd better be quiet. Now, d'you want your precious house or not?'

'I'd live in a tent before I'd let yew near me!'

Graves snapped out his hand and clamped it roughly onto her shoulder.

Beyond Pulditch Gates

'Okay, if you won't give it, then I'll just have to take it.'

His thumb and forefinger squeezed and the pain was blinding. He spun her like a top, forced her arm up her back and pushed her face-down on the settee.

'Me arm! Ye'll break me arm.'

'Well, you nearly broke my ankle so that'll make us even.'

He hauled up the back of her dress. Patsy howled her rage and helplessness into a cushion as she felt him tear at her underwear. Within seconds her sex was exposed and defenceless. Darkness washed over her as she fell backwards into the terror of her worst nightmare. She was back in the factory. Alone. In the storeroom. A rabid animal attacking her from behind. Who could she call for? Who? Who?

Graves reefed the buckle of his belt open. If she wanted it rough then rough she'd get it. The sight of her naked and squirming sent surges of power charging through him. With his free hand he downed his trousers and then threw himself onto her.

'Now, you tight-arsed little whore, let's see how tight you really are.'

He was about to force himself inside her when she cried that one shattering word. It was as if he'd been doused in ice-cold water. Everything stopped as if freeze-framed.

'Who? Who told you about that?'

He spun her around and shook her by the shoulders.

'I said, who told you?'

Patsy stayed silent. He shook her again.

'It wasn't me! It wasn't! It had nothing to do with me!'

Fear left her tear-stained face and cold murderous anger took its place. He slumped back onto his hunkers as she hauled herself upright and fixed her clothing. For the first time in his adult life he was the one who was exposed. He felt an overwhelming need to escape. He didn't have to. Patsy flung him, his coat and his money out into the hall. Then she locked and barred the door.

She checked that Jack was still asleep before tearing every stitch of clothing off her. Standing in a basin of water she washed from head to toe. She was terrified that a single trace of him might still be on her or worse, inside her. She told herself over and over that he hadn't succeeded but it didn't stop her squatting over the basin and washing herself until she was too sore to wash any more. Then she got into a nightdress and stoked the fire until its flames were jumping up the chimney. She burned her clothes, wrapped herself in a blanket, and lay down on the settee. With only the flickering candles and a falling fire for company, she lay shivering and hoping the electricity would come back on. Tears of pain and humiliation came first but were quickly replaced by tears of outrage. She'd go to the police. She'd have Graves charged with rape or attempted rape. Assault. Something. Anything. Then she'd go straight to the prison gates and kick them down and tell Timmy and Timmy would cut that bastard's balls off with a bread-knife. And. And.

'And nothin'! Ye brought it all on yerself. Yewr too uppity t' live in a tenement. Two rooms is good enough for others so it's good enough for yew. Serve ye better t' do right be Timmy and take the kids God sends ye!'

It was only when the voice fell silent that she recognised it as her own.

chapter 9

MOUNTJOY: NIGHT-TIME, THURSDAY, 28 MARCH

Being a tradesman, Saint Joseph wasn't directly involved in the strike; besides, he had grave reservations about anything that smacked of the Kremlin. Nonetheless, he was outraged to hear the boys were locked away like common criminals. He beat his brain for a way to back them up without putting the Pope off his porridge. He was just back from evening devotions when inspiration struck. Despite the night and the cold, he'd go up to the prison and pray for their safe and speedy release. He'd pray all night if he had to. It was to be a one-man vigil, but some ouldwan on her way to bed spotted him and came out to see what he was at. He hated to be interrupted in mid-decade, so he just pointed to the prison thinking the silly cow would understand he was praying for someone inside.

The woman looked at the prison wall and saw the face of Jesus at the window of one of the cells. He was pale and haggard, like he is in most of his pictures.

'My Lord and My God!' she whimpered as she sank to her knees.

The face was crying something over and over. She strained to hear it.

'Prayer! More prayer! Prayer! More prayer!'

Just then a star shot across the sky and it was Lourdes, Part Two. Within minutes she had every neighbour out on the grass and dispatched her husband to fetch a priest from Berkeley Road church. Saint Joseph prayed on regardless. He was delighted to see so many people brave the cold to show their concern for his workmates. They in turn interpreted his unbroken mantra as a sign he was in a trance like the kids in the *Song of Bernadette*.

The ouldwan who prayed beside him was ecstatic too. An apparition wouldn't half block the sockets of the Vincentians and their Third Order lackeys above in Saint Peter's in Phibsboro. They loved to boast that their church had one of the nicest spires in the city. Well, they could sit on it now because Berkeley Road had Fatima and Knock all rolled into one. Ideas danced around her brain. The sick who would bathe in the canal that ran alongside the prison. Crutches, wheelchairs and walking frames discarded after cures would be nailed to the prison gates. The State Cinema would be commandeered and turned into a basilica complete with box office, balcony and stalls. Dunphy's and The Hut would provide discreet alcoholic beverages, while the TTs could get sambos and tea in the Bohemian Café around the corner. Open-air masses would be held in Dalymount Park on Sundays, provided it was fine and Bohs were playing away. Finally she decided that the local library, which was within sight of the prison walls, was a model for a tourist-cum-booking office. Miracles? She'd give them miracles and Green Shield Stamps to boot.

Meanwhile inside the prison, the Governor had been called in. He'd been pulled away from the piss-up after his weekly bridge

Beyond Pulditch Gates

game. So he wasn't a happy camper. He snapped at the Head Warder as he stormed into his already overcrowded office.

'Report!'

'Well, it's kinda complicated.'

'King's English, no big words.'

'For a start there's a prayer vigil on outside the gate.'

'But we haven't hung anyone in years.'

A rookie warder called CJ piped up helpfully.

'They think they saw a vision in one of the cell windows.'

'Jesus!' The Governor dropped his head in his hands.

'Oh, did you see it too?'

The Governor literally bit his tongue. Then the dog-handler threw in his pennyworth.

'There's another thing. The bloody guard-dogs are gone pure yelpin' apeshite. One of them hasn't a tooth left from bangin' his head off the shower-room door.'

'Maybe the bastard doesn't like water.'

'He doesn't.'

'Then what the hell had you got him in the shower-room for?'

'I hadn't! He was outside tryin' to get in!'

The Governor did a Hollywood move and swung his chair to face out the window. He stood up and rocked on his heels like prison governors do in the pictures.

'Okay. Organise a riot squad and break out a shotgun!'

CJ was horrified.

'Ye can't shoot people just because they're prayin'!'

'Ah, no,' the Head Warder explained, 'we'll shoot well over their heads!'

The Governor asked God why he always got stuck with the wankers.

'The riot squad is to put the wind up the Holy Joes. The gun is for the guard-dogs!'

'Will we shoot over their heads as well?' CJ beamed.

'No, no,' The Governor sneered. 'Aim low for their bollocks!'

'That's me snookered,' the Head Warder spat. 'The dog on my landin's a bitch!'

The Governor counted up to five hundred.

'Look, it's simple. If it's an illegal gathering then we can break it up and if it's howling, has four paws and a tail, then we can shut it up. Now we won't actually 'do' anything. We'll just throw a few shapes and get everybody back in line, understood?'

All nodded and got the finger out as instructed.

Minutes later, the crowd outside heard the guard-dogs set up yet another blood-curdling howl. One of the kneelers threw up her hands to Heaven.

'Another sign! Repent, for the end is nigh!'

Saint Joseph was chuffed. Not alone were the boys being prayed for but now he'd convinced all these sinners to turn back to Jesus. It was all peace on earth and goodwill to men, though he did get a little concerned when a riot squad came clattering out of the prison. Sporting helmets and batons, they fanned out along the width of the patch where they were praying. One of them stepped out to the front. He was the leader. He wasn't very bright but he knew how to obey orders and his were that it was an illegal gathering and they were within the law to break it up. All he had to do was wait for a signal. He had only lined the men up when every dog in the prison began to howl and an unearthly wail was silenced by the blast of a double-barrelled shotgun. Thinking it wasn't so much a signal as the whole bloody prison going up, he gave the order to draw batons and charge. At least that was his story and he stuck to it.

Beyond Pulditch Gates

It was CJ who blasted the cats. When the Head Warder handed him the shotgun he said to take no chances. What the Head Warder meant was be careful because the bloody thing had a hair trigger, but CJ took it as an instruction to shoot first and ask questions later. That, and the Governor's earlier warning of rabid guard-dogs, really had him on edge. So when a two-headed creature with four green fiery eyes began screaming and scratching on the laundry roof he let loose and blew it clean over into the exercise yard.

The owners of the tomcat sued for extensive pellet removal from their pet's rump, a splint for his broken leg and a custom-made set of feline earplugs. They claimed that after that night, every time a car backfired, the cat shit itself. As for the she-cat, she told all her mates that if they ever made it with that particular tom they should get a bloody good grip on the roof-tiles, because he certainly finished with one hell of a bang.

DAYBREAK: FRIDAY, 29 MARCH

Seven a.m. and George Keyes was on the phone to Richard Graves.

'A disaster,' Keyes sighed. 'That's what it is. An out-and-out balls-up!'

'You said it,' Graves sneered. 'Imagine those gobshites praying outside the prison.'

'And imagine a bigger gang of gobshites baton-charged them for it! Not only that but one of 'your' men flipped his lid and was taken out of his cell in a strait-jacket.'

'That's hardly our fault, George.'

'Isn't it? Now before this gets completely out of hand we have to find Red Kearns!'

'What for?'

205

'To have a quiet word and do a quiet deal. That way we all get our heads off the block and no one will be any the wiser!'

Graves wouldn't hear of it.

'No way, George! Why should we shit first? They could walk out of the slammer right now if they paid their fines. Anyway, it's the government's show, so let them handle it!'

'Richard, this may have started as a show, but it's rapidly turning into an all-out fucking circus. If we're not careful, we'll have every damned factory in Dublin out in sympathy. Then the same politicians will shit yellow and hang it all on us!'

'Nonsense! We have it from the horse's mouth that they're in this all the way!'

'I'd trust that horse about as far as I'd throw it. Now, we have to cover our arses so find Kearns and tell him we want to parley!'

'And what if he won't come?'

'Oh, he'll come all right! He'll want out of this mess every bit as much as we do!'

MORNING: FRIDAY, 29 MARCH

After the fiasco of the night before, the tune in the prison changed, so when the boys demanded a meeting with Cowboy Flanagan they got it. The Cowboy listened as Timmy explained what happened to Man-in-the-Mirror.

'I was just lyin' there havin' a doze when all of a sudden he went bananas. Started bangin' his head an' hands offa the cell door and howlin' that he had to get out. I was tryin' to stop him and roar for help at the same time. Be the time the screws got the door open he looked like he'd spent a month in the ring with Jack Dempsey.'

The Cowboy shook his head sadly.

'Poor bastard! What 'ospital did they take 'im to?'

Beyond Pulditch Gates

'The Mater but if the main fuse is blown he'll end up in the 'Gorman.'

'I'll folly it up. I know the official that looks after the 'ospitals.'

The Pox spat a gollier of tobacco juice into the corner.

'Any sign o' Kearns? He's like the Scarlet Pimperpoxynel, never there when 'e's wanted.'

The Cowboy shook his head.

'I rang his house before I come up here but his mot said 'e was gone to a meetin'.'

'Must be somethin' cookin' if he's on the move so early.'

The Cowboy stood up to go.

'Youse keep actin' the sack in here and I'll let yiz know if I hear anything.'

He was at the door when Oily called after him.

'Hey, Cowboy, is it true there was a riot outside the place last night?'

'Yea! Some yo-yo started a rumour that Jay Cee was prayin' in one of the windas!'

PATSY: NOON, FRIDAY, 29 MARCH

Jack was at school so Patsy made her way to Fitzgibbon Street police station. She had twigged a clever way to find out what charges she could bring against Graves without telling the police what happened. She'd say it was a friend who had been attacked and that she was only asking on her behalf. That was the line she fed to the sergeant who came to the hatch when she rang the bell. A big red-faced man he took her into a back office that, like him, smelt of stale smoke. She talked and he stopped her occasionally to ask a question. She struggled to hold her voice as she described the actual attack. When she finished he leaned back in his chair.

'Is your friend marked?'

'Her shoulder. She has bruising all over her shoulder.'

'And you say he tore her clothing?'

'Yea, but she burned them.'

'Why didn't she cry out? You said other families live in her house.'

'She ... She was afraid. Her kid was asleep in the next room.'

He looked her straight in the face. There was tiredness in his soft, watery eyes.

'My advice is to tell your friend to forget it ever happened.'

Patsy felt as if she'd been kicked.

'I can't! I mean, she couldn't!'

'I have a wife and daughters so I'm on your friend's side but any solicitor worth his salt would devour her in a witness box, that is, if the case ever got to court.'

'Of course it'd get to court!'

'Look, she invited him in, burned evidence and didn't even cry for help. I'm sorry but she'd lose hands down and then it'd be her name trailing in the muck.'

He walked her out to the door, but just before she left he mused quietly:

'What puzzles me is why did he stop? I mean, to go so far and then just stop?'

'Who knows?' Patsy whispered.

She tried to smile and then walked away.

The sergeant watched from the station steps as she headed towards the raw-spiked railings of Mountjoy Square. He clamped his hands behind his head and cursed bitterly. As he walked her out he glimpsed the yellow-grey bruising on the nape of her neck. Not that he needed to see. He knew the minute she came to the

Beyond Pulditch Gates

hatch. If he had a pound for every woman who walked in saying her friend had been attacked he'd have retired years before.

Cold. Grey. Bleak. Not a leaf on a tree. The playground in Mountjoy Square was deserted. Patsy sat on one of the swings, gripped its cold metal chains, and began to rock. Like a child willing itself to enter a darkened room, she tried to bring herself back to the night before. She rocked. She tried. She rocked. She tried. She could smell him, hear him and feel the pain of her arm bending upwards. He was behind her, ripping at her clothes and she was choking her terror into the cushions. It was just about to happen when she cried aloud. She cried the word again and the sound echoed around the shabby faces of the tenement houses surrounding the square. Ca. Ca. Ca.

The Park Ranger seldom saw anyone in the playground at that hour especially on a bleak March morning. He was concerned for the woman rocking on the children's swings. He kept his distance but then she cried an unearthly howl that echoed to a pitiful plea for help. When he got near her he could see the silvery trickle of tears.

'Beggin' yer pardon, Missus,' he said, 'But ye'll get yer end o' cold sittin' there.'

'I shouted. I shouted something, didn't I?'

'Ye did indeed. Ye called for someone named Monica!'

He twirled his peaked cap nervously in his hands.

'The Jesuits is above in Gardiner Street. If somethin's broke dem boys'll fix it.'

'Not this time. They'd have a better chance with Humpty Dumpty.'

Cold. Grey. Bleak. Not a leaf on a tree. Patsy wandered the streets oblivious to her tears. When she finally pushed open the hall-door, she came face to face with Mrs Coffey. Patsy let her elderly neighbour jump to the wrong conclusion, take her into her room and make her tea. Mrs Coffey put a shot of whiskey in it.

'Don't you be frettin' about Timmy. Many's the man spent a night in Mountjoy and come out the better of it!'

As Patsy sipped the hot punchy liquid her mind was racing. Would she tell Timmy? How could she tell him? What happened to Monica Dillon? Why did the mention of her name stop Richard Graves in his tracks? Suppose Timmy found out? Suppose she hadn't cried out? Suppose he hadn't stopped? Again Mrs Coffey misread her tears and refilled her cup. This time she used more whiskey than tea.

THE FIXY-UP: FRIDAY, 29 MARCH

Keyes and Graves met Red Kearns at lunch-time in a room on the top floor of a quiet hotel. Keyes went straight to the point.

'Our political masters are getting cold feet. The Minister's office wants to know if all avenues were explored before we sought the court injunction. In other words, things are getting sticky so they're trying to blame last night's disaster on us.'

Kearns scraped under his fingernails with a pen.

'I don't care what they're tryin'. We can't rush into a settlement. Not without it looking like a climbdown be one side or the other!'

'We'll have to do something!' Keyes demanded.

Kearns shrugged his shoulders.

'Pay their fines. That'll take us all offa the hook.'

'And lose all credibility?' Graves exploded. 'Why don't you pay them?'

Kearns shrugged his shoulders again.

'Same reason. Anyway, if youse had stuck to the fine an' a fixy-up arrangement we wouldn't be in this shite now. I have shop

Beyond Pulditch Gates

stewards on from everywhere howlin' about strikers bein' in jail! They'd fuckin'well shoot me if they knew I was here!'

Keyes tried to smooth the waters.

'Look, we're all in this together. The likes of Barney Coogan won't pay a red rex of any fine but if they were paid anonymously, say through a solicitor acting for people who just wanted their power back on, then the court might be satisfied.'

'An' then what?' Kearns pushed.

'Then we'd make a no-hard-feelings gesture and ask the unions back to the table.'

Kearns thought about the offer for a moment.

'It might be a runner but how'll it travel with the shaggers in Leinster House?'

'As long as we make no firm offers and they're not left looking like pricks, they'd let us sign the Magna Carta. All they want is this disaster and their faces off the front page.'

Having decided who would handle what, they agreed to meet again later that evening.

Kearns left but Graves wasn't happy.

'George, I just don't understand how we can cave in like this. Those bastards are claiming twenty per cent of an increase! We were told to concede six and no more!'

Keyes had enough of Graves trying to piss on the chips.

'Listen, in '66 they told us the fitters wouldn't get a penny over a pound, but they stuck it out for seven weeks and ended up getting a fiver. That's why they dreamed up this Electricity Act. Typical Civil Service. Brilliant in theory and a parrot's arse in practice!'

Graves watched out the window as Keyes made his way across the street to a nearby café. He was besieged with thoughts about the strike, his career and the two women who could blow it all to smithereens. His father's words roared in his head. Only a gobshite stuffs one of his own staff. In the distance he could see the grey slate roofs of Mountjoy Prison. If Patsy Talbot ever proved what he'd done he'd see them from the inside just as her husband was doing that very minute. His only hope was that they had each other in checkmate. She invited him to her house and it would be his word against hers that he tried to rape her. As for Monica Dillon he'd find out what happened to her and make sure his tracks were well covered.

Just then there was a soft rap on the door. He opened it to a young, fair-haired girl dressed in a black skirt and white blouse. His experienced eye took her in at a glance. Skivvy. Seventeen, eighteen at most. Innocent, almost certainly a virgin. Her face reddened.

'Beg yer pardon, Sir, but I haveta air out the room.'

Graves knew it was madness but the butterflies were already stirring in his stomach. He bowed and waved her into the room.

'Now what is a beautiful girl like you doing in a place like this?'

Mountjoy: Friday, 29 March

After lunch the boys were marched with a crowd of other prisoners into the recreation hall. Within minutes most were playing chess, draughts or cards. Clean Paddy asked to borrow the dog-whistle from Oily. Oily slipped it to him with a whispered warning.

'There's no point in blowin' it because all the guard-dogs is locked outa here except when there's trouble.'

Clean Paddy gave it a few faint sneaky blows anyway.

'By the way, where did you keep it hidden from the warders?'

'Up me arse!' Oily winked at the others.

Beyond Pulditch Gates

Clean Paddy turned green. Oily thumped him on the arm.

'Ah, I'm only messin'!'

'Oh, thanks be to God. An' me after havin' it in me mouth.'

'Naw, I kept it up in me armpit instead.'

Clean Paddy barely made the jacks.

Then Fixit and Fukkit went walkabout and quietly enquired as to where the other prisoners came from. They passed this info on to Hairy and The Child who was bored to his bollix because the windows in the hall were so high he couldn't see out.

Having waited a few minutes Hairy took a big mad-looking bastard from Burtonport while The Child homed in on an equally wild-looking granite-blaster from Wicklow. Hairy broke the ice with the Donegal man by offering him a cigarette and talking about a holiday he once had in Bundoran. On the other side of the hall The Child got into an intense discussion with the Wicklow man about Glendalough. Warders walked up and down oblivious to the fuse being lit behind their backs. A few minutes later Hairy and The Child exchanged eye signals. They armed their missiles, locked onto their targets and fired. The Child leaned in close to the granite-blaster.

'It was bad form o' that Donegal fella to say all Wicklaw men is sheepshaggers. I don't believe all the sheep sits down when one o' them climbs over the fence!'

On the other side of the hall Hairy leaned into the mad bastard from Burtonport.

'Is it true Mary from Dungloe was really a brasser?'

'Whaaat?' the mad bastard was instantly on his feet. 'Who told yew that?'

'That Wicklow fella. He says scorin' with Donegal wimmen is like kickin' a ball into an empty net!'

213

The wildmen were at each other in seconds. As soon as they got swinging Timmy and Barney used elastic bands to launch two hardwood chessmen that whacked two other inmates at the back of their heads. They leaped up together.

'Who the fuck did that!'

The Pox pointed to another table where a friendly game of don was in progress. The don players were instantly attacked and they responded with a will. A wild swipe hit a sitter at a third table, the domino effect kicked in, and within seconds a full-scale riot erupted. Oily waited until the doors were flung open at either end of the hall before he gave a full-force blast on the dog-whistle. Four enraged canines immediately dragged their handlers into the fray and then it was every man and dog for himself.

PANDORA'S BOX: FRIDAY, 29 MARCH

The siren went off as CJ carried in the Governor's lunch. He wasn't impressed.

'I'll have that fire warden's arse for an egg timer! I don't know how many times I've told him not to have fire drills when I'm having my lunch. A pound to a pinch o' shit he'll have one of his minions on in a minute looking for instructions.'

He took a bite out of his cheese roll and then the phone rang.

'See? What did I tell you? No matter who that is tell them I said to keep it going until I'm finished my lunch. Got it?'

CJ nodded and lifted the phone.

'Governor's office. Oh, I see! Well, The Governor says to keep it going until he's finished his lunch.'

He slammed the phone as the Governor put his feet up on his desk.

'Good man, CJ. You'll go places.'

Beyond Pulditch Gates

The roll was almost finished when he called CJ back in.

'You can tell that idiot to turn off that fire siren now.'

'Oh, that isn't a fire siren, Sir.'

'It isn't?'

'No. There's a riot on in the assembly hall.'

'Jesus Christ!' The Governor left his seat like an ejecting fighter pilot.

'There's no need to run, Sir! They'll keep it going till you finished your lunch!'

The Governor arrived in the assembly hall in time to see the last dig thrown. Bodies lay everywhere and only the siren was still in one piece. Warders with batons in one hand and first-aid kits in the other moved gingerly through the bloodied tangle of arms, legs and paws. The Head Warder lay moaning across an upturned card table.

'Tea, Ahh! Tea, Ahh!'

The Governor hauled him up by the hair.

'Dammit, man, this is no time to be looking for tea!'

'Nooo! Tea! Ahh!'

It took a while to decipher that what he was saying was, 'Teeth! Arse!' This led to the discovery that a noise-crazed mutt left most of its incisors in the poor man's buttocks. At the far side of the hall, a whimpering guard-dog had its head firmly wedged between the wall and a radiator, which was where the big mad bastard of a granite-blaster had shoved it. The dog hadn't touched him, but being a Wicklow mountainy man, he had always wanted to worry an Alsatian as much as they worry sheep.

The Governor surveyed the bedlam but then was astounded to see a group of neat orderly men gathered at the far end of what could have passed for an indoor re-enactment of Gettysburg. Lot's wife had nothing on him as Barney Coogan, sided by Timmy and

Henry Hudson

The Pox, made their way towards him through the carnage. Barney planked his hands on his hips.

'We want a parlee with the Minister o' Justice. Me an' my men isn't safe in this kip.'

The Pox backed him up.

'It isn't warders yiz want in here. It's the United Poxy Nations! I'm only here a day an' so far there's been a hunger strike, a baton-charge, a brother taken out in a straightjacket an' some other pox doin' Jesse James with a shotgun! Now we have this heave-ho! What's next? A fuckin' commando raid?'

'Ye have till teatime,' Timmy snapped, 'an' get us the butcher, not one of 'is blocks.'

The ruse worked. Just before teatime, the boys were called to a meeting in the prison canteen. They never thought the Minister for Justice would turn up, and they were right. Instead in walked Red Kearns. The lads all moaned together.

'Ah, Jaysus, its only bleedin' Kearnsie.'

Kearns ignored them and walked to the top of the room where he planked his briefcase on a table.

'Listen up! Yer fines is paid!'

'Be who?' The Child demanded.

'Doesn't matter be who! They're paid and the management is offerin' talks.'

'It's a fanny! A fairy godmother pays our fines an' we sing halleluia!'

'Well, thanks to that fairy godmother youse can all walk out of here right now.'

The Pox wasn't impressed.

'Oh, we can walk out all right an' not a poxy penny better off. I say we stay an' really start poxin'!'

Beyond Pulditch Gates

There was a sharp intake of breath because all that was left was to burn the kip down. Then Kearns threw in the kicker.

'Hold it! Hold it! We're over a barrel on this wan. Youse are out unofficial. Imagine what the press'll say if yiz won't talk and yiz won't go home.'

Timmy leaned over and whispered to Barney.

'Talk about a ventriloquist's dummy! They have their hands so far up his arse they could scratch his ear from the inside!'

Horizontal Harvey yawned his hand in to the air.

'The Cowboy never gave a rat's arse about the press. So why should we?'

Kearns thumped the table in temper.

'Because strikes won't be won at the gate any more. They'll be won in the papers, on the telly and at negotiations. The wild-west act is all over. The Cowboy Flanagan isn't yer union delegate any more, I am!'

'Worse luck,' a voice muttered far back in the hall.

Kearns ignored the insult.

'I'm gonna issue a statement welcomin' the payment of the fines and the offer o' talks. I'm also gonna recommend an immediate return to work.'

'Did Cowboy give all this the nod?' Oily Paddy asked.

'I've arranged to keep him fully briefed. Now, if that's all, gentlemen.'

A sullen silence followed then Kearns picked up his briefcase.

'Good! We'll have yiz outa here in no time.'

He was heading out the door when Mackerel called him back.

'Hey, Kearnsie, how in the name o' jays am I supposed to get home t' Crumlin?'

'Try a bus.'

'At this hour? We want bleedin' taxis an' yer pals in the press can take our picture on our way out the gates.'

GUSSIE: NIGHT-TIME, FRIDAY, 29 MARCH

Three thousand, three hundred and ten. Gussie reverse-counted the notes back into his ammo box, then he hid the box again. He lay on his bed and pleasured himself with mental calculations. He had started saving again after the '59 disaster had cleaned him out. That was nine years ago, give or take a few weeks. Average savings per year three-hundred-and-sixty-seven pounds. Per month? Thirty. Per week? Seven pounds ten shillings. This time there'd be no investing in any get-rich-quick scheme nor would he trust a bank. He'd keep it under the bed like farmers and cattle-dealers. The sluts on the canal wouldn't be so quick to sneer if they knew that at three pounds a throw he could have them one thousand one-hundred-and-three times and still have a pound left over. He reckoned that within six months he could make a move to buy that long-promised parcel of land.

He yawned, closed his eyes, and wondered what he was doing out in Dún Laoghaire. He had avoided the place since the night he press-ganged Josie onto the mail-boat, yet there he was walking towards the very same ship. In the distance he could see two figures standing at the top of the gangplank. His mouth fell open when he got close enough to recognise them. A redhead and a blackhead. Imitation leopard-skin jackets. Cheap plastic boots.

'Yoohoo!' the red-haired one jeered. 'Have a good gawk while yer at it!'

She had his ammo box.

'Nooo!' Gussie cried. 'Ye can't take that! It's mine! It's mine!'

The ship's siren blew. The deck crew disengaged the gangplank. Gussie was frantic.

'Police! Get the police!'

'Yoohoo!' the black-haired one called out. 'Have a gawk behind ye!'

Gussie spun around and came face to face with Josie. Beside her was McBride from the murder squad. Josie pointed an accusing finger towards Gussie and McBride held out a rope tied in a hangman's noose. Gussie had to get away.

The gangplank was cranking away from the ship, so Gussie buffaloed up along it and launched himself out into space. His hands clamped onto a deck-rail, leaving him dangling over the dark murky waters below. He looked down, and just below the surface, the face of Dixie Fanning was leering up at him.

'Guuussiieeee,' it soughed. 'Guuussiieeee!'

Gussie looked up and the sluts had their cheap plastic boots poised over his fingers. 'Nooooo!' he cried. 'Pleeaasseee! Nooooo!'

They stamped hard, he lost his grip and fell downwards into the darkness. Then his eyes jarred open. He was spread-eagled on his bed and lathered in sweat.

'Jesus,' he prayed. 'Oh, thank Jesus!'

He lay motionless, waiting to see if Mrs Gorman would come stomping up the stairs. There was no sound, so he eased himself up off the bed. He prayed as he checked that his ammo box was safe. It was, but he touched it just to be sure to be sure.

FAREWELL: NIGHT-TIME, FRIDAY, 29 MARCH

They could have gone home in taxis, gondolas or Sherman tanks for all the Governor cared. All he wanted to see was the backs of those bloody strikers. He had a pain in his face denying reports that 'the' man himself appeared in a cell window just before the place was plagued with disasters like the time the Egyptians acted the sack with Moses. His denials went directly against the sworn testimony of the hastily-formed M & DPPG otherwise known as the Mountjoy and District Prayer and Penance Group. They insisted that God himself was calling for more prayer and that he was getting it until the bloody prison sent out their riot squad.

The Governor was anxious for an update so he called CJ into his office.

'Are they gone yet?'

'On their way, Sir. I arranged the taxis and they're at the gate right now.'

'Good. I hope you told the gang in Justice we're not paying for them?'

'I gave what you said word for word to the Minister for Justice's secretary.'

'And just what did I say?'

'You said, we'll let that fat-arsed, funeral-faced fucker up in Justice stump up for the Joe Maxi's! Jaysus, he wouldn't pay for a ride in whorehouse!'

The Governor turned green and staggered into his seat.

'I'm not to be disturbed.'

'Gonna do some paperwork?'

'No! I'm going to hang myself!'

'But, Sir!'

'Not to be disturbed! Not even if the fucking place is blazing!'

PATSY: NIGHT-TIME, FRIDAY, 29 MARCH

Patsy put Jack to sleep in her own bed. She had the settee and cushion covers washed and drying on the clotheshorse in front of the fire. She was scrubbing and polishing the floor while watching

Beyond Pulditch Gates

the nine o'clock news on the telly. An industrialist came on demanding that the government should bring in the army to do the striker's work. A spokesman for the farmers was next.

'We've no power to milk cattle or do anything else! The whole country is being held to ransom and the government should take a very firm line with these people. The increase they want is pure outrageous!'

Patsy almost put her fist through the screen.

'It wouldn't be outrageous if they weren't payin' yewr tax as well as their own! Another shaggin' shower that's always up front for Communion!'

Her anger scoured the scrubbing brush across the lino in front of the settee. She had to be certain not a trace of Richard Graves remained. He had tainted everything, including the idea of buying Rose Street. When she was sure the floor was absolutely spotless she took the basin of grubby water out to the back yard and sluiced any remaining trace of him into the sewers.

When the news was over the detective series Mannix came on. Patsy made herself a cup of tea and sat watching the grainy black and white images of Mannix chasing after the bad guys yet again. The sound was lowered so as not to disturb Jack. Suddenly the transmission card of Telefís Éireann flashed onto the screen.

'We interrupt this programme for a news flash! There has been a breakthrough in the electricity dispute. The fines of the imprisoned strikers were paid by an anonymous source earlier this evening. At a specially convened sitting the court accepted that the men were no longer in contempt and ordered their release. Negotiations on their claim will re-open immediately and the unions are asking all staff to report for normal duties. That is the end of this newsflash!'

The card disappeared and within seconds Mannix was after the bad guys again.

Patsy didn't know whether to laugh or cry. She didn't know if she should run in and wake Jack or run downstairs to tell Mrs Coffey. How soon would Timmy be home? Would he be hungry? What could she cook for him? Chips and eggs. His favourite. Within seconds she was on her feet. She'd have to get the covers back on the settee. Peel potatoes. Butter bread. Make tea. Heat the chip-pan. She filled her mind with a million trifling thoughts rather than face the one that was inescapable. What if he came home and wanted her. What if she couldn't, not even with him and even if she could would he know? Would he sense Graves off her? No. She stabbed the peeler into a waiting potato. No. No. She stabbed it again and again. It would be like Timmy never went to prison or Richard Graves ever darkened their door. She viciously excised each imperfection from the potato. Only when it was scrubbed and spotless did she stop working.

MOUNTJOY: NIGHT-TIME, FRIDAY, 29 MARCH

The boys had just reclaimed their gear when the culchie warder decided he'd win at least one round before they left. He picked on Hairy.

'Heaaww, boy! There be no smokin' in dis area or does yee dubs not read too good?'

Hairy was too cute to rise to the bait so he just shrugged and butted his fag.

'Yoo too,' the culchie tapped the bowl of The Pox's pipe. 'It smells like ould socks!'

The Pox saw red.

'Ould socks! That's Danville Plug! Best tabacca this side o' the Missispoxysippi!'

Beyond Pulditch Gates

'I don't care if it's the best tabacca this side o' the misterpoxysippi! Lose it!'

'Where would ye like me ta lose it?'

'Try somewhere dark and smelly!'

The culchie smirked and strutted away. The boys were surprised the Pox didn't go after his tormentor and shove his head up his hole. Instead he headed for a line of wickerwork baskets that were queued along the wall. He pulled up the lid to reveal a nest of ponging overalls that were due for the laundry the next morning. The Pox tapped in the glowing contents of his pipe.

'There, they don't come much darker an' smellier nor that!'

A few minutes later they were at the gate sorting out taxis when The Cowboy came pedalling up. He was drenched in sweat and flecks of foam spittled his lips.

'Where's that short-arsed, snot-gobbling little arserag?'

'Who?' Mackerel stretched to catch the Cowboy's falling bike.

'Kearns! I've been tryin' to catch the little runt for hours!'

He bent over in a hoop. Barney was afraid he was going to have a heart attack.

'We thought he was with you! He left at dinner-hour to meet ye!'

'Me arse! He's given me the slip left, right an' centre! I've a pain in me bollix pedallin' all over the place. Last word I got was to meet t' night at the union hall. So, there I am like a spare prick at a pro's weddin' when the porter comes in and tells me it's all fixed up!'

Timmy nearly had a fit.

'Ye mean, ye didn't know? Kearns told us yew gave it the nod! Otherwise we wouldn't have touched it with the butt end of a bargepole!'

Then one of the taxi men called from his car.

'D' youse fuckers wanna go home or not?'

The boys looked to The Cowboy and he in turn waved them towards the cars.

'G'wan! Yer mots will be wonderin' if yiz are ever gonna show up. I'll see yiz t'morra night in Grealish's. We'll see where we go from there!'

Only Mackerel had the heart to wave to the photographers who snapped each taxi as they turned out onto the North Circular Road.

LAMPLIGHT: FRIDAY, 29 MARCH

She plaited her long black hair as she kept nix for her red-haired mate who was up a nearby lane with a soldier. After a lot of grunting and groaning, she heard her mate wail loudly.

'Aggghhh, Jjaayyssuuss!'

The black-haired one reckoned that either the soldier was hung like a Clydesdale or he'd just run a bayonet through her. Seconds later the soldier, still buttoning up his trousers hurried out of the lane and disappeared into the darkness.

'Yew okay?' the black-haired one called up the lane.

'Yea, Yea!'

Her mate appeared dabbing flecks off her skirt with a tissue.

'Some bloody marksman, he shot everywhere but where 'e was supposed ta!'

The black-haired one handed her a fiver.

'That'll pay for the cleaners.'

'Where'd ye get this?'

'Ye know the weirdo who's always sneakin' by givin' us the once over?'

'Which o' them! There's a regular procession passes here every night. All we're short of is a stand to take the salute!'

Beyond Pulditch Gates

'Oh, ye know this tulip. Remember he walked inta the lamp-post when yew flashed it at 'im the other night?'

'Oh, yea! I'd say his next ride will be 'is first!'

'Ye were just gone up the lane with Sergeant Bilko when he came outa nowhere, hands me two fivers an' says to leave his stuff alone!'

'What stuff?'

'I dunno!'

A car slithered to a halt in the shadows nearby. It was the black-haired one's turn to do business. As she began to sidle towards the car she called back over her shoulder.

'Oh, by the way, he says we're to stay outa Dunleery!'

chapter 10

PULDITCH: DAYBREAK, SATURDAY, 30 MARCH

When word came through that the strike was over, Graves issued instructions to prepare the offload units to go back online. Steam was bled from the running unit to heat the turbine casings on the others. As more and more of the midnight shift reported for work, the motors on the boiler fans and the river pumps were kicked in and run up to speed. Burners were lit with an orange and yellow roar, and the hours that followed were filled with the frantic to and fro of bringing the boilers up to pressure. Graves arrived in his office before daybreak and rang the shift engineer who was over in the boiler-house. Asked how soon they'd be able to put the turbines back on the bars, the engineer said they'd be up to full lash by midday. Just then, a roof-mounted safety valve lifted, sending steam and scores of snoozing birds flapping into the lightening sky. Pulditch One would soon be back to normal.

MOUNTJOY: DAYBREAK, SATURDAY, 30 MARCH

Daybreak. The Governor woke up. He was cold and stiff.

'Bloody CJ! Letting me kip all night in a chair!'

Then he remembered it was his idea not to be disturbed. There was nothing for it but to grab a quick cup of tea followed by an even quicker shite, shave, shower and shampoo and to shag off home. He rang for CJ but there was no joy. Thinking the gobshite was asleep on the job, he kept his finger on the button until CJ tumbled in the door. His uniform was mucky and his face was streaked in black. Admittedly it was early but it was no way for one of his officers to present themselves.

'Tennshun!' he barked.

CJ turned ramrod.

'What in God's name have you been at?'

'Firefighting, Sir! The others wanted to call you but I said you said no way were you to be disturbed, not even if the fucking place was blazing.'

The Governor folded into his chair whimpering like a kicked pup.

'P ... Pa ... Pan ... Pandora's Box?'

'No Sir! It started in a laundry basket!'

GREALISH'S: EVENING, SATURDAY, 30 MARCH

Stuffed and sightless, the mortal remains of the parrot perched above them in his rusty cobwebbed cage. His soul divided between Grealish's and the Caribbean, his glass-button eyes gazed down on the half-full bar. Barney looked ruefully around him.

'Ten year ago every man jack would have been here. Another ten and the only place they'll find the likes of us'll be in a museum.'

Clean Paddy put down his pint.

'It's just how it is, Barney. We done bloody well to get the support we did, but I wouldn't bank on it again. Between mortgages, new cars and Spanish shaggin' holidays, the young fellas comin' up would eat shite rather nor hit the tar. The sooner the better they realise them banks is nothin' more nor jewmen wearin' suits!'

The Cowboy tapped his Woodbine onto the floor.

'They're not the only one's gettin' sucked in. Yer fines wasn't paid be no solicitor, they were paid be the management. Kearns and the politicians was in on it too.'

'Ye have a wrong spy there, Cowboy,' Hairy countered.

'I know the papers say different but it's all winda dressin'.'

'Winda dressin'!' The Pox puffed. 'Sure they're even settin' up a public enquiry.'

'A blind to get each other outa the shite. Like it or lump it, it was a stroke!'

Grealish's turned waxworks. There were plenty of lifelike figures, but no movement or sound. For the first time ever, they saw The Cowboy's head droop in defeat.

'Sorry lads, while they were stitchin' yiz up they had me all over Dublin like a duck with its arse afire! Let's face it. I'm an old grey mare an' I ain't what I used to be.'

He supped silently and laid his glass down. The moment was almost painful. Fixit lifted his voice in defiance.

'Water under the bridge! Let's have a song because whatever went arseways this is neither the time nor the place to fix it.'

'Ah, fukkit,' sighed Fukkit, 'I don't feel like singin'!'

It looked like the night was going to be a total washout, but then an apparition came crashing through the swinging doors. Saint Joseph, a bandage wrapped turban-fashion around his head, was frogmarched in by a big burly copper.

'Anyone o' youse know this article?' the copper demanded.

Mackerel was in like a light.

Beyond Pulditch Gates

'Never seen 'im before, ossifer.'

'It's me!' Saint Joseph shrieked, 'It's me!'

'Hould yer whisht,' the copper snapped.

The Pox thought he was going to wet himself.

'Where did ye pick 'im up, guard?'

'Outside City Quay Church with his head wrapped up like Mohammedan John. He says he got a bang of a baton when Jesus appeared in a window. I know where I'll stick mine if he ever says the like again!'

Joseph wrung his hands together.

'No! No! You see they call me Saint Joseph but I'm not really!'

'There, did ye ever hear the likes? Pure blasphemy!'

Hairy scratched his head.

'Maybe he thinks he's one o' the Three Wise Men.'

'Or The Shaaahhh of Irannnn,' Horizontal yawned.

'Or Ali Bleedin' Baba,' a voice called down the bar.

The copper eyed the boys suspiciously.

'Well, whoever he is, he says he knows yew lot.'

Barney was out in the jacks and came in just in time to twig what was happening.

'Ah, don't tell me they let ye out again.'

He took the bewildered Joseph by the arm.

'It's okay, guard. Last week he thought 'e was Stalin.'

The copper sensed a major fanny but eventually he bit.

'He can be a shaggin' Communist if he likes, but nut or no nut he leaves the Holy Family alone or he'll answer t' me!'

The doors screeched to a close behind the copper's barn-door back and the cheer that followed him lifted the roof and their hearts. The singsong was off like a dog from a trap. Singer followed singer and the spirit of the parrot waited for The Cowboy to lead them into 'yippieeayyee yippieeiioohh'. It was near closing time when he obliged and it took every ounce of strength he had. The doctors had given him six months at the outside so he was determined to leave the boys with all guns blazing. He led them charging on verse by verse and when they hit the final chorus he could barely corral his tears. Saying adios can be hard, even for a cowboy.

PULDITCH: MONDAY, 1 APRIL

Midday. Richard Graves was out on the pump-house wall. He was trying to decide where to start his search for Monica Dillon. He had to be sure she was well out of the frame or else he could never go back near Patsy Talbot. Monica's father had shipped her off to some convent but to which one had he sent her? Back then a legion of convents and homes took in single girls who found themselves up the duff. The trick was to get the information without incriminating himself. He was so engrossed in his thoughts that he never noticed a scowling Timmy Talbot coming towards him. Timmy was carrying a long, vee-bladed jemmy bar and Graves knew that one blow of it and he'd be fish food. He opened his hands in innocence.

'Timmy, believe me! I was walked into it! I mean, it was put right up to me!'

'Save yer breath! Ye weren't the first an' ye won't be the last!'

Timmy brushed past him and into the pump-house leaving Graves clinging to the handrail in shock. He wasn't the first and he wouldn't be the last. Her husband's own words. The bitch was playing with him all the time. How many others had been where he'd never managed to go? If he could be sure that Monica Dillon was no danger to him he'd return to Larnham Street and neither hell nor high water would stop him taking the prize he had craved for years. He checked his watch. He was due at a meeting but he'd escape from

Beyond Pulditch Gates

it as fast as he could because he had made arrangements to collect the young fresh-faced chambermaid and take her out for a drink.

Meanwhile, Timmy had stormed into the pump-house where Mackerel was waiting.

'That shite Graves is outside! Tried the sorry about lockin' yiz up routine.'

'Prick!' Mackerel sniffed.

Timmy wedged the jemmy under the lid of a packing crate.

'They all blame the fella above dem all the way up to de Valera then that blind ould bollix blames the Free Staters or the Brits! I was walked into it he says!'

'Prick!' Mackerel sniffed again.

'I said ye weren't the first an' ye won't be the last. The fucker turned white!'

Tempers had the crate lid off in minutes. Timmy sleeved sweat from his brow.

'Right, we'll unpack it first thing after the break.'

Mackerel took the jemmy from his hand.

'Never mind this yoke! After the break yew be in the painter's stores!'

April Fool: Monday, 1 April

Gussie was delighted. He sat with Graves, Keyes and Kearns in Graves' office. They were having a meeting, eating sandwiches and drinking tea. Keyes called it a working lunch and that thrilled Gussie even more. The meeting was a sort of a post-mortem on the strike and they all had plenty to say about it.

'Youse shudda known not t' trust politicians,' Kearns whined. 'Fuckin' self-servin' shitehawks the lot o' them. Drop their own mothers in it they would!'

'We had no choice,' Graves insisted. 'We had to make a stand!'

'An' see where it got us. I told yiz we coulda worked somethin' out! I still have every hothead in the union bawlin' about men in prison, not ta mention the wan that's lyin' in hospital!'

'That wasn't our fault,' Keyes insisted. 'No one, and I mean no one, on this side had any idea that he'd flip at the idea of being locked up.'

'An' what if yiz did know?'

'Then he'd never have been summonsed at all! Isn't that right, Mister Gallagher?'

Gussie felt sweat trickle down his back.

'Oh, never, never, Misser Keyes.'

'There! You have it from the horse's mouth.'

'Maybe so,' Kearns pouted, 'but youse still oughta do somethin' for him. Okay, he's a bit of an oddball an' a loner, but it'd help me put a skin on things with the others.'

Keyes leaned back in his chair and thought for a moment.

'Fair enough. We'll fix him up somewhere to let him get his marbles back in the bag. I'll have my people talk to his doctors and see what they suggest. Happy?'

Kearns clattered his cup down on its saucer.

'As I'll ever be.'

He stood up to go.

'Oh, there's wan other thing. A little bird tells me there's talk about another station further out in the bay. Is the little bird right?'

'You're well informed.'

'No thanks t' youse! When will it start?'

'Very soon,' Keyes replied.

He stood up and walked Kearns to the window.

Beyond Pulditch Gates

'See? Further down the road, out near the lighthouse. Pulditch Two! Bigger, more efficient than this place will ever be! Once it comes online, this place and the people in it will have to shape up or ship out.'

Graves threw down his pen.

'Well, that strike didn't help. We're talking near a fiver a week of an increase!'

Keyes shrugged his shoulders.

'The money we can handle. It's changes we need!'

'What kind of changes?' Kearns asked.

Keyes ticked them off on his fingers.

'No demarcation, lower manning levels and reductions in overtime.'

Kearns let out a long low whistle.

'That's a hell of a shoppin' list.'

Keyes planked his hands on the table.

'That's where you come in.'

'Me?' Kearns croaked.

'If Lemass wants us up with the Europeans he'll have to let us knock heads together. So, we'll set up review bodies and working parties and you make sure you have your 'boys' at the table. We're going to make pickets and placards a thing of the past!'

'Sure that's what we all want,' Kearns simpered, 'but bringin' them fuckers t' the water is wan thing, gettin' them ta drink is another!'

When the meeting ended, Keyes walked Kearns out to his car, leaving Graves and Gussie to sit in silence. After a few minutes Graves sighed to the ceiling.

'It'll be one royal pain in the arse, Gussie.'

'What will, Misser Graves?'

Henry Hudson

'All that hands across the table shite!'

'Yew said it! Them commies is never t' be trusted, never!'

Graves stabbed his pen into his desk.

'Well, Keyes and Kearns can do what they like but no matter what kissy-kissy goes on in public, back at the ranch it'll still be M W M!'

'I don't folly ye, Misser Graves.'

'Management will manage, Gussie! Management will manage.'

Gussie was so happy he wanted to shit. Management will manage was the battle hymn of his life and there was no better time to go into action.

That morning, Mackerel McKenna had been mouthing off about an afternoon card game in the painters' stores, but he didn't know Gussie was listening. Being a cute hoor Gussie decided to let it get well under way then raid it with Keyes himself on the premises. It would be the capture to end all captures. As soon as Keyes stepped back into the room, Gussie was up on his feet.

'Excuse me, Misser Keyes, I have some important managin' business t' attend to.'

'Off you go, Mister Gallagher. We wouldn't want to stop a manager from managing!'

Gussie swaggered out of the office and almost fell over Barney Coogan's bucket. Barney was mopping further down the corridor. Gussie roared so he'd be heard inside.

'Coogan! Come 'ere! Why isn't this corridor finished? Me granny'd do it faster!'

Barney shuffled up to Gallagher like a chastened child.

'Sorry, Mister Gallagher. It's the ould legs. I'm goin' as fast as I can!'

Gussie leaned down and whispered in Barney's ear.

Beyond Pulditch Gates

'An' have ye no help?'

'I ... I ... eh ... not right now, Mister Gallagher.'

'Well, maybe I'll find ye some over in the paint stores?'

'Oh, no! Don't do that, Mister Gallagher!'

'An' why not?'

'There's.... There's nobody in there!'

'Isdatafact! I'll see about that an' yew keep moppin'!'

Gussie should have smelt a rat, but right then he wouldn't have smelt a fart in a phone-box. He was kite-high as he hopped across the yard. Otherwise he might have noticed Barney hanging out of a window and waving his mop from side to side.

The End of Innocence 1: Monday, 1 April

Timmy finished his sandwiches and drifted over to the painters' stores. He rapped the front door with the toe of his boot.

'It's me, Timmy!'

The door flicked open and a hand pulled him into darkness.

'Whadde...?'

'Ssshh,' a raft of voices hissed.

Then a flashlight flicked on to show Hairy and The Child working on a film projector. The Pox, Mackerel and Horizontal Harvey were beside them. The projector was perched on a crate with its flex connected into the socket of the ceiling light. The windows were blanked and a white square was painted on the wall.

'What's happenin'?' Timmy asked innocently.

'A bluie!' Mackerel rubbed his hands together. 'I hear it's red hot!'

'Right,' Hairy commanded. 'Try 'er now!'

The projector whirred into life, but only a black square slashed by white flecks filled the screen. The slagging and booing were just taking off when a shaky jumble of symbols took their place.

235

'Is it fuckin' Greek or wha'?' The Child demanded.

For a few seconds they tried to decipher the code then The Pox cracked it.

'The poxy projector's upside down!'

In an instant all five were trying to stand on their heads.

'Bedtime with Helga,' they all read together.

Then Helga appeared on the screen, but it looked like she was walking across a ceiling. 'Hold it!' Hairy insisted. 'We'll all be in neck-braces be the time the thing's over!'

A switch clicked, the film froze and Helga hung upside down like blonde bat.

'There's only one thing t' do! Turn the shaggin' thing up on its head!'

The boys quickly did the needful and soon Helga was moving again but this time right way up. Pausing to smile at the foot of a bed she began a slow sensuous striptease. As it progressed, she was joined by two men and another woman, and within minutes all four were naked. They began twining with each other in poses that would put any gymnast to shame. The more intimate their embraces, the more the boys whistled and cheered.

Timmy stayed silent. He always regarded blue movies a bit like leprechauns, heard about but never actually seen. He'd also heard jokes about oral sex but never expected to see it performed in a darkened paint store. When Helga's partner unburrowed his head from between her thighs Horizontal made a vulgar fist.

'Right! Givvit to her quick an' lave her home early!'

The partner gripped Helga's legs and pushed them up and apart.

'Open sesame!' Mackerel cried.

The camera closed in, filling the screen with a huge erection. Hairy inhaled sharply.

Beyond Pulditch Gates

'I hope for her sake that's trick photography!'

'That's nothin',' Horizontal huffed. 'She'd take me before him!'

'Yea! I hear she likes t' start with a cocktail sausage!'

Laughter and cheers drowned Horizontal's reply. On the screen the man began to pump fast and deep inside Helga. He got plenty of encouragement.

'Yeehaw! Ride it cowboy!'

'G'wan ye boy ye!'

'Givvit whiskey!'

In the background, the other couple were in reverse order. The man lay back on a settee and the woman was astride him. Again the camera closed in as she nestled onto the dome of his upright phallus. Then to another whooping cheer she pushed downwards. Timmy watched and wondered if he wasn't so much a saint as a gobshite. Was he really so green, he thought candlelit sex a major discovery? Was he the only one there still falling for the lights off, man-on-top routine? The Catholic half of his mind raged that if he had any shame he'd get up and walk out. The pagan half whispered he'd been a sap long enough. He felt an unmistakable twitching in his crotch and he reddened remembering Mackerel's story of how Quasimodo got his hump from walking around with a bugle in his pants. The coin flipped and flipped again. Stay. Go. Stay. Go. Seconds later the decision was made for him.

The door burst open and Fukkit tumbled into the room.

'Mop wave from Barney! He's on 'is way!'

The others instantly scrambled for the door.

'What's happenin'?' Timmy asked.

'Never mind!' Hairy grabbed his arm and pulled him out the door and into an alcove where Dockets was arming the others with fire extinguishers.

'Careful,' he warned. 'The pins is pulled!'

'What the fuck is goin' on?' Timmy gasped.

'Just evenin' up a score!' Dockets winked. 'Just evenin' up a score!'

Seconds later they heard the unmistakable hop approaching. Gussie ploughed into the stores like a bulldozer.

'Ah ha! Fuckall t' do but play ca...'

He stopped dead, stunned by the flickering vision on the wall. Hairy shot over and slammed the door shut behind him.

Gussie shouted and hammered on the door then stumbled around in the gloom until he found the light switch. He flicked it up and the projector died, plunging the store into darkness. He flicked it down again and Helga and friends were back in business. Then the door flung open again and half a dozen foam extinguishers let loose with a vengeance. Gussie instantly disappeared under an avalanche of froth and bubbles. Seconds later Keyes and Graves came running down the corridor and found what looked like a beached whale thrashing around in a mountain of frog spawn. Above this spectacle four others were thrashing around in a different context.

'What the hell's going on?' Keyes cried.

Gussie rose Lazarus-like from the bubbles.

'Misser Keyes! Misser Keyes! I ... I...'

Then he slipped and fell back into the foamy mass again. Keyes was livid.

'Urgent business, my arse! Bloody pervert!'

Graves could smell fish rotting at fifty paces.

'Who raised the alarm?'

Hairy did the bashful hero.

'I did! I was passin' when I heard all groanin' an' creakin' an' I thought the place was afire! So, I rang Dockets!'

Beyond Pulditch Gates

Dockets took the baton cleanly.

'I'm Fire Warden for this area. Fair play t' the lads, they all fell in with me.'

Graves' eyes narrowed suspiciously.

'Why ring my office? Fire alarms go straight to the Shift Engineer.'

Keyes pulled Graves aside.

'Richard, it doesn't matter who they rang. We had them locked up two days ago and now they've risked their necks to put out a fire.'

'But there was no fire.'

'They weren't to know that.'

'You don't understand, George.'

'Damned right I don't!' Keyes snapped. 'This place ought to be in *Ripley's Believe it or Not!*'

With that, he turned and stormed back down the corridor. Graves turned on the lads who were watching the exchange.

'What are you looking at? Get that half-wit out of there and clean up that mess!'

Then it was his turn to storm off down the corridor.

'Ouch,' Hairy grinned.

'Ouch again,' Dockets chuckled, 'ouch again!'

As The Child fished Gussie out of the slop, Hairy hit the switch on the projector. Timmy caught the final image and something was wrong with it. He hadn't time to figure exactly what it was but something was different. The boys left Gussie in the corridor and went looking for mops. He was dripping like a scarecrow after a snowstorm when Barney shuffled around the corner.

'Moppin's finished up above, Mister Gallagher.'

'Why?' Gussie struggled to contain his tears.

'Why what?'

'You know damned well!'

Barney moved on past him.

'Ask Man-in-the-Mirror, he knows all about gettin' dropped in the shit!'

Gussie was gone by the time Timmy and The Child returned to mop up the mess.

'Pity Barney missed it,' Timmy said innocently.

The Child paused to wring out his mop.

'Oh, he knew all right but he said 'e didn't want to see no filth! I told 'im to come in and have a laugh. As bluies go it was pretty tame.'

Timmy hoped The Child wouldn't notice the flush that rushed to his face.

'Yea, I've seen better.'

'Funny thing, Barney wasn't keen on yew bein' involved. I don't know where 'e gets his ideas. Sure another few year an' *Playboy*'ll be sold like the evenin' paper!'

'The sooner the better!' Timmy agreed, 'We've been in the dark long enough!'

The Child shot him a funny look and Timmy blushed again. Had he been able to bend his boot backwards he'd have given himself a good swift kick for being such a gobshite.

They were in the locker room changing to go home when Barney tipped Timmy the wink that he wanted a word. Timmy followed him out onto the landing. Barney kept his voice low.

'Listen Timmy, I'm sorry ye got caught up in that business with Gallagher. I woulda squared things different but the boys said it'd fuck 'im up good and proper!'

'It certainly did that!'

'But it's not our style, Timmy. I never clapped eyes on wan o' dem dirty films an' from what I hear it's no loss. I mean, them girls

Beyond Pulditch Gates

is somebody's daughter or sister or maybe somebody's wife. Amn't I right?'

For the third time in an hour Timmy felt himself redden.

'Ye are, Barney, but I didn't rock the boat seein' as we were shaftin' Gallagher.'

THE END OF INNOCENCE II: MONDAY, 1 APRIL

It was late afternoon as Sister Frances and some of the girls cleaned out Monica's room. As they worked, it struck her that it was the only room in Saint Jude's devoid of religious icons. Monica's possessions made a pathetic heap when they were laid out on the bed. It was hard to think anyone could die and leave so little. No photographs, no mementoes bar a hairbrush, a cheap costume necklace and a strapless watch. Worst of all, there was neither friend or family to claim them. Her wardrobe held a coat, some well-worn dresses, underwear and shoes. While the girls packed the stuff into bags, Sister Frances slipped the hairbrush, the watch and a piece of the jewellery into the pocket of her habit. The place was soon bare and empty as if Monica Dillon had never existed.

Sister Frances returned to her room after taking Monica's diary from where she had it hidden. In its opening pages Monica recorded the stories of many of the girls who had lived in Saint Jude's. Sister Frances had read them many times, but haunted by their sadness, she kept going back to read them again.

'Annie T. Carlow. Arrived Easter, 1938. Sixteen. Pregnant by father. Twin sons. Adopted. Died New Year's Day, 1960. Buried Hell's Acre. Mary R. Longford. Arrived Christmas, 1942. Eighteen. Raped by uncle. Daughter. Adopted. Died May, 1965. Buried, Hell's Acre.'

A few pages further on, Monica recorded how her baby was fathered by a man named Richard. There was no second name. He

241

was the manager of the factory where Monica had worked. The heartbreak of her mother and the outrage of her father when told she was pregnant was written in two bleak lines:

Mam couldn't stop crying.
Dad wouldn't sit in the same room with me.

Within days Monica had been sent away to the nuns. Only the kindness of the other girls and especially one called Sarah Kelliher carried her through those lost and lonely days. The tragic story of Sarah shook the young nun to the core. Then Monica described her own night-long labour and the birth of her daughter Patsy. She took five pages to describe the time they had together before the baby was taken away. Five Pages. One for every minute.

When she finished reading, Sister Frances finally kept her promise to Monica that no one else would ever read what she had written. She took the papers down to the kitchen, opened the door of the kitchen range and fed them to the flames. As they curled and blackened, her innocence seemed to shrivel up with them. Innocence was the glue that held every illusion together but if that innocence was taken away, what then? She closed the range door and moved outside. The moon was visible against the darkening sky. When she was small, her father told her that it was made of cream cheese and she believed him. Her dream when she joined the nuns was that she would bring comfort and peace into people's lives but now that dream felt as distant as the moon and as real as Santa Claus.

THE END OF INNOCENCE III: MONDAY, 1 APRIL

Patsy was asleep. She lay with her back to Timmy who had his arm draped around her waist. The tribe was spitting scorn.

Beyond Pulditch Gates

'I didn't wanna rock the boat because we were shaftin' Gallagher. Yewr some hypocrite! Yew and that other gang o' perverts! Sittin' in the dark slobberin' and snipin' at real men in action. By Jaysus, they had dem wimmen's undivided attention an' no mistake. Up to the hilt like swords in scabbards! Dem boyos never squirted it onta the sheets!'

Patsy moaned and wormed down into Timmy's lap.

'G' wan man, or did ye learn any shaggin' thing at all today!'

Timmy caressed her breast. She whimpered and the tribe was ecstatic.

'Atta boy! She's horsin' for it! Now givver one ye couldn't tell in confession!'

The antics of Helga and her lover flooded Timmy's mind. He wondered what it would be like. A few minutes later he began to move slowly and easily down Patsy's body.

Patsy was floating in a deep sleep like a ship in a sheltered harbour. Warm rippling sensations washed over her until they were almost seamless. Then a shuddering bolt of pleasure shot through her and she was awake. Her thighs were spread and Timmy was between them with his mouth on her most private place. The Catholic half of her mind was outraged but the pagan half disagreed and arched her back to let him probe deeper. Then without a word Timmy reared up, lifted her hips and pulled her roughly onto him. His mouth clamped over hers smothering her cries as his deep powerful strokes brought him rapidly to a climax. Then he folded on top of her. Her pagan half sighed with satisfaction but her Catholic half was incensed. He was no better than Richard Graves. They were two barbarians who took advantage when she was defenceless. Her precious Timmy never learned a trick like that in a catechism, but then that's what she got for

243

Henry Hudson

going on the pill. No consideration. No concern. She could be bulled like a cow in a field, but at least the cow might have a calf to show for the encounter. The diatribe continued counterpointed by the frantic thumping of Timmy's heart. Patsy was afraid to move because as soon as they sundered they'd have to talk. Then she'd have to choose either to pretend it never happened or else steel herself to ask Timmy some very awkward questions.

Timmy was also afraid to move. As soon as it was over he knew he'd made a terrible mistake. Like a light switching on he suddenly realised what was wrong with the final image on the screen in the paint stores. Helga was with the other man. In the time it took to spring the trap on Gussie, the women had swapped partners just like kids swap comics. Suddenly the image was no longer erotic but shallow and above all, achingly sad. Barney's words echoed in his head. Somebody's daughter or sister or maybe even somebody's wife. The tribe was sniggering in the corner.

'Never mind that stuffy ould bollix. Him and his somebody's daughter! Sure they're all the same lying down! Yer brothers would be proud o' ye and only for those bloody pills she'd be in the Roxy for Christmas!'

Then a chilling vision filled Timmy's mind. It was of a roomful of yahoos cheering him on from the darkness. A paper-seller yelled;

'*Press, Indo, Playboy! Press, Indo, Playboy!*'

Barney was standing at the end of the bed. Sadness and betrayal creased his face then he turned and walked away. It was at that moment Timmy realised the old unwritten innocence was over. In the bedroom, the boardroom, in union halls and even out on the street, the cracks were everywhere. Freedom, if freedom it was, would be bought at a price and he had paid his first instalment. He couldn't stem the tears and when Patsy whispered his

Beyond Pulditch Gates

name he didn't reply. He just wrapped his arms around her and clung to her like a frightened child.

THE END OF INNOCENCE IV: MONDAY, 1 APRIL

The black-haired one was keeping nix under the lamppost. Her mate was up the lane trying again with Sergeant Bilko. She hadn't been too keen, but business was as slack as a rhino's rump. Things were so bad that the black-haired one was almost glad to see Gussie slither towards her out of the darkness. She'd swear she hadn't touched his stuff nor been within an ass's roar of Dún Laoghaire. For another fiver she'd promise to keep it that way. Sure that the coast was clear, he stomped over to her.

'How would yew like t' be covered in bubbles?'

She had met some weird specimens in her time, but this one really was a beauty. On the other hand, her and her mate were behind with the rent. She decided to negotiate.

'Ten in my place, fifteen in yours.'

'What?'

'Okay, I'll throw in a hand shandy while we're in the bath.'

'No! No! No! Ye don't understand! They were doin' it up on the wall an' I was on the floor. Then the door bursts open an' the boss called me a pervert 'cos he thought there was a fire but there wasn't.'

She couldn't stop the smile that cracked across her face. Gussie saw red.

'So ye think it's amusin'! Only for bitches like yew none of it woulda happened! Fair play t' yer man up in court! All sluts should be fuckinwell strangled!'

He made a throttling gesture for effect but she took it for real. She screamed loud and long. Gussie nearly shit himself.

245

'Nooo! Not yeew! Not yeew!'

His clumsy attempt to clamp his hand over her mouth sent her sound level soaring. The red-haired one came tumbling out of the lane followed by Sergeant Bilko. She was pulling down her skirt and he was hauling up his trousers. She ran to her mate, Gussie ran to the darkness, and Bilko ran home to his mammy.

'Whassup? Whassup?' the red-haired one cried.

'The weirdo who gave us the fiver! I think he was gonna strangle me!'

'Ye only think! Either he was or he wasn't! Ye gave Bilko such a fuckin' fright he turned machine gun again. Me knickers is like a billposter's bucket!'

The girls stood silently under the street lamp. Apart from a gunner-eyed gunner and a raving headcase, all they had for their night was a cleaning bill. The red-haired one clamped her hands on her hips and sighed wearily.

'This game is gettin' too dodgy. I think I'll join the nuns!'

'At least ye'll know most o' the priests!'

They laughed, linked each other and began to walk home.

Salvation comes in many forms and theirs came in the shape of a navy merc. They instantly recognised the driver. He was a judge whose favourite fetish was to wear a baby's nappy. He was supposed to be a royal bastard in court, but when he lay gurgling on his back with his white flaccid arse puffed and powdered, he looked the picture of innocence. The ould bollix was money for jam. The girls just had to go topless, pin him into a nappy and sing him nursery rhymes while he babbled back in babyspeak. It was quick. It was clean (apart from wiping cream on his piles) and at a tenner a piece it was lucrative. So what if in the morning he'd crucify some Simple Simon who'd been framed by the coppers. As the black-haired

Beyond Pulditch Gates

one was often heard to say; 'Innocent? Who the fuck is innocent these days?'

MAN-IN-THE-MIRROR: TUESDAY, 2 APRIL

He had been moved to a general ward where smelly old men moaned, groaned, and spat oysters of phlegm into stainless steel bowls. Every day he pleaded to be allowed home, but the doctors kept telling him he wasn't well enough. Then one day, a hospital psychiatrist came to see him.

'How are you feeling?' he asked.

'Grand! Great! I'd like to go home!'

'No doubt but you didn't end up in here because you fell over the cat.'

'What are ye sayin'?'

'After an episode like yours we recommend some time in a secure environment.'

'Ye mean, a loony bin. There's no way I'll sit an' make baskets. The walls! They lock the doors! Jesus!'

The doctor held up a calming hand.

'Hold it! Hold it! I'm told you're a dab hand in the garden. Is that right?'

'Not bad,' Man-in-the-Mirror said modestly. 'Not bad!'

'Well, I know a convent in Wicklow that needs a temporary gardener and...'

'I'll do it!' Man-in-the-Mirror exclaimed.

'Don't you want to hear the deal?'

'I just wanna get outa here!'

'Well, you'd better hear it anyway. The convent supplies bed and board and your employer will pay you sick pay while you're there.'

'How long will that be?'

'A few months, then we'll see where we go from there.'

A few days later, Timmy and Barney collected Man-in-the-Mirror from the hospital. He stayed with Barney while they organised things in Scarfe Terrace. Timmy agreed to look after the house while he was away. When everything was ready, Barney drove him down to Saint Jude's and Timmy travelled with them. They took one suitcase filled with clothes and another filled with gardening books. When they got there, Man-in-the-Mirror could hardly believe the size of the place. He could walk for hours and still not cover it all. A nice young nun called Sister Frances showed him his room and said to make himself at home. Barney had arranged that his sick pay would be paid at the local post office and for his book to be held in the convent safe. Man-in-the-Mirror drank in the place, the air and the space. He could have cried and kissed the ground. The place was his own private Paradise.

His happiness was tinged with regret when he heard what had happened to the girl who looked after the grounds before him. He decided the best tribute he could pay to her was to make them even nicer than she had left them. He spent his days working and his nights perusing gardening books for ideas and tips. Within days he had planted out dahlias and lifted some tulip bulbs for storage until autumn. He put straw mulch under the strawberries and in the greenhouse he planted aubergines, cucumbers and melons. By June he was working on a master-plan for the gardens and grounds. He knew that flowers with soft colours had to be placed so they could be viewed at leisure and from close up. On the other hand hot bright colours caught the eye, but too many too close became overpowering, so the trick was to tone them down by mixing the cooler-coloured flowers in between.

Beyond Pulditch Gates

By July the gardens were a riot of colour and the air hummed with the tireless efforts of bees. Butterflies skipped like silent ballerinas between flowerbeds and birds sang and splashed in the pool in the rock garden. He set up hanging baskets that spilled over with magnificent displays of pansies and other tender perennials. Thinking ahead he planted autumn-flowering bulbs and ordered some more exotic types for the following year. He picked soft fruit and removed the mulch from strawberries that had finished fruiting. In the greenhouse he pinched out the melons and picked early tomatoes and cucumbers. In the flowerbeds he took cuttings of pinks and wallflowers while in the vegetable plot he began to lift some early potatoes. Sister Frances kept on at him to take a few days off. She even invited him to go to Dublin for a break but he insisted he was just too busy.

August was a hot, dry month. Most people sought shade and slept, but Man-in-the-Mirror got himself a straw hat and did battle with the sun. He was determined that not a plant or blade of grass would die for lack of water. The tail of a mountain stream ran through Saint Jude's so he hooked up a pump to the drive of the tractor and took water from the run in barrelfuls. He mowed the lawns, but not too tight or too often. At night he set sprinklers across them, so while the rest of the earth turned brown Saint Jude's looked as if it was covered in a rich green baize. He watched the flowerbeds for signs of pests or disease and deadheaded flowers as they went over. In the vegetable garden he sowed spring cabbage and put in the last crop of lettuce.

There was only one task in St Jude's that bothered him. That was mowing the grass around the graves of nuns who were buried in a plot not far from the main house. Each grave was marked by a small white cross, carved with the name of the nun buried underneath. He used a tractor-mounted mower so the operation took only minutes but it still gave him shivers every time he did it. The other place he avoided was in the furthest corner of the convent grounds. The nuns referred to it as the 'Dolour Plot', but the farmhands called Hell's Acre. Towards the end of the month, Sister Frances asked him to walk around it with her to see how it could be cleaned up. It took him all his courage to go with her, but as they walked around its high forbidding walls, his fear was gradually replaced by an ineffable sense of pain and abandonment. The place hadn't been touched in years. Its walls were surrounded by wild furze bushes and were encrusted with ivy and creepers. They agreed that come September he'd dig up and burn the furze and cut the creepers off the walls. She said that if she was in charge, she'd have the walls themselves cut down. He said that some day she would be and that when that day came he'd have a jackhammer at the ready.

Saint Jude's: Friday, 20 September

Richard Graves drove down the quiet country road that led to St Jude's. In his briefcase were papers that would allow Man-in-the-Mirror to retire into St Jude's. They could have been posted to him, but Graves had volunteered to deliver the papers personally because St Jude's was owned by an order of nuns that took in girls like Monica Dillon, so he reckoned he'd try his luck while he was down there. He had been quietly trying to track her down but was having no success. Many of the homes and convents had been closed down. In those that remained, the watchword had changed from punishment to protection. Records were kept strictly confidential until the *bona fides* of enquirers were established. At the rate things were going, it looked as if he'd never discover what became of Monica Dillon.

Beyond Pulditch Gates

He hadn't been to St Jude's before, but as he drove up the arcing gravel driveway towards the house he got an eerie feeling that the place was almost waiting for him. As he slowed the car to a halt, a young nun came out through the front door. He reckoned her about late twenties. She was slim and had a nice face. Graves couldn't help wondering what his chances might be.

'Mister Graves?' the nun asked quietly.

'What? Oh, yes! That's me!'

He flushed like a schoolboy caught planning a raid on a very private orchard.

'I'm Sister Frances, would you like to step inside?'

She showed him into the library and returned a few moments later with a tray set with coffee cups and biscuits. Graves noticed only two cups on the tray.

'Isn't he going to join us?'

'I'm afraid not. Says he's too busy.'

'I'd like him to be *au fait* with what's going on.'

'He just says he's staying and that's the end of it.'

'He's not giving you trouble?'

The nun began to pour the coffee.

'The only trouble we have with him is getting him to take a break!'

Graves notched up the charm and when she seemed to relax he made his move.

'I'd heard about the place but I had no idea it was quite so big. You're very young to be responsible for it all!'

'Oh, I'm not, Mister Graves. Sister Superior just asked me to look after this business.'

Graves changed tack.

'What is St Jude's used for anyway?'

'It's a sanctuary for what were once termed unfortunate or wayward women.'

'Is that a fact? And where would these 'women' have come from?'

'All over, Mister Graves.'

'Please, Sister, call me, Richard!'

The nun in her knew it was wrong to judge him, but the woman in her couldn't help it. Richard Graves made her skin crawl. She was glad when the coffee was over and she could take him outside to finish their business.

She stayed polite but distant as she led him past lines of crucifixes that ran the length of a neatly tended grass area.

'Our community burial plot,' she explained.

She made the sign of the cross. He followed suit but he was wasting his time. She kept even more air between them until they found Man-in-the-Mirror. He was beside a walled area loading furze cuttings onto a tractor and trailer unit. He stopped loading and eyed Graves suspiciously.

'Howye! Yewr from Pulditch aren't ye? Am I fixed up t' stay here?'

'Yes, I suppose you are.'

'Barney said I'd have ta sign stuff.'

Graves opened his briefcase and took out some papers.

'Mister Coogan vetted these on behalf of the union. He agrees they're in order.'

Man-in-the-Mirror just grunted. He borrowed Graves' pen and used his briefcase as a desk to scribble his signature on them all.

'That it?'

'I suppose so,' Graves mumbled.

'Good! Nice t' meet ye again but I've a ton o' this stuff t' burn so if yiz'll excuse me.' He jumped up into the tractor, fired the engine

Beyond Pulditch Gates

and headed off in the direction of the boiler-house. Graves shook his head.

'Well, that was short and sweet!'

He was just about to add like the ass's gallop but thought better of it. Then he noticed the small wrought iron gateway in the wall.

'What's in there, Sister?' he asked.

'That,' she whispered, 'is known as the Dolour Plot.'

She moved to the gate and gently caressed the bars.

'It's also known as Hell's Acre.'

'Hell's Acre?' Graves felt an icy shiver run through him.

'Yes, Mister Graves. This is where many of those 'wayward' women are buried.'

Graves blanked and blurted out the first thing that came to his mind.

'Ah, well, I suppose God still loves the sinner!'

She turned on him like a tigress.

'That depends on who you see as a sinner! Those women didn't make themselves pregnant but those who did were glad to have somewhere to bury their treachery!'

There was an awkward silence as they walked back towards the house. Graves tried once more to get on terms.

'Your gardens are magnificent, Sister! He really has been working hard!'

'Indeed but most of the original work was done by one of the girls. Unfortunately she died here just a few months ago.'

Graves shook his head sadly.

'Ah, well, at least she left something beautiful behind her.'

'Oh, the gardens are not the only thing Monica Dillon left behind her. She left a beautiful daughter too.'

'Jesus!' Graves gagged as shock washed all over his face.

253

'Are you all right, Mister Graves?'

Graves felt his knees begin to buckle.

'I've just remembered! An appointment ... in Dublin! Terribly sorry! I'll be in touch!'

As he scurried away, the crawling sensation returned to her stomach.

Out on the road Graves jammed the car to a halt and gripped the steering wheel trying to deny the terrifying thoughts that were flashing around in his brain.

'Don't be an idiot! There had to be dozens of Monica Dillon's sent to places like that. Dillon's are all over Dublin and everywhere else as well!'

He gripped the steering wheel even tighter and a full ten minutes passed before he was fit to drive away. On the road back to Dublin he passed some schoolgirls standing at a bus stop. If he had a daughter she'd be about their age. Laughing. Going home from school with her friends. He rammed his fear down onto the accelerator.

'It wasn't Monica Dillon! I have no daughter! I haven't! I haven't!'

EVENING: GUSSIE: FRIDAY, 20 SEPTEMBER

The letter was waiting on the hall-stand in his digs. It was addressed to Mr. Augustus Gallagher Esq. and marked confidential. He knew by the postmark it was from the auctioneers. He took it to his room and savoured the moment before slicing it open. The old homestead was on the market through the same firm who sold it after his mother died. He had seen the ad in the *Indo* a few weeks before, and had learned it off by heart. Three-and-one-third acres with two derelict buildings for sale by private treaty.

Beyond Pulditch Gates

He liked that last part. A private sale would keep the local Mafiosi guessing.

He had sniffed around auctioneers for an idea of a going price and was stunned at the size of their replies. Nonetheless he gathered every penny he had and put in a very generous bid with an N.B. that he wouldn't go higher. Obviously the threat had worked. He ran his thumbnail under the envelope flap. Unfolding the letter like a delicate flower, he cleared his throat and read.

'File 02/22/04/68. Dear Mister Gallagher, Thank you for your bid for the above. I regret to say it was unsuccessful. The property went to an anonymous bidder represented by a London agent. We thank you for your interest and if other such properties should come on the market we will be happy to advise you of same.'

Gussie flopped down onto the bed. Something was wrong. Who in God's name would go higher than he had? Only families got stroppy over land, but his mother was dead and his relations would eat shite rather than pay over the odds for anything. Suddenly the unthinkable flashed across his mind. Maybe it was Josie. Gussie would have none of it. He appealed to the ceiling of the room.

'How could that brainless bitch get that kinda money? Josie Gallagher couldn't tie a lace to keep a bloody shoe on!'

He crumpled the letter into a ball and flung it into the fireplace.

St Jude's: Saturday, 21 September

As deputy shop steward, Timmy volunteered to keep an eye on Man-in-the-Mirror. The day before Graves had offered to bring him down to St Jude's in order to wrap up his retirement but Timmy declined. The thought of sitting with the smarmy prick all the way there and back was too much. Instead he organised the gang at home to go and make a day of it. They took the train to Bray then a

Henry Hudson

local bus service dropped them at the gates of St Jude's. As they walked up the driveway to the house, Patsy checked that the three of them looked tidy. She smiled at the idea. The unquestioning respect for nuns hammered into her at school was as strong as ever. On the other hand, she was at war with the church over the encyclical on birth control released by Rome a few weeks earlier. It was called *Humanae Vitae*. It laid down the law in no uncertain terms. No 'unnatural' contraception could be used by Catholics. All acts of intercourse had to be open to the woman becoming pregnant. Doctors and chemists could no longer hide in the fog of uncertainty surrounding 'the pill'. Many stopped prescribing and supplying it even to women whose lives depended on never being pregnant again. As it was Patsy, had to track to the far side of the Liffey to find a chemist to fill her prescriptions. It was no coincidence that the name over the door was neither Irish nor Catholic.

As they approached the house, a nun swept out of the main doors with her hand extended in greeting. Sister Frances introduced herself then invited them into the house for tea. Jack took only one biscuit as per Patsy's eye-flashed signal. When they finished, Sister Frances directed Timmy towards the boiler-house where Man-in-the-Mirror was burning the last of the cut-down furze. Then she called one of the farmhands and asked him to show Jack around the farm, while she took Patsy around the house. The huge rooms and the wide curving stairs were a million miles away from Larnham Street. Patsy was mesmerised by the polished floors and magnificent hand-carved furniture. The chapel smelled of incense and flowers. Sunlight filtering through a stained-glass window left a muzzy multicoloured wash on the terrazzo altar where a red light glimmered above the tabernacle. As they passed, Sister Frances dropped to one knee and Patsy did likewise. Then

Beyond Pulditch Gates

they walked down a long corridor towards the gardens. Portraits of long-dead nuns hung along the walls, and as they progressed, the paintings were gradually replaced by rows of silver-framed photographs. Only Sister Frances stopped to straighten one of the frames, Patsy would have missed the grainy pinch-faced image lost amongst so many others. It was the nun in the magazine. The nun who called but wouldn't wait.

The copperplate inscription under the photograph confirmed who she was. It read, Sister Mary Hilda, 1908–1958. RIP.

'Sister Frances, who is that?'

'Sister Hilda? Poor woman! She died in a fire in one of our convents in Dublin.'

'I remember that!' Patsy cried. 'It was awful!'

'Actually, a girl who used to look after our gardens saved her friend from that fire. Funny, that's twice in two days Monica's name has come up.'

'Monica?' Patsy asked.

'Monica Dillon,' the nun replied.

Patsy's face turned white.

'Did you say Monica Dillon and that ... she was in the same place as this Sister Hilda?'

Sister Frances thought Patsy was going to faint. She led her out into the garden and sat her down on a bench. It didn't take them long to piece the story together. The factory. The manager called Richard. The baby. The fire. The whole sorry mess. They fell silent for a long time then Sister Frances stood up.

'Come on, Patsy,' she sighed. 'There's something I think you should see.'

Meanwhile Timmy found Man-in-the-Mirror wheeling a barrow-load of cuttings into the boiler-house. When he saw Timmy, he

257

dropped the handles of the barrow and shook him warmly by the hand.

'I'm stayin'! That oul' creepin' jaysus Graves was down here yesterday.'

'I know. Did 'e give ye the read?'

'Didn't ask! I just signed the papers!'

'Ye happy?'

'Pig in shit! No way I'm goin' back t' Pulditch. They're all bloody lunatics up there!'

Timmy smiled to himself. People said Man-in-the-Mirror was nuts, but standing there in the warm autumn sun he couldn't help wondering. Man-in-the-Mirror dabbed his brow with a handkerchief.

'How's the house lookin', Timmy?'

'A bit ropy. It needs paintin' an' the gutters cleaned out. Ye want me t' arrange it?'

'Naw! Now I'm fixed up here I'm gonna sell it. Yew interested be any chance?'

'Yea, I'd be very interested!'

'Great! Prefer someone I know! That way there's no fuckin' messin'!'

He took the handles of the wheelbarrow again.

'C'mon inside! Wait till ye see the job I'm doin' on the boiler-house!'

At the opposite corner of the grounds, Sister Frances unlocked a small metal gate and led Patsy to a corner of a high-walled patch of grass. They stopped at a mound of earth that indicated the presence of a grave.

'Monica Dillon,' the nun whispered.

Patsy blessed herself and fought back the tears.

Beyond Pulditch Gates

'How many girls are buried in here?'

'Over a hundred.'

'Sweet Jesus in Heaven!'

Just then they heard the approaching sound of Jack's voice. He was calling for Patsy.

'Sister, we have to talk,' Patsy pleaded. 'We can't just leave things like this!'

The nun thought for a moment.

'I'll be in Dublin on Wednesday. Wynne's Hotel in Abbey Street. I'll meet you there at midday.'

Sister Frances swung the iron gate closed just as Jack came tumbling round the corner.

'Ma! Ma! I was lookin' everywhere for ye! Ye wanna see the cows an' the baby cows! An' there's pigs and sheeps as well!'

'Sheep,' Patsy laughed.

'Naw! There was loads o' them!'

Patsy hugged him to her. She could let the tears go because tears of laughter and tears of pain are hard to tell apart.

At three o'clock the bus collected them at the gate and Jack knelt up in the back seat waving goodbye to Sister Frances and Man-in-the-Mirror. Timmy guided Patsy into the centre where he could whisper his news in private.

'Man-in-the-Mirror wants us t' buy his house.'

'Scarfe Terrace,' Patsy gasped.

'All we have to do is givvim a fair price an' it's ours!'

For the second time in as many hours Patsy felt tears rush to her eyes. Timmy misread them and threw his arm around her shoulders.

'Ah, c'mon! There's no need t' cry over it! Another few weeks an' at long last we'll have our own hall door!'

Later that night he tried but failed to penetrate her dry tense sex.

'Patsy? What is it? I thought you'd be thrilled about the house. I thought it was what ye always wanted!'

'It is, love! It's just something happened today in that place! I found out what happened to Monica Dillon!'

Then she told him the story except the connection to Richard Graves. That was a mine that could blow all their lives apart. Timmy eased her head down onto his chest.

'It's all very sad, kiddo, but whoever the father was he's long gone and the kid could be anywhere. There's nothin' anyone can do about it now.'

Patsy wrapped her arms around him.

'Timmy, no matter what ever happens remember I love yew an' Jack more than anythin' in the world!'

He felt tears running down her cheek and remembered the night she held him and let him cry his anguish into the darkness.

'Patsy? What can happen to us? Patsy?'

She didn't reply and even when exhaustion took her she shuddered fitfully in her sleep.

Timmy stared for a long time into the darkness wondering what could possibly threaten them. Not that there wasn't plenty of trouble out there in the world. Sometimes he wondered if God had gone AWOL and left the whole lot in chaineys. Everywhere there was war, famine and people at each other's throats. Even the bishops were fighting. The German and American ones were miffed over the Pope putting the kibosh on the pill. Then the Irish ones took the hump at them for putting it up to the Pope. Everything was turning topsy-turvy and even the bloody farmers were threatening to go on strike. That'd be one picket he'd have no bother

Beyond Pulditch Gates

passing. They wouldn't need a riot squad to clear those lines. They'd just have to wave a tax form and they'd vanish like sin on Sunday. Still, it was all small beer compared to what was happening in a faraway place called Biafra. The Nigerians had overrun the headquarters of the Biafran Army at a place called Owerri. Thousands of people were dying of starvation and disease. The pictures on the telly were sickening and the Red Cross had launched an appeal for help. The boys in Pulditch agreed they'd have to do something special to raise a decent wad to send off.

Patsy shuddered again, so he held her close until she settled. As he did so Timmy sighed and wondered if life wasn't just one big repeating circle. Only a few days earlier, a plane came down between Corsica and France. Ninety-five people gone in an eyeblink. Munich all over again. The postal workers and the Aer Lingus clerks were banging the war drums and word was out that the fitters' unions were about to join in. They wanted an increase that would pull them well over ten bob an hour. If they got that, then they'd all be heading back to the trenches again. Strikes, wars, air crashes, famines, football, be born, grow up, meet a girl, get married, have kids, grow old, die. A thousand years on there'd be another Timmy Talbot lying in the dark and wondering where the hell the whole lot was heading. The script would be the same. Only the props would change.

chapter **11**

OPERATION BIAFRICA: MONDAY, 23 SEPTEMBER 1968

Gussie was like a polar bear with icicles on its piles. Losing the old homestead was bad enough, but losing it to some nameless and probably godless Brit made it ten times worse. He was looking for blood and it was just gone noon when Mackerel stepped into his line of fire. He was cleaning out the carpenters' workshop with Barney when Gussie went waddling by.

'Mister Galliger! Mister Galliger! Me an' Barney was wonderin' if it's okay t' do a whip around for the starvin' Biafricans?'

'Biafrans, ye blithern' moron! An' youse are gettin' paid to help the carpenter, not collect money so's dem niggers can buy more guns!'

'But the poor hoors is starvin'!' Barney pleaded.

'No buts! Worst thing we ever did was educate dem wogs! Shudda left them swingin' in the trees with their beads an' bananas! Now, never youse mind the Martin De Porres act! Just do what yiz are gettin' paid to do an' get shiftin' that timber! I'll be back first thing after dinner an' I better see some progress!'

Beyond Pulditch Gates

As Gussie humped off, Saint Joseph shook his head sadly.

'Ah well, Barney, at least you tried.'

Barney swung a plank up onto his shoulder.

'Take a long walk at lunch-time. No rush back!'

Saint Joseph duly took the hint.

Gussie was true to his word. When the siren went for the end of the break he was into the carpenters' workshop like a lion rampant. What he saw did nothing to enhance his mood. Mackerel had Hairy stretched over the workbench with his shirt pulled up around his shoulders. He was massaging a thick brown liquid into his back.

'What the hell's goin' on?' Gussie demanded.

Barney held out a bottle.

'Rub down, Mister Gallagher. Poor Hairy here suffers a martyr with the arthuritis!'

Hairy sighed dreamily.

'Ah, it should be on the Blue Card! The relief is somethin' inhuman!'

Gussie's moaning about his arthritic hips was legendary, as was his refusal to pay a doctor to look at them. He sniffed for a rat but the prospect of a cure, particularly a free one, was too good to miss.

'What's in dem bottles?'

'Special kinds o' rub,' Mackerel explained, 'from the fella what looks after Bohemians. There's mild an' extra strong!'

Gussie's patience was as short as his manner. If extra strong could do things faster then extra strong it was.

'Gerrup!' he barked at Hairy.

He pulled off his shop-coat, loosened his trousers and barked at Mackerel.

263

Henry Hudson

'Gimme full strength an' we'll soon see how good it is!'

'Are ye sure, Mister Galliger? It's very powerful stuff.'

'Lord Jaysus! D'ye want me t' write it out in triplicate?'

'It'll be cold at first then it'll get warmer.'

'Never mind the runnin' commentary! Just get on with it!'

'Now, Mackerel, ye heard Mister Gallagher,' Barney said primly.

Mackerel slapped on a good sup and massaged it into Gussie's hips, making sure a good steady trickle ran down between the cheeks of his arse. At first it felt cold just as Mackerel said it would. Then it turned to molten lava. The Pulditch Book of Legends says that Gussie's roars for water were heard on the steps of Ringsend Church. Now as luck (or rather Barney) had arranged it, there wasn't a drop of water in the carpenters' shop. As Gussie felt his ringpiece singe he rocketed up off the workbench.

'Me aaarse! It's acid! Me aaaarse!'

'Whaddlewedoo! Oh, whaddlewedooo!' Hairy carefully added to the consternation.

'Water! Water! For fuck's sake gemme waterrrr!'

'The fire-bucket!' Barney cried. 'Outside! Quick!'

A four-handed rush-push by Mackerel and Hairy drove Gussie, trousers and long johns round his knees, out into the boiler-house basement. Then, blessed with the roars and curses of their favourite foreman, they shoved his blistering bum into a bucket of cold rusty water. This vessel was painted red and marked with the letters FIRE. It already played host to fag butts, used plasters and various dead and dying insects.

Mackerel was no saint, but he never heard anyone fuck and blind as fast or as furiously as Gussie did when he was jammed into that bucket. Neither did Saint Joseph who arrived back in the middle of the heave. When Barney, Mackerel and Hairy finally

Beyond Pulditch Gates

extracted Gussie from his mucky and inglorious perch he pulled up his trousers and swore they'd have their cards by closing time.

'What for?' Hairy whined. 'Ye told Mackerel to slap that stuff all over yer arse!'

'Yea,' Mackerel put on his best hurt face, 'I was only follyin' orders!'

'Yewr orders!' Barney drove the nail home to the hilt.

Gussie wanted to smack them all in the mouth, but to do that he'd have had to let go of his trousers. Instead he roared in frustrated fury and waddled off under the boilers, taking the long way back to his office in case anyone else might see his predicament.

Saint Joseph was devastated.

'Well, lads,' he sighed, 'we can kiss goodbye to helping the Biafrans now.'

'Ah, I dunno,' Hairy grinned. 'Have a gander!'

Saint Joseph looked up and saw the catwalks above were jammed with bodies. Barney pulled out a notebook.

'Two quid a man if we got Gallagher's arse in a fire-bucket be closing' time! There's forty-five on the book so far. That's ninety quid an' us four'll make it ninety-eight t' send off t' the Red Cross! Whaddya say?'

Saint Joseph shook his head in admiration.

'Put me in for four and make it the even hundred.'

He knew it wasn't exactly what the bishops had in mind when they asked for assistance for the starving millions, but it was a lot more fun than a church collection.

Timmy chaired the locker-room post-mortem on what was generally regarded as one of the best strokes ever pulled in Pulditch. Barney was called out to take a phone call just as Timmy asked Mackerel what he used on Gussie's behind.

'Creosote! Full strength!'

Hairy turned white.

'Fuckin' creosote! Ye said ye got it offa the fella what looks after Bohs players!'

'Naw! I said I got it offa the fella what looks after Bohemians!'

'Bohemians what?' Timmy was almost afraid to ask.

'Goal posts! He uses it on the stands as well. Great stuff! Lasts forever! Look on the bright side. At least Gussie won't ever die o' woodworm in his arsehole!'

Timmy shook his head in admiration. If Mackerel hadn't left school at twelve he'd be sitting in the White House and renting Ireland out for the holidays.

Suddenly the room fell silent. Barney was at the door, shock etched all over his face.

'It's The Cowboy. Cashed in 'is chips at dinner-hour. Massive heart attack!'

No one spoke. Each man was immediately alone with his thoughts and memories of The Cowboy. Some gazed into the nothingness at the backs of their lockers. Others looked at the floor or out the window and downriver to where the first grey stack of Pulditch Two was creeping into sky. Then it started. At first it was a gentle humming, then a work-boot took up the beat, and one brave voice broke the silence.

'An old cowpoke came a ridin' out one dark and windy day!'

The others needed no encouragement. Within seconds they were up and running. Slapping their butts with one hand and holding imaginary reins in the other they circled the rows of lockers singing and whooping in a noisy tribute to the greatest herdsman of them all. Then Barney stood up on one of the long stools and called for order.

Beyond Pulditch Gates

'We all owe the Cowboy Flanagan! That man wudda walked t' Hell an' back for us!'

'Here! Here!' the boys answered as one.

'The Cowboy put a lotta money into our pockets an' inta thousands of others as well so the least we can do is givvim a bloody good send-off!'

'Absopoxyfuckinlutely!' The Pox thumped the table.

Cheers and locker-thumping greeted this spoke and Barney had to call for order again.

'We'll lay 'im down proper and right! Then we'll adjourn t' Grealish's and the last man stannin' can switch off the lights!'

An even louder cheer greeted that battlecry and it hit Gussie Gallagher like a punch as he slithered up the stairs. He was just about to launch a lightning raid in revenge for the fire bucket routine. Though never awash with intelligence, his animal cunning told him that raiding a locker room full of fellas in that humour was at best foolhardy. He stalked back down the stairs in the blackest of black moods. His bum was a mass of blisters and he stank of creosote. Somebody would pay a price for his discomfort and he knew exactly who that somebody would be. He went home early and sat for hours in a basin of cold water. When it got dark, he smothered it in Vaseline and went out looking for the ladies.

THE LADIES: MONDAY, 23 SEPTEMBER

They had just taken up their nightly pitch when the black-haired one saw him coming. She noticed he was walking with his legs wider apart than before.

'Oh, shit, here's that weirdo again! This time 'e can strangle yew!'

'No bother,' the redhead replied. 'No matter what 'e says I'll keep me cool!'

'I wouldn't give that perv a sniff of it. Not for all the tea in China!'

'Ah, yewr too fussy! Stand back an' learn somethin'!'

Gussie walked over very gingerly then planted his hands on his hips.

'How'd yew like to have something hot rubbed on yer arse!'

It was one of the most unusual openers she'd ever heard.

'Wouldn't mind!'

'Ye wouldn't! An' what if next thing was it was rammed inta a fire-bucket!'

She began to get that sinking feeling, but pride wouldn't let her back out.

'I dunno! It might be fun!'

'Fun! Fun! Right! We'll slap a dollop of raw creosote onta yewr pouch, jam it inta a bucket o' rusty water and see how yew like it!'

The mention of creosote was enough. She remembered the state of their neighbour when he gave his pigeon loft a once-over and his agonised roars the day he splashed some into his eye.

'Ye dirty, hoppy-legged reprobate! Ye short-arsed, sick, sorry, fuckin' sadist!'

She drew out and hit him with a right hook Rocky Marciano would have envied. Gussie was caught off-balance and landed flat on his already blistered backside.

'I'm not talkin' about yewr arse! I'm talkin' about mine!'

'Yewr sick! Sick! Sick! Sick!'

Then she kicked him and glared at her mate as she stormed past.

'Say I told ye so an' I'll kick yew too!'

Though she didn't know why, the black-haired one felt sorry for the big baboon.

Beyond Pulditch Gates

'Yew okay?' she called, keeping a safe distance between her and him.

Gussie was bewitched, bollixed and bewildered. All he'd wanted to do was to explain.

'The man in Bohemians said it works!'

'Yea, well 'e might know howta score on a pitch but 'e hasn't a clue otherwise! Ye had some chance with bubbles but, by Jaysus, creosote takes the biscuit! Anyways, don't sit there too long. The cops scout around here all the time!'

Gussie argued with himself all the way back to his digs. The trouble with women was that they changed direction like a weather-cock. The last time he mentioned bubbles to the black-haired one she went bananas, but now she was telling him the bloody things were his only chance. He didn't want a chance, he only wanted to explain. Since the day he was born his mother never listened. Instead she was permanently on his back, and now thanks to his tease of a sister, the murder squad was down on his house. When he got back to the digs the door was locked and he'd forgotten his keys. He'd have to waken Mrs Gorman and she'd be bitching at him for a week.

'Wimmin!' he wailed. 'They'll be the ruin o' me yet!'

GLASNEVIN CEMETERY: WEDNESDAY, 25 SEPTEMBER

It was half-past eleven when the hearse stopped at the bend before the cemetery. The mourners formed up behind it, and six-by-six they carried The Cowboy's coffin the last few hundred yards on their shoulders. Barney was the singer-out who walked ahead, and every few yards he'd stop the carrying six and call on six more to take their places. The flag of The Plough and The Stars draped the plain brown box as it was gently passed between the crews. Hundreds of men came from all over Dublin to pay their respects.

Many knocked off work and wore their overalls, working boots and jackets. There was a fierce unspoken pride as they shuffled quietly along. Their fathers had stood with Larkin, but time and the new trade unionism was making them the Last of the Mohicans. Now they had lost their last great chief. From then on they'd have to rely on the likes of Red Kearns, so they had more than one reason to mourn. Kearns and some other senior union officials were at the front of the mourners wearing suits, carrying briefcases and trying to look solemn. They kept checking their watches as if they had more important things to do but unlike the man they were burying, none had the bottle to break ranks and walk away.

When they got to the graveyard, the cortège wound along the narrow pathways between rows of headstones. The gravediggers walked in the crowd with their spades slung over their shoulders. For the last few yards Timmy, Horizontal and Oily Paddy took one side of the coffin, while Mackerel, The Pox and The Child took the other. Saint Joseph walked behind, feeding his rosary beads through his fingers. In off the pathway, a mound of earth was heaped beside an opened grave. Barney halted the procession and Clean Paddy took the flag off the coffin. There were no wreaths because The Cowboy believed that people should be given flowers only when they could still smell them.

The Cowboy was unmarried. His two elderly sisters and his nieces and nephews moved to the grave and circled around it. They cried, but mostly with pride at the send-off provided for their brother and uncle. At the mouth of the grave, the gravediggers took over, and within seconds the coffin disappeared into the earth cradled on their canvas lowering straps. Then a priest prayed and sprinkled the coffin with holy water.

'I hope that's a Jemmy an' pep!' a voice quipped from the crowd.

Beyond Pulditch Gates

Even the priest allowed himself a smile. Then The Cowboy's relatives threw handfuls of earth down onto the coffin and some of the lads did the same, before the gravediggers slid a board over the hole. There was silence for a moment then a voice rose into the morning stillness.

'The worker's flag it's scarlet red! We'll keep it flying overhead! Though cowards quake and traitors fear! We'll keep the red flag flying here! The worker's flag it's scarlet red! We'll keep it flying overhead!'

Then all voices rose as one. It was an anthem to the end of an era. A farewell to the last great chief of the Mohicans. The white man was coming with flipcharts and business plans and the days of the natives were well and truly numbered. When the singing finished, many had tears in their eyes. Having saluted international socialism, they blessed themselves like good God-fearing Catholics and turned away. Most would stop for a pint to mark the occasion, but the boys from Pulditch had all taken leave for the day. Grealish's was on standby with soup, sambos and extra barmen. The painter's brother was bringing along his banjo and the last man standing would turn off the lights.

As they headed back to the gates, they passed a rectangle of grass about half the size of a football field.

'What's that?' Mackerel asked innocently.

Barney tried to brush off the question.

'The Holy Angels plot. It's where they bury babies if they die.'

'What about the ones that die before they're born?'

'They're buried there as well. Now c'mon, let's pay our respects to Parnell!'

Subject and direction were changed in an instant, but Timmy couldn't help glancing over his shoulder. Three of their children were buried in that place. They seldom talked about them because whenever they did it always ended with Patsy in tears and him struggling to hold them back. He decided to go back up there someday and ask if there was any record of them. Later. On his own. Secretly.

He caught up on the boys as they gazed down into the moat at the gate of the vault containing Parnell's body. Oily looped his thumbs into his lapels.

'Amazin' how a man like that can be shanghaied just be lettin' fagin have 'is head!'

Saint Joseph's brow furrowed.

'Fagan? I don't remember any Fagan being involved with Parnell!'

'Sure everywan knows it was bein' careless with fagin that fucked 'im up!'

'No! No!' Joseph insisted. 'Whoever this Fagan was he had nothing to do with it! Parnell died of a heart attack!'

Heads turned to wipe away tears of stifled laughter. Timmy was never more grateful to Saint Joseph than he was at that moment because tears of laughter and tears of pain are hard to tell apart.

Wynne's Hotel: Wednesday, 25 September

The two women sat in a corner in the bar of Wynne's Hotel. Sister Frances went over the whole story, including how she had kept her promise to Monica and burned her diary. The nun wrung her hands in anguish at the idea.

'If only I'd known what I was doing, Patsy! All the proof we needed was there in Monica's own words!'

'Ye kept a promise, Sister. A pity more people didn't do likewise for the poor girl!'

They fell silent for a while then Patsy came up with an idea.

Beyond Pulditch Gates

'Suppose we traced the family that adopted the baby?'

'Easier said than done. Adoption papers are guarded like the Crown Jewels!'

'Why so?'

'Officially,' Sister Frances whispered, 'it's to protect the children!'

'And unofficially?'

'Too many pillars of society with skeletons in the cupboard. They don't want some stranger turning up twenty years later wanting a share in the business or the farm. Even if we found the child, you may bet Mister Graves will swear blind she isn't his!'

Patsy was willing to try anything.

'Suppose we contact as many Sheridans as we can!'

'And say what? Did you adopt a girl in '58? We'd be arrested!'

'So we never find Monica's baby and Richard Graves walks off scot-free!'

'Looks that way!'

'Is there a God up there at all?'

The nun sighed wearily.

'Right now Patsy, I'm not too sure!'

She reached into her pocket and took out a wrap of tissue paper. It held a hairbrush, a cheap costume necklace and a strapless watch.

'These were Monica's. They were all I could save of her personal belongings. It's a long shot, but maybe someday I'll be able to hand them to her daughter.'

As Patsy ran her fingers over the beads of the necklace, a plan was formulating in her mind. Win, lose or draw, she'd hit Richard Graves with the truth and to hell with the law, the consequences and with him.

When she got home, she checked the phone book and found his address. Later that evening, she took a bus across town to his house. Patsy wasn't sure if the woman who answered the door was the same one she'd met the day Pulditch opened. If it was, then Catherine Keyes had aged thirty years in the space of ten. Her face was drawn and gaunt. Her eyes were circled in black and her hair was matted and unbrushed. A red lurid lipstick was plastered sloppily around her mouth. She looked like an ageing actress clinging to a long departed beauty.

'Mrs Graves?' Patsy said. 'I'm Patsy Talbot, I used to work for your husband.'

A trace of recognition crossed Catherine's face.

'I've met you before, haven't I?'

'The day Pulditch opened. Sorry to call like this but I'd like to see Mister Graves.'

Catherine showed her into the hall.

'Lemme take ... I mean, may I take your coat?'

'No need,' Patsy smiled. 'I can only stay a few minutes.'

Just then Graves stepped out into the hallway.

'Catherine who...'

The words died and his face drained of colour.

'It's Mrs Talbot,' Catherine whispered. 'She ... She wants to see you!'

Patsy stepped forward.

'I'm tryin' t' trace one o' the staff that worked in the factory. Monica Dillon? I thought maybe ye might be able ta help.'

Graves stayed cool enough to observe the niceties.

'Doesn't ring a bell but let's not talk in the hall. Please, step into the sitting room.'

Catherine moved to go with them, but Graves flashed her a look to get lost. Patsy winced at her humiliation. Catherine tried to rescue her dignity.

Beyond Pulditch Gates

'I've just made tea. Would you like some, Mrs Talbot?'

'Don't go to any trouble.'

'It'll only take a moment.'

Graves went on the attack as soon as he got Patsy into the room.

'What the fuck are you at? Coming to my house!'

'Timmy's at a funeral, so seeing he's out of the way for a few hours...'

She began to pull up her skirt.

'Jesus! What are you doing?'

'Pulling my clothes off! Then I'll throw meself down on the couch so your wife can see what you do to women when their husbands aren't around!'

'Stop! Please! Please!'

Patsy smoothed down her skirt then moved slowly to the window. She paused for a few moments then turned to Graves who stood statue-like in the middle of the floor.

'Yew made Monica Dillon pregnant then ye dumped her! She's buried in a godforsaken spot out in the mountains called St Jude's but yew know that already!'

Graves looked like he'd been kicked.

'You'll never prove it! Never!'

'Yewr pathetic! She had a little girl! Don't yew want to know who she is? Where she is? What kind of a man doesn't want to know 'is own daughter?'

Just then Catherine came in carrying a tray on which a tea set rattled noisily.

'Who doesn't want to know his own daughter?'

'No one!' Graves snapped, 'I mean someone we knew, a long time ago.'

275

Catherine wobbled the tray onto a coffee table.

'Imagine anyone being so heartless!'

She raised the teapot, but when she tried to pour she spilled tea all over the tray. Graves shot forward and Patsy saw fear in her eyes. It was the fear of a cur used to seeing its master go for the whip.

'Those pots,' Patsy sighed. 'I have one and I'm always threatening to throw it out!'

They mopped up the spill and filled the cups, then Catherine turned to Graves.

'Well, Richard, will you be able to help Mrs Talbot find the girl she's looking for?'

'I doubt it! Our records were never up to much. Besides, she left in such a hurry and I was busy setting up a new production line.'

Patsy left when she finished her tea. She refused Graves' offer to drive her home but had to let him walk her to the bus. He turned on her as soon as the got outside.

'Don't ever come near me or my house again! I said you'll never prove anything!'

'Ah, ye proved it yerself!'

'What d'you mean?'

'When I came ye said ye couldn't remember Monica workin' in the factory!'

'So?'

'So a few minutes ago ye remembered exactly when she left and that she left in a hurry! Whatever yer wife is, she's no fool!'

A bus heaved itself around the corner. Patsy signalled it to stop. She stepped aboard and never looked back. When Graves got back to the house Catherine was gone.

Beyond Pulditch Gates

CATHERINE: WEDNESDAY, 25 SEPTEMBER

She could hardly believe that she'd finally made the break. Her marriage had been a charade from the start, but from the moment Patsy Talbot arrived, Catherine knew the charade was over. She could tell by his face that Richard knew the girl he was being asked about. That was why she listened outside the door before carrying the tea tray into the room. Forgiving one-night stands and tacky affairs was one thing, but Richard had fathered a daughter by the unfortunate girl then turned his back on both. Only the remnants of whatever pride she had left stopped her from flinging the scalding tea all over him. When he left to walk Patsy Talbot to the bus, Catherine grabbed her handbag, pulled on her jacket and left.

A taxi took her to a bed-and-breakfast place in the centre of the city. The receptionist didn't blink when she arrived without any luggage. He just spun the register towards her and chanted the times for breakfast. It was that kind of a place. Ask no questions, hear no lies. Her room was sparse but clean. She reckoned it could tell some stories. Tourists. Travellers. People like her lying low. Loners passing endless hours or lovers grabbing a few illicit ones. Sitting in that small anonymous cell, she sat staring blankly out the window, and as darkness fell her loneliness was magnified by the sight of couples walking hand in hand towards the cinemas and pubs around O'Connell Street.

A taxi pulled up outside. A young couple scrambled out and the taxi-driver pulled their suitcases from the boot. Spots of confetti in their hair gave the game away. Newlyweds. The girl skipped up the steps and the man followed carrying their cases. Catherine was distracted by a fly beating maniacally against the windowpane. She pushed the window open and brushed it out with her hand. Minutes later she heard voices and footsteps on the corridor outside. A door opened and closed. There was silence for a few moments, then a woman's voice shrieked playfully. A man laughed in reply. She used to shriek like that when Richard chased her round the bedroom when they first became lovers. I'm coming to get you, and he would. More shrieks and laughter drifted down the hall. Catherine couldn't bear to listen. She pulled on her jacket, went quietly out of the room and down the stairs. She said goodnight to the receptionist, but he never lifted his eyes from his paper.

GREALISH'S: MIDNIGHT, WEDNESDAY, 25 SEPTEMBER

They were all maggot-arsed, elephants, twisted, palatic. Even Saint Joseph had overshot on shandy. They'd eaten all the sambos, sung all the songs, told and re-told all the stories. The barman was roaring a time-honoured mantra.

'Time now gents, please! Have yiz no homes ta go ta?'

One by one he moved the boys outside but Barney held on to the last.

'Lass mah stannin'!' he insisted. 'Lass mah stannin' ... swishes off de lise!'

The barman knew Barney of old. It was best and quickest to concede. He nodded towards the light switches that were hidden behind the door.

'Be me guest!'

Barney did the honours, and as Grealish's plunged into darkness, he cried a last farewell.

'G'nite Cowboy! Yippiiayye! Yippiioohh!'

The barman pushed Barney out into the night and locked the door behind him. Timmy Talbot had the boys gathered in a swaying huddle on the path outside. A hand reached out and pulled

Beyond Pulditch Gates

Barney into ruck. On an unspoken signal they gave it one last blast of 'An Old Cowpoke'. It was rough and it was ready, but they stuck together just like The Cowboy always said they should. One for all and all for one. Brothers. Musketeers. Mohicans. A bunch of footless tough guys bawling like lost sheep into the darkness.

CATHERINE: MIDNIGHT, WEDNESDAY, 25 SEPTEMBER

Catherine heard the singing as she eased down the steps of the quay wall. The singers were on the opposite bank, a huddle of shadows made ghost-like by a streetlight over their heads. She was grateful for their unintentional company. If only Richard had told her about that girl. They'd have found her and her the baby and loved them both and everything could have been all right. She moved to the lip of the lowest step. Yippieeayye, Yippieeoohh drifted across the moon-spangled water. Her father often talked about an old union man who used to sing that song. She tried not to think about her father in case her courage might fail. If that happened, she would have to go back to Richard and be like that trapped fly, forever beating her head off an invisible wall of pain and humiliation. She took a long deep breath, and fixing her gaze on the moon, she stepped outwards. Within moments the river had embraced her in darkness, silence and peace.

chapter 12

TIMES OF CHANGE

The Talbots bought Man-in-the-Mirror's house and moved in early in 1969. Scarfe Terrace was a quiet place that sat among a jigsaw of other terraces tucked in behind the unending chaos of the North Circular Road. Number seven had two small bedrooms, a bathroom and a tiny box-room upstairs. Downstairs there was a sitting-cum-dining-room and a kitchenette that led out to a small back yard. Timmy got one of the sparks to rewire the place, then he decorated it from top to bottom. When Patsy moved in she thought she had died and gone to Heaven. They finally had their own hall-door, not to mention a bathroom, a hot-press and swan-necked taps over the sink in the kitchenette. They had a house-warmer, and all the neighbours from Larnham Street came to admire the purchase. Mrs Coffey said Buckingham Palace had nothing on it and that if she ever won the Sweep, she'd buy the one next door.

Exactly one year later, Pulditch Two had its housewarmer as the first of its generators came on stream. It had three times the

Beyond Pulditch Gates

output of a unit in Pulditch One. In 1972, a second unit came online. At first Pulditch held its own against the newcomers, but gradually the cracks began to show. The plant had been flogged for thirteen years and had started to throw up faults that had never appeared before. Lines of burners failed, boilers developed leaks and reliable motors suddenly flashed out. Hard work and overtime kept the show on the road, but it was always an uphill battle. By the end of 1973, the average working week pushed out to fifty-six hours, but the leaks and faults just kept on coming. The place needed a complete refurbishment and the boys were blue in the face demanding that Graves should loosen the purse-strings, but every time they met him, he'd just smile and shrug his shoulders. It was almost as if he could hear the distant sound of bulldozers.

Meanwhile in Larnham Street the bulldozers were already at work. The Corpo had finally conceded that the place wasn't fit for human habitation. They began to move people out to new houses and demolish the old ones as they left. The trouble was that the new houses were in vast, soulless schemes far outside the city. In number fifteen, both Lily Caffrey and Mrs Coffey refused to budge unless they were offered something closer to home. They forged an unshakeable alliance and stuck it out together for a full twelve months until theirs was the only house in Larnham Street that was still standing. The Corpo finally threatened them with an eviction notice, but Mrs Coffey beat them to the punch. Before they could serve it she went quietly in her sleep to join her husband, Padso.

She was waked at home and all the old neighbours turned up to pay their respects. The following evening, the men carried her coffin from the house to Dominick Street Church. They took it in relays, with Timmy out front quietly calling the changes. The women walked behind the coffin carrying mass cards and flowers. Among them a heartbroken Patsy supported the hunched and sobbing figure of Lily Caffrey. During the year she and Mrs Coffey had battled together, Patsy discovered that despite her iceberg exterior there was a brave and human side to the woman after all. They walked together in that solemn procession as old neighbours united in a sad farewell to an old friend, an old street and a way of life that was disappearing all over the city.

Within weeks, number fifteen was levelled and Lily Caffrey was living in an old-folk's flat near the Basin in Phibsboro. Patsy visited her from time to time in the years that followed. They'd sit at her fire and drink tea as they recalled old times and old neighbours. Lily would ask after Timmy and especially about Jack even though Patsy noticed that, whenever they talked about babies or children, she would go quiet and stare into the fire. Those were the times when some great burden would darken her soft, sorrowful eyes. It would take many years, many visits and the country to be thrown into turmoil before Lily Caffrey told her story. That story would launch Patsy Talbot into the eye of what was to become Ireland's second and most unforgiving civil war.

part 3

chapter 13

PULDITCH: THURSDAY, 24 FEBRUARY 1983

It was night-time and Timmy and Hairy were out at the pump-house on the riverfront. They were waiting for a crane to arrive so that they could replace the filter gates on the cooling water pumps with steel blanks. The blanks were to be lowered at extreme low tide and that wasn't due until midnight, so the lads leaned on the safety rail and smoked as they stared out onto the river. Hairy nosed a stream of smoke that ghosted off into the chilly darkness.

'I suppose Gussie was moanin' about the overtime?'

Timmy threw his eyes to heaven.

'Ye'd think the fucker was payin' us out of his own pocket!'

'Ye know, Timmy the more things change, the more they stays the same. Twenty-five year ago Gussie was actin' the sack an' we marched out over a shaggin' theodolite!'

'So?'

'Gussie is still acting the sack an' tomorrow we'll go marchin' out the gate again!'

Timmy took a deep pull on his cigarette.

'The lads in that flour-mill need all the support they can get especially now that some o' them is in the slammer ... and we know what that's like!'

'Is it true the mill was bought out be a gang o' Brits?'

'So I hear.'

'What's their story?'

'They say the place is inefficient, but the truth is that they want to close it down, take Irish wheat over t' England and sell Paddy Gobshite back the flour!'

Hairy spat his anger down into the water.

'Them fuckers were at that durin' the Famine an' now some prick of a judge locks up the workers for tryin' ta stop them! Every man in Dublin should be outside Mountjoy in the mornin'!'

'Well,' Timmy said, 'we'll be there anyway!'

He knew all the lads were behind him on the flour-mill business. Earlier that afternoon, he'd seen flashes of the old spirit as they composed a letter of protest to hand in at the prison. It was good to see it, because the flour-mill lads weren't the only ones facing the road. There were moves on to dump Pulditch One on the scrapheap.

The place was already 'mothballed'. Though Graves insisted that the shut down was temporary, the signs were ominous. They hadn't produced a flicker of power since the day two hitmen, otherwise known as accountants, arrived from head office. Tony Haverty and Robert Black were young, stone-faced and deadly, a pair of ruthless bean-counters intent on listing the scalp of Pulditch One on their CVs. Their first move was to set doubts in the minds of the staff about the future of the place. On the first day they arrived, Haverty said it could only be saved if a third of the

Beyond Pulditch Gates

staff were let go and there was a rise in demand for electricity. A week later, Black was talking of a complete refurbishment and taking on staff rather than letting them go.

Barney and Timmy met with Graves and demanded to know who was running the place. Graves said he was and that Haverty and Black were only advisors. He swore the refurbishment was just awaiting the nod from head office and that when it was finished the place would run for another twenty-five years. A week later he announced the refurbishment was off and sent letters to everyone over fifty offering them an early retirement deal. Barney went ballistic and rang Red Kearns, wanting to know what the hell was going on. Kearns said there was no law stopping people from writing letters.

The meetings in the locker room were long, hot and heavy, but despite the arguments many decided to go. Clean and Oily Paddy were both pushing sixty, so retirement was on their horizon anyway. Fixit's wife had developed heart trouble, so he decided to stay home to look after her. Fukkit was lost without his sidekick and packed in soon after him. The boys reckoned Horizontal Harvey left only so he could stay in bed all day. Barney had only weeks to go, but he stuck to his post right up to the very last. On the day before his sixty-fifth birthday he told Graves to stick his gold watch and farewell speech, handed the shop steward's badge to Timmy and brought the lads up to Grealish's for a piss-up. No one saw or heard from him since.

Timmy's reverie was broken by the blast of a ship's horn as the night ferry to Holyhead slid away from its moorings. It moved downriver towards them, and as it passed, Timmy spotted a woman leaning over one of the rear deck-rails. She had the collar of her coat pulled up around her face. Hairy was watching her too.

'I wonder how many are on it tonight?' he sighed into the darkness.

'Passengers?' Timmy asked.

'No. Women goin' for abortions.'

There was an unusual barb in Hairy's voice, so Timmy picked his words carefully.

'The crowd who wants this pro-life referendum says a few hundred goes every year, but the crowd that's against it says it's as much as five thousand!'

Hairy gripped the rail until his knuckles turned white.

'Five hundred or five thousand they shouldn't have t' go at all. If it has to be done then it should be done here. No way should we be shippin' women off to England for them to do our dirty work.'

'That dog's been sleepin' for years, Hairy, ould son, and we're better off lettin' it lie.'

'Jaysus Timmy, it's not like you to dodge a fight.'

'Oh, I don't mind fightin' if it'll get me somewhere, but that's one row that'll tear this bloody country apart! The Civil War will have nothin' on it!'

Timmy: Friday, 25 February

Timmy had just clocked on when a phone call came through from Red Kearns. Timmy was surprised because, as Kearns's cars and double chins grew bigger, his contact with the lads diminished in proportion. He'd become a head honcho in the union and to show how well he was doing he took to smoking thick Havana cigars. Mackerel said it was like watching short bits of sewer pipe being shoved in and out of a pig's arse. Timmy was imagining that fearsome sight when he lifted the phone.

'Timmy Talbot here.'

'Timmy? It's me.'

'Me who?'

'Red Kearns!'

'Ah, be Jaysus, Lazarus 'imself! When did yew wake up?'

'Don't act the smartarse. It's about this prison protest. Yew know when it comes to contempt o' court this union doesn't want to know.'

'What's fuckin' new, Kearnsie? Yiz left us swingin' in '68 as well. And it's not 'this' union, it's 'our' fuckin' union and we'll say who or what we won't support. We're the breadbasket o' Europe, but the bleedin' Brits get t' grind our flour!'

'Timmy, Timmy! Look at the figures. That mill just isn't efficient!'

'Ah, that's the same shite we're gettin' down here. D'youse just swally everythin' they tell yiz or do they shove it up yer arses when yiz bend over?'

'The word t'day is efficiency.'

'My arse! It's fuckin' profit!'

'Right, go marching! But when the shit hits the fan don't come looking for me!'

'I wouldn't bother me bollix. I swear t' God, Kearnsie but I'd get to see the Dali Bleedin' Lama quicker nor I'd get t' see yew!'

The row was still on Timmy's mind as he led the lads across the junction at Summerhill and onto the North Circular Road. There they fell in behind a line of other protesters and in turn other groups fell in behind them. They'd knocked together a banner using a dust sheet and brush handles. It read, PULDITCH WORKERS PROTEST. A woman waved out from a window.

'Good on yiz, lads! It's about time someone showed a bit o' balls!'

A hundred yards further on the reaction was different. A van driver leaned out from his cab and gave them the fingers.

'Get back to work yiz shower o' wankers! No wonder me light bill's so dear!'

When they reached the junction at Dorset Street, cars, lorries and buses were gridlocked into a massive traffic jam. Timmy checked his watch. It was just eleven o'clock. The crowd was so big they'd fallen behind schedule. He was glad he'd sent The Pox, Hairy, Mackerel and The Child ahead by taxi. They were in their good clobber so they'd look the part when they handed in the Pulditch letter at the prison. They'd be out by the time the rest of them got there. Then they'd all march up to the flour-mill together.

MOUNTJOY: FRIDAY, 25 FEBRUARY

The Governor was only fourteen days from retirement and hoping for a handy sail before tying-up for good. Then the shower in a nearby flour-mill gave the fingers to a judge and got themselves flung in the slammer. His slammer. He still had nightmares about the Pulditch gang back in '68. The crowd in Justice were still scorpy over him calling their boss a funeral-faced fucker, even if he did look like a basset hound that wouldn't get a jump with a fistful of fivers. Honour was bruised and the Governor had been trying to ease the bruising ever since. He had good reason. Justice always asked ex-governors to sit on review bodies in the prison service. Prison Review Boards were known in the trade as the Bisto Express. They never stopped and never ran out of gravy.

Though it was the last thing he wanted he had to invite a delegation up from Justice to see how well he could handle the flour-mill mess. His plan was simple. He'd get them tanked with wine and stuffed with goodies. Then he'd give them a quick scout around the place and get them out before they knew what hit them. He checked his watch. The delegation was late but then the

Beyond Pulditch Gates

roads around the place were chock-a-block with protesters. He rang to check that CJ was at gate to meet them. It took him years to discover why the staff called him CJ. It was short for Calamity Joe. He knew what they meant. The riot in the recreation hall and the fire in the laundry baskets was bad enough, but when CJ closed the wrong valve and almost blew the roof off the boiler-house, it was time to act. The safest thing to do was to promote him out of harm's way, so the Governor made him prison PRO. Then he told him that under the Official Secrets Act he couldn't say a word to anyone. All he had to do was run the Christmas party, the staff sports day and get the 'Jesus Saves' mob to visit the inmates.

He ran over the catering side again. Justice were sending four bodies, so he had more than enough grub laid on. In the room below, canapés, pâté and grapes surrounded a side of smoked salmon. He had even laid on King Edward cigars. He wondered again about the wisdom of leaving CJ in charge even for the first half-hour. He'd gone down earlier to check that the white wine was chilled. When he asked CJ if the red wine was breathing the gobshite put a bottle to his ear to check. Still, he reckoned it was worth the risk. He wanted the Justice mob well soused before he made a fire-brigade entrance as the busiest man in the place.

Happy with the loaves-and-fishes bit, he switched to the security side. The place was surrounded by coppers, and apart from small groups handing in letters, the marchers wouldn't get within fifty yards of the gates. Every landing was manned, so no one could try hara-kiri by beating their heads off a cell door or do another you-know-who from a cell window. Cats, riot squads, shotguns and laundry baskets were either banned or padlocked. Every extinguisher was primed and ready. All he had to do was sit back and let it happen.

PATSY: FRIDAY, 25 FEBRUARY

Patsy usually walked straight up the North Circular Road to Phibsboro whenever she went to visit Lily Caffrey, but Timmy advised her to stay clear of the prison because of the protest over the flour-mill lads. She decided she'd take a detour and while she was at it to take a stroll through Larnham Court. It was wider than the street it replaced. On one side the faces of dour red-bricked flats were slashed with balconies of brightly coloured doors. On their end walls silver-sprayed graffiti proclaimed a raft of messages. Anto luvs Tina, Tina luvs Anto, MUFC, Chelsee, and Gosser issa wankir. The other side of Larnham Court was a hotch-potch of squat offices, a snooker hall, a launderette, a chipper, a pub and a corner shop that overcharged for everything. Patsy paused opposite where number fifteen had stood. It never failed to amuse her that a place that was often without water ended up as a plumbers' suppliers. A man was standing at the door.

'Ye okay, Missus?'

'Just lookin'! I lived here when it was Larnham Street.'

'What's that? Ten year ago?'

'Fourteen. Nearly fifteen. It frightens me t' think about it.'

'Well, ye know what they say, Missus ... time an' tide!'

She smiled. He smiled. She walked on and the memories walked on with her.

Half-an-hour later, Patsy and Lily were either side of the fire in Lily's tiny sitting room. Over tea and toast Lily heard all the news since Patsy's last visit. As ever, her first concern was for Timmy and 'young' Jack. She still talked of Jack as a boy although he was a grown man. As always there was a trace of sadness in her voice whenever she talked about him. Patsy often wondered if she saw him as the son she wanted but never had.

Beyond Pulditch Gates

Lily topped up their teacups while Patsy told her about her latest venture.

'Did I tell ye I'm elected onto a committee for a women's club?' she said.

'Well fair play t' ye, Patsy! And what club is that?'

'It's one we started ourselves. The parish gave us the use of an old school stores. It's not very posh but it does. We have a play-group in the mornin's for the babies, bingo Monday and Wednesday nights, and the last two Fridays people came an' gave talks.'

'What kind o' talks?'

'The first was adult education and second was about credit unions. I was lookin' forward to the one this week but it's off.'

'Why so?'

'It was about this abortion referendum. One o' the committee set it up, but another wouldn't have the word mentioned, never mind discussed. The members split right down the middle, half for, half against!'

Patsy saw a look of deep distress trace across the old woman's face. Lily said nothing as she hauled herself out of her chair and went into her bedroom. Moments later she reappeared carrying a small photograph. She handed it to Patsy.

'I've been wanting to tell somebody before it's too late.'

It was a very old sepia-coloured snapshot of a young, fresh-faced soldier in uniform.

'Who is it?' Patsy asked.

'My boyfriend.'

'Your ... your boyfriend!'

Lily never lifted her eyes from the dancing flames of the fire.

'His name was Johnny Thompson. It was taken in January 1917. He'd just signed up for the British Army. He was eighteen,

293

I was two years younger. The night before he left we were 'together'... and later I discovered I was expecting.'

Patsy was stunned. She fished for words but caught none. Tears began to stream down the old woman's face.

'My mother...'

'Your mother what? Lily? What did your mother do?'

'She brought me to a woman. Did it on her kitchen table. Pain! Awful ... Awful pain! I'm damned, Patsy! I told a priest. He said I'd never see the face o' God!'

'Yew are not damned! Priest or no he'd no right to say that to ye!'

'But he said my baby went to Limbo because it wasn't baptised! I've prayed and prayed. I spent every penny I had on masses. I go to the chapel mornin', noon an' night and I beg God to take my baby inta Heaven!'

Patsy took the shuddering woman into her arms.

'Don't! Don't tear yerself up like this!'

'But it has to be faced, Patsy. The radio says ye could fill Croke Park with them that's had it done in the past few year!'

'I know! They're goin' out every night of the week!'

Lily gripped her arm so tight it was hurting.

'They're out there, Patsy! So do talk about it! Don't leave them t' suffer like I did!'

Patsy just held Lily and let her cry out her loss and loneliness. She knew no words could ease the awful emptiness the old woman was feeling, because she felt the same emptiness every time she thought of her own dead babies. As they rocked together, Patsy realised that Lily's fearsome reputation around Larnham Street was just a moat she created to keep people away. Her sour face and coolness towards neighbours was all a screen to prevent her terrible secret being discovered. Her penny-pinching, once the talk

Beyond Pulditch Gates

of the street, was now a badge of honour, because every one of those pennies had gone to free the soul of her baby from Limbo.

As Patsy walked home, she was haunted by the image of a young girl being pinned to a table while a stranger gouged at her insides with a knitting needle. She thought of all the women she knew, relations, friends and neighbours. Did something like that ever happen to any of them? There was no way of knowing because to the Irish mind no scar meant no scandal. An old rhyme ran across her mind. Seven for a secret that mustn't be told. Couldn't be told. Wouldn't be told. Women like Lily Caffrey had to suffer their pain and shame in silence. Patsy felt an unquenchable anger rise inside her. She remembered a cold, damp morning in 1968 when she wandered the streets with tears of rage and frustration rolling down her cheeks, but this anger was much too cold for tears. She swore a silent oath that the talk on abortion would go ahead in the women's club even if she had to give the bloody thing herself.

SISTER FRANCES: FRIDAY, 25 FEBRUARY

She took over as superior of St Jude's in 1980. One of her first moves was to give the go-ahead for the work on Hell's Acre to begin. Man-in-the-Mirror obliged with a will, and soon the walls around the plot were reduced to knee-height. He put a rose-bed in the centre of the plot and lawned the rest. Sister Frances ordered numbered granite tablets and used these to mark the positions of the various graves. She had been standing at the plot for a long time in the cold February sun when he came and stood beside her.

'A bit nippy t' be out here an' no cloak on ye, Sister.'

The nun smiled, but he could see that she was troubled.

'Somethin' up?'

She sighed and wrung her hands together.

'Well, I suppose you may as well hear it now as later. I've had word from our mother house. St Jude's is being sold to a developer. We've to be out by mid-September!'

'No!' he cried. 'I mean, they can't sell this place!'

'I'm afraid they have to. Our order hasn't had a new recruit in two years. Most of our sisters are elderly, and it costs a lot of money to look after them. We have to get it whatever way we can.'

'But ... what about the girls that's livin' here?'

'They'll be offered a place in another convent or in sheltered housing if they prefer.'

'And these girls?' he nodded towards the grave plaques. 'What'll happen them?'

Sister Frances sighed again.

'They'll be exhumed.'

Man-in-the-Mirror felt his blood run cold.

'Exhumed! Ye mean, dug up!'

'It'll be done slowly and carefully. We'll cremate whatever remains are found and re-bury the ashes in Glasnevin cemetery.'

'That's criminal! Haven't the poor souls suffered enough?'

'More than anyone ever should,' she whispered. 'More than anyone ever should.'

'An' the nun's that's buried under them crosses? Will they be burned too?'

'No, they'll be moved to a plot in one of our other houses.'

'Jesus,' he whispered. 'Dear and merciful Jesus.'

They stood together, each wrapped in their own thoughts. He felt rage and fear in equal measure. Rage at what would happen to the girls who were buried in Hell's Acre. Fear because death, his old tormentor, would soon cast its menacing shadow over every corner of his own private paradise. As for Sister Frances, she fixed her gaze on the plaque above Monica Dillon's grave. As she did so a shiver ran through her. She wrapped her arms tightly around herself but the shivering got worse. There was unfinished business in that place. She closed her eyes and prayed that for good or ill, that business would soon be finished, otherwise it would haunt her soul forever.

GUSSIE: FRIDAY, 25 FEBRUARY

It was fifteen years since Gussie had lost the old homestead to the anonymous bidder from London. He was sure the gods had abandoned him, but as time passed he saw what they were at. While he steadily built up his stash, they solved his problem with Dixie Fanning. Sergeant McBride developed diabetes and had to pack in the murder squad. The cop who took over called to see him but Gussie just repeated the gobshite routine. He didn't bother him again, which was just as well because Gussie was on thin ice in his digs without visits from the cops. Mrs Gorman was getting too old and frail to run the digs so her daughter, Olive, took over. She was a grumpy bitch. She wanted to turn the house into an upmarket bed-and-breakfast, so she set about dumping all the lodgers. She managed to ditch them all except Gussie because her mother wouldn't see her longest-serving guest out on the street. Gussie knew that as long the old girl hung on he'd be safe, but by the law of averages they were already stringing her harp. Once again he pleaded with the gods to help him and once again, they did. The auctioneers who handled things after his mother died put an ad in the *Indo* for a cottage. It wasn't far from the old place.

Gussie rang, but the auctioneer was out and an office junior took the call. Gussie smelt greenhorn, gave a fictitious name and practically offered to buy the cottage there and then. The junior was thrilled and once Gussie had him hooked he began pumping him about other sites around the area. Eventually he described his old home.

'D'ya know that place at all, at all?'

'O' course I do! A woman from England owns it.'

Gussie nearly shit himself. The junior blundered on.

'She's left it lyin' for years, but the builders is just finished doin' it up.'

'Builders?'

'Yea! T' tell the truth ye wouldn't know the place!'

Gussie cut the call and rang to check times for buses to Cavan.

According to the timetable he was supposed to be well out past Ashbourne, but instead the bus was stuck in the middle of a traffic jam that stretched the length of Dorset Street. It looked like every bloody communist in the city had descended on Mountjoy to back up their flour-mill buddies. Gussie fumed but there was nothing he could do about it. All he could do was to clutch his holdall between his feet and go over in his mind how he would handle things. He wouldn't mess about. He'd find out who owned the place and then lob twenty grand in cash onto their table. They might take it, but then again they might haggle. If push came to shove, he was prepared to go as far as twenty-five. He had gradually converted his stash into one hundred pound notes. He was sure that the sight of them bundled in wads of fifty would quickly convince the most reticent seller to hand over the keys.

He sneaked the wrapping off a barley sweet while it was still in his pocket and slipped it into his mouth. Then he pulled his *Indo* from his pocket. He unfolded the paper and began to read and

Beyond Pulditch Gates

crunch piggishly on the sweet. A woman who was sitting beside him craned her neck to see if there was a vacant seat anywhere else on the bus. Stale sweat was bad enough but she drew the line at being drenched in spit and bits of barley sugar all the way to Monaghan. Then the crunching got even more violent as Gussie saw that the front page was filled with nothing but stories about strikes and sit-ins. It was 1968 all over again. Workers had occupied a paper-mill in Clondalkin for over a year and the dockers were in the wars over job cuts. As for the flour-mill gang, they'd dragged their dispute all over the show between sit-ins, injunctions, law courts and jail. At one stage their wives sat in with them. Gussie reckoned if anyone was wearing knickers it was the judges and politicians, but he expected nothing better with the Labour Party in power.

The Brits were way ahead. Rumour had it that McGregor would move from British Steel to their Coal Board. Between him and Thatcher they'd put manners on that renegade Scargill. Once the miners were whipped into line, the rest of the reds would quickly put their hands up. Gussie reckoned Maggie Thatcher had more balls than all the Y-fronts in Whitehall put together. Even though she was a woman and the reds called her Poison Pussy, there was no denying she had it bang on. A good worker was like a good dog. It did what it was told when it was told and was grateful for what it got. Then when it was no longer able or willing, you simply got shut of it. He wished it could be like that in Pulditch One. Graves said they'd both get cushy numbers in head office if they could only dump the place into the Liffey. The problem as usual was the gang in the locker rooms. The fuckers just wouldn't go.

Gussie turned to the inside pages of the paper and his humour improved immediately. Support for Bishop's Abortion Speech, a headline declared. A few days before, one of the bishops described abortion as murder. Now the papers were full of reaction, most of it backing him up. Gussie farted with satisfaction. At long last the lefties and their bra-burning bitches would get their comeuppance. The woman beside him got up and moved to the far end of the bus. He was glad. With her gone he wouldn't have to sneak the sweets out of his pocket.

A View from a Window: Friday, 25 February

Though she was pushing past her sell-by date, the black-haired one still took customers. They were mostly middle-aged to elderly men including a lot of priests and brothers. Her married clients were mostly professionals, members of clubs and all-round pillars of society. Wary of the younger women and rumours of terrible diseases, they stuck to the tried and tested. They were happy with the schoolboy stuff, the suspenders, the fish-nets, the high heels and being told they were hung like a stallion. The latter was invariably untrue but ensured a good tip. The dog collars were as vicious as ever, but she weeded out the real headcases and put up with the rest. Her clients knew the rules. All payments were in cash. Extras were negotiable. For hand shandies she supplied tissues and for anything else she supplied condoms.

Her landlord was her 'organiser'. He didn't like the word pimp. He kept an eye on things for a stiff rent plus two-quid-a-client commission. The two-roomed flat where she worked was above a shop. One room had a door leading out onto a landing where every so often a payphone would ring. She'd answer it. A code word would be given and an arrangement made. At the agreed time, the hall-doorbell would ring. She'd go down, admit the client, they'd go up to the room nearest the landing, do the business, he'd pay up

Beyond Pulditch Gates

and slip quietly downstairs again. Between that and the welfare she made enough to keep the landlord sweet and take care of her mate who spent most of her time sleeping in a reclining chair in the other room of the flat. That room was off limits to the customers.

In there was a woman who was once red-haired but who was red-haired no longer. Her once blazing and curling tresses were now lank and hanging like grey straw on either side of her pinched and leathery face. She was dying, but unlike so many others who'd been on the game, she had somewhere to go and someone to look after her. The black-haired one still made her laugh by describing clients with white, hairless beer-bellies, knock-knees and dentures. Funniest of all were the ones with walnut balls and periwinkle penises who promised not to hurt her. The ones who did hurt her she didn't talk about, but the red-haired one would know when they called. She would hear the stifled cries coming from the room next door and then she too would cry, knowing that some twisted bastard was paying extra to hurt the only friend she had in the world.

The black-haired one had just left one of her regular clients down to the door. He was a barrister, and as always she'd spend ages listening to the gobshite crying for his mother before wanking him into his handkerchief. As usual, she charged him double the going rate and send him packing with the soggy cloth folded into the breast pocket of his handmade suit. She had no qualms about fleecing fuckers who had anything to do with the law, because when it came to fleecing, those bastards wrote the book. She came back upstairs and brought a cup of tea in to her friend.

'Jaysus, there's some traffic jam out there.'

'Somethin's up in Mountjoy,' the red-haired one whispered. 'I heard it on the radio.'

301

The black-haired one helped her out of her chair.

'Here, have a gander at this lot!'

They moved to the window and pulled the net curtain aside. Below them, the north-bound side of Dorset Street was blocked solid. To the right the junction at the North Circular road was alive with bodies and banners all heading up towards Mountjoy. Then the red-haired one gripped her mate by the arm.

'I don't believe it! It couldn't be!'

'What couldn't be?'

'In the bus! Lookit! Readin' the paper! It's him! Bubbles an' creosote!'

Though it was a long time since her mate punched it, the black-haired one knew the big bullocky head straight off. They looked at each other and laughed. They laughed so much that tears rolled down their cheeks. In full view of the world they hugged each other and cried. They cried at first because it was funny but then they cried because of all the hate, pain and loneliness that had been emptied into their bodies. They cried for fortunes they'd handed to pimps. They cried because the red-haired one was dying.

Richard Graves: Friday, 25 February

Haverty and Black were with Richard Graves in his office. Haverty slid a copy of a letter to him.

'We're extending the retirement deal to all staff regardless of age. They'll all get a copy of that first thing Monday morning. What we need from you is more pressure on them to take it.'

Graves threw his pen onto the table.

'I've already put chains on all the main valves and blanked off the cooling pumps. What do you want me to do, put thumbscrews on the fuckers!'

Beyond Pulditch Gates

Black stayed cool.

'We need them chewing their nails and one sure way to do that is to make their day as long and pointless as possible! People in overalls need to feel they've earned their freight. If they don't, they think there's no point in coming to work. When you get them thinking that way, you have them!'

Haverty backed him up.

'We've six months to have padlocks on the gates. Any longer and we'll be sending one of these letters to ourselves! Understood?'

Graves eyeballed the two sitting opposite him.

'And what about me? Where do I sit when Pulditch One is one big padlock?'

Haverty laughed.

'Like we've said, there are plenty of comfortable suites in head office!'

'I don't want that moron Gussie Gallagher hanging out of my neck when I go there.'

Black flipped the lid of his briefcase closed.

'Don't worry, Mister Graves, we'll take care of him! Now, we'll leave you to it.'

They smiled and left.

Graves stood at the window of his office and watched them drive away. He had no problem doing their dirty work. It was them he couldn't abide. No doubt some slick consultant charged a packet to turn them into such obnoxious pricks. On the other hand, if the bods on top were happy with the way they worked, then he'd have to play along. The phone rang.

'Mister Richard Graves, please,' a female voice chirruped.

'Speaking.'

'One moment, I have Mister Kearns on the line for you.'

303

There was a click and Red Kearns came on.

'Howye! It's me! Ye free for a drink?'

Graves was caught for a moment. He hadn't heard a peep from Kearns in ages and he wondered what mischief the little cretin had up his sleeve.

'What's the occasion?' Graves probed.

'A benefit meeting.'

'And who'll benefit?'

'Both of us!'

'In that case Mister Kearns, I'd love to go for a drink!'

'Good! D'ya know anywhere quiet? Somewhere we can talk?'

'Let's say the Ashling Hotel bar, Parkgate Street, at one o'clock?'

'One it is,' Kearns agreed, 'but mum's the word, okay?'

'Fine, I'll see you in the bar.'

THE COMMITTEE: FRIDAY, 25 FEBRUARY

Just before the taxi stopped at the prison, Hairy went over their battle orders. 'Remember what we agreed. No way we're goin' back to tell the lads we handed the letter to some shaggin' gofer! We ask for the main man an' we stick it out to see if we can get 'im!'

'Dead right!' Mackerel nodded. 'Yew do the talkin' and we'll back ye up!'

The Pox popped his pipe from his mouth.

'Keep the poxy protest in yer pocket an' no show until we see Sittin' Bull 'imself!'

They had no need to worry. The police blocking the way to the gates were told by a prison warden called CJ to expect a taxi with four men in it, and to escort them through immediately. So The Pox, Hairy, Mackerel and The Child found themselves being ushered in by a wedge of coppers dressed in riot gear.

Beyond Pulditch Gates

The taxi pulled up. The boys got out and Hairy rapped hard on the gate. Behind it CJ was sweating bricks because the crowd from Justice hadn't shown up. There had been two false alarms but it was only protesters handing in letters. When he heard the firm confident rap on the gate he was sure it was third time lucky. He opened the fly-door in the gate and was delighted to see four flash suits. He stepped forward to greet his distinguished guests. Hairy had his best Dublin 4 accent on.

'Excewse uss! Wee wish to see dee Guvvinor!'

CJ could have kissed them.

'Oh, thank Jaysus! I mean, I'm so glad to see ye all together! Safe! At last! Here!'

Before they could blink he had them inside.

'The Governor sends his apologies. He'd love to have greeted ye in person but the man is just ssoohhh busy!'

The boys eye-signalled each other that no matter what this gobshite tried the letter was going nowhere but into the main man's fist.

Hairy sniffed sniffily.

'Our businezz is with dee persing ing charge!'

'Of course! But before you meet him how about some smoked salmon and cigars?'

'Fuck me,' Mackerel whispered to The Child. 'The bastard's tryin' t' bribe us!'

'One begs one's parding?' Hairy said icily, 'Are yew offering us an indewcmint?'

'Juice, is it? We have orange juice, apple juice and fruit juice. The red wine is breathin' in the fridge and the white stuff is already opened.'

CJ knew there was nothing like an in-depth knowledge of wine to impress people in suits. It certainly made an impression on the boys, in fact, it left them speechless. They were still in the same state when he ushered them into a room that was laid out with a spread straight from the set of Cleopatra.

'Help yerselves, gentlemen. I'll tell the Governor you've arrived.'

CJ whirled out of the room and left them to it.

Mackerel was afraid to move.

'I know they wanta keep the unions on side but this is ridiculous!'

The Child took a different view.

'The grub's improved since the last time we were here.'

'Somethin's stinkin'!' The Pox said suspiciously.

'It's the sammin,' Hairy nodded towards the fish.

'Not that stinkin'! Two minutes ago dem coppers outside wudda bet our brains into a paper bag, an' now we might as well be stannin' in the Gresham Hopoxytel. Dem there's King Edwards!'

'King Edward's what?'

The Pox looked to Heaven. Mackerel didn't give a shite about King Edward. He had a plate in his hand and was loading up faster than a docker on bonus. The others could only follow suit. There was a brief hiatus while they debated whether they'd have red or white wine but like true socialists they decided to lorry into both. The Pox homed in on the cigars. He pocketed three, lit one and blew two lazy smoke rings.

'I've been thinkin' about stranglin' me mot but things is so good in here, I'll think I'll strangle me ma-in-law as well!'

No one demurred. Doing life in a five-star hotel had a lot to recommend it.

'I wonder what's happenin' outside?' Hairy said half-interestedly. 'The boys should be up be now.'

The boys were indeed just approaching the gate. As they did, they saw four fellas in suits arguing with the coppers who were

Beyond Pulditch Gates

barring the way to the prison approach. By the stand of the bluebottles they had two chances of getting past them. Slim and fuckall. Inside the prison the phone rang in the Governor's office. He was taking a leak, so CJ answered it. It was a sergeant down at the front gate. Some fellas in suits were demanding to see the Governor, but CJ was wide to that trick.

'Listen to me, sergeant, never trust lefties in suits. You tell them to hand over their letter and then take a hike!'

The Governor came in zipping up his flies.

'Whassup?'

CJ covered the mouthpiece with his hand.

'A gang at the gate demanding to see you but I'm telling the coppers to take no shite.'

'Good man!'

CJ listened for a moment, then roared into the phone.

'Whassat? They haven't got a letter to hand in? Cheeky bastards! You tell them that if they don't fuck off outa there this minute, there's a cell here with their names on it and that's straight from the Governor!'

He slammed down the phone. The Governor was very impressed.

'Fair play, CJ! I never knew you had it in you! Now, shoot back down and keep an eye on the crowd from Justice. Gimme the half-hour and I'll follow you down'

CJ went and the Governor lay back, imagining himself chairing the next Review Board into prison reform. Months and months of meetings, expenses, flash hotels and mileage at five times the cost of the petrol. All he had to do was keep the gang from Justice sweet and it was in the bag.

chapter 14

SAINT JOSEPH: FRIDAY, 25 FEBRUARY

Saint Joseph 'marched' up to Mountjoy on his pushbike because the walk from Pulditch would have murdered his bunions. Slow pedalling behind the lads, he was thinking about the collapse of his deal with God. For years they'd had a gentleman's agreement. He looked out for God and God looked after his two abiding interests, being a carpenter in Pulditch and the lead trumpeter with the City & District Brass and Reed Band. Then, on his fifty-first birthday, God welched on their deal. He allowed him to volunteer to do a church-gate collection and there he met Henrietta.

Big-boned, blue-rinsed and dressed in a severe navy suit, she was recruiting for the Legion of Mary. She was visiting from another church where she was secretary of the White Star League, the Altar Guild, the Young Priest's Society and the Women's Sodality. As formidable as he was timid, she annexed him like Hitler did with Poland. She decided it would be nice if they went out for tea. He didn't agree or disagree, he just went. Before long she said they should 'walk out' together. He didn't agree or disagree, he just walked. Then she decided they ought to become engaged. He

Beyond Pulditch Gates

didn't agree or disagree, he just bought the ring. Then she announced they'd get married, she'd sell her house and they'd live in his. It was only then he realised that what he was facing was not so much a marriage as a military coup, but it was too late to back out.

In the weeks before the wedding, the boys in the locker room gave him some ribbing about sampling the goods before purchasing. The truth was that he hadn't even seen the goods never mind sampled them. All her hooks, zips and buttons remained securely fastened. Only once did she allow his hand to stray but her corset was so stiff he wasn't sure if it was bra-wire or breast he squeezed. On that basis their honeymoon coupling was their first. Performed in the dark, it was an unqualified disaster with his knotted pyjamas and her ankle-length nightdress only adding to the confusion. His abiding memory of his wedding night was of a frantic joust with a leathery hymen and her piercing shrieks when it finally gave way. Being his first time out, or rather his first time in, finding his stroke was difficult. Keeping it was bloody impossible with her yelping and begging the saints to make haste to help her.

After two more chaotic attempts, she declared sex pointless and messy. She reckoned that at their age it was more the companionship that mattered, though she had carefully hidden that opinion before the wedding. Passion was quickly replaced by an endless succession of illnesses, all of the feminine variety. These strange maladies allowed her to be utterly unreasonable, to scream and throw tantrums, but she expected him to understand that it wasn't her but her hormones that were to blame. It was shite. He knew it, she knew it and so did the doctors who charged a king's ransom to encourage what was nothing more than pig ignorance and pure bad temper. It was amazing how her hormones settled the minute a priest or nun called. They did likewise when her coven of toad-faced friends surrounded her bed while he played a B-movie butler moving amongst them with tea and scones.

In fairness, the City and District Brass and Reed Band gave him plenty of slack but when he continually missed practice they got a new lead trumpeter to take his place. After that he was stranded up a narrow, high-walled creek with no reverse on his paddle. He even thought of jumping ship, but Henrietta was formidable and well-connected. He'd have had every priest in the city on his head and every wit in Pulditch on his back. He finally accepted he'd just have to endure the tea-making, her bad temper and illnesses, not to mention the draughty churches and the sermons about the spread of lust, greed and general immorality. As long as he had Pulditch and the lads he had something to save his sanity but retirement, either natural or forced, was a terrifying prospect. He'd work till he was ninety if it kept him from being at home with Henrietta.

His thoughts were scattered by the sound of a rising argument between a sergeant and four men in suits who were trying to get through to the gates of the prison. Whoever they were, they were rightly pissed off at the copper, but he was taking no nonsense. He didn't have to because he was backed up by a line of blue uniforms in riot gear. A corps of press and photographers were pushing in on this little pantomime. They were pissed off because the marchers were keeping rank and discipline and there was damn all news in that. Joseph was pissed off too. Pissed off at life, his nightmare marriage, Pulditch, and a God who had reneged on their bargain. For the first time in his life he was in humour for a bloody good row so he decided he'd start one all by himself.

'Cheeeaaarrrge!' he cried. 'Cheeeaaarrrge!'

Within seconds all hell broke loose between the coppers, the pressmen and the men in suits. The marchers paused for a moment,

Beyond Pulditch Gates

but Timmy Talbot saw the danger of even stopping to look.

'Keep movin'! Nothin' to do with us! Keep in line! Keep movin'!'

The boys did as he said, although Saint Joseph waited to admire the results of his handiwork. The first ambulance was arriving when he realised how far he'd fallen behind. He had to pedal like hell to catch up on the Pulditch banner which had already disappeared around Dunphy's corner.

Meanwhile back inside the prison, the Governor finally made his grand entrance as the busiest man in the place. The minute he saw them he knew that whoever they were they certainly weren't from the Department of Justice. What they were was gee-eyed drunk on his Chablis and Beaujolais.

'Gentlemen,' CJ beamed, 'may I present dee Governor!'

The Pox rammed his big muttony paw forward.

'Very poxy pleased t' see ye again. Ye haven't changed a bit.'

'Issa fact!' Mackerel tried not to slur. 'Shome sphread! Fair do's!'

The Governor tried to scream but he couldn't. Hairy stepped forward pulling the letter of protest from his pocket.

'Maayy I shaayy ... dash on beehalf o' meeself an' the lads I wish tooo preesent yew with dis spar ... dis sparstition on behalf o' the lads what yiz have banged up!'

'Herefuckinhere!' The Child punched the air. 'What are ye havin', red or white?'

The Governor remembered where he'd seen them before.

'How the hell did you get in here?'

Mackerel pointed at CJ.

''E assed us!'

The Governor dragged CJ into a corner.

'Geddem out! Geddem out now!'

'But Boss, if I do that these four'll shaft ye for the review body!'

311

That brought the Governor to a galloping halt. CJ was pleased that his quick thinking had saved his boss yet again.

'Four of them? Did yew say four o' them? Oh, no! Oh, sweet Jesus in Heaven!'

'Whassupnow, boss?'

The Governor caught him by the throat.

'The four at the gate who you told I had a cell with their names on it! That's what's up!'

The boys swayed gently, wine glass in one hand, cigar in the other watching the drama unfold. It got even better when the Governor whipped up the phone.

'It's the Governor! Gemme the gate!'

Later versions would vary but it was generally agreed that his conversation ran something like this.

'Whose in charge down there? Yew are? Right! There were four men at the gate earlier, where are they now? No! No! Not those four fucking idiots! They're up here! These four would have had briefcases! Yes! Yes! Those four!'

There was what is often described as a pregnant pause then his knees were seen to sag.

'On their way to hospital? All four? Baton-charged? Photographers? What photographers? Pleased? Oh, yea, I'm absoshagginglutely delighted! Why didn't they go the whole hog and smash their cameras while they were at it? They did? How many? Oh, shit!'

He dropped the phone into its cradle. CJ tried to rescue something from the fiasco.

'D'ya still want me ta throw this lot out, Boss?'

'No, No! Why don't ye help them carry some goodies down to the gate!'

Beyond Pulditch Gates

Then, without as much as a farewell, cheerio, kiss-me-arse or *arrivederci*, he stormed out and went up to his office.

He thought about breaking out a shotgun to blow his brains out. He'd have blasted CJ's years before if the mindless cretin had any to aim at. He remembered when he was at school how he learned about algebra. If you wrote down the number ten then put a little two beside it meant ten multiplied by ten. This was called ten squared. If you used a thousand it was a thousand times a thousand and this was known as a thousand squared. Well, he was fucked with a little thousand beside it. The odds on him ever warming a seat on a review body were as good as Ian Paisley asking The Pope out for a pint. He scribbled 'I quit' on his notepad, skewered the note to his desk with a letter opener and put on his coat to go home. Like the soppy bit at the end of love pictures he paused to look out the window one last time. He half-laughed, half-whimpered when he saw CJ struggling across the yard with a box full of goodies. He was leading the four uninvited but well-oiled guests of the nation towards the main gate.

On the way down to his car the Governor thought about how he'd fill in his time. He could open a little garden centre, but with his luck the grass would grow down, the weeds would grow up and the plants would grow sideways. Then it clicked. His mate in the golf club was always on about the fight between Betamax and VHS to supply tapes for those new-fangled videos. His mate had the wire that Betamax would wipe the floor with VHS. That was the shot. He'd pool every penny he had, his pension, his lump sum, his shirt and open an agency for Betamax. As he slid into his car the sun finally peeped through a crack in the clouds. It was an omen. When he had made his first million, he'd ring the gang in Justice and tell them to stuff their review bodies as high as they could get them.

On the other side of the prison wall, the boys marched back down from the mill wondering where the other four had got to and if their letter of protest had been delivered. They got their answer when they turned around by the State Cinema. The four were leaning against the wall of the place. They had a box at their feet stuffed with smoked salmon, cigars, wine, bunches of grapes and a candelabrum. Timmy brought the Pulditch battalion to a halt.

'Howyiz,' The Child saluted sloppily. 'We givvum the letter!'

'In ee's hand,' The Pox confirmed. 'The posht poxshee office cuddna done it better!'

Mackerel held up a flat orange shape.

'Anywan wanna sammin?'

Timmy tried hard to sound stern.

'Geddem outa here! Talk about pissin' in front of the palace!'

Willing hands shored up the four horsemen of Pulditch and hauled them into the line of protesters. Saint Joseph pedalled behind them with the box of goodies on the carrier of his bike. The ragged line moved off again in the direction of Summerhill and their ultimate destination, the North Quays and Grealish's. Saint Joseph knew there'd be a brilliant session and sing-song but to Henrietta piss-ups were strictly taboo and besides she wanted him home early. There was a meeting in the church hall on abortion and she had to be there. That meant he'd have to be there too, but at least there'd be no rogue hormones driving her to a frenzy when he got home.

THE BLACK-HAIRED ONE: FRIDAY, 25 FEBRUARY

A group of protesters crossed back over the junction at Dorset Street and the Circular Road. A man cycled behind them with a box on the carrier of his pushbike. A few doors up from the junction a black-haired woman sat in a window watching them. Her friend

Beyond Pulditch Gates

was dozing in a chair behind her. She often wondered why women like them never formed a union and made the government legalise the game. So what if they'd be hit for PAYE. It was fuckall compared to what pimps took off them. They'd get pay increases, bonuses, danger money for taking on weirdos, and at sixty-five they'd retire with a party, a watch and a pension.

The phone on the landing rang. She ignored it. It was probably the bank manager. He rang most Fridays at lunch-time. His hobby was golf and his thing was to have her lie on the floor with her legs raised and apart so he could practice his putting across the room. Playing into the rough he called it. Though no stranger to humiliation, right then it was more than she could cope with. Her friend moaned in her sleep, disturbed by the insistent ringing of the phone. The black-haired one draped a blanket over her and went out and lifted the phone off the hook. Being in that kind of a mood, she went to her wardrobe and lifted out a small sewing box. In it was a fuzzy photograph of her mother who had died of TB shortly after she was born. She knew nothing about her father. Also in the box were receipts and papers, among them the deeds to a family grave in Glasnevin. Her granny and granduncle were the only ones buried in the plot, so she'd get it opened for the red-haired one when the time came. The grave was in a shaded spot under a tree not far from the entrance to the cemetery. The fourth and last space in it would be hers. She fingered the sewing box and the memories came flooding back.

Her granduncle had lived with her and her granny in their tiny corporation house. He died when she was twelve. She remembered him as a po-faced bachelor who didn't drink or smoke and who went to Mass every morning. People said they never heard him utter a foul word but she knew he did. He would say it whenever they played their secret game of yip-yip-a-horsy. He'd give her a shilling to take off her knickers then he'd bounce her up and down on his lap until his face turned funny and his legs shot out in front of him. He'd grip her botty really tightly then he'd jerk, jerk and jerk again. Then he'd let her botty go and sink back into the chair with a long low groan.

'Ohhhunnnsweeeetjeessuuusss!'

She knew that was kind of a curse, but she couldn't say anything because her granduncle said her all teeth would fall out if she ever told anyone about their game.

When she was fourteen the man next door played yip-yip-a-horsy with her for real. Only then did she realise the truth about her granduncle but by then the twisted ould shite was dead. The man next door said she was a grand girl and paid her ten shillings every time, though he made her swear on her granny's life that she'd never tell anyone about their arrangement. She had a great thing going until one day his wife came home early and caught them. There was an awful row between the man, his wife and her granny but it was kept between them in case the neighbours found out. The man and the woman stayed in their house, but her granny sent her to live in a hostel for wayward girls.

The people there were mostly nice but then one night one of the male wardens caught her alone and made her play yip-yip-a-horsy. He did it from behind and it was rough and very painful. Unlike her granduncle and the next-door neighbour, he didn't give her money, but like them he warned her not to tell anyone. He did it again a few days later, so she ran away. She lived rough for a while then one night in a cafe on the quays a very nice woman bought her tea and cakes. Then she took her to a man who said he'd give her money and somewhere nice to live if she worked for him. She agreed so the woman took her to a house, gave her a new dress, did her hair and took her out onto the quays with her.

Beyond Pulditch Gates

The first man who approached them was fat and smelly. He had black crooked teeth and when she was told to go with him she turned on her heel and ran. She didn't get far. The man she was working for stepped out of the shadows and dragged her into a lane. He beat her senseless, and when she came to, the fat smelly man was standing over her. Two other men played yip-yip-a-horsy with her that night. She was very sore but she earned fifteen pounds. The man she worked for took twelve and left her three and that, more or less, would be the share out for the rest of her life.

The red-haired one moaned in her sleep, so the black-haired one put away the sewing box and tucked the blanket in around her, quietly praying that she wouldn't suffer very much longer. She'd already suffered too much for too long. Her father was an alcoholic and a gambler who 'rented' her to his mates from the time she was ten. When she was thirteen she became pregnant so he took her to a quack who botched an attempt at an abortion. For weeks she lay in hospital while doctors battled to save her life. They succeeded, but she was no longer pregnant and never would be again. When she was fifteen she left her father to work for a pimp who was equally vicious, but at least she didn't have to face him across the breakfast table.

The black-haired one let her friend sleep on for a while, and then went out to the landing to replace the receiver of the phone. It rang immediately. It was the bank manager. He'd bought a new putter and wanted to try it out. She was going to tell him to get stuffed but she remembered she had a light bill to pay. She told him to be at the hall-door in an hour.

GREALISH'S: FRIDAY, 25 FEBRUARY

When they turned onto the quays, the boys saw a lorry outside Grealish's. It was stacked with gear and a man was tying it down.

Henry Hudson

Two others were carrying stuff out onto the path. As they got closer, Timmy recognised the man on the lorry. It was Paddy Hennessy. His family lived near the technical schools in Bolton Street.

'Aye, aye, Paddy! Glad to see someone earnin' a crust!'

The man spun around and recognised Timmy.

'Ah, be Jaysus! Timmy Talbot!'

He reefed home a knot then flipped down onto the path. The men shook hands.

'What's happenin'?' Timmy asked.

'Kip's closin'.'

'Closin'?' the lads all cried together.

'We're homeless!' Hairy wailed.

Timmy shook his head in disbelief.

'We were in here on Tuesday night an' no one said a dicky bird!'

Paddy shrugged his shoulders.

'It was all done on the QT! We only got the call t' clear it out this mornin' but that was up be the time we got here!'

He pointed to a sign nailed above the door.

'Sold.' The Child said sadly.

'Can we go inside?' Timmy asked.

'Help yerselves!' Paddy hauled himself up into the driver's cab. 'See ye, Timmy!'

'Mind yerself, Paddy!'

The lorry farted a sideways cloud of unburnt diesel as it lurched away.

Timmy led the boys inside. No one spoke. A million memories lay scattered on the floor. Upturned bar stools were scattered like tank traps and tables lay at crazy angles like giraffes with their front legs broken. A buckled tray claimed 'Guinness is goo' on one

Beyond Pulditch Gates

side and 'd for you' on the other. Beside the tray lay a bollixed-up cash register and a mouldy stuffed parrot in a cage.

The Child shook his head sadly.

'If The Cowboy was alive now he'd be turnin' in 'is grave!'

The Pox produced and lit a King Edward.

'Funny how this place is closin' the same as ours is. Closin' places is gettin' to be a national poxy pastime!'

After a brief powwow they decided to seek asylum in Reagan's of Tara Street.

Reagan's was a sister ship of Grealish's in that it asked nothing of its customers other than that they behaved. The lads arrived, settled down, rounds of drinks were called, and as Timmy waited up at the bar, he asked the barman what happened to Grealish's.

'That whole site,' the barman declared, 'from the Custom House t' the Sheriff Street flats, will be worth a fortune in a few years' time.'

'Gerroff! The coppers go down there in tens!'

'I'm well in with one o' the planners in the Corpo an' he says the wide boys is already movin' to get their hands on it!'

'Why so?'

The barman planked three pints onto the counter.

'Because it's within pissin' distance of the city and the railway an' river's beside it!'

'So?'

'So, the wide boys buy up all the buildin's they can an' leave them t' rot. When they're in a bad enough state they get the okay t' knock them down. Then they join all the sites together, wrongfoot the locals, an' bingo, yer up to yer arse in office blocks!'

'How d'ya mean, 'wrongfoot' the locals?'

'Promise them jobs when the offices is built. Ye know, security, cleanin' the jacks and makin' the tea but it'll be live horse an' get grass. Once dem boys have what they want they'll tell the locals to go fuck themselves!'

Timmy carried the pints back to their table where Hairy was on his feet reliving their prison visit for the benefit of the others.

'Issafact! The warder fella is like a fish with its tit in a trap an' the Governor fella is goin' ballistic. Then The Child asks 'im, whaddya havin', red or white?'

The place exploded into laughter. Timmy laughed too but his mind was elsewhere. What applied to Grealish's applied to the flour-mill and could soon apply to Pulditch. The gospel according to Thatcher made flesh by men in suits. Just wrongfoot the locals and you're laughing.

RICHARD GRAVES: FRIDAY, 25 FEBRUARY

Richard Graves once spent a lot of time in the bar of the Ashling Hotel. It was a quiet place near the entrance to the Phoenix Park where people could meet unnoticed and undisturbed. Now he was in there again sipping a gin-and-tonic and waiting for Kearns to show up. A woman was drinking coffee at a table at the other end of the bar. A sheaf of papers was on the table in front of her. Though she was well dressed, she wasn't anything great to look at. Well into her forties, plumpish with blonde hair straight from a bottle. On the plus side, she was wearing a wedding ring and to Richard Graves a married woman alone in a bar was always worth investigating. Watching her reminded him of all the other women he brought there when he was on the hunt behind Catherine's back. He wondered where they all ended up. Probably married with a couple of kids. He imagined them dressed in white and gliding tight-legged up the aisle. Here comes the bride and the poor thick at the altar thinking he'd be first to burst her balloon when she'd already had more mounts than Lester Piggot.

Beyond Pulditch Gates

Not that he blamed the poor thicks up at the altar. All men are blinded by pussy at some time in their lives. Even in his old age, his father just couldn't resist it but unfortunately Theo's final dalliance cost him everything, including Richard's inheritance. The first he knew of it was when Theo rang crying and cursing that he'd been swindled by a fiery little French piece less than half his age. She'd sucked him into her bed and then into bankrolling a property deal in France. Of course, there was no property and no deal only her and her fraudster boyfriend who had set up the sting. Theo snuffed it a few weeks later and Richard had to pay for his funeral but what could he say? It was genetic. To be a Graves was to have you brains wired direct to your bollocks.

Kearns arrived and apologised for being late. Graves offered him a drink. He called a pint of shandy. Fuss glistened on his brow. His double chin mooned downwards, hiding the knot of his tie. Rings of dry sweat whitened under his armpits. Graves sipped at his gin.

'Well, Mister Kearns, what's this with the cloak-and-dagger routine?'

'Monkee no see, monkee no say. Now, I hear there's them that wants t' put the boot in down in Pulditch. Make life very uncomfortable for people.'

'You're well informed, as usual,' Graves quipped.

'Look, the gang down there is a breed apart. Push them too hard and there's no tellin' what they'll do. I told them not to picket Mountjoy this mornin' and they told me to go fuck meself. We haveta keep a lid on things or we'll all end up in the shite!'

A lounge boy brought Kearns his drink. He grabbed it and gulped greedily. Graves was disgusted by his hoggish slurping and the noisy belch that followed. He could smell his fetid breath as Kearns leaned in close to him.

321

'When it comes to Pulditch better carrot nor stick! Squeeze but do it gentle.'

'How gentle?' Graves asked.

'Another few months gazin' at the walls an' there'll be only a handful left, if that.'

'And what do we do with this 'handful', may I ask?'

'We'll cross that bridge when we get to it. But for now it's softly, softly, catchee monkee. They know the writin's on the wall.'

'And where do you fit into the frame?'

'I don't!' Kearns winked.

'Very convenient!'

'It's closin' regardless. No point crucifyin' ourselves over it!'

Kearns glugged the rest of the pint down his throat then looked at his watch.

'Sorry, I haveta go. Thanks for the drink!'

Graves was about to remind him that it was Kearns who invited him out but he let it go. It was enough to have the little cretin licking his dick.

He wondered if the woman at the other end of the bar might be persuaded to do the same. If he got her well-sauced, anything was possible. He decided to open with the standard, 'Don't-I-know-you-from-somewhere' routine but as he got close he saw money. Real money. Big money. There'd be no quick, drunken hump there. He immediately changed tack. Stopping a discreet distance away, he coughed politely to get her attention.

'I beg your pardon, might you be resident in the hotel?'

'No, just finished a meeting actually. Doing up my notes.'

'Ah, pity! Never mind. Sorry to have intruded.'

'Is there some way I can help?'

'Oh, it's silly, I shouldn't have bothered you.'

Beyond Pulditch Gates

'It's no trouble,' she insisted. 'Honestly.'

'I was just wondering if the restaurant here is open to non-residents?'

'It is and it's well worth a visit.'

'Ah, good. I dine out so seldom these days, I'm never sure where to go.'

He turned away, stopped then turned back as if he'd just thought of something.

'I don't suppose... No! No! Totally stupid idea!'

'What is?'

'Are you hungry?'

She laughed like a schoolgirl, her face flushing red.

'As a matter of fact, I am a bit peckish!'

'Then have lunch with me or would your husband have my head for breakfast?'

Her face darkened for an instant.

'Hardly, Robert died two years ago.'

'Oh, I'm very sorry. Actually I've felt the pain of that loss myself.'

'You're a widower?'

'Fifteen years. Anyway, I'm Richard, Richard Graves.'

He put out his hand and she took it warmly.

'And I'm Doris, Doris Greer.'

'Well, Doris Greer may I get you an aperitif?'

'Campari and soda would be nice.'

Graves didn't bother the lounge boy and strolled up to the bar where he called their drinks himself. He needed a few minutes to gather his thoughts. An afternoon ride off a lonely woman was one thing, but sinking the log with a wealthy widow was a different case entirely. Wealthy widows were like specimen salmon, rarely found and very difficult to land. He'd have to reel her in bit by bit,

323

but it was hard to control his excitement. Her wedding and engagement rings were chunks of gold and diamonds and her wristwatch was a Rolex. On the middle finger of her right hand she was wearing a blue sapphire ring. The stone was transparent and Graves knew that was the most expensive kind there was. Her clothes, her jewellery, even her shoes cried cash and lots of it. Greer. Greer. Greer. The name had a familiar ring to it and he repeated it several times. Then it hit him like a blow from a sledgehammer. She said her husband's name was Robert and Bobby Greer was one of the biggest property speculators in the city. He owned rows of houses, office blocks and even a hotel. It made headlines in the papers when he dropped dead on a golf course in Spain. If she was Bobby Greer's widow then he was about to have lunch with Ireland's answer to the Klondike. The barman put up the drinks.

'Are you all right, Sir?' he asked quietly.

'Me?' Graves could barely find his voice. 'I'm fine! Fine!'

'You look a little pale, if you don't mind me saying so.'

'To tell you the truth,' Graves grinned, 'I've never felt better!'

He made sure Doris could see him casually toss a twenty spot across the counter and when the barman brought back his change stuff a generous tip into his fist.

'Have one on me,' Graves said loudly.

The barman was well-versed at the game.

'Thank you, Sir,' he boomed, 'very generous of you!'

Despite his best efforts, the ice cubes in the glasses rattled like chattering teeth as Graves carried the drinks back to the table. Doris Greer smiled warmly as he set them down. She was looking at a rare find. Richard Graves appeared to be a quiet, sensitive and cultured man, a man who had known his fair share of sorrow, a considerate man who wouldn't head straight for her knickers the

Beyond Pulditch Gates

minute they were alone. Richard Graves smiled back at Doris Greer. He too was looking at a rare find. She was a nice plump sheep that was only crying out to be shagged and then sheared of every penny she possessed.

GUSSIE: FRIDAY, 25 FEBRUARY

The bus finally passed through Ashbourne. Leaving the church and the grain stores of Dardis and Dunn's behind, it headed on out for Slane and Ardee. Gussie had read his *Indo* from cover to cover and was rooting high in his left nostril for snot. The farms they passed were dotted with sheep and cattle who kept their heads slanted downwards into the lush Meath grass. It reminded Gussie of a dream he had many years before. His feet tightened around the holdall. He was going to buy back the old homestead and the begrudgers could whistle Dixie. He wouldn't forget the monument for his mother's grave either. He'd slap up the biggest one in the county. People would come for miles to see it. It would say in big bold letters, Here lies the mother of Augustus Gallagher, Landowner and Investor. The bus hit a bump, his finger shot upwards and he nearly de-brained himself. He decided to report the driver when they got back to Dublin.

When they got to Ballyjamesduff, a policeman directed him to a garage that provided a hackney service. He had to bargain hard with the owner. The roads around where he wanted to go were deadly on suspensions and exhausts. Eventually they fixed a price and Gussie was on his way home. Once outside the town, the earth was as raw and as black as ever. Twisted leafless trees gnarled their spleen at a world that never seemed to dry out. Furze bushes ducked down out of the sharp February wind. A jackass scanned the horizon. He recognised some of the houses they passed. Roofless mostly. The thatch caved in. Families scattered. Some of the names came to him. Kiernan, Cooney, Quinn, Malone. Not all were gone. One or two places had new houses built beside the old ones. A few Paddy Reillys who managed to stick it out.

They passed a hatchery. The long rows of grey squat huts made it look like a concentration camp. The smell was awful. Turning off the main road, the car wove and twisted for another mile along a side road before turning down a rough potholed track. He got the driver to stop so he could walk the last hundred yards to the house. Whoever owned it had spent thousands on the place. He barely recognised it with its white skimmed walls and sturdy hardwood windows. The roof thatch was perfect and a newly laid lawn was cut in two by a pebbled driveway. A Merc and a Land Rover were parked at the front door, both were new and had English registrations. Gussie felt his stomach drop. It had to be Josie. Who else would pour a fortune into what was never more than a glorified cabbage patch? He quickly realised that what he had in his holdall wouldn't be worth a fiddler's so he switched to the repentant brother routine. He'd blame their mother. The neighbours. The priests. The times that were in it. He'd swear he had known no peace since he pushed her onto that mailboat. He moved wearily towards the house, a man bent in sorrow.

He rapped on the door and she answered it. Gussie gagged in fright. She hadn't aged at all.

'Ulloh! Can I 'elp yoou?' she smiled.

'Josie?'

''Fraid not! I'm Angie. It's my Mum you want.'

A voice called from inside.

'Angie? Who is it?'

'There's a man 'ere wants to see yoou, Mum!'

Seconds later she was there. Josie. Older. Older but beautiful. Tall, elegant, hair still black as ebony. A woman you'd look after in

Beyond Pulditch Gates

the street. She stood for a moment staring at the brother who abandoned her all those years before.

'Angie, go get your brothers,' she whispered.

The girl hesitated but then went back into the house.

'H ... How?' Gussie whispered.

Josie smiled and shrugged her shoulders.

'Hard work,' she whispered. 'Hard work and sandwiches! I was in London a few days when I got a job in an airport. I made sandwiches. Thousands and thousands of them. I worked every hour God sent up to the day Angie was born.'

She threw her head back and laughed.

'No wonder she detests coleslaw!'

Gussie spotted her wedding ring.

'Yewr married?'

'Come on, Gussie, only Irishmen shag rings round them and then want a virgin to walk up the aisle. Dutchmen are far more honest!'

'Ye married a Dutchman?'

'Dieter Van Harr. We moved to Amsterdam and I opened my own sandwich bar. Then I opened a whole string of them. In 1966 we moved back to London and now my company makes sandwiches for the airports. Not bad for a witless bitch. That's what you used to call me wasn't it? Or was it a dough-faced cow?'

'Please, Josie! Please! I...'

She raised her hand like a policeman stopping traffic.

'When you pushed me up that gangplank I swore I'd find a way to tear your heart out. I joined the Irish Club in London and they kept copies of the *Indo*. That's where I saw the ad for this place. Lucky, wasn't I?'

'Ye slut! Ye hoor! I'll swing before I'll let ye have it!'

'Oh, you could swing all right! I heard you swear you'd have Dixie Fanning's life for making me pregnant!'

Gussie was trying to decide if she was bluffing when a voice boomed behind his back.

'Is everyfin' all roight, Mum?'

Gussie spun around and faced himself as a young man but without the bendy legs. The man was a Gallagher. He had Gallagher eyes, Gallagher hair. Beside him was another young man but he had sallow skin and dark curly hair. Gussie hoped Josie wasn't hitched to a nigger. The girl stood in beside them. Josie did the introductions.

'My sons James and Hans. Angie you've already met!'

Josie moved over beside them.

'And this specimen, is your uncle Gussie! Remember I told you how he put me out so he could have this place for himself?'

'Wha?' Gussie choked. 'Issa lie! I did no such thing!'

James, his mirror, his rebirth, stepped forward.

'Roight! You're trespassin'!'

'This is my house.'

'Was your 'ouse! Now it's our Mum's so on yer boike!'

Hans began to roll up his sleeves. Josie shook her head.

'No, that won't be necessary. Your uncle is leaving.'

She took Gussie by the elbow and led him towards the gate.

'What was it you said, Gussie? You remember, at the end of that gangplank? Never darken our doorstep again? As far as me and mine are concerned, you're dead!'

Gussie stumbled in shock but she shunted him on out to the gate.

'If you don't want to end up in a neck-brace don't ever come here again!'

She walked back to her children, ushered them inside and closed the door. Revenge, like white wine, was best served cold.

Beyond Pulditch Gates

It was late by the time Gussie got back to the bus terminus at Busáras. He was too sick to eat and knew he wouldn't sleep. He decided to have a drink before he went to bed. Just the one. Just the once. He went to an off-licence and bought a naggin of cheap brandy. When he got back to his digs he found a note from Olive Gorman pinned to his door. Graves wanted him in Pulditch at nine o' clock the following morning. There hadn't been a Saturday worked in Pulditch for ages, but if Graves wanted him then Graves would have him. He put his money back into its hideout, set his alarm clock, got into his pyjamas and said his prayers. Then he took three good slugs of the brandy. He climbed into bed, closed his eyes and tried to sleep but words just ran around and around in his head. Hard work and sandwiches. Josie, the slut, the dough-headed cow had everything. The brandy ignited in his empty stomach and had to fan the blankets to disperse the smell. It took a long time before exhaustion finally pulled him down into sleep. Slowly, slowly he fell away. Backwards. Downwards. Into the dark-ness. Then he realised he was being lowered into a grave. Josie was looking down at him. He cried out to her in terror.

'No! I'm alive! We're not finished! I'm a Gallagher! I have money! Moneeee!'

He thrashed around for his holdall. He couldn't find it. Josie's sons were pushing a massive tombstone over him. The world was dark and getting darker.

'Help meee! Oh, Jesus! Please! Help meeee!'

Then his eyes were open and he was being shaken by Olive Gorman.

'Mister Gallagher! Mister Gallagher! For God's sake, wake up!'

She was all housecoat, curlers and fury.

'You've woken the whole house with your roaring!'

'Sorry, Miss Gorman! A nightmare! I'm sorry!'

'You were at this before. If you start again you can pack your bags!' She sniffed suspiciously.

'Have you been drinking, Mister Gallagher?'

'Me? Never! Never in all the years I'm here!'

She gave him another look then stormed out. When Gussie was sure she was gone he checked that his money was safe. Then he fished the brandy bottle from under his pillow and downed the rest of it.

PATSY & TIMMY: FRIDAY, 25 FEBRUARY

It was late when Timmy got home to Scarfe Terrace. The house was empty. After a long day on the protest march followed by a skinful in Reagan's he was only fit for bed. He was making himself a sandwich when Patsy arrived. She'd been at a meeting of the club committee pushing for the talk on abortion. Timmy shook his head.

'Why d'yew always haveta be out the front? Haven't ye enough on yer plate just runnin' that club.'

'It hasta be talked about.'

'Ye heard that Bishop, abortion is murder!'

'Easy for him to say. He'll never get pregnant!'

'True but be careful not t' shite in yer own shelter. Youse might run the club but the parish owns the hall. Anyways, I don't know why people can't leave things as they are. This abortion act will ditch us all in the shit!'

'I thought youse trade unionists were all on for freedom. Ye know, liberty, equality, all that stuff!'

'Well, we are and we aren't!'

He slapped two slices of bread together then began to break the sandwich roughly with his fingers.

'Oh, here!' Patsy snatched up the bread-knife.

Beyond Pulditch Gates

She took the sandwich and split it down the middle.

'If ye ask me yiz are all dry-day socialists. Yiz don't think twice about marchin' on a bloody prison or even gettin' locked up in one but mention a real fight an' yiz all run for cover!'

'We never run from anything but we know a bloody minefield when we see one!'

'Me arse! Men are terrified they won't have women for brood mares any more!'

Drink and the tribe launched Timmy out of his chair. The chair shot backwards and brought down a vegetable tray in the corner.

'Nobody drags them into the bed! If they don't want kids they don't have ta have them. No one knows that better than yew!'

'Meanin'?'

'Meanin' that for years we couldn't do it this night or that night but we could do the night after! Then as soon as those clinic things opened, who was first in the queue? Yew were and then ye went tellin' the world and its mother about them too. Between pills and creams it's like goin' to bed in a chemist's!'

'Those pills and creams bloody suit you too! D'ye want me to be like your sister-in-law? Forty-three and gone again. She has eight as it is!'

'At least she's havin' kids not helpin' people to kill them! Jesus, can there be anythin' worse nor little dead babies!'

As soon as he'd said the words he was sorry. He would have given anything to call them back but the missiles were fired. Patsy was hit and hurt to tears.

'If a girl's pregnant because she's been raped or fooled by some two-faced little shit then I'll do whatever I can for 'er! An' neither yew nor anyone else will stop me!'

Just then the door burst open and Jack barged in.

'What the hell's goin' on? I could hear yiz out in the street!'

331

He got it all in an instant. The upturned chair. Vegetables scattered all over the floor. His mother brandishing a breadknife to keep his drunken father at bay. Then he saw she was crying. He lunged at Timmy and Patsy had to hold him back.

'No! No! Jack! It was nothing! A silly row! It was nothing!'

'Nothing? An' yew with a knife in yer hand!'

He pointed a furious finger at Timmy.

'If yew laid a hand on her I'll do time for ye!'

Timmy stood in a daze. His son, his mate, his best friend was threatening to punch his head in. All three stood looking at one another unsure of what came next. Then Timmy grabbed his jacket and stormed out into the night. A crescent moon hung in the blackness like an upright slice of melon. He wished he was on it. Millions of miles away. Looking down on the madness.

The morning after the row, an awkward truce descended on the house. Silence thawed over breakfast to small talk. Jack apologised to Timmy who apologised back and they all agreed everyone got the wrong end of the stick. Jack buttered himself some toast.

'Stupid, wasn't it? Fightin' like that over this abortion act? I mean, why bother?'

Patsy almost jumped at him.

'Because chances are this pro-life thing is gonna be passed and if it is then that becomes the law!'

'Since when did Irish people give a shit about the law? If they have the bread and their daughter gets caught then they have her on the next plane to England!'

Patsy slammed down her cup in exasperation.

'That's the whole point, Jack. It shouldn't be down to money or the law. The woman should decide if she wants to keep the baby. No one else has any right to interfere!'

Beyond Pulditch Gates

'Ah, hold now on, Ma! If a girl's pregnant for a fella she can't just decide to end it without even asking him how he feels!'

Timmy left them to it. He went up to the jacks to read his paper. As he moved slowly up the stairs he sighed and shook his head. He knew the signs of impending civil war. It always began with petty little spats. Brother arguing with brother. Sister with sister. Husbands with wives. Mothers with daughters. Fathers with sons. He knew if he looked into a thousand other kitchens, bars or bedrooms, the story would be the same. The fateful questions being asked. The poison starting to drip. Whose side are you on? If you're not with us, you're against us. Fence-sitters or peacemakers would be treated as traitors. Civil war didn't allow grey only black and white, yes or no.

He flopped down on the toilet seat and opened the paper. Across the front page was a banner headline: FARMERS AND SELF-EMPLOYED OWE EIGHTEEN MILLION IN UNPAID TAXES. Further down was another headline: GOVT TO CUT WELFARE BENEFITS. He turned the page where he found an article by the Minister for Social Welfare. Though he was from the Labour Party, he was justifying why benefits to workers had to be cut. In the opposite corner of the page, the unions were threatening tax protest marches for April. It was all window dressing. The Labour boys would soon stop that gallop. Protesting about tax was a sacrament while the followers of Larkin were in opposition, but minister's Mercs soon changed their tune. A page further on, another headline proclaimed that the hierarchy had come out in favour of the wording of the abortion amendment. Timmy threw the paper into the corner. He contemplated having a shit. He decided he would but he'd do it quietly. Otherwise the government would tax it, the unions would march in protest and the bishops would moan about the dangers of enjoying carnal pleasure. He wondered when the

333

farmers' reps would demand a shite grant seeing that they managed to get grants for everything else. Hairy said farmers thought tax was what you used to hold down carpet. Downstairs the discussion was edging ever closer to yet another row.

PULDITCH: SATURDAY, 26 FEBRUARY

Gussie Gallagher arrived in Pulditch at nine o'clock. He looked like he hadn't slept all night. When Dockets Hannigan asked him why he was in, Gussie told him he was paid to be a watchman and not a secret agent. Richard Graves arrived at ten. He talked with Gussie in his office, then Graves left and Gussie set to work. For hours he moved between the workshops and stores pulling connections, fuses and disconnecting lights and phones. He finished at three o'clock and ignored Dockets as he pedalled out the gate. Dockets raised a two-fingered blessing to his back, then hurried across to see what he'd been at. He discovered that only the fire escape lights were lit in the workshop. Everything else was dead. The drills, the lathes, the milling machine, even the overhead crane had red HOLD OFF tags attached. He checked the stores and it was the same story. The padlock on the soap and towel stores had been changed. Dockets walked back into the cold and unlit workshop.

'Bastards! Poxy pack o' bastards! Jaysus, this isn't playin' the game!'

His angry bellow echoed through the air ducts and then died away. He walked slowly back to his hut and slammed the door behind him.

When the boys arrived on Monday morning they discovered that not alone was the place in chaineys but that their clockcards were missing and had been replaced with letters offering each of

Beyond Pulditch Gates

them a redundancy package. Panic ran through the ranks, so Timmy called a meeting in the big locker room. Everyone piled in and started talking and arguing together. Timmy rapped his mug on the table.

'Let there be no panic! This is only more o' their psychological warfare!'

'Sykofuckinwhatical warfare?' Mackerel gulped.

'Poxin'!' The Pox explained. 'Turnin' up the heat so we'll stew in our own juice!'

'They can stew me t' apple sauce as long as they're payin' me wages!'

Hairy sighed to the ceiling.

'It's a long day just scratchin' yer bollix. We'll be crawlin' the walls in a fortnight!'

Someone suggested reconnecting the electrical supplies but The Child put them wide.

'They're all signed 'outa service' be management, namely Megabolix Gallagher. If we reconnect and anyone gets a belt they'll be fucked for insurance and we'll be up to our neck with the law!'

Another suggested snaring gear from the stores so they could nixer to pass the time, but The Child spiked that idea as well.

'Too risky! Everythin' that's ever gone missin' would be down t' us!'

Timmy laid it on the line.

'We'll haveta play this be the book. Watch the tea breaks. Don't bunk off early and don't let Gallagher say ye weren't willin' to do yer work. Meanwhile, we'll get onto the union an' see what's what.'

'They'll do fuckall as usual,' a voice called from the back of the room. 'Let's get the pickets out! We'll put out the lights an' fuck them!'

Henry Hudson

'Fuck who?' The Pox exploded. 'The only wans we'll fuck is ourselves and we'll have every poxy right-winger in the country down on our necks t' boot!'

Silence fell. They knew the Pox was right. Then Saint Joseph stood up.

'To leave men all day with nothing to do, surely that's immoral? I mean, years ago we knew what we were fighting against. This way if we fight they'll say we have nothing to fight over but if we do nothing then they'll break us bit by bit! It isn't right! It couldn't be!'

Mackerel paused then thought aloud.

'It's like this abortionin' thing. Everyone says it's not happenin' but everyone knows that it is!'

They chewed at the log for another hour but got no further. Timmy was exhausted by the time the meeting finished. He made his way up to the boiler-house roof for a breath of air. Below him groups of men wandered around the grounds, their hands waving in inaudible argument. Downriver, steam and smoke pumped out of Pulditch Two. He looked towards the mountains and wondered how things were going for Man-in-the-Mirror. He paced the roof while he figured out his options. It was near lunch-time when The Child stumbled out of the access door.

'Well, fuck ye anyway. I've been all over the kip lookin' for ye!'

'What's up?'

'Gallagher, that's what! He's goin' ballistic! He has half the crew out lookin' for ye!'

'Where is 'e?'

'In the loadin' bay beside the lift. I dunno what ye done on 'im, Timmy but whatever it was, it worked!'

When Timmy stepped out of the lift Gussie was waiting for him.

'It was yew! Talbot! Ye black-hearted hoor ye!'

Beyond Pulditch Gates

Timmy hadn't a clue what Gussie was on about and neither had all the others who were watching from behind girders and ductings.

'What did I do?'

'Whaaattt did Iiiiii doooo? Two ton o' ready-mix cement, that's what ye did! Dumped on the path outside o' me digs! COD t' Mr. G. Gallagher! Me landlady is threatenin' t' throw me out in the street!'

Timmy caught the whiff of drink as Gussie went eye-ball to eye-ball with him.

'Ye think ye'll shake Gussie Gallagher? Well, think again ye smartarse jackeen bastard! I haven't long t' do it but by Jaysus Talbot, I'll nail yewr balls t' the wall before this place is closed!'

As soon as he went, the boys surrounded Timmy and hailed him a hero.

'But it wasn't me!' he insisted. 'I didn't do it!'

'Oh, no?' The Child chuckled. 'Ye go missin' straight after the meetin' and before ye can blink Gussie has cement all over his path!'

The Pox puffed happy smoke-signals from his pipe.

'Brilliant! Brilliant! Poxin' par excellence!'

With congratulations coming at him from all sides, Timmy had to go with the flow. Saint Joseph toddled round the corner to see what all the fuss was about.

'I was out oiling my bike,' he explained. 'Did I miss something?'

During the lunch break, Hairy and The Pox took Timmy for a walk.

'Okay,' Hairy said earnestly, 'how'd ya do it? How'd ye set it up so fast?'

Timmy stopped and planked his hands on his hips.

'For the last time, it wasn't me'

The Pox was like Sherlock Holmes but without the hat.

Henry Hudson

'It wasn't? Then what pox was it?'

They eliminated themselves and went through the likely suspects. Hairy even suggested Saint Joseph.

'After all, how long does it take t' oil a bike?'

Timmy thought about that.

'Knowin' Joseph, about two hours!'

That put the carpenter out of the frame so then The Pox wondered if Mackerel could be the culprit. Hairy shook his head.

'Naw! Sure the poor hoor can barely read an' write so how could he order the stuff?'

Like an Agatha Christie mystery the more they thought about it the more puzzling it became. Timmy walked with them, half-listening to the conversation. Gussie swore he'd nail him and that he hadn't long to do it. What did that mean? May? June? July? A bird flapped out from an air duct on the roof. A rat scurried along a pipe. The weeds were sprouting through every crack in the ground. The place was one long death rattle. The Pox stopped to re-fire his pipe.

'What d' ye do when there's two ton o' cement on yer path?'

'Shovel like bejaysus,' Hairy chuckled. 'Shovel like bejaysus!'

High above them a man watched their progress. He was almost invisible behind the grimy window at the back of the boiler-house. He knew what they were laughing about. The cement rocked Gussie but it hadn't rolled him over. One or two more surprises would do the trick. He decided he'd wait. String them out. He'd already hit Gussie in the stern. Next he'd hit him in the bow. He'd finish him at mid-ships.

338

chapter **15**

PATSY TALBOT: MARCH

Patsy sat in the kitchenette reading the paper. She was studying the outcome of a trial where a gang of youths was accused of killing a man in a park. They claimed they thought he was gay so they did a spot of 'queer bashing'. Unfortunately the 'bashing' got out of hand. The dead man's family claimed he was just a quiet, inoffensive creature who had been battered to death by thugs. Now there was uproar because the youths were convicted but given a suspended sentence. On one side of the page a spokesman for the Council of Civil Liberties wrote backing the decision. He reckoned everyone was sadder and wiser after the event. Beside this was a photo of a gang of youths marching beside the park where the man was murdered. They were celebrating the release of the killers and an historic 'victory' over the 'queers'. Patsy thought back to 1968 when a man accused of strangling a woman got off after his defence painted her as a tease. In fifteen years, only the props had changed. Underneath things were as twisted as ever. Patsy threw the paper into the waste-bin.

That month, other groups went marching too. One Saturday Patsy stood on the footpath and watched the Pro-lifers pray their way up O'Connell Street. They carried candles and little white crosses symbolising the souls of aborted babies. Their placards read 'HUMAN LIFE IS SACRED' and 'LET THE BABIES LIVE'. A week later, the Pro-choicers were on the move but their placards demanded 'THE RIGHT TO CHOOSE' and 'DEFEND THE CLINICS'. Patsy had finally managed to get her way on the talk about abortion in the club, but on the Sunday before, the Parish Priest made his feelings clear from the pulpit. Though the bishops were calling for open and honest debate, he insisted that even talking about abortion was irresponsible. It was wrong and that was the end of it. He prayed that those who wanted to unstitch the fabric of Irish society would get no audience in his parish. Patsy felt every eye in the church flick in her direction. It was a direct challenge to cancel the talk but she never flinched. She had made a secret promise to Lily Caffrey and that promise would be kept.

The talk went ahead and the club was packed. Patsy noticed that a lot of those present were strangers, but she put this down to the fact that so many women were anxious about the whole abortion issue. The invited speaker was a journalist who specialised in women's issues. She was to give both sides of the argument and then take questions from the floor. Her talk had only begun when the heckling started. It came almost on cue from every corner of the hall. Patsy was asking people to be quiet when a woman in the centre of the crowd jumped to her feet.

'Abortion is murder! We will not be quiet!'

Beyond Pulditch Gates

She hoisted a poster up over her head. It showed a dismembered foetus. Some women screamed and looked away but others snatched the poster from her. She called them devils. They called her a twisted bitch. Within seconds a hoover of anger sucked the whole hall into the fight.

Posters popped up and were dragged down. Insults and obscenities flew. There was chaos and the mêlée even spilled out onto the street. The police were called. The papers sent reporters sniffing for a story. The kickback was swift and public. The Parish Priest barred the club from using the hall as long as 'a certain irresponsible person' remained on its committee. Patsy knew how much the club meant to the women of the area so she resigned. It was game, set and match to the PP. Patsy licked her wounds for a few days but then she saw an ad asking for volunteers to help the Anti-Amendment campaign. She decided that if she couldn't fight on one battlefield she would fight on another. She signed up the following morning.

LILY CAFFREY: APRIL

April brought showers and more about abortion. It crept onto the radio, into the papers, it came from the pulpit at mass. A Protestant bishop claimed the amendment was the policy of the Catholic Church. Other religions had problems with it too. The term 'unborn' didn't exist in Jewish doctrine, while the Muslims allowed abortion where a pregnancy threatened the mother's life. They worried that if the amendment were carried, any of their people involved in such an operation could be up for murder. An Anti-Amendment barrister asked what would happen if a young girl was raped and became pregnant. Would she have to carry the baby to full term and delivery? A Pro-Amendment spokesman accused him of scare tactics.

Lily Caffrey felt too weak to go to Mass so she stayed in listening to the radio. Mid-morning, a studio debate began and the subject yet again was abortion. She froze every time she heard the word in case somehow, someone might discover her terrible secret. As ever, the debate quickly descended into a row. It was at its height when a Pro-Amendment speaker shouted that abortion was nothing less than godless murder. The words seared into the old woman's brain. She'd had an abortion so she was godless and she was a murderer. Her fingers gripped the arms of her chair and tears trickled down her face. Then the presenter questioned a priest who was on the panel.

'Father, do you approve of the amendment as it stands?'

'Yes, I do.'

'And you believe the wording to be watertight?'

'Absolutely.'

'And you believe it should be passed?'

'Obviously.'

'What about claims that if a young girl of thirteen or fourteen was raped, that this amendment would force her to carry the baby to full term?'

'You and I know that's never going to happen. Our aim is simply to save the souls of both the born and the unborn!'

'The souls of aborted babies? How do they stand?'

'I believe God's love is merciful.'

'But can the souls of aborted and therefore unbaptised babies ever go to Heaven?'

'As I've said, I believe God's love is merciful.'

Lily Caffrey's head dropped onto her chest.

'Say it!' she sobbed. 'Say my baby will go t' Heaven!'

Asked for the third time, the priest repeated that he believed God's love was merciful.

Beyond Pulditch Gates

Gussie Gallagher: May

When May came, Gussie began his annual novena in honour of Mary, Queen of Peace. He prayed fervently for a whole list of things including the gift of sleep without having to murder naggins of brandy to get it. Instead what he got was two hundred breezeblocks stacked five high on the path outside his digs ordered C.O.D. as a rush delivery to Ms Olive Gorman. She went apeshit when she saw them. She went apeshit with cream when she saw that the delivery lorry had gouged two ignorant tyre marks along the grass verge outside the house. It was apeshit with cream and cherries when she read the delivery docket and discovered it was a Mister Gallagher who had ordered the bloody things. Gussie swore on the Bible, on his knees, on his mother's grave that he was innocent. Again old Mrs Gorman saved him, but he was told in no uncertain terms that if there were any more unwanted deliveries, he'd be homeless.

That night after the novena finished, Gussie walked for miles. He argued with God, with himself and with the world. He prowled the canal in the hope of seeing the red and black-haired ones although it was years since he'd laid eyes on them. Others were doing business but they'd never understand like those two that it was all their fault. If women weren't sluts, then his sister wouldn't have been shafted and he wouldn't have had to put her on the boat, and he would still have the farm, and his landlady wouldn't have cement or blocks or tyre marks the length of her green patch. Only for women and communists everything would be hunky-dory. He knew Timmy Talbot and his gang were behind the blocks and cement routine. They were resisting every attempt to push them out. He wondered why God was testing him again especially after he'd volunteered to work for the Pro-lifers. He signed up after he read in the *Indo* that a Jewman doctor called Solomons was one of the leading lights against them. A mouthy woman lawyer called Robinson was rocking the boat as well. Even the Arabs were asked where they stood, as if any decent, god-fearing Irishman gave a tiddling fuck what half-baked niggers, yids or pushy women thought about anything.

The Pro-lifers needed people to steward marches and to collect funds. Gussie opted for the stewarding because when it came to whipping people into line he was a pig in shit. As long as they had parades he'd steward them and when they won the referendum God would have to come across. It wasn't as if he was asking the earth. All he wanted was Pulditch closed and Josie and her brats to shag off back to wogland with her half-wog husband. Then he'd warm a seat above in head office until he retired to do the squire around his old hometown.

Despite his prayers, the month finished with a disaster and the appearance of the howling coyote. The disaster was that old Mrs Gorman had a heart attack. She survived, but only just, and her family was told she wasn't to be distressed under any circumstances. Gussie learned all about distress when the coyote began ringing his office. It never said anything, it just went Uuuhhoohoohooo. When he'd be in the lift it would drift up the lift shaft behind him. Uuuhhoohoohooo. When he went to have a shit it would be lurking under the shithouse window. Uuuhhoohoohooo. He roared after it, waddled after it, threatened to sack it, shoot it, fuck it, fire it and folly it home but he never caught it. The coyote was like a Scotsman's promise to give to a collection, heard but never seen. When he asked Graves if he got any calls from a coyote, Graves told him to go home and sleep it off.

Gussie was glad when June came. He began a special novena to the Sacred Heart for the well-being of sick landladies and another

Beyond Pulditch Gates

to St Patrick to banish coyotes as well as the snakes. He also began
to take a second naggin of brandy to work every day.

THE BLACK-HAIRED ONE: JUNE

She spent all her money on a funeral for the red-haired one. She
got her a coffin with flash handles and a bouquet of roses to sit on
top of it. She couldn't afford a limo to follow the hearse, but she
knew two decent skins who ran taxis. They did a nixer and carried
some 'girls' from the old guard who turned up to pay their respects.
One of them knew a kindly young priest and arranged for him to
say a funeral Mass. He offered it in a tiny side-chapel off the
church where he was serving. With his long hair, unkempt beard
and white flowing vestments he looked like JC himself. The black-
haired one cried when he said that her friend would find rest and
love in Heaven. After the burial in Glasnevin, she finished things
right and brought the mourners back to the Addison Lodge for soup
and sambos. The Lodge usually had the blue-rinse battalion in at
lunch-time. She got a great kick watching their sideways gawking
at the priest holding court among 'ladies' who called a spade a
spade, a shite a shite and who always gave a decent corpse a
bloody decent send-off.

It was late afternoon when she got back to the flat. The landlord was looking for his money and a flutter of bills was skewered
on a hook inside the door. The payphone on the landing rang. It
was one of her politician clients. This one was an ouldfella well up
in one of the parties. She often saw him on the telly giving out
about the state of the country. He called her Miss Whipsey because
he liked to use his belt on her buttocks until he raised a decent
weal. It was agony but it was fifty quid. A fiver a stroke. If she
used a gag and cried real tears he gave her an extra tenner.

345

She always moaned and wriggled as much as she could in the hope he'd manage an erection, because whenever he emptied himself he always emptied his wallet in gratitude. She told him Miss Whipsey would expect him at teatime. She had the gag, and with the day that was in it, Miss Whipsey would have no trouble crying.

Man-in-the-Mirror: July

On the last day of July, workmen arrived at St Jude's in a navy van. They had long metal boxes with them. Man-in-the-Mirror knew they were for bodies. They were about to dig up the graves in Hell's Acre and then they'd dig up the nuns from under their chiselled white crosses. He watched from a distance as a priest led the nuns from grave to grave praying briefly over each one in turn. When they left, the workmen surrounded the first of the graves in Hell's Acre with a high canvas screen. A JCB moved in and dug for a few minutes before it pulled back and the thuck, thuck, thuck of picks took over. Then that stopped and he could hear earth being shovelled before the men put on masks and carried a box in behind the screen. A few minutes passed, then the box was carefully lifted into the back of the van. The men stopped and had a smoke, but soon the awful digging started again.

Man-in-the-Mirror wanted to run, but an irresistible power held his eyes on the macabre scene. Death was being dug from the ground as he watched. His heart hammered his anguish that, having kept it at bay for fifteen years, it was back walking at his side yet again. Sister Frances had offered to fix him up in a place just north of Dublin. She said it was called a hospital but it was more like St Jude's. It was by the seaside and it had grounds where he could walk for hours. He asked if it had walls, gates and if they made baskets. He knew by her face that it had or did all three and

Beyond Pulditch Gates

he secretly vowed that he would never set foot in a place like that. Not then, not ever. As another box was taken inside the canvas, he turned away and he didn't stop walking until he was high on a hilltop overlooking the valley. Up there the air was cold and clean. He drank it in like a drunkard.

TIMMY: AUGUST

That month Timmy saw nothing but figures. The lads constantly debated the figures on the exit package and the odds on how long it would be around. Dunlop's tyre plant in Cork was in trouble, and six-hundred-and-eighty jobs were on the line. In Dublin, Lemon's factory was going after 141 years and seventy-three jobs would go with it. In the abortion row, the government announced that the referendum on abortion would be held on Wednesday, 7 September. The Pro-Amendment side claimed they were all out to win and would do so by a margin of two to one. The Antis insisted that thousands of women went to England for abortions every year, and if the amendment was carried, it would only make things worse. Timmy felt as if the whole country was gearing up for war. He thought they were all mad, but then late on August he suddenly got a war all of his own.

Management stopped issuing soap and toilet paper. Heat and hot water were cut off from the toilets, showers and locker rooms. The payphone in the workshop was disconnected. Light bulbs were removed from their sockets. Graves began calling people to his office on Friday afternoons to say the retirement deal was being withdrawn and that if they didn't go they would end up with nothing. Some stewed in their fears over the weekend, came in the following Monday and signed up to go. Timmy went gunning for Red Kearns, but the little bollox had gone on leave and then disappeared to a conference in England. Timmy knew Kearns was

347

staying offside so the little fucker was up to something. He swore that as soon as the fat little shit showed again, he'd gatecrash his office and drag him down to Pulditch by the head.

PATSY: TUESDAY, 6 SEPTEMBER

Sister Frances had written to Patsy about the arrangements to rebury the girls from St Jude's on the following Friday in Glasnevin, so she was surprised when the nun rang and asked if they could meet. Patsy knew from the tone of her voice that something was amiss, so she was already sitting in the bar of Wynne's Hotel when Sister Frances walked in. Her hair was cut in a modern style, and instead of a nun's habit, she wore a navy business suit. The only clue to her profession was a tiny gold crucifix pinned to the lapel of her jacket. Patsy had ordered coffee and Sister Frances looked liked she needed it.

'Sister Frances,' she whispered as the nun flopped down beside her, 'are you okay?'

The nun went straight to the point.

'Monica Dillon's daughter is on her way to Dublin!'

'Oh, my God! How did you find her?'

'I didn't! She contacted our mother house, and as I'm in charge of St Jude's, they passed her on to me.'

'What happened to her? Where has she been?'

'Her family moved to Australia when she was ten but she spent the last year working in London. Now she's coming here to ask about her birth mother ... and father!'

'Oh, hell!'

'Oh, hell again!'

A waiter brought their coffee and the two women were silent until he left.

348

Beyond Pulditch Gates

'So, when is she coming?' Patsy asked as she poured out the hot steaming brew.

'She flies into Dublin Airport tomorrow.'

'Tomorrow!' Patsy cried. 'Oh, my God! Monica! Friday! Oh, my God!'

The nun eased a spoonful of sugar into her cup.

'A freak coincidence or maybe the closing of a long-opened circle. I always said there was unfinished business!'

Patsy planked the coffee-pot firmly onto the table.

'Then let's finish it and let Monica lie in peace!'

'My sentiments exactly! Now, I need to ask a very big favour.'

'Shoot!'

'Our order votes *en bloc* at midday tomorrow. Orders from the top. It's a show of solidarity for the referendum but our girl flies in at midday, and I was to collect her.'

'No problem. I'll get Timmy to leave the car. Jack's on a few days leave so he can do the needful!'

'Thanks, Patsy, I'd appreciate that.'

Patsy toyed nervously with a paper serviette.

'Are you going to tell her who her father is?'

'Tell her?' the nun sighed. 'I can't even mention his name without his permission!'

'That's ridiculous!'

'It's the law!'

'Surely there's something we can do?'

'We could try one more time with him. Give him one last chance to come clean.'

Patsy wrung the serviette into a knot.

'I haven't laid eyes on Richard Graves in years and I'd be happy to keep it that way!'

Henry Hudson

'And who could blame you?' the nun said quietly. 'Who could blame you?'

Just then a woman's voice shrilled across the bar.

'Sisteerrr Francesss! Yoohoo! Sisteerrr Francesss!'

The nun cringed down into her seat.

'Oh, no! Not today! Not that gang!'

'Who is it?'

'Marion Hastley and her friends. I met them in one of our convents a while ago. The Pro-lifers call them storm troopers. If you need a row over abortion just call them in. They'd start a heave in Heaven!'

Patsy looked around. She froze and the posse of women froze too. The last time they'd seen each other was the women's club, the night they ruined her talk on abortion. Patsy saw red and stormed across to their table.

'Which o' yew bitches is Marion Hastley?'

Like most bullies they were great in a mob but one-on-one they were useless.

'I ... I am,' one of the women choked.

Patsy was just about to savage her when she remembered a trick Timmy told her about negotiating. When you're unsure, bluff.

'I know who sent yiz to the club that night and be the sweet livin' hand o' Jesus wan fine day I'll hang them on a meat-hook!'

One of the other women dived in.

'You foul-mouthed trollop! How dare you threaten your own Parish Priest!'

The bar sank into silence as Patsy walked back to an open-mouthed Sister Frances.

'I'll talk to Graves,' she whispered. 'Maybe I can hang him on a meat-hook too!'

GUSSIE: 6 SEPTEMBER

He took two days off work and stayed dry to help in the referendum and was glad he did. The forces of evil were everywhere. The busmen, a shower of closet commies, were going on strike, so people couldn't get to the polling booths to vote Yes. Even The *Indo* wouldn't say vote Yes and be done with it. They'd even let Malcolm bloody Muggeridge whine about the wording of the amendment. Gussie always said English Catholics were like Roy fuckin' Rogers, able to ride two horses at once. At least the Pope had nailed his colours to the mast. There'd be no contraception and no women priests. Women were for having kids and cooking and a priest had to have a prick, full stop and no commas.

He was handing out Vote Yes leaflets when he spotted the black-haired one walking along by the Adelphi Cinema. At first he wasn't sure, but as he got closer he was certain it was her. He'd have grabbed her there and then only he didn't want to accost a brasser in broad daylight. His bootlace opened and he bent down to tie it. When he looked up again she was crossing O'Connell Street into Lower Abbey Street. Then the crowd surged in behind her and he lost her in the sea of bobbing heads. He went after her again and knocked a paper-seller flying as he thundered past. Cars blasted as he hobbled across O'Connell Street, but Gussie didn't give a shite. He wasn't going to lose her. He knew there was no point in checking the bank on the corner because everyone knew brassers had no business in banks. He checked along the street all the way up to the Abbey Theatre, but he knew there'd be no call for her in there either because everyone knew all actors were queers.

He back-checked every shop, but there was no sign of her. Then it hit him. He read in a book that her type often used hotels. He tried to get up the steps of Wynne's, but a gang of ouldwans was surrounding two others who were having a right go at each other.

'You shouldn't have said anything, Agnes,' one bitched.

Agnes wasn't having any of it.

'It was Marion started it. Calling like a fishwife across the bar to that nun!'

Gussie had to squeeze past them into the hotel foyer. There was no sign of her. He waddled into the bar. Nothing. His eyes passed over two women sitting in a corner. He thought he recognised one of them but he hadn't time to wonder how. He shot back out to the reception area. A man in a morning suit was writing in a book.

'Howye!' Gussie barked.

'Good morning, Sir. How may I help you?'

'Did ye see a tall, black-haired one comin' in her in the last few minutes? Ye know, she's wan o' them!'

The man looked at him blankly. Gussie knew the shagger would say nothing without a dropsie. He pulled out a pound and pushed it into his hand.

'Just tell me what room she's in and we'll say no more.'

The man threw the pound back at him.

'This is a respectable establishment. We do not cater for the type of person I think you are referring to. Good day, Sir!'

Gussie slithered out of the hotel past the women who were still going at each other like she-cats. He slunk into the laneway beside the hotel. Harbour Court stank of stale piss and cooking fumes that spewed from surrounding restaurant kitchens. He steadied himself against the wall and wished he had a naggin of brandy with him.

Only yards away, the black-haired one stepped out of the bank on the corner. She had just withdrawn the last fifty she had in the

Beyond Pulditch Gates

world. She'd hung on to it in case of a really rainy day and that rainy day had arrived. Since the red-haired one died, she had lost the heart to work. She was so far behind with the landlord he told her to pay up or pack up. The fifty quid would keep him quiet until the end of the week, but after that she'd either be on her back or homeless. She wasn't sure which option appealed to her less.

She was crossing the street when Gussie looked up and saw her. He followed her up O'Connell Street, giving out the odd leaflet as he went. They passed Clery's, the Gresham Hotel and then headed up into Parnell Square. From the Square she headed up into North Frederick Street, past Walton's music shop, the LSE Garage and then around into Dorset Street. Gussie never let more than fifty yards of a gap open up between them until she stopped at a hall-door near the junction of the North Circular Road. She pulled out a key and let herself in. Gussie rubbed his hands together. Now that he knew where her lair was, he could go off and attend to his other concerns. He had a station to close and a referendum to win.

A little while later, the black-haired one left the flat again and walked to the Cross Guns Bridge where she bought some flowers in a shop on the corner of Mobhi Road. From there she walked to Glasnevin Cemetery where she stood at the grave and told the red-haired one all her troubles.

'The priest said ye'd be up there so put a word in for us! I'm on me uppers! Just ask how the hell I can get over this hump!'

She stayed there for a long time chattering away in the warm September sun. It was peaceful and the high cemetery wall barred the shittiness of the world outside. The roses from the funeral were withered so she threw them into a waste-bin and arranged the fresh flowers on the grave. She promised herself that if she ever came into money she'd have the red-haired one's name carved on the headstone in big gold letters. She had to go then. The barrister who cried for his Mammy was booked in for later that evening.

He turned up just after teatime and she spent twenty minutes trying to get him going but he was still lying to the left, pink and floppy like a half-cooked sausage. Undoing her suspenders and sliding out of her stockings didn't work and neither did letting him sniff her red high-heeled shoes. She was getting desperate. Her hand was starting to cramp but a week's rent was riding on him having lift-off. Then she had a brainwave. She sat him on her lap and sang him a nursery rhyme. Ba, Ba, Blacksheep, Have you any wool? He was like the Eiffel Tower by the time she reached the little boy who lived down the lane. She had only time to clamp his monogrammed handkerchief over his helmet.

'Oooooohhhh! Oooooohhhh! Mmaammeeee!' he cried.

Then he came like special offer washing-up liquid, twenty per cent extra.

He was crying with gratitude as she zipped him back into his pinstriped trousers.

'If there's anything I can ever do for you please, don't hesitate to call me!'

She folded his handkerchief back into his pocket and the plan hit her like the belt of a baton. It was mad, outrageous and illegal but she was desperate enough to try it. She put on her best Shirley Temple pout.

'There is somethin' ye could do for me and if ye do it the next time ye call I'll sit ye on a potty and read a whole story book to you!'

'For a whole storybook I'd do anythinggggg!'

'Who's a good little boy then?'

Beyond Pulditch Gates

He blushed and went all shy and ripe for skinning, but when she told him what she wanted he nearly needed the potty there and then.

'I ... I couldn't! It would be totally unethical!'

'Oh, well, in that case I couldn't get your little jellyman to stand up and do woopsie for Mammy ever, ever again!'

'Nooo! We have to do woopsie! We have to!'

She looked at her toes and continued the sulk.

'All right! I'll do it but you have to be the jellyman's friend again!'

Trying not to laugh she unzipped him again, fished for and found his sardine penis.

'Well, if a good boy helps me out, of course I'll be the jellyman's friend!'

When she closed the hall-door behind him she leaned her head against it and shook like a leaf. If she pulled off the stunt she was planning she'd be made. If it backfired she'd be in shit so deep she could bag it and sell it for fertiliser.

Timmy: 6 September

When Timmy got in from work he found a note from Patsy saying that she was off on one last canvass and that Jack was out with his mates. He made himself a mug of tea, a sandwich and sat down to watch the teatime news on telly. The doorbell rang, and when he answered it, Red Kearns was on the doorstep.

'Well, well,' Timmy exclaimed. 'The Scarlet Pimpernel!'

'Very funny! We haveta talk!'

'Bloody sure we do, I've been huntin' yew for weeks! Is this official?'

'Yes an' no!'

'Fuck this, Kearnsie, I should have some of the lads with me!'

'Not this time! What I'm gonna tell ye is strictly between us, understood?'

Timmy hesitated but then led him into the kitchen where they sat on opposite sides of the table. Kearns planked his briefcase up beside him.

'First off, yiz are all gettin' offered jobs in Pulditch Two.'

'What? That was always a no-no!'

'Yiz'll get letters on Thursday from two fellas outa head office, Haverty an' Black.'

'I know them pair o' shites!'

'Shites they might be but they're runnin' the show now!'

'What about Graves?'

'Never mind him. Youse just get goin' to Pulditch Two. No Custard's last stands! Just pick up yer beds and walk!'

'We will in our arse just walk!'

Kearns pulled a thick bound document from his briefcase.

'This hits the papers tomorrow. Consultants did it when Finny Fawl was in power. It wants to close a dozen stations and cut a thousand jobs.'

'Bloody hell!'

'That's what I said too but most o' the stations is turf-burners in the midlands. Now the Fawler's was cute enough to know they'd be roasted everywhere east o' the Curragh come the next election so the word went out, back off the turf-burners!'

'What about Pulditch?'

'There's no votes in Pulditch One stayin' open!'

'But the Fawler's got turfed out last October! Why didn't the Labour gang shred it when they got in?'

'They couldn't.'

Beyond Pulditch Gates

'Whaddya mean, they couldn't?'

'It'd look like the Labour tail waggin' the Finny Gael dog! The Fawler's would have had a fuckin' field day over it!'

'So?'

'So, we all needed an out.'

'Whose we?'

'The management, the government and the unions!'

'And what 'out' did 'we' agree on?'

'Close Pulditch. That way it looks like the report's bein' implemented and the Fawler's is fucked!'

'An' the unions went along with that?'

'What choice did we have? It's a hit of two hundred jobs instead of a thousand. It's nothin' personal, it's just politics!'

'Politics me bollox! It's jobs down the tubes!'

Kearns scratched like a mangy dog.

'This is only the start, Timmy. There was a time the likes o' Scargill ran the show in England but not any more. Thatcher's payin' the piper so it's dance or get trampled!'

'Yea, but in the old days...!'

'The good ould days is gone! Cowboy Flanagan's gone, Barney Coogan's gone an' Grealish's pub is gone too! Now, youse aren't bein' sacked, youse are just bein' moved! So, do yerselves a big favour an' walk down the road to Pulditch Two!'

'Or else?' Timmy demanded.

'Or else march up the road with yer cards up yer arses! I can't put it plainer nor that.'

Timmy looked Kearns straight in the eye.

'There hasta be somethin' in all this for yew, Kearnsie.'

Kearns thought for a moment then flopped his hands down on the table.

357

'Okay! Givvit another few year and there'll be only one union worth spit in this country. There's moves on already to set it up. It'll be a kinda 'superunion' for labourers, tradesmen, clerks, yew name it. Thousands an' thousands o' members.'

It was Timmy's turn to slap his hands on the table.

'All payin' up every week no matter what. There'd be nice jobs in a set-up like that.'

'For people who can deliver without spillin' blood.'

'The likes o' you?'

'Timmy, yew say I've lost two hundred jobs; I say I've saved eight!'

'That's bollox, Kearnsie, an' damned well you know it!'

Kearns slid the report across the table at him.

'Ye don't believe me? Then have a gander at that!'

PATSY: EVENING, 6 SEPTEMBER

Richard Graves sat on a bench opposite the National Art Gallery and waited for Patsy Talbot. She had phoned him earlier and asked to meet him. She said it was very important. He recognised her as soon as she turned the corner, still beautiful, distant, challenging. As she approached there was no smile and no handshake.

'Timmy thinks I'm out workin' on the referendum so we met by accident, okay?'

'Would you like to sit down?'

'I'd rather walk.'

He stood up and fell in beside her. Pasty wasted no time.

'I'm meeting yer daughter tomorrow.'

'Whhaatt? No! That can't be!'

'Her name's Patsy Sheridan. Spent most of her life in Australia, but then she moved to London. She's comin' here t' find out about her birth parents. Understand?'

Beyond Pulditch Gates

'Jeeesuuus!' Graves moaned but Patsy was all out of sympathy.

'Straight question, will ye meet her, yes or no?'

Graves stopped dead.

'I can't! I couldn't! What would I say to her?'

'Sorry?'

'Sorry wouldn't be enough! I'd have to tell her about Monica and how I ... I....'

'Abandoned 'er? Well, ye may have a chance to make amends there too.'

'How d'you mean?'

'Saint Jude's is closing. Monica and the other girls who were buried there are being reburied in Glasnevin on Friday at noon. Your daughter will be there and she can have you with her or she can stand there alone. It's up to yew!'

Patsy walked on. Graves followed like a kicked pup.

'She.... She'd never forgive me!'

'Ye'll never know unless ye ask.'

'If I don't meet her, if I say no, what then?'

'Then I'll tell her that as far as I know, yewr dead.'

'But I'm not dead!'

'For chrissake! I'm not letting that girl come halfway round the world to tell her that her father is within spittin' distance but doesn't want to know her! Now, for once in yewr miserable, useless existence do somethin' decent! Be with her ... or be history!'

'It's not that simple. There's other things! Complications!'

'Like?'

'I'm in a relationship.'

'Someone's wife I'll bet!'

'Doris is a widow!'

'Wealthy, is she?'

359

'She's.... She's comfortable.'

Patsy shot him a poisonous look.

'Ye always land on yer feet, don't ye?'

'Doris and I have a very special relationship.'

'Special enough to tell her about yer daughter?'

His face turned sheet-white. Patsy shook her head.

'I thought so. I'm in the phone book. Talbot, Scarfe Terrace. Ring me tomorrow, otherwise forget it!'

Saint Joseph: Wednesday, 7 September

Henrietta made him take the day off to help with the Vote Yes effort. He felt like a right dick outside the polling station with all the ould-wans. One of them was reliving a row she was involved in the day before. It had happened on the steps of Wynne's Hotel. Henrietta and the others oohed and aahed as she described how two women from her prayer group went at each other like she-cats. Joseph eased away from them only to hear an all too familiar voice cycle up behind him.

'Lord God, is it yerself? I never thought one o' youse would do somethin' decent!'

'Morning, Mister Gallagher,' Saint Joseph mumbled.

'Gussie! Gussie! Sure we're all on the wan side t' day. Now, have ye enuffa leaflets an' stickers? I'm goin' station to station to make sure we don't run out!'

'Actually, it's very quiet here.'

'In that case,' Gussie flung a copy of the *Indo* at him, 'ye'll have time t' read that!'

Saint Joseph opened the paper and his heart stopped. A report had been leaked that said a fistful of stations and a thousand jobs were to go. Pulditch One was finished for sure and he'd soon be

Beyond Pulditch Gates

home with Henrietta. He was so busy contemplating this disaster that he never noticed her looming up behind him.

'Well,' she boomed, 'aren't you going to introduce us?'

Joseph did and in an act Gussie was in among the ouldwans doffing his cap, shaking hands, shaking hands, doffing his cap. The ouldwans loved him. Henrietta asked how he thought the vote would go.

'Two to one for us! Maybe even three to one!'

Henrietta rubbed her hands together.

'Archbishop McNamara says it's a foregone conclusion and Eamon Casey will swing everything west of the Shannon!'

Gussie whipped off his cap and held it over his chest.

'That man'll be Ireland's first Pope! Yew mark my words!'

The ouldwans loved him even more. Saint Joseph was mortified and five agonising minutes passed before Gussie decided to push off. He had just thrown his leg over the crossbar of his bike when the ouldwan who had been reporting the row outside Wynne's started up again.

'Anyway, as I was saying, it was all that woman Talbot's fault. Threatening to hang the PP on a meat-hook!'

'Doesn't her husband work in Pulditch?' Henrietta snapped.

'I believe he does,' Saint Joseph mumbled.

Gussie heard and dived back in among the ouldwans to get the goods on Timmy Talbot's missus. A few minutes later, he cycled off happier than a bee in bloomtime.

Joseph was still stunned by what he had read in the *Indo* and let two voters by without giving them a Pro-life leaflet. Henrietta tore strips off him. He said he was sorry. She just said 'hummfffhhhh,' and went back to her coven. He noted that her backside had bloated to the size of a barrage balloon, but on the

361

other hand the few days over the referendum would keep her fibrositis and flatulence under house arrest. Even on the worst of days it was right to give thanks for small mercies. He hoped to Christ the Vote Yes crowd would win, otherwise Henrietta would take it out on him. Though he was only a humble carpenter with just three chaotic jumps to his credit, she would hold him personally responsible for all abortions, past, present and future.

TAINTED: WEDNESDAY, 7 SEPTEMBER

Graves paced his office. Neither Haverty nor Black could look at him.

'The deal was that I was to close this place then take over a section in head office!'

Haverty fiddled with the top of his pen.

'We only do what we're told.'

'Where the fuck am I supposed to go? Where? Tell me!'

'There's always the redundancy package!'

'You can't get the gang down there to take that!'

'They won't have to. They'll be working in Pulditch Two.'

'They wouldn't take that shower! Not in a million years!'

'They will, when they're told to. Now, please, sit down and listen.'

Graves hesitated but then sank back into his seat.

Black took over.

'Right now closing stations is a political hot potato so we've been told to tie up the loose ends here and then vanish.'

Graves reddened with temper.

'So I'm just a loose end! A piece of shit to be swept up with the rest of the dung!'

Beyond Pulditch Gates

'Remember what you told the men you hauled into your office. The place is closing. There's no job so take the package because it won't be there forever!'

'But I gave everything! I did anything I was told! Surely there's something for me?'

'There's nothing, Mister Graves, and there's nothing for Mister Gallagher either!'

'Fuck him! Let him fuck off to that pigsty of a farm he's always on about!'

Haverty stood up.

'We didn't want to say this, but you're tainted.'

'Tainted? With what?'

'The good old days. Demarcation, overtime, walkouts, sit-ins and God only knows what else. I wish I had a pound for every story I've heard about this place. Now, we'll say it was your idea to go. You'll have a presentation, speeches, the lot!'

'Bollocks!' Graves snapped.

Black pushed back his chair.

'It's like this abortion row, Mister Graves. Most people don't give a damn how things are, they're far more concerned about how they look!'

Graves moved to the window. An Aer Lingus plane screamed low overhead. He watched its wheels unfold as it dropped steadily towards the airport.

'What if I insist on going to head office?'

'You'll be counting paper clips. Everyone will know you shafted men in Pulditch then got shafted yourself. You'll be a laughing stock and a pariah. A very lonely pariah.'

Graves watched the plane shrink to a speck in the sky. The other two thought he was in shock but he was playing for time. Doris was

Henry Hudson

taking him to a villa in Spain for a week of sun and sex. He intended to use it to set his feet well into her concrete, but it could all go arseways if she discovered he was for the chop. He turned to face Black.

'I'll go but on two conditions. One, I get the top lash lump sum and pension'

'No problem, and the second?'

'I'm away for a week starting this Friday. When I come back you offer me the job in head office but I'll decline and opt to get out instead.'

'Why the delay?'

'It's personal.'

Black raised his eyebrows to Haverty.

'Okay,' Haverty nodded, 'we can live with that!'

When they left, Graves rang a friend who ran a wholesale jeweller. He wanted to buy Doris an engagement ring. He'd give it to her while they were having dinner under the stars. She'd dive on it, he'd leave Pulditch and they'd get married. He'd hammer her through the mattress for a few weeks then get her to buy him a pussypuller of a car. With his lump sum in his pocket it'd be just like old times again.

Before he left he threw a few mementoes into a cardboard box. They included photos of the day the place opened in 1958. There was one of George Keyes with his arm around Catherine's shoulder. He was beaming at her and she was beaming back at him. He never got over her suicide and lasted little more than a year after her. Graves stared at the picture and thought of his own daughter. For a moment he wavered, wondering if there was any chance Doris might understand. Deep down he knew she wouldn't so on his way out he threw the box and its memories into a skip.

364

Beyond Pulditch Gates

DUBLIN AIRPORT: WEDNESDAY, 7 SEPTEMBER

The plane from London touched down on time. Patsy and Jack waited in the Arrivals Hall. Patsy wondered if Monica's daughter would look like her. Just in case, she had a cardboard sign with her name in block letters. After a while people carrying bags with Aer Lingus tags began to funnel out of the arrivals gate. Patsy held her sign up but no one stopped. Then another wave of passengers came out. Patsy didn't need the sign.

'Jesus,' she whispered.

'Is that her?' Jack gulped. 'Bloodeee Hell!'

The girl was magnificent. She was tall, dark and tanned. She had rich, nut-brown hair and almond coloured eyes. Wearing faded blue jeans, tan boots and a white Aran sweater, she could have come straight from a fashion shoot. She had a hiker's backpack over her shoulder. Patsy was riveted to the spot. The girl didn't look like her mother, but she was the living image of her father. She shook herself, stepped forward and smiled.

'Miss Sheridan?'

'That's me, but folks at home call me Pat!'

Patsy introduced herself and explained that Sister Frances couldn't make it. Then she introduced Jack.

For the first time ever, Patsy saw him stuck for words. He reached out as if to touch some priceless treasure while Pat Sheridan took his hand in a warm confident grip.

'Glad t' meet ya, Jack. My Dad says Dublin's a great place to visit!'

'Oh, it is! Anywhere ye wanna go, pubs, restaurants, just shout! I know them all!'

'First things first,' Patsy laughed. 'Let's get home and get something to eat.'

365

Jack took the girl's backpack and guided her through the crowds towards the car park. Patsy couldn't help notice the number of heads, especially male, that turned to look as she passed.

Patsy sat in the back of the car on the way home to Scarfe Terrace. The girl sat in the front with Jack. She had the same gentle laugh as her mother, but when Pat Sheridan turned back to say something, Patsy couldn't help the shiver that ran through her from head to toe. Facing her were the dark, smouldering eyes of Richard Graves. They passed a school that was being used as a polling station for the referendum. Outside people were handing out leaflets. Posters were crucified along the railings pleading Vote Yes or Vote No. The visitor was fascinated.

'Is there an election or something?'

They were almost home before Jack finished explaining the situation.

'Strewth,' she whispered. 'I 'ope I never get pregnant over 'ere!'

Patsy was ashamed to hear herself pray likewise. Jack stopped the car at a traffic light.

'Pat, I've just had a great idea!'

'Whassat, Jack?'

'Stay with us for a few days until you find your feet.'

'Oh, no! I'm booked into an 'ostel in Gaardyner Street or is it Square? I dunno, somethin' like that.'

Patsy tried to be diplomatic.

'Sister Frances has arrangements made, Jack. We shouldn't interfere.'

'But she'll be far more comfortable in our place than in a hostel.'

The girl shrugged her shoulders.

'Oh, don't worry about me! I hiked across Aussie using 'ostels. Did Zealand too. D'you trek yourself, Jack?'

Beyond Pulditch Gates

'I've done me share!'

Patsy smiled to herself. Jack thought hard of walking to the shops. Either way he wouldn't hear of Pat Sheridan staying anywhere but in Scarfe Terrace. They pulled up at the house and he ushered them inside. While he took Pat's kit upstairs to the box room, Patsy put on the kettle. Pat Sheridan asked her where she kept the cups and set about laying the table. Now she was Monica Dillon's daughter. Helping. Being useful. No frills. No flounces. Jack came into the kitchen and Patsy may as well have been invisible. He could see only the beautiful, dark-haired visitor. After they'd eaten, Patsy rang Sister Frances to say that the girl was staying with her. They agreed they'd meet there the following morning.

When Timmy came in from work he found Patsy and Jack knee-deep in photographs.

'Yiz'll want a bloody big album!' he laughed.

'Ssshhh!' they snapped together. 'Ye'll wake Pat!'

'Pat?'

'Pat Sheridan. The girl from Australia! She's asleep upstairs!'

Timmy knew they were to collect her at the airport but nothing about her staying with them. Years of experience told him to say nothing. Patsy leaned back on her hunkers.

'It's no use, Jack. There's not a sign of it.'

'What are yiz lookin' for?'

'A photograph of an outin' when I worked in Graves' factory. I just remembered that Monica Dillon might be in it. Ah, it's years since I seen it.'

'There's a trunk in the attic we never unpacked after we left Larnham Street. There was a mountain o' photos in that.'

Jack was on his feet in a flash.

367

'I'll get the stepladder and have a look.'

Timmy watched him go.

'I've never seen him so anxious to help.'

'Yew haven't seen Pat Sheridan!'

The edge in Patsy's voice told him to walk in slippers in case he cracked the eggs.

'Does Jack know the story there?'

'I've told him all he needs ta know.'

'And?'

'He's very understandin'! Just like 'is Da!'

Timmy smiled and Patsy leaned her head against his chest. In her mind she was wishing that some day she would be able to tell him everything.

Suddenly they heard a muffled call from the top of the stairs.

'Fouuunnnddd somethinnn!'

Then there was a howl, a crash and a rumble of thunder on the landing. They ran up the stairs to find Jack clinging onto the trapdoor of the attic. The stepladder had collapsed under him and a snowfall of photos littered the landing. Timmy and Patsy creased in laughter. Then the box room door flung open and Pat Sheridan, resplendent in a tee shirt nightie, stepped out onto the landing.

'Ohhmyyggooddd! Jack! What are you doing?'

'Lookin' for a photograph but I'll be lookin' for a bloody ambulance if yiz don't get me down outa here quick!'

Realising that only his dignity was hurt, she too began to laugh. Then Jack began to laugh. It was Keystone Cops who replaced the ladder to get him back onto the landing again.

Pat Sheridan got dressed and reappeared in the kitchen a few minutes later. Timmy and Jack stood at the window. Patsy sat at

Beyond Pulditch Gates

the table. She had a photo in her hand. When she looked up, Pat Sheridan saw tears in her eyes.

'What is it?' she whispered.

'Come here, love.'

She sat down and Patsy put her arm around her shoulder.

'There. On the left. That's your mother. That's Monica Dillon!'

The girl's lip began to quiver. Her finger gently traced over the smiling face in the photo and then she buried her head into Patsy's shoulder and cried as if she would never stop. When her sobbing eased Timmy winked at Jack.

'Right then,' he said quietly. 'I think we could all use a drink!'

Timmy got out the glasses and Jack got out the whiskey. As he poured, Pat Sheridan wiped her eyes.

'Sorry I got so upset. I always hoped I'd have a photo. This is worth a million dollars to me. Thank you! Thank you so much!'

'Oh, don't thank me,' Patsy smiled. 'Thank Jack, he nearly killed himself finding it.'

She stood up, went over to Jack and kissed him on the cheek. He blushed and looked down at his feet.

'I told ye,' he mumbled. 'Anything ye want, ye just ask!'

chapter 16

PULDITCH: THURSDAY, 8 SEPTEMBER

Timmy and the boys spent the day before debating what Red Kearns and the newspapers said about the imminent closure of Pulditch One. Now Timmy had them all gathered in the big locker room to decide what, if anything, they were going to do about it. Some were on for a fight, but Timmy had to tell them they'd be pissing against a snowplough.

'We all knew this day was comin' and we all read yesterday's papers. Now as the man said, there's no sense stickin' yer dick in a meat-slicer, and even less sense leavin' it there. So, I'm goin' to Pulditch Two. If anywan wants to stay I'll do everythin' I can to help them, but they'll be fightin' the management, the unions and the fuckin' government as well!'

The Pox and his pipe stood up.

'Timmy's right! We often fought with wan hand tied behind our backs but now the other wan is pinned to the poxy flagpole. I wanna go t' Pulditch Two as much as I want me arsehole reamed be a full-grown yeti but it's the only option we have!'

Beyond Pulditch Gates

At that moment the door opened and Gussie Gallagher stomped in. Dressed in his best 'Sunday' suit and 'going-out' cap he looked like an extra from *The Quiet Man*. He walked straight over to Timmy.

'Well, well! If it isn't the babbykiller's husband!'

Timmy jumped up, but The Child gripped his sleeve.

'Don't, he's not worth it!'

Gussie's eyes were flashing triumph.

'D'yee know that this man's wife threatens priests and runs meetin's for antichrists what kills five thousand Irish babbies every year! But we, us, the plain people of Ireland gave them their answer yesterday!'

He hauled his transistor from his pocket.

'Two t' wan! It's comin' in already! I always said I'd nail ye, Talbot, and at long, long last I have! It'll gimme the greatest o' pleasure to put me boot up yer arse and send ye scurryin' up that road and the rest of yer godless butties along with ye!'

Timmy and Gussie were still eye to eye when Mackerel came breezing in from the jacks. Gussie turned on him.

'Ah, ha, Mackerel McKenna! The block-headed moron 'imself. Who'll read yer letters for ye now?'

'Oh, I don't haveta be able ta read, Mister Galliger. I learns offa the radio!'

'Bah, a prize eejit like yew?'

Mackerel looped his thumbs into the pockets of his overalls. His voice became that of a jaunty radio announcer.

'Still breaking your back mixing cement? Forget it! Ring Quickmix now on eight, four, eight, seven, three, seven! Just tell us how much, where and when you want it and we'll deliver. Account or cee ohh dee customers welcome. And remember use the Golden Pages and....'

Henry Hudson

He began to sing a familiar little jingle.

'... let yer fingers do the walking!'

Gussie turned white. He tried to speak but couldn't. Neither could the rest of the room and Mackerel wasn't finished.

'Now say ye wanted t' order two hunnerd breeze blocks, then this is the ad ye want!'

He became the radio announcer once again.

'For all your building needs, timber, tiles, mortar or blocks ring Handy Brothers on eight, eight, seven, seven, four, oh. We deliver cee oohh dee to your door and remember....'

He turned and conducted the boys who sang with gusto.

'... letttt yer fingers do the walkin'!'

Gussie went for Mackerel but Saint Joseph jumped in his way.

'Oh, be Jayysuss!' Gussie roared. 'Ould go-be-the-wall's feelin' brave is 'e? Yer good lady wife won't be too happy about this!'

Saint Joseph pulled himself up to his full height and let rip.

'Frankly, Mister Gallagher, I couldn't give a rat's bollox what that moon-arsed, horse-faced farting-bucket thinks!'

The room was again doused into silence. Saint Joseph had cursed and now he was stabbing his fingers into Gussie's chest.

'And another thing, Mister Gallagher! We are not going to be sacked! We are all going to work Pulditch Two! So fuck you, here, her and the referendum!'

Panic washed over Gussie's face.

'Naw! Naw! Youse is gettin' sacked! Me and Graves is goin' ta head office!'

'I wouldn't bet on that,' Timmy said icily. 'I wouldn't bet on that at all!'

Gussie knew they were winding him up. They had to be. Nonetheless he could feel his ring-piece loosen as an old, familiar feeling

Beyond Pulditch Gates

trembled from his forehead to his toes. It was the same feeling he got when Dockets upended Saint Joseph's bag that day in the snowstorm. Creosote, bubbles, cement and breeze blocks all flashed before his eyes. He buffaloed out the door and headed for Graves' office. Behind him the locker room erupted in those old familiar cheers and laughter. It was a wind-up. It had to be. Even though he had a hard, mean mouth Graves wouldn't drop him after all they'd been through, after all he'd done for him. No. Graves had even picked out suites for them above in head office. Picked them out he did. Next door to each other.

SCARFE TERRACE: NOON, THURSDAY, 8 SEPTEMBER

The photo of Monica Dillon lay on a coffee table beside her hairbrush, her necklace and strapless watch. Patsy and Sister Frances sat opposite Pat Sheridan who sat on the settee beside Jack. She wanted the story told from the start so Patsy began from the time she first met her mother.

'I went into Graves's factory in 1954 and I met yer Mam. She was quiet and gentle, but great gas when she was out. I left when I married Timmy in '57, so we lost touch. A year later Jack was born so I decided to bring him up to 'er house. She lived with her Ma and Da up near Binn's Bridge.'

'They'd be my grandparents?'

'They moved away a long time ago but I can show ye the house if ye like. Anyways, that day they didn't want anythin' to do with me. I shudda twigged something was wrong but I never thought yer Mam was in so much trouble.'

Patsy then told of a snowy day when a small, pinch-faced nun called to Larnham Street. Pat Sheridan followed every word.

'You reckon my Mam was trying to contact you from the home?'

Henry Hudson

'No doubt,' Patsy sighed. 'I'll regret to me dyin' day that she never succeeded.'

Then Sister Frances took over. Step by harrowing step, she took the young woman through the rest of the story. She told of Monica's heroism in the convent fire and how she came to live and die within the walls of St Jude's. She told of reading Monica's diary but how, to keep her promise, she had destroyed it. Finally she explained that St Jude's had been sold and that the ashes of the girls who were buried there would be reburied in Glasnevin the following day. There was silence for a long time, then Pat Sheridan asked the dreaded question.

'D'you know who my father was?'

Sister Frances looked to Patsy.

'No,' Patsy answered firmly. 'We have no idea.'

Pat Sheridan touched the trinkets on the table.

'I've always felt she was out there trying to find me but I never felt that way about my father. It was as if he didn't know I existed or even if he did, he didn't want to know.'

'Then he doesn't know what he's missed,' Jack said bitterly.

Patsy didn't know whether to kiss or kick him but she settled for a third option.

'I think we could all use some hot strong tea! I'll stick on the kettle.'

'I'll give you a hand,' Sister Frances insisted.

Both women went into the kitchen where they talked in a whisper.

'You talked to Graves?' Sister Frances asked.

'I did! He was to ring if he wanted to meet 'er.'

'And?'

'No show, not that that surprises me.'

Beyond Pulditch Gates

The nun filled water into the kettle as Patsy began to lay the table. As she did so, she picked a bread-knife out of a drawer and gazed at its serrated blade.

'I swear t' God,' she sighed, 'if I ever get the chance I'll gut that bastard!'

Sister Frances gently took the knife from her hand.

'Tell you what, Patsy ... if you ever get the chance just give me a shout ... and we'll knife him together!'

Patsy could see from her eyes that she meant it.

MAN-IN-THE-MIRROR: THURSDAY, 8 SEPTEMBER

The workmen had returned to dig out the last of the nuns' graves. Man-in-the-Mirror stayed well clear as he did when they dug out Hell's Acre a few weeks before. Around noon dark clouds began to tumble in from the East, so he headed back to the garden shed for his rain-gear. When he got there, he noticed one of the undertaker's vans parked behind it. The van drew him like a magnet. The back doors were open and a long, box-like shape lay inside. It was covered in a rough canvas sheeting. Though his mind screamed at him to run, some irresistible force made him climb into the van, grip the corner of the sheet and pull it back. The skeleton was caked in wet, clinging earth. It was looking straight at him and its bony claws were reaching up to pull him in beside it. He screamed and scrambled out of the van only to find himself face to face with death. It was masked, gloved and walking towards him. It was carrying a shovel to dig his grave.

He ran blindly down the driveway towards the main gates but just outside them death lay in ambush. A poster was fixed to a telegraph pole on the far side of the road. His stomach emptied at the sight of the dismembered limbs of tiny, barely formed babies.

Desperate to find safety he headed for his hilltop retreat. His mouth was dry and his chest was aching but he called up every ounce of his courage and strength to keep himself moving. He didn't look behind in case death was following. By the time he got to the top of the hill his lungs were screaming for air and he was soaked in sweat. He dropped to his knees, closed his eyes and searched for an image to give him comfort.

As ever, he returned to the one of his mother humming to herself as she packed their suitcase and his father sitting at the table reading his paper. His mother saying she'd never fit everything in. His father saying she would if she didn't take the kitchen sink. His mother laughing. His father laughing. They were going on holidays to Wexford. He was five. He was happy and safe but then his father died and his mother was taken away. Only the lads in Pulditch or the walls of St Jude's ever gave him that kind of comfort again. Now St Jude's was sold and he'd be sent to a place where they locked doors and made baskets. He had only one option. Go back to Pulditch. When his strength returned he drank some water from a stream then he headed down the far side of the hill towards the road that would lead him back to Dublin.

GUSSIE: THURSDAY, 8 SEPTEMBER

Haverty and Black were in Richard Graves' office when Gussie barged in.

'Right!' Gussie cried. 'I'm ready an' rearin' to go!'

'Go where?' Black asked.

'Head office, o' course!'

Haverty and Black exchanged looks, but Gussie ploughed on regardless.

Beyond Pulditch Gates

'Me an' Misser Graves! Sure hasn't he picked out two grand rooms for us, wan beside t'other! Oh, there's no doubt but ye can't keep a good team down!'

Haverty asked Gussie if he'd like to take a seat.

The word went around like wildfire. Graves had ditched Gussie and left him to be shafted. Hairy eventually found him huddled in the corner of his office. He could see that the big baboon had been crying.

'Mackerel is awful sorry about that messin' with the blocks and stuff, Mister Gallagher, and to make it up he asked me t' do him a big favour an' drop ye home!'

Not knowing if his arse or his elbow was up Gussie allowed Hairy to lead him to the car park where sure enough the station pickup was waiting. As they passed out through the gates, Dockets gave them a wave. Gussie was too stunned to wave back or notice that Mackerel McKenna was in the gate-hut feverishly dialing the phone. Neither did he notice that Hairy took the longest way home to his digs.

He was still in deep shock when Hairy left him at the corner of his road and drove away. It got even deeper when he approached the house and saw an ambulance pulling away from the door. It got deeper still when he saw Olive Gorman heading for him with her sleeves up and her eyes spitting fire.

'Yew are one sick, twisted bastard!' she screamed. 'Sending an undertaker to measure my mother for a coffin! She's had a relapse she got such a fright! I swear t' Jesus if yewr not out of that house by the time I get back I'll set the dogs on ye!'

'But it wasn't me, Miss Gorman! I swear!'

'Then who was it?'

'I ... I don't know!'

377

'Liar!'

Then the lights flashed on in Gussie's bewildered head.

'Oh, no...! No...! It was.... It was that bloody Mackerel!'

'Since when can a fuckin' fish ring an undertakers? I mean it! Pack yer bags an' go!'

She leaped into her car and burned rubber as she raced off after the ambulance.

Shortly afterwards Gussie left his digs for the last time. In one hand he had his old battered suitcase, in the other a holdall. In the suitcase were his good 'going-out' suit, shirt, tie, cap and boots. In the holdall was thirty-eight thousand pounds in cash.

He walked aimlessly for hours but by evening the suitcase and the holdall were weighing a ton. Unable to eat anything he bought himself two naggins of brandy and headed for Gardiner Street where he took a room in the cheapest bed and breakfasts he could find. He lay down on the bed, wrapped himself and his holdall into a blanket, slugged the brandy and turned on his pocket radio to keep himself company. A Pro-lifer came on crowing that there'd never ever be abortion in Ireland. He praised the plain people for the magnificent result and said God would reward them a hundred-fold. Tears of frustration trickled down Gussie's cheeks. He could just see them all up in the Archbishop's Palace drinking champagne while he lay alone drinking pig piss. Worse again, the Archbishop wouldn't even notice he was missing.

He didn't sleep, nor did he wash before breakfast when he passed on the flakes and fry and settled instead for tea and a slice of toast. Though it killed him to pay for food and then not eat it, he knew his stomach would lose it as quickly as he took it in. When breakfast was over he left his case in his room, took his holdall and went walking again. Everywhere he looked newspaper fliers

Beyond Pulditch Gates

claimed victory for the Pro-lifers. At noon he folded onto a bench in Stephen's Green. His feet were a union of blisters, his knees two clicking knives of agony. Wrapping his holdall tightly inside his coat he lowered his head onto his chest and drifted in and out of sleep.

He imagined a tall black-haired woman walking towards him from the far side of the duck pond. Josie. He snapped awake but there was no one there. His head drooped again and he wasn't sure if he was asleep or not. Then he was walking. Or was he? Yes. He was on the road to the old place. He could see the house. The door was open. It was his. All his. BAAARRRPPPP! His eyes snapped open and he was standing in the middle of a busy junction. The bumper of a taxi was only inches from his feet and the taximan wasn't pleased.

'Fuckin' madman! D'ye wanna get killed! Go back t' the doss ye bleedin' waster!'

The taxi powered away, leaving Gussie like a bewildered statue in the middle of the road. An old lady took his elbow and led him onto the safety of the path.

'There,' she said gummily as she stuck some coins into his fist. 'Go on up to the Iveagh Hostel like a good man. They'll give ye somethin' hot to eat!'

She walked away before Gussie could reply. He looked at the coins for a long time and then he walked on. At an off-licence he bought another two naggins of brandy and downed one of them in a few choking gulps. His pain and tiredness eased but black-haired women were everywhere he looked. Then a skinny little runt with a crew-cut hairstyle tried to grab his holdall. Gussie had the strap of the bag double-wrapped around his left wrist and for a split second the two faced each other. Gussie roared and rammed his

379

free hand into the snatcher's face. Shovel-sized, it sent the snatcher flying backwards over the bonnet of a car while Gussie scrambled to the safety of the toilets in a nearby public house. Hiding in a cubicle he tucked his trousers into his socks, took his money from the holdall and stuffed it down into his long johns. He finished off the second brandy and then he left the toilets, walking even slower than he did before.

GLASNEVIN: NOON, FRIDAY, 9 SEPTEMBER

The undertaker's van pulled up beside a plot where a chest-deep rectangular trench had been excavated. The van held urns containing the cremated remains of the girls from St Jude's. Jack and Patsy stood either side of Pat Sheridan. Around them were relatives of some of the other women who were being reburied. Sister Frances stood by the graveside with sprays of small white flowers at her feet. A priest looped a purple stole around his neck as a gravedigger eased himself down into the grave. Then the undertaker carried the first of the urns to the edge of the grave where Sister Frances waited. The urn had a tab with a number and four names on it. The number was the number of the grave in Hell's Acre. The names were of the women who had been buried in it. Sister Frances read the tab aloud.

'Grave number one. Carty, Anne Eileen. Jones, Mary Jane. O'Sullivan, Frances. Cullen, Rita.'

The undertaker lowered the urn to the gravedigger who placed it in the grave. Then Sister Frances handed the gravedigger a spray of the flowers and these were placed beside the urn. One by one the urns followed, often accompanied by quiet cries of sorrow from relatives in the crowd. It was only a matter of time before the dam burst.

Beyond Pulditch Gates

'Grave number sixteen,' Sister Frances called. 'Agnew, Joan. Allen, Geraldine Mary. Toolan, Katie. Brennan, Frances Alice.'

A racking sob came one of the women mourners.

'Oh, Jesus! She was my sister! Oh, Jesus, Franno! I'm sorry!'

Patsy had to look away from the pitiful scene. That was when she saw Richard Graves lurking in a clump of trees not fifty yards away from where they stood.

An instant of panic shot through her, but she locked her eyes on his. For a full ten seconds they dared him to step out into the light but then he fell back into the shadows.

More urns and flowers were placed and then the last urn was lifted from the van. It had only one name on it. Sister Frances paused as if afraid to say the words.

'Grave number twenty-eight. Dillon, Monica.'

Pat Sheridan moved towards the urn with her hand outstretched. She caressed the rounded container for a moment then turned her head into Jack's chest and howled. Her cries finally ripped the curtain of restraint around the graveside. Cries and sobbing rose until it seemed the sky itself was grieving. When the cries eased, Sister Frances handed down the last spray of flowers, the priest gave a final blessing, and the gravedigger hid the urns and flowers under rolls of artificial grass.

For a while nobody moved, but then the crowd slowly began to sunder. Jack was still rocking Pat Sheridan in his arms. Patsy nodded to him that it was time to go.

'C'mon, Pat,' he whispered. 'There's no more we can do here now!'

She let him lead her away, but every few steps she stopped to look back.

'I have to come here again! I have so much to say to her!'

Jack stared into her tear-filled eyes. From the moment he saw her at the airport he suspected, but now he was absolutely certain. He loved her.

The Black-haired One: noon, Friday, 9 September

She wanted to run the plan by the red-haired one. Just to be sure. As she was walking to the grave, a man came hurrying from a clump of trees and brushed past as if she didn't exist. Through the trees she saw a crowd around a grave. She reckoned somebody important was being planted. When she got to her mate's grave she knelt down and whispered so no one else would hear.

'I'm gonna hit that politician ouldfella this afternoon! Ye know the bastard that belts yer arse till it bleeds! Well, I'm gonna 'bleed' him for a Corpo flat an' a few quid t' do it up! I rang 'is office an' fed them a load o' shite about writin' an article for a local rag. He'll get some lemoner when Miss Whipsey walks in, but even so, I could do with a bit o' back-up!'

There was nothing for a moment then a warm feeling began to ripple through her. She could sense that the red-haired one was there with her, opening all doors and turning all lights to green.

She took the long way back to the gates and passed rows of old graves that looked rough and abandoned. She knew lots of people who ended up in graves like that. They were the three L's as her mate used to say – loners, losers and loopers. The one thing they all had in common was that they died alone and potless, so the Health Board had to bury them. They used old plots where people had paid a deposit on a grave, buried a relative and then disappeared. It was a cheap way of ditching Uncle Joe and the cemetery could hardly dig him up and send him back. As a result, four total strangers could end up in the one grave with only a cemetery ledger to record where they lay. The black-haired one never worried about death or dying because one of the few consolations she had was that when her time came she'd be buried with her best mate. If they went to heaven that would be fine, but if they were sent to hell, then that wouldn't be too bad either. There'd be plenty of priests, politicians and pillars of society to keep them company.

Two hours later she strode into the politician's office. He nearly shit himself. It was mutual. She'd had thousands of men on top of her, under her and behind her but she was still petrified when facing one behind a desk. He threatened to throw her out so she threw him the barrister's card. She told him to ring the number and ask about the Whipsey file. That changed his tune. He rang and the little boy barrister confirmed he had photographs of a certain political person entering and leaving the premises of a certain Miss Whipsey. The politician put down the phone and asked exactly what she wanted. She said a flat and a grand in cash. His face unlocked with relief. He asked if she wanted the flat north or south side and if she'd take the grand in twenties. She said northside and twenties would be fine. Before she left he made her swear an oath that the photographs and their negatives would be shredded. She swore they would be, when she had the key of her flat in one pocket and a grand in cash in the other.

Pulditch: noon, Friday, 9 September

Timmy, The Child, The Pox and Saint Joseph took one last walk around the place before they packed it in for good. Apart from the dull slow thud of their boots, there was silence in the turbine hall. They were being watched by pigeons that roosted quietly on the boiler-house girders. The turbines lay like a line of bodies on mortuary slabs. The lads moved on down the hall in silence, then Saint Joseph sighed wearily.

'It's hard to credit that this place will never run again.'

'Aye,' The Pox agreed. 'Twenty-five year gone like a poxy puffa smoke!'

He puffed a puff to emphasise the point. Saint Joseph wondered aloud.

'Whatever happened to Richard Graves?'

Timmy shrugged indifference.

'He slithered outa here on Wednesday. Word is that he got himself fixed up and dumped haybarn head in the shit!'

Saint Joseph was puzzled.

'Who's haybarn head?'

'Gussie!' The Child explained. 'The dopey bollix really thought Graves was gonna lift him inta head office! He got some kick in the mebs an' no mistake. He was in such a state that Mackerel got Hairy to drive him home in the van.'

The Pox nearly exploded.

'After that pox spent twenty-five year callin' him a gobshite an' a brainless prick! I'da got Hairy all right! To fuckinwell run 'im over! What was Mackerel at?'

'There's the man,' Timmy replied. 'Ask him yerself!'

Mackerel was walking down the hall towards them. The Pox went for him.

'Did yew organise a lift home for that poxbottle Gallagher?'

'I did,' Mackerel grinned. 'I wanted him arrivin' at 'is digs just after the undertaker!'

Saint Joseph nearly choked.

'Undertaker! What undertaker?'

'The wan I sent ta measure 'is landlady for a coffin!'

'Jesus Christ!' The Child gagged.

'Naw,' Mackerel winked. 'Golden Pages!'

He joined his hands and tried to look solemn.

'At your time of grief Duggan and Sons will handle funeral arrangements with tact and sensitivity. Call us eight, four, three, one, double two for our complete home service!'

He sang the ditty himself.

'Lehheettt yer fingers dooo the walkin'!'

The Pox gave credit.

'Fair poxy play! Sherwin Holmes cunna done it better!'

'Sherlock!' Saint Joseph dived in. 'His name was Sherlock Holmes!'

'It cudda been Ideal Holmes for all I care! Mackerel, I'm awardin' ye the Pulditch Grand Prix for poxin'!'

The Child led them to the stairway that led down off the floor to the locker rooms.

'I suppose we should say somethin',' he mused.

'Like what?' Timmy asked.

'A farewell speech?'

'We could say a prayer,' Saint Joseph offered.

There weren't any takers.

'A poem!' The Pox exclaimed.

He looked serious and even Saint Joseph was impressed.

'Ideal! Nothing like a bit of culture to say *adieu*!'

The Pox shuffled his feet to give himself a head start. The boys lowered their heads and the pigeons did likewise. It was a touching moment like the bit at the end of war pictures where the chap says farewell to his comrades.

'"The soldiers farewell to 'is horse."' The Pox gave the piece its full title.

385

"'The soldiers farewell to 'is horse! Good luck ... an' fuck ye!'"

There was a moment of stunned silence. Then The Child collapsed with laughter and Timmy and The Pox joined in. Even Saint Joseph couldn't keep his face straight. They doubled up over the handrails and tears rolled down their cheeks. They could let them go because tears of laughter or tears of pain are impossible to tell apart. Then as their laughter died away, Mackerel cupped his hands round his mouth.

'Ooohhoohhoohooo! Ooohhoohhoohooo! Ooohhoohhoohooo!'

His howls coyoted down the turbine hall, raced along catwalks and girders, bounced off burners, pumps and motors, then hunted into dark unlit chasms at the back of the boiler-house. They summoned old ghosts, the hours of overhauls, breakdowns, the laughs, the rows, the triumphs and defeats. All were called to stand-to for a last march past. Silence returned and the boys stared down the vast and lifeless hall, mind-mapping so they would remember. It was one of those moments that men carry with them into eternity. Then pigeon fluttered its wings and a rogue drop of water plinked from a leaking flange. It was time to go.

chapter 17

ESCAPE: NIGHT-TIME, FRIDAY, 9 SEPTEMBER

The plane banked out over the bay and turned south towards Wexford. Below it the roads leading to the airport were lit by daisy chains of twinkling roadlamps. Doris Greer admired her engagement ring for the hundredth time since Richard surprised her with it that afternoon. Before he gave it to her, he had made raw and violent love to her. It had upset her because in the time they had been sleeping together, he had always been gentle and considerate. Though she begged him to go easy, he just grabbed her hair and drove himself in even harder. Then he climaxed with a snarl and collapsed on top of her. She started to cry and asked why he'd been so rough. He said it was because she turned him on so much and then gave her the ring to prove it.

The plane levelled out and she turned and touched his face.

'We'll be at the villa by daybreak.'

'Great,' he smiled, 'I can't wait!'

'And then, when we go into Barcelona, I'll buy you a Rolex to match mine.'

Henry Hudson

'Silver or gold?'

'I shouldn't buy either. You were very naughty this afternoon!'

She giggled, kissed him on the cheek then turned to get a last look at the city lights before they disappeared. Graves closed his eyes and thought of his daughter.

He just had to go and see her. He wanted to take a mental snapshot before he turned away from her for good. He was admiring and drinking her in but then as usual that bitch, Patsy Talbot, spoiled it on him. She caught him hiding in the trees and her fiery glare dared him to step out into the light. Like a rabbit caught in the beam of a powerful light, he froze for a few seconds, but as ever his instinct was to escape. He slithered away, though he was seething that yet again she had dismissed him like a dog from a door. As the day passed, he grew ever more angry that he couldn't have his daughter and Doris's money too. That afternoon he buried that anger deep inside Doris. Her pleading and whimpering only made him even more brutal. It was only when he finished that he realised she was crying. Afraid that he'd blown things, he immediately produced the engagement ring. She cried even more and smothered him in hugs and kisses. Graves played along until he finally escaped to the refuge of the shower while Doris rang all her friends to tell them her news.

The plane's engines lowered a tone and he opened his eyes. Dark wisps of cloud drifted past the window. The moon was a high distant disc of yellow. A hostess walked along the aisle towards the cockpit. She was young, blonde and moulded into a tight green skirt. Graves had never had an air hostess, at least not that he knew of. He wondered what they were like in the sack and just how much it would cost to get one of them into it. That was another thing to add to the list of all the things he'd do when he finally got his claws into Doris's loot.

The Black-Haired One: night-time, Friday, 9 September

Her nerves were still jangling after the spat with the politician, so she slipped down to the pub, got a naggin of whiskey, and headed back to the flat. As she passed a laneway, a hand reached out and hauled her into the darkness. She heard a smash as the naggin exploded on the path. Her attacker reeked of sweat and drink. He had her by the throat and jammed against the wall. With his free hand, he began to loosen his trousers. Fear paralysed her. She'd be found in the morning. Raped, strangled, maybe even mutilated. It'd get just a small mention in the papers. The deceased was previously known to have worked as a prostitute. That would make it okay because prostitutes were never raped and strangled. They just got what was coming to them. The attacker suddenly relaxed his grip.

'Now 'oor! Donshoo move!'

The voice jolted her memory, her eyes adjusted to the light, and she knew who it was.

He pulled open his trousers and began to grope inside his long johns. The smell was revolting but she told herself to just let him do it. Then he told her to hold out her hands. Relief ran through her. Maybe he only wanted a peddle. A wad of money planked into her palms. Then another and another. The thought struck her that she'd be wanking him till the year two thousand and ten. She closed her grip on the cash.

'Waish!' he snapped. 'There's shmore!'

He kept pulling cash from his long johns until her arms were full. Then he grabbed her roughly by the hair.

'Yer a black-'aired 'oor 'n' slut! Whash are ye?'

'I'm ... I'm a black-haired hoor an' a slut!'

'Sho eew find thash udder black-aired 'oor an' givver mee monneee ... an' shay ... shay fug off ouumee f ... farrrm! Whash ye haffa shay?'

'Fuck off outa me farm?'

'Nun! Nun! Nun! G ... Gusshhiiee shays!'

'Gussie says ... fuck off outa me farm!'

He closed his hands around her neck. The smell of his breath was month-old milk.

'Gemmee dem deedsh or ... or I'll sthrangle yeeew! Dyeunerstan'.'

He let her go and she ran away. Gussie downed yet another naggin of brandy, swayed for a moment, then collapsed on the path in a heap.

It was a hundred yards to the safety of her hall-door. She ran the first fifty, dropped some cash, stopped to pick it up and let the whole lot fall. Whipping off her coat she parcelled the lot inside it. Every second she expected a hand to haul her back but she made it to the doorway. Panic hammered the key all round the lock but then it found the slot, slid home and twisted. The door fell open and she was safely inside. She tore open the coat to expose a hillock of cash banded in wads. She had a quick flick through one and found it contained twenty one-hundred-pound notes. Two grand! Her hands shook as she counted the wads. Nineteen. Nineteen by two was thirty-eight. Thirty-eight-thousand pounds! Leaning against the wall she asked herself what the red-haired one would do. It took two seconds to decide. She'd keep the cash.

Within the hour a taxi pulled up outside the door and she jumped into the back seat with an overnight bag and a suitcase stuffed with the money. After a night in a decent hotel she'd buy a complete new wardrobe and have her hair dyed flaming red. On Monday she'd collect a grand and the key of her new flat from the politician. She'd keep the grand for pocket money and take the rest of her stash to her golf-playing bank manager. She'd have him sink it so deep a submarine wouldn't find it. The taxi disappeared around the corner into Gardiner Street and the black-haired one disappeared along with it.

Beyond Pulditch Gates

Piss-up: night-time, Friday, 9 September

They were all in Reagan's pub and the sing-song was flying. Timmy had contacted all the old gang, Fixit and Fukkit, Horizontal Harvey, Clean and Oily Paddy. To a man they all turned up. All they were missing was Barney, Saint Joseph and Man-in-the-Mirror. Hairy was MC and he passed an empty ale bottle around. Once handed the bottle the bearer had to sing, recite or make a bollox of himself by forgetting the punchline of a joke. If he didn't oblige, the boys instantly struck up.

'Sing, sing or show yer ring! La! La! La! Lalala! Sing, sing or show yer ring! La! La! La! Lalala!'

That convinced even the most reluctant to try, though The Pox muttered that some singers sounded like bulls giving birth to gas bottles. Hairy gave them 'Moonlight Becomes Yeeeww', having first recalled that famous day back in '58 when Saint Joseph was nearly done for the theodolite. Someone asked where Saint Joseph, was but The Child gave the thumbs down.

'His mot was a warder in Alcatraz. There'll be no gettin' off the rock there!'

Timmy was at the bar calling his round when The Pox was prevailed upon to do 'The Cremation of Sam McGee'. Feet and pipe in poet position he began.

'There's strange things done in the midnight sun be the men who moil for gold!'

Timmy had a few drinks taken but the line hit a chord with him. Strange things had happened since the day he first reported to the site of Pulditch One. He'd seen the place rise from the muck to a massive structure that pushed out power around the clock. Memories flooded his mind so that it was like looking back on Christmas as a kid and being unable to separate one from another.

The happy from the sad, the crazy from the sane. It felt like it had all happened in twenty-five hours rather than twenty-five years. The barman slid a posse of pints to him along the counter.

'Heard they closed yiz down.'

'Yea! How's it goin' around here?'

'They're buyin' everythin' east o' Butt Bridge. Like I said before, givvit ten year an' ye won't hear a Dub's voice between here an' Ringsend!'

He hisspissed a collar of cream onto another two pints and put them up beside the others. Watching the bubbles fade into the blackness of the pint, Timmy remembered what The Child said the day they covered Gussie in bubbles. Givvit ten year an' ye'll see *Playboy* on sale beside the *Herald*. It hadn't happened but it was just a matter of time. It was a slow, steady drip. Things changing. Bit by bit. Unseen. Unnoticed.

'Was that night on the marge of Lake Lebarge, I cremated Sam McGee!'

The Pox finished to a rousing cheer and was just about to hand on the bottle when the bar doors pushed open. An elderly man walked in. His shock of wild hair was snow-white, his face a puzzle of lines, but the eyes were as fiery as ever. The Child jumped to his feet.

'Barneee Coogan! Fair play! I knew ye wouldn't let us down!'

The place erupted, men were on their feet cheering, clapping and whistling. The old man shook hands, slapped and thumped shoulders. His eyes swept the bar until they found Timmy.

'Howye, youngfella!'

'Good t' see ye, Barney!'

'Good t' see yew too, ould son. Thanks for the invite.'

'We couldn't have this piss-up without the main man aboard!'

Beyond Pulditch Gates

They sat together and it felt as if Barney never retired at all. They laughed about strikes fought, stunts pulled, jobs tackled, stupid mistakes and ingenious solutions. Their conversation stopped when Mackerel took the bottle and retold the story of how he sent a lorryload of cement, two hundred concrete blocks and a real, live undertaker to Gussie Gallagher's digs. The whole bar joined in for 'Let yer fingers do the walking' bit and the barman said it should have been on in the Abbey.

MAN-IN-THE-MIRROR: FRIDAY, 9 SEPTEMBER

It was dark when he got to the gates of Pulditch One but they were padlocked. Apart from the odd wall-light, the building was in darkness and the briars crept over the wall like black snakes waiting to grab him and swallow him up. The gate hut looked lost, alone and sinking in weeds. He gripped and rattled the rusting bars of the gates.

'Dockets! Dockets! It's meeee! Let me in! Please let me in!'

The briars, the blackness and the breeze circled him, waiting. Then a rat skittered across his foot and disappeared into the undergrowth. He leaned his head against the bars. He had been walking for close on thirty hours and he was weary, weary to the pit of his soul.

'Where are yooouu? Barneee! Timmeee! It's meee! Let me innn!'

He slumped down onto the ground unable to understand why the boys wouldn't answer. Then suddenly it came to him. They were on strike! And where did they go when they went on strike? Grealish's. He forced himself to stand upright and to face back up the road towards the dull distant glow of the city. He hoped he'd remember the way, that he'd make it on time, that the parrot still squawked and the cash register was still stuck on '9d'.

SAINT JOSEPH: FRIDAY, 9 SEPTEMBER

Saint Joseph stunned a lot of people that Friday night. First into the frame was the unsuspecting Henrietta. It was just before teatime when he climbed into the attic and pulled down his trumpet box.

'Alfred,' she snapped. 'Alfred! What are you doing?'

'Taking down my trumpet.'

'Whatever for?'

'Because I'm about to rejoin the City and District Brass and Reed Band!'

'You are not indeed!'

'Oh, I am indeed and what's more, I have attended my last evening devotions, prayers for the conversion of China, abortion referendums or any fuckin' thing else! And as for that poisoned dwarf of a priest who's always on about the dangers of sex, I recommended a big ouldwan with short legs!'

For the first time in her life Henrietta was dumbstruck. Alfred John Jameson pulled on his coat.

'From now on, Henrietta, you make your own tea, butter your own scones and your fat, rubber-arsed friends can do likewise!'

He lifted his trumpet box.

'I'm going down to meet the lads in Reagan's after practice. I'll be late but you make bloody sure there's a decent sandwich ready for when I get back!'

Henrietta's mouth was still hanging open when he walked out and slammed the door behind him.

Standing up to Gussie Gallagher had broken the mould of his life. He felt alive, unafraid, invulnerable. He got a huge cheer when he stepped into Reagan's bar, then he stunned the place by calling for a pint and a large cigar. He stunned it again by lowering half the pint in one go before whipping out his trumpet and launching

Beyond Pulditch Gates

into an all-out Al Jolson medley. He hit 'Swanee', 'Toot Toot Tootsie', 'California Here I Come' and then lifted the ceiling with a full-blooded version of 'Mammee'. At the finish, the boys were all on one knee, arms outstretched.

'I'd walk a mih hillion miles for one o' yewr smiles, myhh Maa ... haa ... haa ... meeeee!'

He backed every singer as the bottle moved around and he was still blowing strong when the barman began to tour the bar banging a glass on the tables.

'Gerrouut an' go homme! Homme nooww gennnts, plleeaase!'

It was time. Timmy handed Barney the bottle in an unspoken request.

'Yiz'll haveta help me,' he wheezed. 'All o' yiz!'

Heads nodded. Horses were saddled. The cowpokes were ready. Barney started to tap his foot then he threw back his head to set the herd moving.

'An old cowpoke came a ridin' out one day an' windy day! An' upon a ridge he rested as he went along his way!'

By the time he hit yippieeiiaayyeee, yippieeiiiohh the herd was in a full and furious stampede. The floor shuddered under their thundering hooves. All over the bar, blind drunk gringos slapped their rumps with one hand and let out the reins with the other. The spirit of The Cowboy had returned to lead them all in one last charge before they became names in a ledger or in the stories of old men gassing about the days when men were men and ye could drink all night on a wanser.

PATSY: FRIDAY, 9 SEPTEMBER

It was just past midnight when Jack and Pat Sheridan arrived back in Scarfe Terrace. He had taken her out for a meal to cheer her up. When Patsy opened the door they were beaming and holding hands.

Henry Hudson

'Yew two look like yiz had a good night!'

Jack whipped Patsy up in his arms.

'Ma! I'm goin' to Australia.'

'Ye can't! What about yer job.'

'Ah, I was gonna jack it anyway.'

'Ye can't just walk inta Australia!'

'I can get a visa to stay over there for a few months! Pat says I'm mad but then you've been tellin' me that for years!'

Patsy looked over at Pat Sheridan who smiled and shrugged her shoulders. Like father, like daughter, the bitter phrase lashed Patsy's mind. She was instantly ashamed. The girl had a decent mother even if her father was an out-and-out bastard.

'What'll yer Da say?'

'What he always says! Bejays, I hope it keeps fine for ye!'

An icy dread took Patsy in its grip. If Jack and Pat Sheridan married she would be tied by blood to a man she hated beyond words. The idea almost made her sick.

Then she realised Jack was waving his hand in front of her eyes.

'Ma? Ma, ye still with us?'

'You seemed to be in a trance,' Pat whispered. 'Are you all right?'

Patsy had to sit down. Jack moved beside her.

'Maybe we're rushin' things but I always knew I'd meet someone special. The minute I laid eyes on Pat I knew it was her!'

The girl sat on the other side of her.

'Only for Jack I'd never have made it through the last few days. It took twenty-five years for all the bits to fit, but now I've found my Mum and Jack and me are together!'

Jack took Patsy's hand and held it tightly.

'It's like a circle closin'! We're endin' somethin' that began a long, long, time ago!'

Beyond Pulditch Gates

Patsy had just seconds to think. They were looking at her, begging for her blessing. She thought of all the Monicas and Sarahs who suffered because no one told the truth about men like Richard Graves. On the other hand the truth might shatter everything for her son and the woman he loved. She knew what she had to do. Like so many other Irish women she would carry a secret that could never be told. She hugged them together and to her.

'Be good to each other,' she whispered. 'Just love and be good to each other!'

Then she hugged them close and closer still.

Dawn: Saturday, 10 September

The first hints of daybreak were touching the eastern sky when Man-in-the-Mirror finally got to Grealish's but only the façade remained. All the rest was flattened. He stood on the path and looked at it for a long time. He was too tired to cry and too afraid to sit down for fear he might never get up again. St Jude's, Pulditch and now Grealish's were gone. He had nowhere to go and no one to turn to. Death was sure to catch up and take him. Looking over at the black silent river he thought about going to meet it rather than wait till it hunted him down. Then he remembered Scarfe Terrace. Timmy Talbot was there and Timmy always looked out for him. Beyond exhaustion and pain he walked along the quays and turned right up into O'Connell Street. From there he was sure of his way to Scarfe Terrace. As he limped across the junction at Talbot Street, a tramp was roaring and stamping around the island in the centre of the street. His coat was open and the flies of his trousers were undone. He was baying like a hurt dog.

Wherrrssmeeemmmonnee! Whhooohasssmmeeemmonnneeeee!'

Then he threw his arms up into the air.

'Blaggaair wwimenn issss ssluuus! Sluuus I shayyy! Ssllluuss!'

Folding onto all fours the tramp wailed in despair.

'Wherrrssmeeemmmonnee! Wwhhooohasssmmeeemmonnneee!'

Man-in-the-Mirror thought the voice reminded him of someone who used to bawl like that. He might have stopped but he was just too tired. He walked on and left the madman baying and cursing at the fading disc of the moon.

Daybreak found him sitting on the path outside number seven Scarfe Terrace. At the end of the terrace the flat tinkly dink of milk-bottles being delivered told him he wouldn't have to wait much longer. At the first sign of movement in the Talbot's house, he'd ring the doorbell. Timmy would take him in and take care of him like he did before. He'd sleep and eat then Timmy would find him a place that had no walls, no locks, no gates and that didn't make baskets. It would be a big place in the country where he could walk and breathe, a place where he'd never have to look behind him again.

Scarfe Terrace: Saturday, 10 September

Patsy opened her eyes and saw that Timmy was awake.

'You okay?' she whispered.

Timmy propped himself up on his elbow.

'I was just thinkin' that I'll be the shoppie that led the lads outa Pulditch One.'

'Ye had no choice, love.'

'Maybe, but I can't help wonderin' if Barney or The Cowboy would have done it or would they've stood their ground regardless?'

'Barney and The Cowboy never fought a war they couldn't win!'

'I dunno, Patsy ... I just keep thinkin' I shudda handled things different.'

She moved in close to him.

Beyond Pulditch Gates

'We all think that sometimes, Timmy.'

'Even you?'

'Even me!'

They were silent for a few moments then Timmy ran his hands slowly through her hair.

'D'ye ... D'ye still love me, Patsy?'

'Quietly,' she said and pulled him down on top of her.

She wrapped her arms tightly around him and thought of how much she loved him and loved Jack and all the people she cared for. She wanted to be able to shield them all from pain and heartache. When she stood by Monica Dillon's grave she had made a solemn promise that from that moment on she would fight for the ones who had no one to fight for them. No matter what the odds, no matter what the cost, she'd take their part. When it was time, Timmy pushed deep inside her and whispered her name as he always did, and she welcomed him as before, as always.

When it was over she kept him inside her. He was like a baby in her arms, sleeping, trusting her to take care of him. Daybreak washed the flat, flawless ceiling in pale pink light. She thought of the times she held him and gazed at the ceiling in Larnham Street. That was an honest ceiling showing all its cracks and carbuncles. A ceiling that hid nothing. What you saw was what you got. Like their love was when it was new and innocent. Someday she might be able to tell Timmy all that happened and ask him if she too might have handled things differently. Just then the flat tinkly dink of milk-bottles being delivered told her it was time to rise and face a new day, but she decided that for just a little while longer she would hold him and let him sleep.

PULDITCH: DAWN, SATURDAY, 10 SEPTEMBER

The security van slowly circled the grounds of Pulditch One allowing the driver, do a visual check that all was in order. The place was eerily silent. Apart from the odd fluttering of a bird or a rat scurrying down a drain, there was no sign of life or activity. Weeds were already encircling the bottoms of the oil tanks and a sour fishy stench hung around the river pump-house. Satisfied that all was in order, the driver headed back to the main entrance. He drove out onto the road, stopped the van, got out and pulled the big road gates closed behind him. He twined a heavy chain through the bars of the gates and used a padlock to snap the ends of the chain together. He smiled as he noticed that someone had chalked a farewell message on the wall of the gatehut. It read simply, Mackiril wurked here 1958–1983. Under that again was the legend, Dokits did to.

The security man eased back into his van and lifted the handset on his two-way radio.

'Car fifteen to control, over.'

'Control, go ahead fifteen,' the radio cackled in reply.

'Pulditch One all secure, over!'

'We read that fifteen. Pulditch One all secure, over.'

'Fifteen out,' the driver sighed and dropped the handset back into its slot.

He looked downriver. The roof of Pulditch Two was clouded in steam as its generators powered up to meet the breakfast-time demand. Further out in the bay dawn was washing a sash of pink onto the horizon behind the Kish Bank lighthouse. He sat for a few moments watching the daybreak then he fired the engine and drove up the road towards the wakening city.